Lives
explosive

MICHAEL BRANT—Aging ~~p~~ ...ily descended from the legendary Mohawk Sachem Aaron Brant, one tragic act of anger will set in motion the drama that will make this daughter a fugitive and his son-in-law a traitor.

CRAIG MILLER—Proud warior son of an Assiniboine Indian woman and an outcast frontiersman, he has vowed to protect his people's birthright with a daring plan that can put his own head in a hangman's noose.

MEU BRANT—Tempestuous daughter of a proud line, her devotion to one man may drive her from her home, her desire for another may lead her to tragedy.

KEVIN O'CONNOR—Hot-tempered, high-spirited member of the Irish Brotherhood, his soul belongs to his cause, but his heart belongs to a sinfully beautiful woman who seduced him as a lad . . . and then betrayed him as a man.

ALLISON MILLER—Lustful wife of a cruel but wealthy man, her lovely face hides the evil behind the clever mask.

ALEX MILLER—A frail boy who grows into a bold, treacherous man, he would kill once for passion, once for greed, and once for pure blind hate.

BROTHERHOOD

THE CANADIANS

by
Robert E. Wall

VII
BROTHERHOOD

BANTAM BOOKS
TORONTO · NEW YORK · LONDON · SYDNEY · AUCKLAND

*This Book is Dedicated
to My Teacher
Edmund S. Morgan.*

BROTHERHOOD: THE CANADIANS VII
A Bantam Book / September 1985

The map of "The Fenian Raid in Ontario" from *Fenianism in North
America* by W. S. Neidhardt. Copyright © 1975 by The Pennsylva-
nia State University. Reprinted by permission of the Pennsylvania
State University Press, University Park, PA.

ISBN 0-553-24872-3

Published simultaneously in the United States and Canada

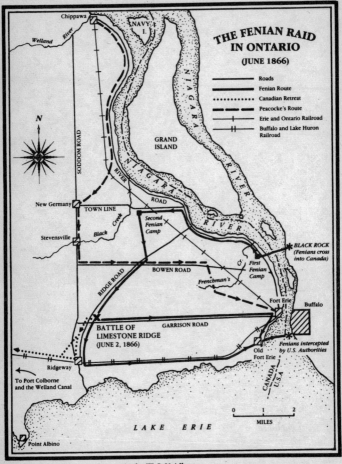

THE FENIAN RAID IN ONTARIO
(JUNE 1866)

Roads ─────
Fenian Route ─────
Canadian Retreat ·········
Peacocke's Route ─ ─ ─ ─
Erie and Ontario Railroad ─┼─┼─
Buffalo and Lake Huron Railroad ─╫─╫─

Chippawa

NAVY I.

Welland River

GRAND ISLAND

NIAGARA RIVER

N

SODDOM ROAD

River Road

New Germany

TOWN LINE

Stevensville

Black Creek

Second Fenian Camp

First Fenian Camp

BLACK ROCK (Fenians cross into Canada)

BOWEN ROAD

Frenchman's

RIDGE ROAD

Fort Erie

Buffalo

BATTLE OF LIMESTONE RIDGE (JUNE 2, 1866)

GARRISON ROAD

Old Fort Erie

Fenians intercepted by U.S. Authorities

Ridgeway

CANADA
U.S.A.

To Port Colborne and the Welland Canal

0   1   2
MILES

Point Albino

LAKE ERIE

From: *Fenianism in North America* by W. S. Neidhart

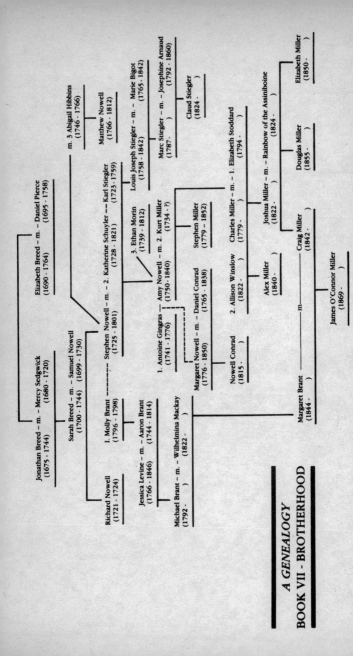

A GENEALOGY
BOOK VII - BROTHERHOOD

I

Ireland, June 1860

The young man stared at the surface of the lake, his eyes almost blinded by the glare of the early morning sun on the brown water. He blinked and continued his search. Water lilies, their gold centers just bursting into bloom, covered the surface. A frog poked its head from behind a lily pad. It was almost perfectly camouflaged by the greenery.

Kevin O'Connor had removed his shoes and stockings and now stood knee–deep in the pond. His black hair was damp with sweat at the temples and on his neck. He was strong for fifteen, and much of his strength was in his legs. He could outrun all the boys in the village and had done so many times. When he was younger he had run away from them. First they would taunt him for being his lordship's bastard, then he would respond with rocks or whatever else was at hand. The older boys would chase him, and some could have broken him in two if his speed had not saved him. But now it was Kevin who did the chasing. Many a time he had collared a youth who had besmirched his birth. The taunts came less frequently now.

It was not so easy, however, to quiet the sneers of the adults. His mother, Mary O'Connor, was an enigma to him. With her light red hair and blue eyes, she was at once his shelter and the source of all his pain. He silently cursed her foolish love for the Anglo–Irishman who was the lord of this manor, yet he could not deny her affection for him or that it was her plump arms that encircled him when the hurt grew too large for a mere boy to endure.

Well, this morning he would be inflicting pain on her, not that it was his intention. He only wanted to catch some frogs. The heathen Canadians who were guests of his lordship had professed a desire to eat frogs' legs, and he was of a mind to catch some, hoping for a small cash handout from the cook.

1

His lordship's steward had ordered the sluice opened on this Sunday morning, and the water pounded noisily on the rocks. The lake in front of the house seemed to sink into its own mud as the water spilled into the lily pond below the cascade. The raised water level of the lower pond usually distracted the frogs and made them easy to catch. And the cascade of water drowned out much of the noise Kevin might make.

It also drowned out the sound of the village church bell. Mary, Kevin's mother, would be searching for him up and down the dirt road and in all the nearby pastures. She might even stay home from church herself, claiming the croup for both of them, before she would let Father Doyle, the pastor, know that the lad had missed Sunday Mass. Kevin thought her pride silly. On Saturday, as sure as the devil had a forked tail, he, O'Connor, the bastard boy, would be marched off to church, and in the dank gloom of Father Doyle's confessional, Kevin would proclaim his absence as a mortal sin as sure as any committed by the giant simpleton who had sired him.

But that would be next Saturday. Right now he had a frog or two to catch. A green head emerged farther out in the water. The frog inched its way up onto a lily pad. Kevin remained perfectly still. The frog had to be lured into complacency by the sun and the distant pounding of the water. Then he struck. His hand shot forward. His fingers touched the wet body of the frog. But he was not fast enough. The frog's slimy body squeezed free of his fingers, and the animal was in the water and out of sight before he could act again.

Kevin cursed. Instinctively he looked about him. He had tasted his mother's brown soap for a less foul word. But there was no one to hear him except Prince Albert, the gelding that grazed on the tall grass at the pond's edge. Prince Albert was Kevin's private name for this horse with no balls. It was his own private tribute to the recently deceased Prince Consort. His lordship called the horse Warlock, but the horse responded to the caresses of the stable boy, Kevin O'Connor, and answered to the name Kevin had secretly, and with some malice, given to the beast.

Kevin kicked the water several times just for the fun of seeing the water lilies stretch on their long stems. He kicked again, and this time dislodged the escaped frog from its hiding place. The amphibian made a giant leap for deeper water. Kevin bounded after it, but his foot slipped on the muddy bottom, and he fell forward into the water. When he came up sputtering and wiping the muddy water from his face and eyes, he did not give a thought to Saturday confession.

"Goddamnit," he swore. Again he looked about him, shaking water from his clothes. There to his left was a clump of hedge. He had often placed his clothes on that hedge when he wanted to cool off under the cascade. Well, Mass was just beginning. He had about an hour before he had to return, more if the old windbag Father Doyle warmed to the topic of his sermon. It should be more than long enough to dry his clothes in the morning sun. He pulled his wet linen shirt up over his dark hair. He undid the buttons on his woolen trousers as he climbed up onto the dry bank of the pond. He stepped out of his pants and laid them and his shirt on the hedgerow to dry. He wore no undergarments. His mother said they were only for gentry. On hot summer days when the wool began to itch he wished he were gentry.

Kevin stretched out on the short grass behind the hedge. He looked up into the sky. Giant clouds seemed to whirl across the heavens. His mother told him that Irish poets saw images of battles, giant faces, portents of the future in those puffs of vapor. Well, he was no poet. He saw only clouds. When the heat from the sun had baked his front he flipped over onto his belly. He was reminded of the story old Doyle loved to tell about the saint, (St. Lawrence, he thought it was) who was grilled to death by the Romans. In his suffering he had quipped that he was done on one side—would they mind turning him over. He shuddered. He was terrified of pain, especially the pain of fire.

The warm sun dulled his senses, and he did not hear the sound of the horses until they were almost on top of him. He looked up to see the two women riding sidesaddle approaching the pool. Both were dressed in dark riding dresses. Kevin recognized one as Barbara, Lady Carringdon, his lordship's young wife, a haughty Englishwoman whom he disliked and who had tried to have Lord Carringdon remove him from his job in the stables for no other reason other than it offended her to have her husband's bastards around the house. She was a gaunt, pale woman whose face bore a strong resemblance to that of the mare she rode.

Kevin recognized the other woman as one of his lordship's guests. He had never seen her so close before, though. She was older than Lady Carringdon, but far more beautiful. Her blonde hair was pulled straight back into a bun, accentuating

3

the beauty of her long, straight throat. And her eyes were green, as green as the hills overlooking the sea on a day full of sunshine such as this one.

"My God, it's that O'Connor woman's bastard and he's naked," Lady Carringdon cried out.

Kevin rolled toward the hedge and grabbed for his clothes. He retrieved his shirt, but his pants fell to the ground on the other side of the hedge beyond his reach. He quickly fled around the corner of the shrubbery out of sight.

"You, boy, why are you parading around indecently out here, offending innocent women with your foulness? His lordship will hear of this, as will your mother and your priest."

Kevin groaned. He could bear a tongue–lashing, and even a few strokes across the rump, by his lordship's steward, but the priest would ramble on and on about his soul with his breath stinking of onions and home brew. He hated the boredom of the sermon and its interminable punishment. He was sure St. Lawrence had quipped in his pain in the hope of shortening it.

"Don't pick on the boy," said the blonde lady. Her English was strangely accented. She was not Irish, not even Anglo–Irish like his father. Nor did she have the clipped speech of the English like Her Ladyship.

The Lady Carringdon stared at her companion in surprise.

"It's the first warm day we've had," the lady said with a note of impatience in her voice. "I don't blame the lad for wanting to soak up what little sun you get here. Back in Canada, after the long dark days of winter, the little boys are frequently tempted to go swimming in the lakes and the streams."

"Kevin O'Connor is not a little boy," said Lady Carringdon.

"So I've noticed," responded Allison Miller with a smile.

"I must still tell my husband about the boy's neglect of duties," the English woman snorted. She pulled on the horse's reins and cantered away from the pool up onto the pasture leading to the lawn of the manor house.

Kevin peered out and was surprised to see Allison still there. He ducked back down.

"Kevin," Allison called, "come out, come out, wherever you are."

The boy hesitated, then finally he stood up, wrapping his shirt foolishly about his middle.

"You were right, my lady," he stammered. "I was only soaking up the sun and drying my clothes."

The woman stared at him, unnerving him. The sleeve

4

slipped from his grip behind his back and his shirt fell down around his knees. The boy was tempted to dive back into the bushes but the lady was not at all shocked by his nakedness. In fact, she smiled at him. It was a smile that riveted him in place.

"Tonight," she said. "Meet me here at eight o'clock." Then she too turned her horse and galloped away.

Kevin gave a low whistle. Surely the woman was a slut. Just as surely he intended to be standing in exactly the same spot at eight o'clock that very night. He had never had a woman, unless he counted the time he got Mary Gardner to lie on her back and lift her skirts. It had all been over for him the moment he touched her, and the virgin Mary remained one through no fault of her own. It was as if leaning over the precipice had frightened her. She had never again been so accommodating. Surely tonight he would know bliss at last. No matter that this woman was a loose one; she was the most beautiful female he had ever set his eyes upon.

He retrieved his shirt and trousers and his shoes and stockings. He walked over to Prince Albert as he buttoned his shirt. The wicked witch of the manor had not even noticed the gelding. He was not supposed to help himself to a mount whenever he wished, but he felt it was only right that the better horses in the stable be ridden by an expert on occasion, instead of by the tight–assed, weak–thighed Englishmen who usually rode them. He swung himself up onto the horse's saddleless back. At the slight pressure of his legs the horse sprang forward. Kevin threw back his head and a loud yell of wild abandon came from his throat.

The great manor house came into view. It was built of pale yellow stone and was bathed in sunlight. Its giant windows caught the reflection of the sun and flashed like huge mirrors. Kevin leaned over the side of Prince Albert, gripping the horse's mane. He kept his seat merely by the tension of his calf muscles as they grasped the sides of the beast. The grass had been allowed to grow in this pasture and Kevin always played this game of daring when he rode through it. He slid down farther and farther. He could see the violence that the gelding's front hooves did to the soft turf. Kevin reached for a handful of grass and pulled at it as he straightened himself onto the horse's back, grasping the horse's flying mane even tighter. The gelding complained in pain and its mouth snapped, if only

5

halfheartedly, at the source of its torment. As had happened so many times before, the horse's teeth sank into nothing but air.

Kevin waved the handful of grass above his head before he realized that a clod of dirt still remained attached to its roots. Dirt showered onto his black hair and down his face into his eyes and mouth. He pulled the gelding to a quick stop as he spat out the dirt and rubbed his eyes with the backs of his sweaty hands. He looked about him as the Prince snorted and pounded the grass with his hoof. There were no prying eyes. No one had seen his riding feat, and as a result no one had witnessed his humiliation. Price Albert, however, was angry. He tossed his head and continued to pound his hoof. Kevin knew what would follow next. The horse would feign lameness in an effort to force Kevin from his back and to prevent anyone else from climbing aboard until he, Prince Albert, was ready to tolerate him. Just as the boy had expected, the horse began to limp. Kevin had an elaborate ritual already worked out. He slid off the animal's back and knelt in front of him. He took the "sore" leg in his hand and began to rub it gently. He reached into his pant's pocket and found the wet stump of a carrot. He raised it in his hand. The horse snorted, then sniffed the bribe, which quickly disappeared into his mouth. Kevin then walked beside the animal as it limped across the rest of the pasture toward the green lawns of Carringdon Manor and the stable block at its rear. The horse would not lose the limp until proximity to its stable and the prospect of a bagful of oats blanked out the memory of this morning's mistreatment.

The closely clipped lawn showed the scars of many a horse's hoof. Lord Carringdon and his Canadian guests had been riding all week. The woman with the golden hair and the green eyes had an ancient husband, bald except for some grey fuzz about the temples. He was bent forward and seemed weak. He had to be helped by his son, a blonde–haired youth slightly older than Kevin. This other boy had done no riding. Could such an old man have sired so young a colt? Kevin wondered. But there was no denying the dam. The boy looked the image of his mother. Kevin shook his head. "Tonight, meet me here at eight o'clock." The words rang in his ears still.

Albert snorted again, bent his head down and sniffed at the pile of dirt left in the middle of the grassy lawn by an industrious mole. The limp grew less pronounced as they walked. Kevin could hear the hounds baying in their pens. They must already be sniffing the scent of fox. Tomorrow morning Lord and Lady Carringdon and their guests would ride the hounds. Kevin doubted that Alex Miller, the Canadian boy, would join them. He had never seen him sit on a horse. He always stayed in the manor watching, standing next to his father's chair.

Desmond, the gardener, greeted Kevin with a wave from the rose garden.

"Old man, come to the stables with your shovel and get some food for your roses this afternoon," Kevin called.

"It will have to season a bit before it is useful. Why don't you spread it on your mother's cottage floor? The way you O'Connors live, I doubt you would notice it at all," the gardener quipped.

Kevin laughed.

"And, Kevin, my boy, I admire the way you handled Warlock." He pointed at the gelding with his trowel. "Keep riding him that way and you could end up gelded just like your mount once his lordship gets finished with you."

"Is that what happened to you, Dessy?"

"No, I wore them off by constant use."

Kevin laughed even louder as the image of Desmond and his gnomelike wife flitted into his mind.

They were at the stable now. Kevin led Prince Albert to his stall. The limp was totally gone. The boy reached for a bucket, filled it with oats and placed it in front of the horse. He brushed down the animal, then watered him. Finally he patted the gelding's nose and stepped out of the stable into the brilliant sunshine.

He walked along the dirt road back toward Carringdon Village. The road was still muddy from yesterday's rain. Kevin took off his shoes and shoved them under his arm. The mud was warm as it squished between his toes. He came to the top of the knoll that overlooked his village. Of the thirty houses, only about half were filled. The empty ones were ghostly reminders that less than a decade before the Irish nation had been destroyed by a potato blight and by the uncaring British relief efforts. One or two of the houses had stood empty ever since the men fled their vengeful British masters after the "troubles" back in 1848. Many a survivor of the potato famine and the troubles was now living free in America.

Kevin envied them. He could do little to emulate them. Most of his family had not been survivors. Their pitiful graves could be found in the churchyard; his grandfather and grandmother O'Connor and all their offspring except his mother lay in one grave together. It would have been unmarked if Kevin himself had not done chores for Desmond the gardener in return for a plain square board with the name O'Connor carved lightly into it. The rain and the wind would wear away their identity before the earth stripped their bones. No, he was the last of his line, sole protector of his mother. God knew his father did nothing for her other than hire him for stable work. It was difficult for Kevin to think of that large vain man as his father. He disliked Lord Carringdon almost as much as his mother continued to love him. His lordship had not gone near her since before his birth, yet she continued to pine after him.

He walked down the slope toward the village. The parish church stood at the end of the dirt road. The pastor liked the fact that the only road in town inevitably led to the church. Kevin liked to think of Carringdon Village Road as leading nowhere. The bells started to ring again.

The boy cursed. Now all the parishioners who had not attended the early Mass would come pouring out the door. Kevin started to run. If he could make it to his cottage before the assembled worshipers came out, then he would have to answer only to Mary O'Connor and that was bad enough. He ran through a large puddle in front of the Widow Collins's house. He ducked behind her cottage. He cut through her garden patch. He was sure he had trampled some seedlings. He would have to offer her some free weeding later in the summer to make it up. She would be puzzled by his generosity, since her dead Mick had been no friend of Sean O'Connor, his grandfather's. Well, the hell with her, let her wonder.

His mother had lit a small fire before leaving for church. It still smoldered and filled his nostrils with the aroma of burning peat. The single room was stuffy. The heat of the day had been intensified by the cooking fire. Kevin went to the pile of bound straw that served as his bed. His shirt and pants were still damp from their morning dousing. The only other clothes he possessed were his church clothes. He was tempted to put them on anyway and bluff his way through her inquisition about his whereabouts. But the temptation was soon dissipated by the appearance of her face at the window. Tension seemed to drain from her ruddy face when her blue eyes lighted upon him sitting on his bed. But then her brow furrowed. She disappeared momentarily and then stormed through the door.

"Kevin O'Connor," she cried out as the cottage door struck with a thud against the dried mud wall of the house. "What are you doing with your lazy arse in bed on a Sunday morning, and Doyle himself waiting to lay the word of God Almighty on you? Jesus and Mary have mercy on me for raising such a lout."

"Mama—"

"Don't you 'mama' me." She approached him with anger in her eyes. As she passed her kitchen work table she picked up her favorite wooden spoon.

Kevin covered his head with his arms. His head was her favorite target, despite Grandmother O'Connor's admonition that to hit the lad on the head might rattle his brains. She swung the spoon mightily and it cracked across his knuckles.

"Shit, mama," Kevin yelled. "That hurt."

Mary turned to an absent audience and pleaded her cause. "Listen to the little shithead, say 'shit' before his own mother. Mother of God, I don't know what I'll do with him."

The spoon swung again, but this time Kevin was taken by surprise as the spoon smacked smartly against his thigh. He rose, rubbing the welt. It was a mistake. He had exposed his rump and two more quick blows fell on him. Kevin had had enough. He started to move away toward the safety of the door. Mary's pride would never let her follow him outside. Never must her neighbors see what only deaf old McGuire could not have heard. But suddenly the assault stopped and the spoon was returned to its proper place on the kitchen table. Kevin knew what would follow. Mary silently fixed her apron over her church dress and went to the cupboard in silence. She took three precious potatoes and an onion from the shelf and began to peel and slice. She wiped the tears from her eyes with the back of her hands.

"Don't cry, Mama," Kevin said finally after watching her for some minutes.

"And who's crying!" she sniffled. "It's the onions that are watering my eyes."

"I'm sorry I embarrassed you by missing Mass."

"It's not the embarrassment, boy," she said defensively. "It's my awful fear for your immortal soul. You'll be burning in hell with the heathens."

Kevin dearly wished to point out that by her own church's

9

definition her beloved lord was one of those very heathens. But he did not wish to cause her any more pain.

"I'll see Doyle on Saturday."

She turned on him angrily. "It's Father Doyle to you, you snip, and you'll not be waiting until Saturday to rid yourself of that mortal sin. You'll make it to the box this very day. I'll never sleep this night knowing that my only child has a smirch on the lovely soul that my own love brought into this world."

Kevin knew it was useless to argue with her or to point out that her love, which produced his once-innocent soul, was also in the light of her church a mortal sin, one deserving eternal damnation. He walked to the table and took the knife from her hand.

"I'll peel," he said.

She put her beefy arms about him. "Oh, Kevin my boy," she said squeezing him, "I know you'll feel better about it yourself when you've unburdened. Old Doyle announced he'd be hearing confessions tonight at eight."

"At eight?" Kevin asked, a momentary look of pain crossing his face.

"Eight o'clock sharp. He doesn't like to sit in the box waiting for sinners to stroll by. He expects them waiting for him. 'Get it over and done with,' she said. 'No sense in letting sin drag on. Make your peace, be shrieved and be on with your life.'"

Kevin said nothing. He continued to slice the skin from the potatoes. Mary slapped his hand.

"You're cutting too deep," she complained. "By the time you finish, that spud will be as small as a grape."

"Mama, stop hitting me!" Kevin complained.

"Stop doing things that make me want to hit you."

"What can I do to make you stop?" he asked good naturedly.

"You'll see the priest tonight?"

"I'll see the priest."

"Good. Now go wash yourself. You smell like a swamp."

"Mama, I always stink."

"You usually stink of horses, which isn't altogether a bad smell. Today you smell like his lordship's pond."

Suddenly it dawned on her. "So that is where you were instead of at holy Mass. You were swimming!"

She hit him again with the spoon but this time just lightly atop his black curls.

Kevin was growing impatient. The village church clock had

10

struck the hour at least ten minutes before. He could hear the water falling over the cascade. It had been reduced to a trickle now that the sluice had been closed. He could see nothing. The moon had not yet risen, and even if it made its appearance it would have little effect on the night. The clouds had blacked out the stars completely, and a fine mist was falling. At least it was not pouring, leaving him soaked and miserable. It was bad enough he had to wait for the Canadian woman. He was sure now she would not come. A fine lady need not seek out stable boys on a cloudy, misty, Irish night. He turned away from the cascade and the hedge to find his way in the darkness up toward the manor house and the village. Maybe he could catch Doyle before he fled the chill in his box.

"Where are you?"

He was startled by her voice.

"Boy?" she called anxiously.

"Here, ma'am," he said, his voice cracking.

She came to him out of the gloom. She wore a dark woolen cloak over her narrow shoulders. She had pulled the cloak's hood about her face so that only a small portion of it was visible. But he had no trouble recognizing her. She held out her hand. He took it in his. It was cool and soft. He was embarrassed by the calluses on his own palms. He was glad it was dark, because he could not remember if he had washed his hands before leaving for this rendezvous. He had intended to, he could remember that.

"You came," he said stupidly.

"Not yet," she said laughing. The toss of her head caused the hood to fall onto her shoulders. She wore her hair loose. The moisture on the air had curled it at the ends—at her temples and at the nape of her neck.

Kevin had never seen a more beautiful sight in his life. He stood gaping at her.

"Boy," she said, "I've forgotten your name. What is it?"

"Kevin. Kevin O'Connor."

"And is it true that you are Lord Carringdon's bastard?"

Kevin looked away from her in embarrassment.

"Don't tell me you're ashamed of it? Why, my dear Alex would give his left nut if he could be anyone's bastard. Unfortunately he is the legitimate son of Charles Miller, my dear, dear husband. Unfortunately for me, that is."

Kevin had never heard a woman speak in this manner and it embarrassed him even more.

11

"Enough chatter," said Allison. "Where can we go to get out of the rain?"

Kevin was at a loss. He had assumed that the woman either had some place in mind or was prepared to tumble in the bushes like the Gardner girl.

"Quick, boy," she said pulling the hood back up over her head. "It's chilly!"

"I don't know," he said finally.

She looked at him in amazement. It would have shattered him had he seen it but he was saved by the darkness.

"There's a gazebo down at the foot of the pond. It's supposed to be like the ones they have in China."

"Lead on, Ling," she demanded.

He took her hand and led her along the edge of the pond. He was becoming aroused by the very presence of her. She periodically squeezed his hand, and when he stopped to let her step around a puddle in the path, she deliberately placed her hand on his rear as if to steady herself.

Kevin was grateful when they reached the darkened wooden pagoda. He was having some difficulty walking because of the bulge in his pants.

"Why, it's more than a gazebo," Allison cried out in delight. "It just might be the spot for us. I was sure this afternoon that you would take me to the stable and we would roll in the hay as you do with the little girls in the village. Quick, let's get inside."

The door of the pagoda creaked as Kevin opened it. There was a whir of wings as a pair of doves that used the place as a night roost flew out the open sides. Allison sniffed loudly.

"My God," she exclaimed, "the place does smell of pigeon. Ah well, the stable too would have had its own odor. Besides, it's all so natural."

She reached over and placed her hand on Kevin's groin. "Oh yes, so natural," she repeated. "How shall we go about this? I was really counting on the straw—some fine Irish hay for a bed."

"The floor is wooden here, miss."

"It's Allison, dear boy."

"Miss Allison," he repeated.

"God, you make me sound like a schoolmarm. Well, on with it, Kevin," she said, squeezing him.

He gulped. "I'm really not very experienced," he croaked.

"Do you mean to tell me *a strong Irish lad* like yourself is not going to show me how they do it in the Old Sod?"

He said nothing, but backed off into the darkness.

"Well, I guess Allison will just have to show you how it is done back in Canada." She stepped toward him and slid her hands about his waist. Soon she had forced his woolen pants down to his knees. He gasped as he felt her mouth on him.

The board floor was hard, although Kevin was scarcely aware of it. He lay on top of Allison's hooded cloak. She lay naked next to him. She rested her hand upon his belly. Her long, polished nails played with the line of dark hair that grew there. His pants were still entangled about his knees, trapping his legs. Never in his life had he experienced the explosion of feeling of that first time. Allison had looked up at him. He was about to apologize for ending it so quickly but he was halted by the smile that crossed her face. She was not at all angry with him, nor did she agree in any way that it was all over.

Now he lay exhausted next to this naked woman. He hated the feel of her fingers on his hairy belly. He tried to inch his way up in the hope that she would allow her hand to stray downward. Three times in succession he had felt that welling up and the convulsive release that followed. But exhausted as he was, he could feel the stirring in his groin at even the thought of her touch. He reached down to push his pants farther down and release his feet from the entrapment.

Allison groaned and then raised her head to look at him. "Where are you going, my boy lover?" she asked him. "Ah, you seek to escape my web?"

"No, ma'am, I just want to get my feet loose," Kevin responded in a whisper.

"Kevin, you just made love to me three times. How can you continue to call me ma'am?" Allison said in a loud tone. "And stop whispering. There's no one around, and if there were they could hardly have missed your shouts when you came the last time!"

"I didn't shout," Kevin said covering his embarrassment.

"And I don't like boy's cocks," Allison responded.

He grew silent.

"What's wrong?" Allison said raising herself on her elbows and presenting Kevin with an eye–level view of her beautiful breasts.

"Does my stable boy find me shocking? I hope so. I truly hope so."

"You're going out of your way to embarrass me, aren't you?"

"I am going out of my way to arouse you. I've found some men like me to use such language with them."

"A lady isn't supposed to talk like that," Kevin said sheepishly.

"I am no lady. I was taught that by a master teacher. He taught me all sorts of exquisite things until they all became memory to him and he left me unsatisfied."

"Who was that?"

"Never mind. What is it that you like, my handsome stable boy?"

Kevin leaned his face forward until his nose began to nuzzle the soft skin of her breasts.

"Ah, you like to play baby. Never mind, my child, mama will feed you to your heart's content." She stroked the back of his head as he sucked first one nipple and then the other.

"So unlike my Alex," she said aloud. "He found his own mother's milk hard to bear."

Kevin staggered along the road toward the village. He could see the church spire outlined in black against the dark sky. He ached all over. One part of him in particular had been abused to the point of rawness. The woolen trousers made him groan each time he took a step.

He wondered if Doyle had waited for him to come to confession. Well, he hoped the old man had caught a bad chill waiting in the damp church while he, Kevin O'Connor, his lordship's true but unrecognized bastard, was having himself one hell of an evening of sin. Next Saturday old Doyle would get himself an earful. He'd probably spend the next two weeks trying to figure out who would allow a boy the chance to have her four times in one night.

Kevin stopped in front of his cottage and listened. He opened the door slowly. With any luck he would hear his mother's soft snoring from the bed on the far side of the room. Instead he saw his mother's ghostly white–nightgowned figure sit up in the bed.

"Is that you, son?" she called out, fear clearly dominating her voice.

"Who else?" he said cheerfully.

"You were gone so long."

"The old man kept me in that box for what seemed like half the night. There was not a soul else waiting for penance and he gave me five full rosaries as a penance—not just five mysteries, but all fifteen five times—and just for missing Mass."

14

Mary O'Connor smiled to herself. She could not see her son in the night gloom of the cottage but she could hear his outrage at the priest. Thank God for men like Thomas A. Doyle. Without them, what would widowed mothers with growing sons do? She liked to think of herself as a widow, even if her darling was still alive and up at the big house. He was dead to her.

"Get your things off and climb into your bed, Kevin, my boy," she said. "Remember, his lordship and his guests will be riding the hunt tomorrow. It will be a big day at the stables."

"Yes, mama." Kevin sighed. She had bought his story. He dropped his pants on the floor by the straw mat. He took off his shirt and dropped it onto the pants. He climbed into bed and pulled the coarse woolen blanket up about his chest. The dampness in the cottage made him shiver. He should say his prayers, especially an act of contrition. If he should die in his sleep, especially tonight, not St. Patrick and St. Bridget together could get him out of Satan's clutches.

"Oh my God, I am heartily sorry for having offended thee." He whispered the prayer to conclusion. Now maybe he could sleep in peace. Without thinking, he reached his hand down to his groin, then gasped with pain. He would have to go easy, but he could never fall asleep unless he could gently caress his "privates" as Doyle referred to them. Tonight he would only hold himself until sleep came. His last thought was of the golden-haired Canadian woman. Half asleep, he wondered if his act of contrition had been sincere enough.

The baying of the hounds filled the morning air before the sleepy-eyed boy was halfway down the muddy road toward the stable block. He could see lights in several windows of the manor. Lord Carringdon's guests, including Allison Miller, were in all probability shivering as they groped their way out of their warm beds into the early morning chill of their large and unheated bedrooms. Kevin had entered the house only once to help sweep the chimneys, and had never been allowed in any of the upstairs rooms. He had difficulty placing Allison in the proper surroundings in his own mind. But the woman was indelibly fixed in his brain—her hair, her throat, her breasts—all of her. In his mind he saw her step out of her sleeping garments and stand in the center of the room just as he had seen her last night.

"Oh, Christ," he said, as he realized the image had had a natural effect on him. It would be hard to carry out his duties as a stableboy on hunt day as long as Allison Miller was around. In the light of the early morning, with his night fears behind him, he knew his act of contrition had not been sincere enough.

The rich green lawn of the manor house was wet with dew, and ground fog still lay in low-lying sections of its broad, rolling sweep. Both the dew and the fog would burn off early this morning, Kevin thought, squinting as the first rays of the rising sun struck his face.

"Kevin, move your arse."

O'Connor knew the hoarse rasp. It was a sound as familiar to him as his mother's soft humming, which he had first heard at her breast.

"For sure, your excellency," the boy responded with an exaggerated bow in the direction of the stable.

"Bow like that again, lad, and I'll see to it that there's a horseshoe firmly wedged in place with a horse attached to it."

Kevin laughed, but he could tell that O'Hagen, the master of the horses, was in a foul temper. The old man's mood had very little to do with Kevin. It was the dogs. A pack of nearly thirty-five were rushing around the stable yard. Some sniffed at bales of hay being made ready to feed to the royal tenants of the barn, the horses of the hunt. As Kevin watched open-mouthed, one hound hoisted his leg and urinated into a bale. O'Hagen moved slowly at first but then his strides lengthened until he seemed to fly across the stable courtyard. He timed his arrival perfectly and his right foot swung with precision directly toward the offending dog. But the dog was too quick. He raced away, temporarily guaranteeing the possibility of his having issue and at the same time causing O'Hagen to slip and fall with a thud onto the cobblestones.

"Oh, I've broken my back," O'Hagen moaned, "and all because of Muldoon's piss hounds. Muldoon," he screamed. His yell frightened more of the dogs, who responded by baying all the louder.

Kevin ran to his master's side and helped him up. He stifled a laugh when he saw that O'Hagen had fallen on a small pile of dog droppings which had smeared all over the seat of his pants.

"What is it?" O'Hagen asked, his massive black brows rising

to form a complete arch on his craggy red face. His nose told him.

"Oh, good Jesus, Muldoon, I'll have your balls for this. There is nothing that smells worse than dogshit unless it's Muldoon shit. Give me horse droppings or cow manure any day. They're healthy–smelling, not like something that's died and been allowed to bloat in the sun." He started to wipe his pants with his hands, then caught himself.

"I've got to get to my rooms and change," O'Hagen shouted at Kevin. He pointed to the windows of the second story of the stable building. O'Hagen lived there alone in two sparsely furnished rooms. Kevin had never visited O'Hagen's rooms, no one had, although it was rumored in the village that at least once or twice a month lamps burned until late in his rooms and a woman's laughter was heard coming from the direction of the stables.

As soon as the cursing O'Hagen disappeared through the barn door, a small, thin man peeked around the far corner of the stable block. He possessed a large hook nose and his ears stuck straight out from his head, a deformity enhanced by a flat tweed cap which was jammed tightly onto his wiry red curls. He glanced about to see if O'Hagen had disappeared. He sighed with relief, then began to walk boldly across the cobblestones toward Kevin. As soon as the hounds saw him, they formed a solid pack and howled a greeting.

"How is it with you this morning, Master Muldoon," Kevin greeted the older man.

"Fine, my lad, truly fine. A fine morning for the hunt, now that certain foul–mouthed and foul–smelling individuals have left the scene."

Kevin merely smiled. He liked both these men and tried to avoid being caught in their endless rivalry, although, since he worked for O'Hagen, he knew the horse master better and naturally sided with O'Hagen's preference for horses over dogs.

"The vixen was active last night," Muldoon reported. "She raided the Meighan chicken yard up on the ridge. She took a hen but killed three more. Aye, she's a vicious one."

"How do you know she's a she?" Kevin asked. "Did you see the tracks of some pups?"

"Not at all, lad, but I know it is a vixen. No male fox would kill like that. It's the female of the species, of all species, that kills wantonly."

17

Kevin started to laugh. He knew he was about to be treated to one of Muldoon's endless misogynous lectures. O'Hagen said it had begun with Muldoon's mother. She must have had sour milk, he said. Kevin's own mother had told him that as Muldoon got older the girls of the village had made fun of his gangly legs, skinny body and protruding ears. O'Hagen also said that Muldoon had once tried to court a girl but her father had chased him off with a razor strop. He had never married. Instead he took charge of his lordship's hounds and, according to O'Hagen, "he slept with the bitches."

"Watch out for the female, Kevin," Muldoon droned on. But the word triggered in Kevin's mind the image of Allison and he tuned out Muldoon's disappointments. Muldoon misinterpreted Kevin's silence for boredom with the topic and so he switched to a subject he thought, mistakenly, was closer to the boy's heart.

"Are the filthy beasts ready?"

"What?" Kevin asked absentmindedly.

"O'Hagen's filthy dumb beasts which his lordship and his misguided friends insist on riding. Are they ready for the day? Are they prepared, lad? Are they prepared to try to keep up with my beauties? To bear on their backs the witnesses to the kill?"

Muldoon reached down and patted the soft brown head of one of his dogs.

"They have the vixen scent already. I have all I can do to keep them from taking off after it. I wish the gentlefolk would hurry up." He continued to stroke the hound as he spoke.

Kevin was amused. "Muldoon, that's a bitch that you're stroking there."

"Indeed," said Muldoon, "and there is little better than a bitch hound."

"It's a female."

"A bitch is no female," Muldoon said as he straightened up to look Kevin in the eye. "Female is deceitful. It's saying one thing and meaning another. It's guile. None of my bitches have any of those characteristics."

"But you possess them all. And have no balls whatever. So it would do me little good to try to remove what you've not got in the first place."

Both Kevin and Muldoon looked up in surprise as O'Hagen, in clean trousers, came out of the barn.

Muldoon seemed to shrink backward in the presence of the larger man.

"And you continue to insult the noble steeds of the hunt. I wish his lordship could hear his master of the dogshit talk about his true love, his horses. Could you conceive of a hunt without them, Muldoon? Imagine watching thirty filthy hounds tear apart one poor fox who up to that point was merely minding his own business killing a chicken here or there in order to feed his belly."

"That's what it's all about," said Muldoon, his eyes darting from O'Hagen to Kevin.

"Aye, you poor bedraggled spirit, Muldoon, down in the offal with your filthy beasts. The hunt is about noble folk, lords and ladies sitting astride God's finest creatures. The hunt is all about courage, muscles of iron, the charger of ancient legends. The hunt is a combination of noble human folk and their noble steeds, racing together across open fields, leaping hedges and fences, climbing hills, jumping gulleys. Oh, God, it stirs my blood."

"And to what end, O'Hagen? In the end the hounds catch the fox and tear it to pieces."

O'Hagen was about to tell Muldoon what he could do with his hounds when the strange howl of a flat-sounding horn penetrated the silence of the early morning air.

O'Hagen was startled. He cursed under his breath. "That will be Mr. Morrison, the master of the hunt, and here we are flapping our jaws. His lordship's party will be upon us any moment. Kevin, get into the stables and prepare horses, boy. There will be twelve in Lord Carringdon's party and seven from Sir Thomas Wilson's estate. Hurry, boy. They'll be coming down from the kitchen any minute with the kippers and the champagne. Some will want to be in the saddle while they eat and his lordship will insist on champagne being served to the mounted only."

Kevin rushed into the great stone building that housed the horses. O'Hagen had already prepared some of the mounts. Kevin patted Prince Albert's rump. He would save the best for Allison. She would ride the Prince today.

Two younger boys from the village arrived to help Kevin for the day. Usually Kevin took his time selecting bridles and saddles and showing the others how to polish them and place them on the horses. But today no one had much patience for teaching. They were behind. At one point O'Hagen came rushing into the stable and screamed at Kevin to prepare the carriage too.

"Who the hell is going for a ride in the middle of a hunt?"

"No one tells me anything," O'Hagen screamed out. "Just demands and more demands."

Outside in the courtyard, servants were setting up kitchen tables covered with white linen cloths. On them the cook placed great silver serving dishes and chafing pans. Chilled bottles of French champagne were uncorked, the popping frightening some of the more sensitive horses and sending the hounds scurrying for cover with Muldoon in hot pursuit.

Mr. Morrison, the master, was a straight-backed thin man. He sat atop an enormous white stallion. He looked elegant in his red coat and white riding breeches topped off by a black hunting cap. Under his arm was the brass hunting horn that had first announced his arrival. He patiently awaited the arrival of Lord Carringdon and his guests. The troop of seven led by Sir Thomas had just arrived in the courtyard and had already begun to take breakfast.

Kevin led Prince Albert out into the courtyard. If anything, the scene was one of greater confusion now. The iron shoes of the horses clanked on the worn cobblestones. The smells of fish and eggs stirred the juices of Muldoon's charges as they barked and nipped at each other and then scurried away from the kicking feet of Sir Thomas's unfamiliar mares, geldings and stallions.

Kevin saw his father, dressed in his red and white hunting outfit, leading his young horse-faced wife who was dressed in a black riding dress. A riding hat covered her brown hair, and she wore a veil over her face. Whenever he had the chance, Kevin searched his father's face and form for recognizable signs of their relationship. He did not know why. He had never doubted his mother's word about who his father was, nor had his lordship done anything to squelch the rumors that Kevin was his bastard. On the other hand, he had never shown Kevin by word or by gesture that he meant anything to him. As he approached, Kevin could not help staring. Lord Carringdon was a big man, some would say fat, but he was so tall, well over six feet, that he could carry his weight well. A smile lit up his ruddy face when he saw the pandemonium in the stable courtyard and he started to push his wife gently along to hurry her up. She looked sourly first at him and then at the confusion of the courtyard.

Kevin looked beyond his father. He saw Allison. She was

dressed all in black, like Lady Carringdon, but there could be no further comparison. Her blonde hair was drawn back from her face and neck and held tightly in a bun so that the black riding bonnet could fit firmly in place. Kevin stared at her green eyes, her honey–blonde hair and the beautiful pale white flesh of her throat. She laughed at the handsome blonde young man who walked beside her, pushing a high–backed wheelchair in which sat the bald–headed old man. Kevin recognized them as her son and her husband.

His lordship's party entered the courtyard. Greetings were shouted between Sir Thomas and Robert, Baron Carringdon. O'Hagen led a black stallion, his lordship's preferred mount, out of the stable. Without waiting for any assistance, Kevin's father placed his left foot in the stirrup and hauled his large frame up into the saddle. The stallion pulled to the right as if to bolt but Carringdon handled him expertly.

"O'Hagen, old fellow, my wine," Carringdon called out.

One of the grooms immediately rushed to his lordship with a long thin champagne glass.

His lordship sniffed at it as if expecting it to be bad. On discovering it acceptable, however, he drained it in one gulp. "Another," he called out.

When Kevin saw Allison walk toward the mounting block, he led Prince Albert to the platform of cobblestones held together with mortar which was used to assist the ladies mount their horses sidesaddle.

"Robert," Lady Carringdon called to her husband, "tell the boy that Warlock is too frisky for our Canadian guest. After all, she is a city girl and not accustomed to this."

"Oh, I don't know," Carringdon looked admiringly at Allison. "I'll bet she has a good seat."

His wife looked at him strangely, then began to berate him. Carringdon was in no mood for a public debate.

"You there, Kevin," he called to his son, "let her ladyship ride Warlock."

A smug smile broke across Lady Carringdon's face. Kevin would dearly have loved to loosen the saddle and watch the Englishwoman fall on her face but he could ill afford the consequences of such a fleeting pleasure.

The Englishwoman offered him her black–gloved hand, which he held as she climbed the steps to the top of the mounting platform. Kevin steadied the horse's head as Lady Barbara mounted sidesaddle. The horse shied a bit and Kevin whispered in his ear, "She's a bitch, Albert, my Prince. Not like our Allison."

He handed the reins to her. The horse kicked out and she pulled in, forcing the bit deeper into his mouth.

"Behave yourself, Warlock," she commanded.

Kevin chuckled when he saw the wild look of Prince Albert's eyes. Lady Carringdon was going to have an interesting ride today.

"Boy," Allison's voice rang out over the din of the horses, men and dogs. "Get me a sweet horse."

"Yes, ma'am, a gentle mare," Kevin responded.

"Get a gelding for Alex," the old man in the chair said with a cackle.

The young man seemed not to notice the quip. "I won't be riding," he said softly.

Kevin returned to the courtyard with the mare O'Hagen normally gave to the inexperienced. She was gentle and lazy and past her prime, but she had been dam to many of the best of his lordship's stable and O'Hagen was fond of her.

"Ah, now, that's my horse," Allison said as Kevin led the mare to the mounting block.

"It doesn't suit you," her husband called out.

"Ssh, Charles. You know nothing of horses. With you it is always ships, and now those awful steam engines belching ugly smoke."

Allison took Kevin's hand as she climbed up the steps. She removed her gloves and Kevin could feel the warmth of her hand. She squeezed his fingers.

"Good morning," she murmured. "I hope you slept well."

"Like a baby," he responded.

"I'm not sure how to take that. I prefer to think of my lovers pining away from love in my absence."

Kevin blushed. She had spoken too loudly. He was convinced all the hunters and grooms had heard.

Allison mounted gingerly. When she took the reins, her face broke into her beautiful smile.

"There," she said, "I've done it."

Lord Carringdon rode up next to her. He offered her his glass.

"A sip, Allison, my dear."

Allison took the glass and raised it to her lips. Just at that moment Prince Albert—Warlock—shied out of control and crashed into the rear of Allison's mount. The champagne

22

spilled and dribbled down Allison's chin and soaked the bodice of her riding costume.

Charles Miller, who watched from his chair, snorted with glee.

"I am so sorry," Lady Carringdon apologized. "I don't know what's wrong with Warlock this morning."

Allison glared at her hostess, then quickly flashed her smile once again. "Perhaps the beast suffers from a bad case of the green envies," she suggested.

Again Charles Miller chortled.

"Have you eaten, my dear?" His lordship addressed whichever woman wished to respond to his term of affection. Without waiting for a response, he turned his stallion to face Sir Thomas and Morrison, the master of the hunt.

"Gentlemen, have you satisfied your appetites?"

"For food and drink, my lord," Sir Thomas said laughing.

"And what other appetite could you have in mind?"

"In polite company, my lord, I'll mention only the appetite for blood. I long to see the kill."

"Muldoon," Lord Carringdon called, "are your hounds scented? Where was the fox last seen?"

"It's a vixen, my lord, and it was up at Meighan's ridge."

"Are we all in the saddle?" his lordship called.

"Everyone but Alex," Charles Miller said.

Lord Carringdon looked at his Canadian guest. "God, these colonials," he muttered. He wouldn't have let him in the front door of Carringdon Hall had Charles Miller not had more money than any man ought to have. He treated his son with contempt. Not that it was hard to blame him for that. If he had a son like Alex Miller, he would treat him with contempt as well. The boy had no spirit, no virility, no manhood. He stole a quick glance at Kevin O'Connor. He did have a son, thank God, and not one like Alex Miller—although he could hardly say he treated the boy any better than Miller treated his son. At least Alex was a Miller. Oh, well, it was all unavoidable. But the Miller woman. Wasn't she something else? She dabbed at her bosom with a lace handkerchief. Lord Carringdon found it hard to keep his eyes off her bosom even when covered by unrevealing riding garments. Kevin, he noticed, was having a similar difficulty.

"Muldoon, release your hounds," he called.

"Aye, my lord," replied Muldoon and signaled the pack

leaders. The volume of the dogs' howls increased, as the animals rushed from the courtyard toward the uncultivated pasture fields below the ridge where their quarry was last scented. Morrison raised his horn to his lips and the strange notes of the horn reverberated off the stone walls of the stable. Someone yelled. Sir Thomas's contingent were the first to race away toward the narrow gateway through which the hounds had just disappeared.

"Let poor Sir Thomas have a head start." Lord Carringdon called out to his friends and guests. "He'll need it once my horses start to work up a lather." He nudged his stallion forward. The others followed at a slow trot toward the gateway. Allison was the last guest to leave. She was followed by O'Hagen on a high-spirited stallion. He would not, of course, get ahead of any of the hunters. He went along only to be there in case his lordship needed him. As they left the courtyard he called back to Kevin, "Drive the carriage for the Millers."

Kevin led the horse and carriage from the stable. He opened the door, then offered to assist the old man.

"I'll take care of it," Alex said. "Come, Father."

"Get your bloody hands off of me. Go paw someone else. I can stand on my own. I may be eighty but I can still stand on my own two feet. By God, I stood on a quarterdeck and faced American cannon with those two feet. That was back in '13. But none of you remember anything about that."

Alex looked bored. "Do tell us the story *again*, Father," he said.

"Don't give me any of your smart-ass lip. I know your mother told you that I ran when it got hot and heavy. For the life of me I can't think how she got that idea. Maybe your brother Joshua told her that. Men will do strange things when caught up with women. But then you wouldn't know what I'm talking about. Christ, how I'd like to see your brother again. Or is he your cousin?"

He tried to lift his foot onto the first step of the carriage. Kevin could see that he would miss it and yet he hesitated. Alex saw the misstep too, but did not move. At the last second, Kevin lunged and grabbed the old man before he fell onto the cobblestones.

"You prick," the old man shouted at his son. "You'd have let me fall."

"You said you could do it yourself," Alex said calmly.

"I always say I can do it myself even when I can't. You know that. Here, get your dumb Irish hands off of me," he said to Kevin.

O'Connor did not know if it was more of the same bravado. The old man frightened him with his yelling and cursing, but he was not about to let him fall and have to face O'Hagen.

"I said let me go," Miller complained.

"Not until you're safe inside," Kevin said as he lifted the old man up and placed him in the seat of the carriage.

"Stop it," Miller shouted. Too late, he was safe. He sat there like an old rooster with ruffled feathers. Kevin took the woolen blanket that had covered him in the chair and tucked it around his legs. Then he stepped back to allow the younger Miller to climb in. It did not take Charles long to fix his attack onto his normal target.

"Now that's what I call taking care of me. That young fellow, dumb Irishman that he is, paid no attention to me and got me to where I was supposed to be."

Alex stared ahead and offered no defense.

Kevin got into the driver's seat and clucked at the horse. They drove smartly through the gate and out onto the driveway of Carringdon Hall.

"This is not the way the horses went," the old man shouted.

"I know that, sir. They'll be going up over the ridge toward Meighan's farm."

"Well?"

"We'll get there by the road, sir. Carriages were not meant for cross-country jaunts."

"But I want to be there for the kill. Don't you, Alex? Don't you want to see the mutts tear the belly right out of the fox and slash the jugular with their teeth?"

Alex turned visibly paler.

"No, I guess you don't. Blood frightens you, doesn't it? Well, not your brother. I'll venture to guess that he has lifted one or two scalps in his day, but then he was always more like your Uncle Stevie. Lusty, that's what they called Stevie. Bloodless, cold, and calculating, that was old Charlie. Do you calculate, Alex? Are you more like me? I'll bet you calculate. All those dollars and pounds sterling will be yours and your mother's once I am out of the way."

"Don't agitate yourself, Father. You know it's not good for your heart."

"If that's the case, why don't you just rile me up? Never can tell when the old ticker might just give up."

Alex continued to stare at the back of Kevin's head.

"Driver," Charles Miller called out, "what's your name, boy?"

"Kevin, sir."

"Kevin what? Or don't you Irish have last names?"

"Kevin O'Connor, sir."

Miller savored the answer for a moment. "You're Lord Carringdon's bastard, aren't you?" he said finally.

Kevin's shoulders slumped lower. "I don't rightly know, sir."

"Don't know? Of course you know. Everyone else does. My wife told me you were and she knows everyone's business. You know my wife, don't you?"

Kevin was tempted to respond that he knew her better than the old man would want him to.

"Would you believe that a vixen like my wife could produce a washed-out pup like this one here next to me?" Then the older man started to guffaw. "I guess 'vixen' wasn't the best choice of words, given what we're up to. I certainly would not want my beloved Allison to end up like the object of today's search."

Kevin began to feel sorry for Alex. If one had to have a father like Charles Miller, it would be better to have no father at all.

"Must be in the blood. Not hers. Mine. Well, Kevin O'Connor Carringdon, will we be in for the kill?"

Kevin snapped the carriage whip a good foot above the chestnut mare that pulled them. The horse quickened her pace. "I'll take us up to Meighan's ridge. We'll see what we can see from there. It all depends where the fox is brought to bay."

They rode on in silence. The road took the long way about toward the more gradual slope of the hill. When they reached the top of the rise, they could see the dark seas of the North Atlantic as they crashed against the high cliffs of the Irish coast. There were gulls circling and squawking.

"That's more to my liking," Charles Miller said wistfully as his rheumy eyes stared off at the seascape. "Let's sit here for awhile."

"But the hunt," Kevin said.

"To hell with the hunt. Carringdon and that other fellow, Wilson, can keep their foxes, their filthy dogs, their bloody horses, their shit, their stench, I wouldn't trade one moment of looking at the sea for any of it."

They remained silent. Only the distant whisper of the surf and the far-off cry of the gulls mixed with the closer snorts of the horse to disturb their reverie.

"Drive on," Charles finally said.

Kevin flicked the carriage reins and the mare plodded along the ridge road. As the road turned to the east, away from the coast, the sound of the surf was replaced by the baying of the hounds.

Kevin stopped the carriage and stood in the driver's seat. "There they are, across Meighan's field, beyond that clump of hedge and into the apple orchard."

Kevin thought of poor Bill Meighan. His potato crop would be ruined by fifteen or twenty horses galloping across it. No matter that Lord Carringdon owned the field anyway and would allow Meighan to tap the Carringdon Hall larder this winter, the sheer frustration of watching a whole season's plowing and planting trampled under by some aristocrats playing a game would be hard for anyone to bear in silence, and Bill Meighan was not a silent man.

"I want to get down there," Charles said.

Kevin remained motionless still thinking of Meighan's plight.

"Do you hear me? Alex, push that boy. Get him moving."

Kevin needed no pushing. They began to move forward again toward Meighan's cottage.

When they arrived in the Meighan yard, they found Lady Barbara standing next to Prince Albert. The horse had his right hoof raised in the air. She had dismounted and she was clearly enraged.

"This wretched beast has ruined my day," she complained. "He's gone lame on me. I shall miss the kill."

Kevin had to suppress his smile. He knew Prince Albert hated to be ridden sidesaddle. He could have whispered in the Prince's ear and the hoof would have come down to the ground as good as new. But he had no intention of helping her ladyship. He climbed from the carriage and took the reins of the horse in his hands instead. In turn, Lady Barbara climbed into the carriage. Her face was screwed up in anger, and she missed the obvious leer that Charles Miller gave her.

Within minutes they were joined by another hunter. Allison Miller, sidesaddled on her mare, came cantering into the cottage yard.

"You're going the wrong way, my dear," Charles called out. "The hunt is the other way."

Allison looked flustered. "I can't control this horse."

Again Kevin smiled. The mare was notorious for heading straight to the stable if she felt she could get away with it, and it was obvious to everyone that for once in her life Allison was not in charge.

Kevin moved in front of the mare and took the reins.

"Thank you, dear boy. I must reward you for saving my life," she said.

Charles Miller snickered. "Well, you are in for a treat," he said to Kevin.

Kevin went several shades of red. The old man caught on immediately.

"That's a new practice. The reward is given before the good deed. My Allison is always innovative."

Lady Carringdon paid no attention whatsoever to the exchange between the Millers and its effect on Kevin. She was still complaining, and since only Alex had been willing to listen to her, she complained to him.

"And that Meighan; that lout, you have no idea what he said to me about his stupid potatoes. My goodness, Lord Carringdon owns this land. This fellow is a tenant yet he had the nerve to speak to me the way he did. Then he and his wife went off to complain to my husband about his hunt. The woman didn't even offer me a cup of tea, not that I would have taken one from her. These Irish are so filthy. God knows when the cup might have last been washed."

She looked about uncomfortably. Lord Carringdon, who was Irish, did not approve of her English snobbery, but there were only these colonials to hear her. They probably barely understood her. They were only a notch better than the Irish themselves. She had forgotten about Kevin altogether.

Allison was developing a strong dislike for this Englishwoman and growing weary of the country life. She wished Charles would conclude his business with Lord Carringdon and let them get out of Ireland and off to London. She had been advised that June was the best season for London.

"My goodness, Barbara," Allison said, the malice in her tone obvious. "It appears I am not the only one who couldn't control her horse. Were you thrown? I hope you weren't hurt. I see the horse was."

"I was not thrown! The horse went lame. I had to dismount."

"Just what I intend to do. Kevin, lad, help me down."

Kevin reached up and offered her his hand.

28

"Alex, you dolt, don't you see the boy is about to manhandle your mother? Go over there and stop him."

Kevin's fingers were inches from her waist. How he would have loved to reach up and touch her body once again. But Charles Miller's voice forced him to stand frozen. He stepped aside as Alex Miller reached up and helped his mother dismount. Then he returned to his customary place at his father's side in the carriage.

"Well, here we are. Not much when it comes to the hunt, are we? What do we do now?" Charles Miller asked.

"I know what I'm doing. I'm going home," Barbara interjected.

"Oh," Allison smiled, "do take my trusty steed. It seems my horse has the same intention."

"I would not be seen dead on that nag," Barbara said haughtily.

"It was good enough for me."

"Mrs. Miller, you do not understand. I am a woman noted for her seat."

Kevin watched Charles Miller's eyes dart to Lady Carringdon's rump. He knew the old man rarely checked his tongue but suspected he might this time.

Barbara swung up onto the driver's seat of the carriage. "I am also noted for my driving. We're all going home. Kevin, you take care of the horses. Are you coming, Allison?"

"I rode out. I shall ride back. I'll be along shortly."

Barbara did not even wait for Allison to finish her sentence. She snapped the reins and the carriage bolted ahead, forcing back the heads of both of the Millers, father and son.

"Alone again," Allison said smiling as soon as the carriage had gone.

"But not for long," Kevin responded. The howling of the dogs told him that the prey had been found and the kill begun. "They'll all be back shortly with their trophies."

Allison laughed. "I hope it's all bloody and gory."

"It won't be too bad. They'll take the tail and the hounds will eat the rest."

Within minutes the victorious hunters returned led by Lord Carringdon and Master Morrison. Behind them rode the red–coated men and black–frocked women. Sir Thomas brought up the rear with O'Hagen and Muldoon and his dogs.

"O'Hagen," Lord Carringdon called, "give my greetings and a guinea to that fellow Muldoon. His dogs were superior, yes, superior. You tell him that for me. Yes, superior."

O'Hagen scowled but said nothing. He did not wish to confront that weasel–pussed bitch master, much less give him the guinea from his lordship's coffers, but Muldoon had heard him and there was no avoiding it.

"Kevin, how is it that you are holding Warlock? Nothing has happened to Lady Carringdon, has it?" Lord Carringdon asked.

"No, sir," Kevin answered. "She claimed the Prince, I mean Warlock, had gone lame. She returned to Carringdon Hall with the two Canadian gentlemen in the carriage."

"Claimed he went lame? What do you mean? Is he or isn't he?"

"He's all right," Kevin responded.

"O'Hagen?" Lord Carringdon called. His horse master dismounted and knelt beside the horse.

"Nothing broken, sir, that I can feel."

"Well, watch it like a good fellow. None of my horses must suffer at all. If he has gone lame, shoot him."

Kevin went white. "My lord?"

The aristocrat had already turned his mount for the leisurely ride home.

"What is it?" he responded turning in the saddle.

"There's nothing wrong with the horse. It's a trick I taught him. He goes lame deliberately."

"That's a hardly funny thing to do, lad. In fact, it cost her ladyship an opportunity to be in on the kill. I don't think she'll be very happy about this at all," he said with a note of self-concern in his voice.

"Well, my lord," Sir Thomas teased, "don't tell me that little bit of an Englishwoman has got you worried?"

Carringdon gave his neighbor a withering look.

"Aha, look at his face. I knew I was right. His lordship is fast turning from Galway's prime ladies' man and eligible bachelor into Galway's typical henpecked Irish male."

Lord Carringdon spurred his stallion and raced ahead of the others. Sir Thomas continued to chuckle, but most of the other hunters looked embarrassed as they followed Carringdon to Sir Thomas's estate for luncheon.

Muldoon, the master of the hounds, called for his pack leaders, but they were still too far off.

"What's wrong with you?" O'Hagen shouted to his rival. "Can't you hear the bloody beasts . . . ? Oh, excuse me, Mrs. Miller. I forgot myself. Can't you hear the beasts howling

30

off a good half–mile away? They'll never hear you here, man, and all you'll do is give us headaches with your blasted whistling."

"You know nothing about dogs, O'Hagen."

"Aye, it is something I am proud of."

"You're an ignorant man. Pride is the downfall of the ignorant."

O'Hagen bristled. If Allison Miller had not been standing before him he would have let Muldoon have the answer he deserved.

"Dogs hear more than we do," Muldoon continued.

"That's pure nonsense, Muldoon. If it's there, we'll hear it. If the sound is not there, we'll not hear it."

"I suppose you'll deny that they smell things better than you and I do. It would be logical to say that if the scent is there, we'll smell it too. I've got me an idea. Instead of one of my bitches, next time we have a hunt we'll give the scent to O'Hagen and let him track the vixen." He slapped his thigh with amusement.

"Get on with you, you wild fellow, before I ride you down. Find your bloody . . . your filthy beasts."

Muldoon started to move off still laughing. He trudged through Meighan's destroyed potato crop, whistling loudly all the while.

O'Hagen watched him disappear, and then turned solemnly to Allison. "I'll accompany you back to Carringdon Hall, Mrs. Miller. Kevin, help the lady mount."

Kevin offered Allison his hand. Her mare stood between O'Hagen and herself and Kevin. Kevin put his hands together to make a step for her foot. As he did so she reached over and patted his groin. And then as she mounted she looked down and smiled at the embarrassed boy. But Allison had misjudged what O'Hagen could see and could not see. He was shocked by her brazen behavior. No lady who had stayed at Carringdon Hall and had ridden one of his mounts had behaved in such a fashion. If the truth be known, he thought, this was no lady at all. He felt sorry for Kevin if he was involved with her.

"Kevin, you've caused a disagreement between Lord and Lady Carringdon. I suggest you keep out of sight for awhile and take Warlock with you. I've seen Lord Carringdon grow muleheaded before. I don't want him to get it in his head to blame the horse for his problems."

"My, you are frank, Mr. O'Hagen," Allison quipped. "Do

31

you frequently discuss the personal business of your employer in front of guests?"

"No."

The bluntness of his response shocked Allison into silence. Kevin had never seen O'Hagen be rude to a lady before. He was puzzled by O'Hagen's behavior and his request.

"It was Sir Thomas who riled him up, not me," he said.

"But he can't take out his anger against Sir Thomas, my lad. Do as I say."

"I won't go far. I'll take the horse to the edge of the property, near the summer house. There is water and grass there for him. I'll stay there until I hear from you. Get word to my mother."

"That I'll do," O'Hagen said coldly. His annoyance grew even greater when he saw the smile on Allison's face. He knew that Kevin's announcement of his whereabouts was meant more for Allison Miller than for Mary O'Connor.

Kevin was bored. It had been one of those rare days in the west of Ireland when there are no winds from the sea. Everything was quiet. The leaves of the trees seemed to droop in the heat of the sun. Kevin had stripped and waded into the lake below the cascade. Then he dropped down into the chilly water to cool off his body.

Now evening had fallen and Kevin was back in his clothes. He found an old canvas mat that had once graced the wooden side benches in the summer house. It was stuffed into a full-length closet in the far wall of the structure. It smelled of mildew, but it was more comfortable than the splintered, unpainted planks of the summer house floor.

He was bored waiting for O'Hagen's word to come back to Carringdon Hall. And he was disappointed. He had told Allison where to find him, and she had not come last night. He had sat up most of the hot evening waiting for her. Even today he had hoped she would come but there was no sign of her. He still had hopes for tonight but he was prepared to be disappointed.

The sky was still light in the west, but the summer house and the woods and fields around it were deep in darkness. Kevin could barely make out the forms of the trees and the bushes around him. He could locate Prince Albert by his occasional snort. The horse had come closer to the summer house with nightfall as if seeking Kevin's company in the darkness. Off in the distance he could hear the trickle of water over the cascade as it bounced on the rocks beneath it. The waterfall was loud enough to block out the sound of night birds and insects. Kevin wished the moon would rise so that he could see better in the darkness.

Suddenly, over the noise of the cascade, Kevin heard the sound of the horse's hooves. It had to be Allison coming to him at last. He was about to call out when he realized there were two horses. He checked himself. Prince Albert heard the horses too, and whinnied a greeting.

"What?" A voice came out of the darkness. "Who's there?"

The horses rode over to where Prince Albert stood. "So this is where that vile stable man has pastured you, you damned beast."

Kevin recognized Lady Carringdon's nasal twang, but the man with her was not Lord Carringdon. This man was smaller and thinner. The two riders dismounted. The man helped Lady Carringdon from the saddle. Once her feet were on the ground, the forms of their two bodies seemed to merge. Kevin realized that they were kissing. He drew back farther into the darkness of the summer house. Somehow or other he had to find a way out of the pagoda and reach Prince Albert and get away from here. Perhaps the noise of the cascade would cover the sound of his escape.

Kevin slipped his legs over the railing of the open porch and slid down the far side of the building. He dropped to the ground with a thud and waited for a moment and listened. He could hear his own heart pounding but nothing else. He started to crawl toward Prince Albert.

"Halt, you scoundrel!" A voice rang out in the night. "With my wife no less."

Kevin recognized the angry voice of his father, Lord Carringdon, coming from the other side of the summer house where he had last seen Lady Barbara and her lover.

There was a woman's scream and then Lord Carringdon cried out in pain and fear.

The pain—racked voice of his father froze Kevin in his tracks. He turned and hesitated. He couldn't just stand there, he thought. He made up his mind and raced around the summer house. He could barely make out the forms of the others in the night as he approached them. When his eyes finally adjusted he stood in horror.

Lady Barbara leaned against the wall of the summer house.

Her gloved hand covered her mouth and prevented her from screaming. His father lay coatless on the ground; the front of his white shirt was stained black. Protruding from his chest was a thin–bladed knife. Lord Carringdon was trying to pull the stiletto from the wound but managed only to cut his fingers on the sharp blade. His eyes were shut and his face was contorted in agony. A dark trickle of blood oozed between his lips and down his quivering chin.

"My lord," Kevin said, as he knelt beside his father. Lord Carringdon's eyes opened and focused on Kevin's face.

"Good boy," he whispered. Then his eyes opened wide in fear. Kevin realized that something behind him was frightening his father. He started to turn—too late. A red, blinding pain came crashing into his head. The boy staggered and fell forward across his father's still legs.

He seemed to be floating in blackness. His horse was calling to him from out of the billowing black smoke. The screams of dying men mingled with the screams of others who celebrated their deaths. He could see better now. Giant birds, their bodies painted bright colors and their feathers askew, bent over and tore with their beaks at the contorted, quivering bodies of their victims. The victims screamed soundlessly as the long beaks pierced their eyes.

Kevin could see the form coming toward him. He tried to cover his eyes with his hands, but could not move. He struggled. Maybe if he turned over he could save himself, but it was hopeless. He could not move. He was helpless. The giant form leaned over him. He expected the bird's breath to be as foul as the stench of death but it was not. He was enfolded in the scent of jasmine. The face came closer. He could feel the feathers touch his skin. Suddenly his eyes fluttered open and he looked up into the curve of Allison's breast. As she lifted his bloody head up to her chest, he moaned half in pain and half in relief.

"Kevin, wake up." She spoke softly but the pain in his head made it seem as if she was shouting at him. He thought he would pass out again.

"No, Kevin," she said shaking his shoulders. "You must wake up. You're in trouble. But I can help you."

He still had difficulty focusing his eyes and then he remembered and he was awake.

"My father?"

"Lord Carringdon is dead."

"Who?" He tried to clear out the fog and pain from his mind. He tried to recall what had happened. Who was the other man? He must have been the one who attacked him. He looked at the corpse, which lay next to him. He thought of his mother. She would grieve for Lord Carringdon probably for the rest of her days. Now she could truly be a widow.

Again Allison tried to bring him to his senses. "Kevin, we must do something. You're in trouble."

"What do you mean?"

"Your father is dead and you have obviously been in a struggle. You are covered with your own blood and his. People are going to say you did it."

Kevin looked at her in surprise. Did she too think he could kill his own father? "I tried to stop whoever did this and he knocked me out."

"Did you see who it was?" she asked.

"No, it was too dark. He rode up with Lady Carringdon. They must have been lovers. My father must have followed them and surprised them. The man knifed him." Kevin turned again suddenly to look at the corpse. It was still there. "We could find out who owns the knife," he offered. He was more alert now. "They can't blame me for this. I wouldn't kill my own father. Besides Lady Barbara knows who did it."

Allison smiled at him sadly. "You really don't think she'll 'fess up do you? Not that cold-blooded bitch. It would cost her everything. No, she would let you hang before she'd utter a word in your behalf." She avoided the issue of the knife.

The word "hang" struck him like a blow in the stomach. "But I didn't do it!"

"I believe you," she assured him. "I came here and found you like this. I wouldn't hesitate to state that in any court. Some might suspect why I came here and might besmirch my reputation, but what's that when a life's at stake?"

Kevin looked at her adoringly. "You'll save me then?" he said.

"I don't think I can, Kevin. What could I say? I found Lord Carringdon dead and you unconscious and bleeding. I saw no one else. He could have struck you after you stabbed him and then fallen down dying with you unconscious on top of him."

"But people here know me. They wouldn't believe I killed my father."

"Who did then? Whom could they blame but his unrecognized son Kevin?" She said this last almost in a panic. "No, I

35

don't think even my testimony could help you. You must flee. I could not bear to see anything happen to you."

Kevin knew she was right. They would blame him because there was no one else to blame. He was afraid. His head pounded, and he was overwhelmed by the feeling of nausea that welled up in him. He was going to throw up. He tried to stand up. He stumbled and fell to his knees. He could hold it no longer. The vomit shot from his throat with the first heave. He retched again and again even after his stomach had nothing more to give up. Finally the waves of nausea stopped. Allison handed him an ivory–colored lace handkerchief to wipe his lips. When he finished, he did not know what to do with it. He couldn't give it back to her soiled in that fashion.

"Keep it," she whispered.

He smiled at her in gratitude.

"Do you have a place you can hide?" she asked him. He could not think.

"Perhaps someone with a grievance against his lordship would not be outraged by his killing."

Kevin still did not respond.

"What about that farmer whose fields we tore up yesterday? My God, that was only yesterday, wasn't it? What about him?"

"Meighan?"

"That's the name."

"I guess he'd hide me. It's out of the village but he's Irish and he knows my mother."

"Good. You must go there immediately. Can you ride?"

He nodded.

"Then get your horse. We'll ride like the wind. We'll go to Meighan's cottage. Then I'll go back to Carringdon Hall and make arrangements for you to flee. You must leave Ireland. You must leave immediately."

They did not ride like the wind, not on a black night like this one. They rode slowly and on one occasion they actually walked the horses along the ridge road. Within an hour, however, they saw the lights of Meighan's cottage.

"I can go no further," Allison said. "Give me your horse's reins. I'll take him back to the stables."

Kevin did as she asked.

"I'll be in touch with you before morning." She stepped closer to him and they stood looking into each other's eyes. She kissed him on the lips. She opened her mouth and he tasted her. She pulled away from him and she was gone.

The Meighans put him up for the night without question. He told them he had argued with his mother and needed a place to spend the night. He said nothing about the murder. He hoped Allison would come back with his escape plans before his lordship's body was discovered.

Meighan was a grey-haired, pinch-faced little man who sucked continually on an old briar pipe. He never smoked. No one was sure whether he detested smoking or just refused to purchase tobacco. He was notoriously stingy. When asking for lodgings, Kevin wisely had indicated he would repay him with labor in the field to help him salvage as much of his crop as he could.

Margaret Mary Meighan, his wife, was rumored by the village women to nip occasionally. If Kevin had any doubts about those stories they were soon dispelled. She sat on a stool by the peat fire, her skirt up about her thighs and her legs askew. She removed a jug of Irish whiskey from its hiding place under a hearthstone and immediately began to drink. An hour or so later, she dozed off and started to snore. Patrick Meighan looked over at his wife and made a disgusted sound.

There was a soft rap on the cottage door.

"Now who the hell can that be at this hour?" The old man started to rise from his chair but Kevin was far more alert. He dashed from his place by the single window in the cottage and was at the door before Meighan could raise his rump entirely off of his chair.

The violence of Kevin's reaction awoke Margaret Mary and sent her earthenware jug falling to the cottage dirt floor. The woman looked at the jug in surprise and then mumbled something about the blessings of poverty which had kept the cottage floor dirt and soft.

Kevin threw open the door. "Allison—" he blurted out. But it was not she. Standing in the doorway, his old coat up about his ears, was Muldoon, the hound keeper.

Kevin's initial shock gave way to disappointment.

"Don't leave me standing in the night air, lad. Besides, you shouldn't be exposing yourself to any prying eyes."

"Muldoon," Meighan called from his chair, "you're as welcome as the cholera in me house."

"The warmth of your greeting moves me, Meighan."

The friendly banter surprised Kevin, who had rarely heard

the two men exchange a word, much less greet each other with friendly irreverence.

Kevin stuck his head out into the dark and peered into the dark. There was no sign of Allison. What was delaying her?

"Why so anxious, lad?" Meighan asked Kevin.

"He has reason to be anxious. He has murdered his lordship."

Margaret Mary took in a giant gulp of air at Muldoon's words, but her husband continued to suck on his pipe.

"Like hell I did," Kevin shouted.

"Why don't you announce your presence here to the whole village? They're all out there looking for you now already," Muldoon whispered harshly.

"Jesus save us." Margaret Mary crossed herself as she prayed.

"I did not murder Lord Carringdon."

"That's not what Lady Carringdon is saying."

Kevin sat back down by the window. He was frightened, but at the same time he was angry. He had done nothing wrong but to go to his father's rescue. So much for the Good Samaritan. He looked over at Muldoon still standing in the middle of the room.

"Why do you just stand there?" he asked. "Why don't you go and bring the bailiffs here?"

"What do you think, Meighan?" Muldoon asked, ignoring Kevin. "Is he worth saving? Is he worth anything to us?"

Meighan took his pipe from his mouth. "He's not a bad lad, Muldoon, and if he did remove that large hunk of Anglo-Irish shit from this mortal pale, he did the cause some service."

"Indeed," said Muldoon. "But a lad who would kill his own father?"

"A bastard whose mother had been wronged could do little else."

"What are you two talking about?" Kevin protested. "I've killed no one."

"Perhaps," Meighan said nodding, "but since no one will believe you you may as well have done it. You can't win, lad. They'll be hanging you for the murder of Robert, Lord Carringdon."

Kevin was near panic.

"Unless . . ." said Muldoon.

Kevin looked at him. His eyes searched the man.

38

"Unless what?"

Muldoon looked over at Meighan. The other man nodded back at the master of the hounds.

"I think we can save you, lad, provided you're a loyal Irishman and you're willing to work for the cause and you keep your mouth shut."

Suddenly it dawned on Kevin. "You're Republicans," he blurted out.

"He says it like it was a dirty word, Muldoon. Maybe we've misjudged him."

"Listen, lad," Muldoon said to Kevin. "We fight for Irish freedom against the aggressor, especially Anglo–Irish like your father—Protestant Englishmen who pretend to be Irish. We rose up in '48 to avenge the loss of our nation at the hands of the bloody English."

"But all the men of '48 were exiled or executed."

"Not by a long shot. Many of us went underground. We wait for another day, for a better time to strike." Muldoon stiffened and turned his head toward the door.

"What is it?" Meighan asked.

"Ssh, ssh, I heard something."

"It's my dear drunk Margaret Mary snoring."

"No, it isn't. It's my hounds. Someone has set them loose. They must have scented them, given them something of the lad's. I didn't think anyone would try that without me."

"I don't hear anything," Kevin said.

Muldoon turned to him. "If I'm to save your worthless Irish life, boy, you'll stop doubting my word as of this very moment. You'll have to start doing as you're told."

Kevin stared at him.

"Well, what's it to be? Are you with us, or do you prefer to hang?"

"I was waiting for Mrs. Miller to help."

"You mean the slut?"

Kevin bristled. "She's no such thing." He rose to his feet, his fists clenched.

"Irish chivalry. There's no accounting for it," Meighan chuckled.

Muldoon joined him in his joke. "Listen, Kevin my boy. That lady is no doubt moving hell itself to get assistance for you but I don't think she's going to succeed before my hounds find you here in the Meighan 'castle'. You've got to make up your mind, lad. Are you with us or not?"

Kevin bit his lip nervously. Now, he too could hear the dogs baying off in the distance—just as they had yesterday morning when they tracked the fox. But now he was the intended victim.

"All right, I'm with you," he said finally.

Muldoon breathed a sigh of relief. "I can divert the dogs. They are my beasts and they will do as I signal them, scent or no scent. We'll get you out of here and on your way to Galway in a flash."

"Then what happens to me?"

"Then you're off to America on the first ship we can safely hide you on."

"America? What will I do there?"

"You'll follow your oath and work for the cause."

"In America?"

"Of course. There are those who feel that since the oppressor of our nation is so strong here the place to strike a blow against Britian might well be in America. There is a bloody war going on there now—Northern nigger-lovers against southern slavemongers, a plague be on both of them. But there is many an Irish lad in the Northern Army, learning his trade, you might say, and preparing for the day when that war is over, for the day when armed Irish lads will march thousands strong across the border into British North America and strike a blow for Mother Ireland. I believe Irish independence will be won in Canada."

"That's not the brotherhood policy," Meighan protested. "If Stevens could hear you he'd drum you out, Muldoon."

"He can't hear me, and I don't have time to argue policy with you, Meighan."

"All right," said Meighan, "administer the oath."

"I haven't time for ritual now, either."

"No oath and he is not a brother and we won't spend a shilling on him." Meighan insisted.

"All right. Kevin, are you with us?"

"I have no choice."

"That won't do, lad. It will have to be of your own free choice."

The dogs seemed to get closer all the time. "All right," Kevin sighed.

"Raise your right hand, and repeat after me."

"I, Kevin O'Connor, solemnly pledge . . ." Kevin repeated the words Muldoon spoke. His head was reeling. Was all of

40

this really happening? Two days before his main worry was missing Mass and trying to avoid his mother's anger. Kevin continued to repeat Muldoon's words. "My sacred word of honor as a truthful and honest man that I will labor with earnest zeal for the liberation of Ireland from the yoke of England and for the establishment of a free and independent government on Irish soil."

"That will do. We haven't any more time for him."

"There's more," Meighan said. "Do you swear by the rest, Kevin O'Connor?"

"I do," said Kevin.

"Then it's done. Now stay here. I must greet me beauties." Muldoon ran out the front door. He whistled and the baying of the dogs seemed to lessen and then stop altogether. Soon the only sound was Margaret Mary's snores.

It was Meighan who first spoke again but not until the baying of the dogs renewed but this time clearly retreating from Meighan's cottage.

"You'll stay here for another two hours, brother, then Muldoon will lead you to a house we have in the outskirts of the city. You'll be in Galway for two days and aboard a fishing boat for Cork within a week. From Cork, it's America and godspeed."

The room was black except for the glow of the small enamel coal stove. One of the double doors opened a crack and allowed a beam of light to pierce the darkness. The door opened wider and Allison Miller stepped into the room, her black form outlined in the white light. She stopped at the foot of the bed. She heard Charles speak from the darkness.

"'Oh! Thus,' quoth Dighton, 'lay the gentle babes:' 'Thus, thus,' quoth Forrest, 'girdling one another within their alabaster innocent arms: their lips were four red roses on a stalk, and in their summer beauty kiss'd each other.'"

Allison stepped backwards at first as if frightened at the sound of her husband's voice.

"Are you awake?" she asked.

"No, I must be dreaming," responded the old man. "My wife comes to my bedroom at night only in my dreams."

Allison ignored his complaint. "Charles, I need your advice."

"Ah," he said in mock disappointment, "and all along I thought it was my cock that attracted you to me. How unfortunate to learn after all of these years, that it was really my brain that you lusted after."

"Charles, this is serious. Lord Carringdon is dead."

The old man was silent for a moment as he absorbed the information. "Which was it—overeating or overwenching?"

"Neither. He was murdered."

Again there was silence.

"It had to be a crime of passion. Nobody who really thought about it would bother killing him."

"It was!"

"Good. You see, we should have reached this understanding about my mind sooner. We could have avoided all of those years of fucking and really done something interesting. Who knows, we might even have avoided having Alex."

"That's whom I have come to talk to you about."

"Already the intellectual level of our conversation has fallen."

"Charles." There was a note of panic in Allison's voice that shut her husband up immediately. She sat next to him on the bed. "It's Alex, he's killed the baron."

All the mocking left Miller's voice. "How do you know that?"

"I was there. I saw him do it."

"Explain!"

"He went to meet Lady Carringdon at the summer house down by the lake. His lordship followed them and discovered them. Her ladyship's position was compromised."

"That's one way of saying it. Compromised, that's nicer than saying her legs were wide apart and our son had mounted her."

"Your description is more accurate if less delicate than mine."

"Little Alex. I would not have believed it of him."

"Why not? He's your son."

"Is he really? I have always wondered. That is a question I face with both of my sons. I do believe men should have the babies. That way *we* could be sure. But you were saying, our dear boy murdered our host."

"Please contain your cynicism. For once deal with me without your suit of armor."

Again Charles was sobered by Allison's plea. "Tell me what happened."

"It was so quick. Lord Carringdon came upon them bellowing like a bull. Alex defended himself and stabbed the baron in the chest. Alex panicked and ran, leaving Lady

Barbara in a state of shock. She and I talked. We finally agreed on a way to cover for both of them, saving her reputation and Alex's neck."

"My, my, and how did you do all that?"

"We put the blame on the stableboy—Kevin."

"His lordship's bastard?"

"Yes."

"Very clever, my dear. But will it work?"

"I hope so. You see, he came upon the scene and was struck on the head with a rock. He bled all over his father's corpse. I convinced him that everyone would blame him, so he ran. They are out looking for him now. I know where he is, and I sent them there to find him."

No sound came from the blackness of the canopied bed for some moments.

"Charles, speak to me. I am frightened," Allison pleaded.

"You've done well, my dear, but whom did you speak to about the boy's whereabouts? Will that tie you to the crime and implicate Alex?"

Allison smiled. "It was to old Muldoon, the hound master. I knew they would call on him. All I said was that I had seen the boy on the ridge road heading toward Meighan's farm where we were this afternoon. I didn't volunteer. He asked me."

"Good. But you'd have done better to send him in the opposite direction."

"What do you mean?" she asked in surprise.

"We really don't want the boy found, now do we? At least not alive. Is there any chance of arranging an accident?"

"Why?"

"Because if he is found, he'll talk and implicate you."

"He wouldn't!"

"Ah, the stableboy is a gentleman! He would not compromise his lady's reputation. I'll bet he wouldn't. I'll bet he's compromised you in the same way Alex was compromising Lady Carringdon when Lord Carringdon found them."

"I thought we had agreed not to allow these details to come between us."

"We did. It's just that it's so one-sided. You get to use our agreement all the time and my little escapades are only memories—fond memories, mind you, but still memories."

"Charles, what about our son? I'll do anything to protect him."

"Mother love, it's such a force in our lives. It's a shame no other woman ever loves you again as your mother loved you."

"Charles! Alex?"

"All right. We must try to help the stableboy escape, since we can't kill him. Get him to Europe, or even better, to America. Somewhere where he can't be questioned. All will agree that his flight is an admission of guilt. You were very clever about that, Allison. You have learned much from me."

"You are a master."

"Our Alex will be safe as long as the O'Connor boy is not caught. He will need friends and some money. We cannot be seen to be his friend, but we can see to it that he gets the money and make sure he gets enough to take him as far away as America. There is a billfold in my trunk. And, by the way, the weapon—what did you do with it?"

"I recovered it and gave it back to Alex. He says he won't be without it."

"Stupid move by our boy."

Allison rose from the bed and went to the old sea chest Charles still kept from his days as a captain on the lakes.

"And, Allison, I know how much is there. Give him enough to get him to America and no more. A lad like that will never earn enough to make his own way back."

"Do you really think I'd steal some from you?"

"Yes!"

"There are times, Charles, when I really find you even more than offensive."

"Do I ever reach loathsome?"

"Yes."

"Oh Lord, you may now dismiss your servant."

She fumbled in the trunk. She found the wallet and removed the pouch of gold coins. She started toward the door.

"You took the coins. I told you to take the paper money."

He amazed her. She was astounded that he could see in the dark. She looked at him in surprise.

"I was right, wasn't I?" he said, as she returned to the sea chest and replaced the coins with pound notes from the billfold. "I couldn't see, in case you're wondering. I just know my Allison."

She was angry now and stormed toward the door.

"Allison," he called her, "tell little Alex to control his appetites a little more. I have allowed you to bail him out once again, but, really, he must grow up. He can't just go around killing lords, not even Irish ones."

44

She slammed the heavy door behind her and went down the hall to her own bedroom.

She wondered finally what Charles had quoted to her when she first entered the room. He had seemed almost frightened. She liked that tone in his voice. She wondered what she could do to make it a fixture in their relationship.

The next morning Lady Carringdon secretly informed her that no trace of Kevin O'Connor could be found. Meighan's place had been searched, but not until Muldoon's dogs had been sent off in the wrong direction, costing hours of delay. Lady Carringdon was tense but seemed to be holding up. His lordship's estate would provide well for her even if the title passed to a nephew. Now she would be free to dally with other boys like Alex, only better than Alex.

Allison sent no one to look for Kevin. If he had got away without her help and her money so much the better. She could use the money herself.

The bell from the village church tolled mournfully. At Carringdon Hall, his lordship's Anglican chaplain led the prayers for the dead before his lordship's widow and family. He would be entombed in the crypt beneath the chapel. In the village, his tenants poured out of their cottages and trudged slowly toward Doyle's church to hear a Mass for the dead. True, his lordship was a Protestant—a heretic—but all the more reason he would need a Mass. He would need a miracle for sure to escape the devil's clutches. But the tenants stopped dead in their tracks when Mary O'Connor left her cottage. She was dressed totally in black and wore a black veil across her face. These were her widow's weeds, and she was not entitled to them.

The widow Deagan complained loudly for all to hear that she was the man's slut, not his widow. But Mary ignored the widow Deagan. She walked straight and tall despite her grief. Everyone was dead now. He was called to his coffin. She had no son. No son of hers could be alive to her after what he had done. All she had now was the grief, and there would be some consolation in it. She would allow the memory of her love to control her. She would seek out the priest in confession and do penance for her sin with her lover again and again. That way the sin and the love would be kept alive even if the sinner and lover could not be. Doyle and his confessional would give her something to live for. She had nothing else.

She lowered her head and dropped her gaze toward the dirt road that led to the church. She walked steadily and solemnly ahead. Even the widow Deagan was silenced, unable to ignore the power of a grieving widow. The village stepped aside and allowed her to head the procession into Doyle's church. Mass would not begin for half an hour.

Thomas Doyle was in his box awaiting her. She entered the darkness and gloom of the old stone building, dipped her finger into the holy water fountain and blessed herself. She genuflected before the red vigil lamp that hung over the tabernacle. The villagers filed into the pews. In full view of all of them, she entered the confessional. She pulled aside the purple cloth which covered the sinner's side of the box. The little door opened, and the familiar smell of Doyle's onions filtered across the little grilled opening. There was also the faint odor of whiskey about him. But Mary forgave him his weaknesses. She would forgive everyone. She was so much closer to Jesus now. There were the penances she would perform for her sin, the physical loving of her beloved. But now that was over. There was to be no more physical loving. Her lover was cold in his tomb. Now there was only a memory to be cultivated and suffered over, a spiritual loving to be cherished throughout life, throughout purgatory, into heaven, a loving suffering in which all sin would be purged.

"Bless me, Father," she confessed, "for I have sinned."

II

Halifax, Nova Scotia, May 1863

The cannons of the Citadel roared, signaling the lowering of the Union Jack and the end of daylight. Behind the hills to the west the sun turned the sky pink briefly, then dropped out of sight. Darkness did not fall rapidly in these northern parts. Every day the dusk would linger longer. By the end of June it would seem as if night delayed its arrival to coincide with the first obliterating light of dawn.

Wilhelmina Brant sat by her writing desk in her bedroom. In front of her was the ledger book in which she kept her household accounts and the books for her husband's law practice. She had served as bookkeeper and accountant since the days when they lived in the old Breed-Nowell mansion in Charlestown, Massachusetts. Those days seemed so long ago. In truth, almost a generation had passed. The thought of time passing forced her to look up from her books and into the mirror which stood on its own base on the desk.

She pushed her brown hair away from her cheek. There they were—those tiny lines running from the eyes toward the temples. "Smile lines" her husband Michael called them. It was not fair, she thought. He was thirty years older than she— seventy this year, to be exact—and he had not a single wrinkle. True, his black hair was now white, and his skinny legs and narrow chest looked funny supporting a belly that protruded over his belt. And then there was his heart. Dr. Stockard said it had to be watched carefully. It worried Michael, she knew. His father had died of a bad heart.

She sighed and looked away from the mirror. She had never been a vain woman and she wasn't going to start now. As a girl she had never thought herself pretty. In fact, she had done her best to hide the fact that she was a girl. Little Willy Mackay, the waif of Toronto. For years, she'd dressed in breeches,

47

cursed, played truant from school, and dodged her unloving father's "tokens" of affection. Then fate and the failure of the Mackenzie Rebellion of 1837 had thrown her into the arms of Michael Brant, the half–Mohawk, half–Jewish liberal leader of the reformers. They had fled Canada together in Willy's sailboat and lived in exile at Brant's cousin's home in Massachusetts.

She did not believe they ever really fell in love. He was just there, a replacement for her murdered father. She had not left Michael for even a day ever since. When she came of age, it was natural that he would ask her to marry him and natural that she would accept.

The days in Boston had ended fifteen years before. A pardon for his offenses in 1837 arrived for Michael and allowed him to return to British North America. But Michael would have no part of his old home in Upper Canada. He never told her why, but she could guess. His father, the Mohawk sachem, Kenonranon, and his mother Jessica, the daughter of a New Hampshire peddler Moishe Levine, might both be buried in the family plot in Toronto but Michael could remember only the hatred and the bigotry of a community which would turn on and persecute people because they were different. Later, enriched by a bequest from his cousin, Margaret Nowell Conrad, she and Michael had come to the port of Halifax in Nova Scotia. They had purchased this house and Michael had resumed his practice of law.

There were four bedrooms on the second floor of this house. It was an extravagance she had resisted at the time of purchase but now fifteen years later she was relieved by Michael's foresight. She and Michael kept separate bedrooms, partly in deference to his age and partly because she needed some place where she could do her own books and read in private. Her books were not the kind of books that Michael and Meg would discuss for hours. She never entered those discussions, nor did she allow her husband and daughter to know that she understood their talks. It was enough for her to know that she understood.

Their daughter, Meg, had been born in Boston. She was eighteen now. She was bright, witty and highly educated—far beyond most young women. Michael had seen to it that she learned as much as any boy.

There was a time when Willy had been jealous of the care and education showered on their daughter. All Michael had taught Willy, beyond reading and writing, was the simplest of accounting techniques, and most of those she had learned by doing rather than by theory. But she took pride in her daughter's native intelligence. Sometimes she worried that Meg's intellect and biting tongue would drive away potential suitors. But then she would laugh aloud. Imagine Willy Mackay worrying about her daughter getting a man. If Willy Mackay could get a husband, anyone could.

The fourth bedroom in the house became occupied last year. She had answered the door bell and found a leather–clad, dusty–faced, brown–eyed young man.

"Mrs. Brant?" he had addressed her. "My pap sent me to get some learning."

She knew who he was just by looking into his face. The eye color was wrong, and the flaxen blonde hair of Joshua Miller had turned dark, but it was his face, the face of the boy she had loved.

"You're Joshua's son, aren't you?"

"Yes ma'am. My name is Craig Miller."

And suddenly they had another child and no empty bedrooms. Michael had taken the boy under his wing. He knew what the son of a white man and an Assiniboine woman faced. He had faced it all his life and he had been raised in one of the finest houses on Bay Street, Toronto. This boy had been born in an Indian village on the open prairies, and raised along the shores of Lake Manitoba and along the banks of the Red River where his father had a farm.

The half–breeds, the two of them, were soon as thick as thieves. The boy was a quick learner, and now he was ready for admission to King's College in Windsor.

The dinner bell rang. The cook and the housemaid were the only servants Willy employed, and there were times when she resented even their presence. She liked doing things herself. She rose from her desk and walked out into the hallway. The oil lamps had already been lighted downstairs in the foyer, even though darkness had not yet fallen and would not for at least another hour and a half. They cast flickering shadows on the pale blue and white wall covering she had had installed two years earlier. It went so well with the black–lacquered foyer table with its painted scenes of Chinese ladies and gentlemen. Willy had a fondness for things Chinese, including her cook, the only Chinese cook in Halifax or in Nova Scotia for that matter. Willy would not have been surprised to learn that Chou was also the only Chinese person, much less cook, in all of Nova Scotia. She had found him on the harborfront, penniless. She smiled to herself as she descended the curved stairway to the foyer. Ever since she and Michael had been taken in as refugees by the Conrads back in '37, they had tried to repay Cousin Margaret's kindness by taking in refugees themselves. So far, it had worked to their advantage. Chou was a brilliant cook. And even if the family was never quite sure what it was they ate, it always tasted delicious.

Michael, who had been in the parlor, awaited Willy at the foot of the stairs.

"What's the dinner tonight?"

"I don't know. I think it is pork," she responded.

"My Jewish grandfather is flipping in his grave," Michael teased.

She put her arm through his and he led her into the dining room. It was Willy's favorite room in the whole house. It was paneled in dark, rich, grained walnut. The rug was deep maroon. It covered almost the whole floor and revealed, at the edges, the wide floorboards of walnut–stained hardwood. The large, oval dining table was covered with a fine lace cloth that matched the lace of the window curtains. Chou had set out their good china, brought all the way from Jessica Brant's home in Toronto after her death back in 1846. The cook had also decanted a fine red wine from Michael's modest cellar to celebrate Craig's acceptance by the faculty at King's. This would be the boy's last month with them. In late summer he was off to the college.

Meg sat at the table. She wore her reddish hair piled high on her head reminding Willy of her namesake and godmother Margaret Nowell.

"My dear," Willy said as she entered the dining room.

Meg rose to greet her parents, but before she could speak, the front door opened and closed with a slam. Craig Miller came racing into the room breathing heavily.

"Aunt Willy, Uncle Michael, sorry I'm late." He plopped himself into the chair opposite Meg.

Michael looked annoyed at the boy but Willy smiled indulgently. The young man immediately launched into a description of a near riot that had delayed his return from the Brant law offices where he had been doing research.

"What started it?" Meg asked.

"A ship came into the harbor. It was a blockade runner

heading for Charleston in South Carolina. Some of the black dockworkers refused to load it. They got into a fight with the whites, most of whom were Irish," Craig responded.

"I thought the Irish in the United States were fighting for the North?" Willy interrupted. "It would seem they should have a common cause."

"I am not sure whom the Irish fight for," Michael replied laughing. "All I know is that they fight anytime, anywhere. On the other hand, the blacks of this town and province have had families living in Nova Scotia since the American Revolution. The British armies, leaving places like Savannah and Charleston, took slaves with them to Halifax and set them free."

"You teach me that," Craig said.

"I *taught* you that," Michael corrected him.

"That's what I said," he went on, "but lots of blacks have come to Halifax via the underground railroad. Some have gone back to join the Union armies now that the war is on, but those who stayed behind have sympathy only for one side, the North."

"What else would you expect?" Meg interrupted. "Would you sympathize with a society that kept your people in bondage, sold you like chattels and beat you at whim?"

"Sounds to me much like what the white man did to the red man," Michael said.

Craig laughed at his cousin Meg's discomfort.

"Daddy, you know what I mean. I don't see why the Irish would be fighting the blacks. They too are a oppressed people. Look at what the English have done to them."

"The Irish are supposed to be loyal subjects of Her Majesty, Queen Victoria, just like you and me."

"So says the man sentenced to hang for rebellion back in 1837," said Craig looking at Michael Brant in admiration. "My father told me all about how you and he fought against the queen under William Lyon Mackenzie."

Michael looked a bit squeamish at the mention of hanging. "Your father and I drifted into the rebellion without a great deal of conviction. It was something to do with a girl for your father."

"And who could forget her? Allison Miller, the Toronto whore," Willy said this last with such vehemence that the two younger people looked up at her in surprise.

Michael started to laugh. "They were all children together. Joshua, Allison and your mother." Then he leaned over to Meg and in an exaggerated whisper said for all to hear, "Your mother never cared for Allison. I can't say the same about Joshua though."

"I was never a child," Willy said with some pain in her voice.

The kitchen door opened and Chou brought in a tureen of soup. They proceeded to eat.

"What is this stuff?" Michael finally complained. "My mouth and lips are stinging."

"Don't ask," Willy responded.

"Why don't you get a decent Christian cook like every other family in Halifax?" he continued.

"So says the Jewish Mohawk."

"I am a Christian, madam," he responded haughtily. "I am a confirmed communicant of the Church of England and I have been one all my adult life."

"I think Chou's a Methodist," said Willy, teasing her husband.

"Damn it, he should cook like a Methodist."

They ate on for some more minutes in silence, interrupted only by Craig's occasional forgetful slurping.

"The Irishmen invited bystanders to come to their meeting tonight down at MacSorley's tavern near the docks. Do you think I could attend?"

"Why would you want to go?" Michael asked him.

"I don't know. I am curious I guess. My father told me to learn everything I could while I was in the east. He told me he could afford to send only one of us. I will have to teach everything I learn in turn to my brother Douglas and my sister Beth. Even my mother wants to learn everything she can. My father is too busy farming our land or hunting buffalo or just going off with my mother's people, the Assiniboine, to do much to help anyone else."

"What do you think the Irish can teach you?"

"Some of the same things you've taught me, I suppose. How you can't just sit back and let yourself be pushed around. You have to stand up for your own rights."

"Is that what I've taught you?" Michael asked, his brow wrinkling in concern.

"No, you've taught me the importance of the rule of law and how to go about changing things by changing laws rather than trying to overthrow governments."

"A practice your Irish friends have never quite taken to their bosoms," Michael joked.

"There are times, even you must admit," Meg interrupted, "when even the rule of law is insufficient and all must take up arms for a just cause."

"Those occasions are very rare," Michael insisted. "And as I get older I think they become more rare."

"We are watching one of those times play itself out across the border."

"I cannot believe a civil war is ever justified, Meg," Michael responded.

"Don't you believe in just wars, sir?" Craig asked him.

"Yes, if I'm attacked I'll fight back. When the Americans invaded our homeland back in 1812, I stood with Brock at Kingston Heights."

"Oh my God," Willy said, "don't get him started on that story; how he saw Brock fall. I've heard it more than I can bear."

"The cause of the northern States, the Union, is just, Father," Meg said angrily. "I don't see how you could defend slavery."

"I don't defend it," Michael responded angrily. "But I don't believe you must destroy the South in order to abolish slavery. It was going to fade on its own anyway."

"Justice can't wait until people acknowledge it," Meg cut him off.

Michael shrugged. "By my analogy, the South is the invaded nation defending itself. There is some cause for saying that they have justice on their side. I see no Southern armies invading the North. They are merely defending their homes and families just as the York militia did back in 1812—against those same Yankees, I might add."

"I don't believe you're saying these things, Father," Meg said in exasperation. She turned to Craig. "Instead of going to listen to those vulgar Irishmen, you should be trying to give succor to the black men."

Craig nodded at his cousin. He still was not comfortable with the give-and-take between Michael and Meg. In his house his father always had the last word, even if they all did what his mother decided, including his father.

Chou entered the room carrying a platter of steaming meat and chopped vegetables over a bed of boiled rice. He placed the platter on the table and then bowed to the family and departed. The food smelled delicious. Michael dug into it with

53

a serving spoon. The aroma of meat tickled his taste buds but he could not resist a complaint.

"Willy, we may as well throw out the table knives as long as you insist on keeping this Chinaman in the kitchen. We're never again going to have the chance to cut into a solid piece of meat." With that he plopped a piece of sliced pork into his mouth.

"Well, Craig, my lad," he continued after swallowing his first mouthful, "are you going to the Irishmen's meeting?"

"Michael," Willy warned.

"No, my love, he's a man. He must make his own decisions."

"You don't say that to me," Meg complained.

"Because it would be inaccurate, by God. You're a woman." He grew silent. He had participated in this conversation before when he was a lad. Only then it was his foster sister, Elizabeth, complaining that Michael could go off to war and she couldn't. He said no more to Meg but gave his attention to Craig's answer.

"My father says that the white man will not leave us in peace much longer in Rupert's Land. Once the American war is over they will pour into the west. They will slaughter all the buffalo and drive the Indians before them just as they did the Iroquois and the Abenacki. They'll move north into the valleys of the Red and the Saskatchewan unless the English keep them out. The Canadians, he says, will force the English to keep the Americans out. The Canadians will want the land for themselves so that they may slaughter the buffalo and drive the Indians before them."

Michael laughed. "Age has made your father a wiser man. It is true, the Canadians do covet Rupert's Land just as the Americans do. Canada will want all the possessions of the Hudson's Bay Company from the Great Lakes to the Rockies. The Canadians will demand a confederation, mark my words, to bring together all the British possessions on this continent, Newfoundland, New Brunswick, Prince Edward Island, Nova Scotia, Victoria Colony. We are all to be gobbled up by Upper and Lower Canada into one country sea to sea. The prairies of Rupert's Land will make a transcontinental Canada a possibility."

"But my father also said it will be a country without room for Métis like me and my brother and sister or red people like my mother."

"He's right, you know," Michael said shaking his head. "The

only Indians who will find a place in this nation are those who become more white than the white—people like me."

"Oh, daddy, you're hardly Indian," Meg said.

"My father was a Mohawk war chief, son of Molly Brant, grandson of Nicus Brant and great grandson of Old Brant, sachem of Schoharie, the Lower Castle of the Mohawk."

"And his father was Stephen Nowell of Boston, whose father was the Reverend Samuel Nowell, and my mother was Jessica Levine Brant, daughter of Moishe Levine of Cracow, Poland."

"So, I'm a mongrel."

"All three of you can claim that distinction," Willy laughed. "Now, me, I'm pure Scots-Irish. While you, Meg, and the half-breeds have been raised in improper houses by your equally mongrelized parents, I was raised a good white Protestant by my drunken Baptist minister father."

Michael laughed and turned to Craig. "So, son, what have the Irish to teach a mongrel like you?"

"I don't know for sure, except maybe how to fight the English Canadians as they have fought the English English all these centuries."

"Let's hope it doesn't come to that, son."

"I'm sure it won't," Willy said.

"Let's hope," Craig repeated but without any conviction in his voice.

Craig stepped out of the bathtub and grabbed the soft towel that was draped across the sink. The greatest wonder in coming to live in the Brants' home was the indoor plumbing, and having hot water at your disposal. As a boy he had bathed frequently in the lake and rivers in the summer. He loved to swim and cavort in the waters. Both his parents and later Beth and Doug, his tagalong little brother, joined him, but the luxury of a hot bath, even in the dead of winter, had been unknown to him until now. Now he bathed as often as he could. It did not bother him that the servants complained to Willy and would no longer heat his water for him. No matter, he heated his own water. He liked doing things for himself anyway.

He wrapped the towel about his middle and stepped out of the bathroom and into his bedroom. There was a soft knock on his door. He grabbed the old bathrobe Michael had given him and wrapped it around him.

"Who is it?" he asked.

The door opened and Meg slipped in.

"I didn't say for you to come in. I'm not properly dressed."

"Oh shoot, Craig, I'll bet you aren't such a prude back home."

"My mother would respect my privacy, and has done so ever since I became a man."

"You're hardly naked. Only your feet are showing."

Without thinking, Craig looked down at his toes.

"My goodness, cousin, you are such a simpleton."

He blushed. "Did you come here to admire my feet?"

"Touché." She laughed. "No, I want to come with you to the Irish workers' meeting."

He grinned at her and turned his back. "There are no women allowed."

"I suspected as much, and have anticipated that unenlightened attitude. You'll lend me some of your clothes."

"I really should take you, you know. It would do you some good to rub elbows with real people. It might teach you more about life than all the books in your fancy library."

"Since when have you turned anti–intellectual?"

"I haven't. I just know there is more to be learned than can be found in books."

"Like what?" she questioned.

"Like knowing where to find the herds, and how to cut up a cow for the tenderest meat, or how to skin an antelope, or when to cut the wheat to avoid a killer frost."

"I don't need to know any of those things. They'd be of little use to me here in Halifax. I need to know what is happening here, what the men who make their living from the sea can teach me."

"You can't come with me."

"Damn," she said stamping her foot, "why not?"

"I've told you why. Besides I couldn't take you without betraying the trust of Uncle Michael and Aunt Willy. Now, get out of here so that I can get dressed. You're going to make me late for my meeting."

"I hope you're good and late, Craig Miller," Meg said petulantly. She turned and ran from the room.

Craig smiled. He liked her. She was immature and insolent, but that was because she had been so protected in this household. He wondered how any of them, Michael, Willy or Meg, could survive without their luxuries in this civilized town. Far be it for him to condemn them. He had gotten used to those baths and indoor plumbing and he had gotten used to them very quickly.

He pulled on his pants and tucked the tail of a clean shirt into his breeches. He would need only his light jacket, since the evening was mild. He saved the shoes for last. How he had hated wearing them at first, so hard and unbending when compared to Indian moccasins. He still hated them, but by now he was used to them too.

He trotted down the stairs two at a time. He stuck his head into the parlor, and found his uncle reading. He could hear his aunt conversing, shouting really, with Chou in the kitchen.

"I'll be leaving now, Uncle Michael."

"Take care," Brant responded without looking up from his text.

"Where's Meg?" Craig asked.

Brant looked up over the top of his spectacles. "She said she was tired. She's not joining me tonight for our evening declaration of war. Instead she's off to an early bed."

Craig smiled. "Well, good luck in case she changes her mind."

Michael gave him a look of mock hurt. "Young man, I'll have you know I've taught that girl everything she knows and I can still hold my own with her."

"I'm glad *you* can. It will be a long time before *I* can."

"Nonsense, can't let the women bully you, my boy. You must put them in their place, which is properly the kitchen."

"I heard you," Willy said as she came out of the kitchen. Michael rolled his eyes upward.

"But, damn it, you may be right, especially if the cook is Chinese. Michael, you must go out there and speak with that man. He's brought a monkey into the house. He bought it from a sailor down at the docks. When I yelled at him that I would have no pets he just smiled. 'No pet, missy,' he said. 'You eat, make good supper'."

Michael blanched. "God knows what we've been eating!"

Craig decided that it was time to depart. He could shock them with stories of fighting with his brother for raw buffalo liver and intestines but he saw no point to further shocking their sensibilities. He stepped out the front door and walked along the street and down the hill toward the harbor. MacSorley's was around the corner near the docks. Craig could see other men moving along the street in the same general direction. There would be a large crowd at the tavern tonight. He turned the corner.

The tavern was at the end of a narrow street. Actually it was on pilings over the water. The front door had panels of cheap stained glass. It was difficult to tell what was drawn on the glass because it was covered with the grime of the waterfront and years of neglect. All that Craig could identify looked like a bow with many strings, a clumsy thing he thought. He had no prior experience or knowledge of a harp.

The taproom smelled of whiskey, stale whiskey. It was lighted by oil lamps and some candles on the tables. He had guessed right about the crowd. There was barely room to move. He worked his way into the room and found himself leaning against the bar.

"What will it be for you, chap?" He was addressed by a large woman from behind the bar. She must have stood just under six feet tall. Her arms rivaled the small kegs of whiskey that were piled behind her on the bar, and her bosom protruded over the bar itself.

"What's your pleasure, boy?"

Craig pointed at himself.

The woman's eyes rolled up toward the ceiling in exasperation. "What are you drinking," she said sighing.

"Nothing."

"Yes, you are, or it's out you go. I love the cause but I love Bella MacSorley better. You come to a meeting in my tavern, you drink."

"In that case, I'll have a mug of ale," Craig said to the proprietor.

"That's more like it." She drew ale from the tap and slapped a pewter mug down on the bar. The foam started to run over the side. She stuck her finger into the ale. "You don't mind, do you? That finger ain't been any place it shouldn't have been and I've misplaced my sponge."

Craig was not too certain of her assurances. The woman was a mess. Huge stains spread from her armpits down the sides of her blouse, and she stank badly. Yet there was something about her that appealed to him. He couldn't place it. There was something familiar. He smiled at her.

"Wipe that shit–eating grin off your face," she said angrily.

He did as she demanded, yet she continued to stare at him.

"Why did you smile at me?" she said finally. "No one smiles at me. Were you trying to make a pass at me?"

58

He bent almost in two with laughter.

"Why, you little pecker! I suspect that's exactly what you've got! You think that's funny?" She reached across the bar and grabbed him by his brown locks. "Why, I could take everything you've got and still have to ask you if you were in yet!"

"I wasn't laughing at you. Ouch, let go," he laughed. "I wasn't making fun of you. It's just that I finally remembered who you reminded me of."

"Who?"

"My grandmother."

Again the barrellike arm shot forward and her fingers entwined in his hair. His head was moving toward the bar for a good slam when he stiffened his neck and shoulder muscles and braced his arms on the bar, bringing her motion to a sudden halt.

"No insult intended again," he said laughing.

She was more impressed with the strength of his muscles than with his words.

"Most young cubs come in here all puffed up and that's all they are—hot air. Where did you get muscles like that? You must be a dockworker. But if you were I'd know you."

"I got my muscles from working hard, from harvesting wheat and hay, paddling canoes and hauling buffalo meat to make *pemmican*."

"Not in Halifax you didn't do none of those things."

"You're right. It was out west, and the grandmother that you remind me of is an Indian chief's wife, a great woman, with the name of Warrior Woman, who has taken scalps in her own right."

"A fighting woman, eh? So long as you weren't trying to call me an old lady. You're part Indian, eh?"

"My mother is Assiniboine."

"That makes you one of them fellows out there they call Métis, half breeds."

Craig couldn't tell if she was trying to mock him. He started to move away from the bar.

"No, wait," she said. "No offense meant. You fellows have much in common with us Irish. I assume that's why you're here. O'Connor," she called. "Where is that kid? Kevin O'Connor," she yelled.

"Here, you old battle-ax," a young man screamed drunkenly from across the room.

"Lucky, you're where I can't reach you," Bella screamed back.

"It's indeed my good fortune."

"Well, do something to earn your keep. We have a young guest. I want you to take him under your wing and explain our cause to him." As she spoke she pointed to Craig.

The flushed face of the black-haired youth broke into a grin. "Make your way over to this table, guest."

Craig started to move when he felt Bella's clawlike grip on his shoulder.

"You'll be going nowhere without paying first."

Craig reached into his pocket and handed her his shilling. She nodded at him and turned to serve another customer.

"Does an ale cost a shilling in this tavern?"

"No, it's two pence."

"Well, I'll be going nowhere without my change," he imitated her brogue.

Now it was Bella's turn to laugh. "And here I thought you enjoyed my company so much you were rewarding me with a generous gratuity."

"I love the cause, Bella, but the cause of my own pocket must come first."

Now she let out a roar of laughter. "Kevin O'Connor, you old misbegotten bastard, you take good care of this one. I like him."

She handed Craig his change. He took his mug of ale and joined O'Connor and his three companions at a table across the taproom from the bar.

"My name's O'Connor, Kevin O'Connor, though how you could miss the name with that tub of lard screaming it all the way across the taproom I don't know. And these louts are my companions. Jim Hickey."

A large, freckle-faced man merely nodded at Craig.

"And Sean Lavery."

The second young man actually rose from his seat and made a sweeping bow.

"The lad is a bit daft," Kevin explained. "He was on the stage in Dublin before he discovered a sudden necessity to be on this side of the ocean."

Craig nodded to the three young men. "Craig Miller," he said extending his hand.

O'Connor shook it, as did big Jim Hickey, but Lavery

concluded that his bow was more than sufficient greeting, besides he had concerns.

"Miller, Craig Miller, that's not an Irish name. Have we a Judas in our midst? I'll be damned if it's not an English name."

"You're right. My family is from good Loyalist English stock."

"Shall I bash him and throw him out?" Hickey muttered.

Craig started to chuckle at this joke until he realized that the big man was serious. "That's on my father's side. My mother's an Assiniboine, a tribe that's been fighting the English since before Montcalm and Wolfe."

"This Boyne, does it have to do with the Orangemen?" Hickey looked even more menacing now. "My family lost everything it had at the Battle of the Boyne."

"Shut up, Jim," Lavery insisted. "Your family never had anything to lose in the first place."

Hickey looked as if he had been kicked in the shins but he said nothing more. Craig realized that, like a giant puppy dog, Hickey did whatever Sean Lavery commanded him to do.

"So you're not just another homeless man looking for something to belong to. No wonder Bella sent you over," said Kevin. "You Indians and us Irish are natural allies."

"How so?" asked Craig.

"Because of the common enemy."

"Bella," Lavery called out.

"What is it, squirt?" she responded.

"Bring another round of drinks for us all."

"Not without seeing some coin of the realm first."

"You know it's against my principles to carry anything bearing the image of the English monarch. I have no money."

"Convenient principles you've got. Convenient for you, that is. Well, I've got one of my own principles. No money, no drink. Why don't you hit the Indian? He took some pence off me just a few minutes ago."

Craig nodded.

"Hooray," Kevin O'Connor shouted, "the drinks are on the Assiniboines."

From the whole of the taproom rose a mighty cheer. Craig panicked momentarily, then realized that he had a half-crown in his watch pocket. That should be enough. Even big Jim Hickey rose and clapped him on the back.

Bella's assistant started bringing trays of whiskey and ale

from behind the bar. Men grabbed at the glasses and at Bella's assistant, a pretty red–haired girl of about seventeen.

"Keep your hands off her," Bella screamed.

"I know," Sean Lavery called out. "She's reserved."

Bella gave him a wicked look. "I'll fix it so that, as they say in the Bible, your line shall no longer piss against the wall, Lavery."

Sean laughed and stuck his tongue out at Bella. She was about to step from behind the bar when Lavery, realizing he had gone too far with her, suddenly turned his attention back to Craig.

"Big Jim and I are going to the States next week. We're joining up."

"With the Yanks?"

"Who else?"

"But why?" Craig asked.

"We Irishmen must get our training," Kevin chimed in.

"We're going to learn tactics from the Yanks. Then we're going back to Ireland and fight for a Republic. We'll all be officers in an Irish republican army," Lavery said. "Can't you see me now? General Sean Lavery."

"Me too," said Hickey.

"No, Jim. I'm sorry, but there can only be one General Sean Lavery."

Jim was confused for a second. Then his face broke into a big grin. "I didn't mean I'd be you."

The front door of MacSorley's swung open just as Craig glanced in that direction.

"Oh no," he said staring at the newcomer. The three other men looked in the same direction.

"Who is it?" Kevin asked. "It's surely not a man, and boys are not welcome."

"That's no boy either," Craig said angrily. He rose and squeezed his way through the crowd of Irishmen. He grabbed the newcomer by reaching over someone's shoulder.

"Hold it, cousin," he said, taking a handful of his own jacket which hung loosely from the newcomer's shoulders. Meg Brant turned her face toward Craig.

"What the hell do you think you're doing here?" he shouted at her. The sound was drowned by a cheer as Bella's assistant finally reached the far side of the taproom with another tray of drinks.

"Get yourself out of here and back home. What will Uncle Michael say if he finds out?"

"I'll tell him you took me with you," Meg said haughtily.

"He won't believe that of me," Craig responded without conviction.

Meg pouted. "Maybe you're right," she said finally. "But I won't go unless you come with me. I thought I was a free spirit, Craig, stealing your clothes and sneaking out of the house, but I'm not as brave as I thought. I was really frightened out there in the dark street alone."

"I can't go now," Craig protested. "Oh damn, come sit down with us for a few minutes. Then we can go home."

He took her by the hand and led her through the crowd back to his table.

"Kevin, Jim, Sean, this is my little cousin Mark. Mark Brant."

"He doesn't even look Indian," Jim said studying Meg's face.

"Well, I am. My father was a Hebrew Mohawk."

"Aha," Sean laughed, "one of the descendants of the Lost Tribes."

Kevin studied Meg suspiciously. "There's more mystery here than we are being told. I suspect it is not age that would bar you from these premises," he paused and then said, "sir."

There was a commotion at the front door of the tavern again. The double doors flew open with a crash. Some of the stained glass clattered to the floor.

"Hey, what the hell—" Bella called. She did not finish. A young man came flying through the doorway and crashed into a table, overturning it along with mugs of ale and sending them and patrons scurrying in all different directions. The first man was followed by a second, and then there was a rush of the largest black men that Craig had ever seen. Some swung clubs made from barrel staves. One blow crashed on an Irishman's skull, sending blood flying through the air. Suddenly about ten Irishmen were down and bleeding.

Bella vaulted over the bar. Her enormous leg swung up into the crotch of the nearest black man. He screamed in agony and fell to his knees holding his groin with both hands. A huge smile crossed Bella's face.

"Smash up my place, will you, you black bastards." The knee rose again. This time it smashed his face beyond recognition.

A woman screamed, and Bella, thinking it was her assistant

63

who had been hurt, went berserk. She tore into the attacking crowd in the direction of the scream. In fact, it was Meg who had screamed as one of the black dockworkers came charging toward their table. Craig grabbed her about the waist and pulled her from her seat. The attacker was greeted instead by big Jim Hickey who rose to his full six feet four inches. As Jim rose, the expression on the black man's face changed from anger to awe and then finally to fear. He turned to retreat and smashed into Bella.

"Has this prick hurt my Phoebe?" she shouted. She reached for him but was cut down from behind by a flying table. The reprieved black man picked up a loose chair, turned swiftly and brought it down on top of Jim's skull.

Hickey blinked in astonishment and then shook his head. His reactions were slowed but his intention was unaltered. He moved toward the attacker. The black man cursed and started to run away. His foot was grabbed from below by Bella, who reached out from under the fallen tables and chairs. The bone in his ankle snapped with a sickening crack and the black man screamed in agony.

Kevin stood next to Craig. "I think we had best get out of here," he said, "A fellow could get hurt in here. Lavery," he called to his friend who was sampling drinks on other tables vacated by a great rush of his fellow Irishmen, "get Hickey to lead us out of here."

Lavery pulled his cloak from the back of his chair and theatrically turned it about on his shoulders.

"Big Jim," he called, "let's be gone."

Hickey halted his pursuit of screaming victims and turned back to his friends. His eyes spread wide in surprise when he saw Meg. Her father's old hat, which had hidden her long hair, had been knocked from her head in the scuffle. If Sean Lavery was surprised, he hid it well.

"We must protect the lady. Irish chivalry—our honor demands it, Jim my boy," he called out.

With Hickey in the van, the little group inched their way toward the rear door of MacSorley's. Kevin had fashioned a club out of a chair leg and brought up the rear immediately behind Meg, who stayed as close as she could to Craig's back.

Hickey kept clearing people out of their path, white or black. On his way he saw Phoebe lying on the floor. He picked her up and threw her over his shoulder. One large black arm came crashing at him. He caught it in midair with his fist and twisted it. Craig could not tell if the owner of the arm screamed or not. The noise in the tavern was deafening and it was impossible to distinguish one scream or shout from another.

Finally they reached the side door. It was locked. Hickey handed the unconscious form of Phoebe to Lavery and threw his shoulders into the door, shattering it. It was a mistake. Outside were at least fifteen black longshoremen kept out of the fray by the obstacle Jim had just removed. They came rushing forward with a force that even Hickey's enormous power could not resist. Jim, Sean Lavery, and poor Phoebe were knocked backward into Craig. They all fell to the floor and were trampled by the onrushing black men.

Kevin reached around Meg's waist and pulled her off to the side. When all the black men had rushed through the shattered side door, he calmly led her through it into the pitch black alley.

"Quick, hold onto me," he ordered. "If we can get out to the street, we may just get out of here without getting our heads bashed."

"I can't," Meg objected. "Craig's still in there."

"Tough. It's each man for himself in there. My chivalry stops with saving women and children. Beyond that I don't go." He stiffened when he heard a constable's whistle. "I've got to go. Are you coming with me?"

"No," she responded, "not without Craig."

"Listen, whoever you are. I've got very good reason for not wanting to fall into the hands of any of Her Majesty's bloody loyal officials so I'll see you around."

"Don't leave me alone," she cried out in panic.

Kevin stopped. "I'm not staying," he repeated. "So I guess that means you're coming with me."

He held out his hand. She hesitated at first, then reached for him.

Craig pulled himself to his knees. He was groggy. Suddenly the room was filled with constables and redcoated troops from the Citadel. An officer was shouting orders. Someone shoved aside tables and chairs, and a battered and bruised Bella MacSorley emerged from under the rubble.

"Bella," a British officer addressed her. "I've warned you again and again about these brawls. This time I'm taking you in."

Bella paid no attention to him. She searched the room with her eyes until she spotted Phoebe sitting on the floor laughing at a joke Sean Lavery had just told her. Lavery looked as unruffled as he had before the attack occurred. He said nothing about the wooden splinters that had pierced his buttocks when he was sent sprawling by Hickey's fall.

Bella rushed to Phoebe's side and helped her to her feet. She covered her face with kisses.

"Bella," the British officer yelled again. "I'm talking to you. Didn't you hear me? I'm taking you all in."

"What else could I expect from an English pig like you?"

"This is a den of Irish republican thieves. You all belong in a jail cell. For some of you that will be the first step toward a noose. One need not be a prophet to predict that."

Craig grew wary as he listened to this exchange. It dawned on him that the officer meant him as well. Even worse, he meant Meg. But where was she? He rose to his feet and moved quickly toward the rear door. But it was too late. The officer had seen him.

"Constable, block that doorway and arrest that man trying to escape."

Kevin stopped at the corner of the alley and checked in both directions. Meg was gasping from the exertion.

"Come," Kevin whispered. He took her even more firmly by the arm and stepped out into the street.

"Halt." The call came from behind them, from out of the shadows. "You two, stand where you are or I'll shoot."

Kevin forced down an overwhelming urge to make a break for it. The side alleys were darker and close at hand. But he could not make it with the girl. He could, of course, abandon her. But no, he reasoned, she might be an asset after all. He stood still.

"What will happen to us?" Meg said, close to tears.

"Be quiet and do as I tell you," Kevin hissed at her. He placed his arm familiarly about her waist. She started to pull away but his strong arm forced her even closer to him. "Don't play Miss Prim and Proper at a time like this."

Kevin swung Meg around and together they faced the muzzle of a single–shot pistol held in the hands of a dark–coated Halifax constable. The policeman held a ship's lantern in front of him. It cast a ghostly glow on his face and on the faces of his two captives.

"Where do you two think you're going?" the constable addressed them.

Kevin smiled nervously and began to stutter. "Constable, you frightened us. I . . . I . . . My girl . . . We thought . . ."

"You thought what, lad? Out with it!"

"I thought you might be her father. You see he's Irish and I'm not." All trace of Kevin's Irish brogue had disappeared, his accent was pure Anglo-Saxon, just like the constable's.

A knowing look crossed the constable's face. It was followed by a broad smile.

Kevin squeezed Meg's waist even tighter.

"Irish, is she?" the policeman repeated. "I've heard about them Catholic girls, but I thought you had to be a priest in the confessional to get anywhere with them." He broke out into a loud laugh.

Kevin looked shyly at his feet.

"Tell me, lad, did she do what you wanted her to do? Will she be nice and damp in the right places?" He reached over to touch Meg but she backed away from him.

"Oh, she's a teaser," the constable said angrily.

"Carlson," the call came from down the street, back toward MacSorley's.

"Damn," the constable muttered.

"Let me take her home, constable," Kevin pleaded. His hand was thrust into his pocket and gripped the handle of his knife.

"Carlson!" the voice was less patient.

"Coming!" Carlson called out. He leaned over toward Kevin, and at the same time patted Meg's chest with his open palm. "Give the bitch a good one for me, lad," he turned and disappeared into the darkness.

Meg stifled a sob. Kevin held her by the elbow to prevent her from sagging to the ground.

"Are you all right?" he asked.

"Why didn't you stop him? How could you let him touch me?"

"Listen, miss," Kevin responded, "as I told you, I've got reasons not to let the officers of her majesty the queen get hold of me. All he did was touch you. There is no way Kevin O'Connor gets himself a noose as a reward for protecting some wench's virtue."

"You disgust me. You're no gentleman."

"Is that a fact?"

"Take me home," Meg said haughtily.

"I thought maybe you'd like to come to my room. It's really close by."

Meg was furious. "I want to go home."

"Go, then."

Meg hesitated. "Alone?"

"Alone!"

"I don't know where I am."

"Well, I'm going home. You can stay here if you want, or you can come with me." Kevin started to walk off into the darkness.

"Wait," Meg called.

"Coming?"

Meg did not respond but instead reached out tentatively for his hand.

Kevin stepped aside to allow Meg to enter the room first. He could hear her breathing heavily—the result of the long climb up the rickety wooden steps to the third floor. The dank smell of unwashed clothes and bed linen struck her as she entered the room. She wrinkled her nose with disgust.

Kevin closed the door behind them. The room was lighted only by the moon, which filled the one window with its silver glow. Kevin stood with his back against the door. His face broke into his boyish grin, and he pushed his hair back away from his eyes.

"What a night," he exclaimed. "Good ale, good brawl and now a good woman in my room."

"Take me home," Meg said softly.

"I will, lass, in due course, provided you tell me where you live."

"It's near Citadel Hill, the Brant house, Mr. Michael Brant, Esquire. He's my father. He'll reward you well, He's a lawyer."

"I hope I'll never be needing his services," Kevin laughed. He reached out and touched her. She stepped back.

"You don't really want to go home right now, do you?"

He stepped close to her and placed his arms around her waist. She lifted her head up and looked into his handsome face. He lowered his face to meet hers and their lips touched. He tried to force open her mouth with his tongue but she pulled away. His hands reached up to undo the buttons on the man's shirt she wore. She pulled away again, but the action ran counter to what her body wanted. Again Kevin reached

68

forward his hands, this time touching her gently through the shirt and ignoring the buttons she seemed determined to protect.

Meg was frightened, but his touch on her breast sent chills through her body. She could feel her nipples stiffen. She reached over to touch his chest. He smiled at her.

"It doesn't do for me what it does for you. Now if you want to feel what a man is all about, you do this." He took her hand and moved it to his groin.

Meg was repulsed and attracted at the same time. She knew she was in grave danger, yet she didn't want it to stop. She shook her head. Tears started to fill her eyes and run down her cheeks.

"You're crying," Kevin said in surprise. "They must be tears of joy, for sure as I'm standing here, I've not been hurting you."

"I don't want this," Meg nearly broke into a sob. "Not this way, in a dingy room with a stranger."

Kevin stepped back from her, anger flashed in his eyes. "Why did you come with me then?"

"I don't know. I was afraid to be alone. And I suppose I was excited at the idea of being alone with a man for the first time."

"Don't tell me you've never been with a man before?" exclaimed Kevin, shaking his head with disbelief.

"Never," she whispered.

He touched the tears on her cheeks with his fingers. She melted under the gentle stroke of his hand. She moved to place her face against his chest but this time it was Kevin who backed away.

"How could anyone blame me? There you were, a lass all dressed up in man's clothes, one who walks the streets of Halifax at night alone and comes into a tavern. How could anyone blame me for taking you for a simple 'lady of experience'? Oh no, not me, lass, I'll not be responsible at all." He grabbed her hand. "Come on. I'll be taking you home. Who is that fellow, Craig? What is he to you? Why didn't you send you packing just as soon as he saw you enter Bella's place?"

"Craig is a fine man," she shot back angrily. "He's my cousin."

"Oh, I see. I perceive a little more than cousinly feeling between the two of you." Kevin realized to his amazement that he was actually jealous of the half-breed. If that's the way it is between you, then all the more reason for me to take you home."

The girl started to deny any feeling for Craig but then realized that what Kevin said was true. She did not wish to be with this handsome and lighthearted Irish boy. She wanted instead to be with Craig, dark and brooding, so anxious to belong, but not sure what it was he wanted to belong to. She did not resist when Kevin took her hand and led her out of the room, down the stairs and out into the moonlit streets.

The cells were dank and smelled of urine. Craig sat on some damp straw. His head pounded from the cut in his scalp. Almost everyone else had been released. The first to go were Bella and Phoebe. Bella paid a lawyer to keep her out of jail or trouble of any kind. Then, one by one, the Irishmen had been questioned and released. The few blacks to be arrested were kept in another cell. Craig did not know what happened to them.

Finally even Jim Hickey and Sean Lavery were told to be on their way. They had been released because they produced enlistment papers for the American army. The officials were ready to say good riddance. Lavery swung his cloak about him as he was led from the cell followed by the plodding Hickey.

"Don't touch me, sir," he said to the jailkeeper, who tried to rush him along. "I shall soon be a soldier in the victorious Army of the Potomac, Fifth Michigan Cavalry."

"You could easier ride your ape of a companion than you could a horse," said the jailkeeper.

"There is nothing to riding a horse," Lavery insisted. "I know. If there was something to be learned from it I would have tried it before now."

"You joined the cavalry, and you've never been on a horse in your life?" Now the jailer was roaring with laughter. "No wonder the Rebs keep licking the Yanks and your glorious Army of the Potomac. We just got word that the Rebs have done it again in someplace called Chancellorsville down in Virginia. The Yanks, they say, are still running, falling back on Washington again."

"That will all change, sir, once me and my companions join the Union forces."

The jailer slapped his knee. "What kind of a unit can the Fifth Michigan Cavalry be when it takes one trooper who can't ride and another who is bigger than the horses?"

As he left the cell, Sean turned to Craig. "You should join us. Kevin promised to teach us all about horses. Join with us for free labor and a free Ireland and a free Indian people."

Craig could only wave in reply. His new friends' departure depressed him even more. He sat with his head in his hands. He did not know how much time elapsed before the cell door swung open again. The jailer reentered.

"You Craig Miller?"

Craig looked up. "Yes," he responded.

"You been released. Someone is waiting for you in the front."

Craig followed the jailer out of the cell and down the long stone corridor. He entered the reception hall. It was bright here. The sun had risen. It was morning. Craig's eyes stung and his head throbbed. He saw Michael Brant. Never had he seen any man look as angry as his uncle.

"Miller," he bellowed at Craig. He walked up to the boy. There was anger even in his stride. "Craig Miller. Your father asked me to take you into my home. I did so because of a great fondness for him. It will grieve me greatly to have to write to him that I can no longer allow you to live with us. You are no longer welcome in my house."

"But, sir, what did I do?"

"What did you do?" Brant spit the words out in anger. "You took my daughter, my child, my only child, whose life is dearer to me than my own, and you led her to some public house. There, you became involved in a disgraceful brawl and endangered her in the process. Her mother and I were frantic with worry. It was almost dawn before she came home."

"Is she all right?"

"What do you mean? How should I know? She and I argued. She became hysterical and I sent her to bed."

"But didn't she tell you what happened?"

"She told me she was with you. I depended on you to protect her like a sister. You have betrayed that trust."

"But—" Craig protested.

"But what?" Brant stood glaring at him.

Meg had lied and blamed him for what had resulted from her own wrongheadedness. It was she who had betrayed a trust—not he. The rage surged within him—but he would not betray her as she had betrayed him.

"Well, but what?" Brant repeated.

"Nothing," the young man said finally.

"I'll send your things once you've found some place to stay."

The enormity of what his uncle said to him finally struck Craig.

"I have no place, Uncle. School does not begin until the fall."

"Go home then to your father. You explain to him why I cannot accept you in my home. Save me that difficult task."

"I can't go home a failure."

"You should have thought about that before you subjected Meg to all this." Michael Brant turned on his heel and began to walk away.

"Uncle Michael, how could you do this to me?"

Brant hesitated a second, but he did not turn around to face Craig. He resumed his stride and stepped out into the morning sunlight. He would walk home and hope the fresh spring air would cool his head.

Craig waited until his uncle had disappeared. His rage grew stronger. Michael Brant had been grossly unfair. True, he was partly responsible for what happened, but so was Michael Brant. It was he who had given the girl her head. If he had wanted to protect her from the real world, he should have raised her differently. And he should have instilled in her the courage to speak the truth.

Craig was released by the constables. He stepped out into the street and turned left, back toward the harbor. He did not know where else to go. After he had walked two blocks, he found Kevin O'Connor at his side.

"Where did you crawl from?" Craig asked in anger. He had not seen the Irishman since the fight.

"I ducked out just as soon as the little disturbance started to attract the law. Didn't the lass you sneaked into MacSorley's tell you?"

"I did not sneak her in. She came all on her own," Craig said gruffly, "and besides I haven't spoken to her since last night. What's more, I never want to speak to her again."

"You sound like someone else who's got troubles," the Irish boy said.

"Troubles? Nothing much. I've just been kicked out of my uncle's house, and I have no place to live. His loving daughter blamed me for taking her to MacSorley's."

"Is that all?" Kevin said goodnaturedly. "That's not real trouble. I've had no real place to live for the last three years, ever since I left my mother's cottage."

"At least you left of your own free will."

"You must be kidding," Kevin said with some emotion. "She'd turn me over to the British the minute she laid eyes on me. I had Bella send her a letter via New York. It came back undelivered. So, until recently, I was stuck in Bella's back room. It wasn't so bad except when she went after that girlfriend of hers. You know, I never knew women did things like that until I met Bella. But why not, if that's what you like. And I sure can understand her liking that Phoebe. I could go for a piece of that myself, but Bella knew that. That's why she kicked me out. Now I've got a room of my own."

"Your friends are leaving for the army today?"

"Me, too," Kevin said happily. "I decided to join up. Somebody had to keep them from breaking their necks. Can you imagine Lavery signing up with the cavalry unit? He's never been on a horse in his life."

"Why did he do it?"

"He said it suited his sense of the dramatic. He wanted to ride into battle, not slog through mud. Of course, Hickey does whatever Lavery says he should do."

"Do you ride?" Craig asked.

"Like nobody else you've ever known."

"I suspect I know a few better," Craig said quietly.

"Who?" Kevin asked belligerently.

"Me, for one. I've been on a horse since before I could walk. My mother climbed off of one to give me birth."

Kevin looked at the Métis warily. He realized that the Indians and the half–breeds of the Canadian and American West practically lived in the saddle. As good as he, Kevin O'Connor, was with horses, he decided to soften his bragging until after he had seen this one in the saddle.

"Look, I've got an idea," Kevin blurted out. "You've no place to go. Why don't you come with Lavery, Hickey and me. Join the Yanks and fight for free labor. You'll do more for your own people learning cavalry techniques than you'd ever learn from a book in school. That's what you were planning, weren't you?"

Craig nodded.

"To hell with book learning. You should join our brotherhood. We're Fenians."

"What's a Fenian?"

"A Fenian is a supporter of a free Irish republic."

"Kevin, I can sympathize with your cause but I'm not an Irishman. How will an Irish republic help my people?"

73

They were almost at the waterfront now. They turned down the street to Bella MacSorley's.

The early morning wind was chilly coming in off the harbor. Craig pulled his coat collar up about his throat. He felt his scalp. It was still sore, and there was dried blood caked in his hair. He felt grubby, and he wanted a hot bath. He thought longingly of his old room back in the Brant house. A room with its own private bathroom. The wind did not seem to bother the Irishman. He had two days' growth of beard, maybe more. Craig had to shave only rarely and he was not a good judge of such white man's matters.

"Not all Fenians want to go back to Ireland to fight," Kevin said finally. "In fact I'm damned sure I don't ever want to go back to Ireland."

"What do you mean?" Craig asked.

"Here we are," Kevin said as they came before the battered door and broken stained glass of the entry to MacSorley's. Kevin pushed open the door. It stuck halfway, the hinge was bent.

"Bella," he screamed out.

She did not answer him. She merely looked up from the bar. Her giant, neckless, head was resting on the smooth surface of the bar and great tears rolled down her eyes.

Kevin stepped sideways to get through the half–opened door. Craig followed him.

"Come on, Bella. You've got enough stashed away to fix this place up in no time at all. You know the brotherhood will help with the labor."

"I don't give a damn for you and your bloody brotherhood. Phoebe is leaving me. She says she can't take any more of what happened last night."

"We've always had fights in here. Certainly since I been in Halifax, and that's been for three years."

"It wasn't the fighting," Bella sobbed. "It was some son of a bitch at the jail. He felt her up and tried to take advantage of her."

Kevin controlled the urge to laugh which gripped him. Jesus, he thought, this old cow was feeling her up constantly, to say nothing of everyone in the Fenian movement in Halifax. You'd think she'd be used to it by now. Instead he put his arm halfway around the woman's shoulders and tried to comfort her.

"Do you want me to talk to her Bella?" he asked.

74

"Would you?" She smiled for the first time. "You're awfully good with words, lad. Maybe she'll listen to you."

"How about a little drink for my friend Craig and me?"

She looked over and saw Craig for the first time. "He pays?" she asked.

"No, not this morning." He could see the resistance growing in her face. "All right, free for me but he pays for his own."

She smiled in agreement.

Kevin turned to Craig. They righted a table and some chairs and sat down.

"Sorry," Kevin said, "she insists that you pay."

"I don't want anything," Craig said.

Kevin shrugged his shoulders.

"You were saying that there were some of you who didn't want to fight for Ireland in Ireland."

"Right," Kevin said, "and it makes sense. How are we going to raise troops and supply an army in Ireland? The damn British have control of the seas. They'd cut us off from all the help while their army cut us up on land. Then they'd turn the damn Ulstermen loose on us. Creating an Irish republic like that is a vain dream."

"Where is all this leading?"

"Patience, lad," Kevin said, "I met this fellow, William Randall Roberts. He is one of us, a Fenian here in America. He disagrees with the Head Center, Stevens, back in Dublin. Stevens can think only of Ireland, but Roberts says our strength is in the United States. Americans could never turn their backs on people in revolt against Great Britain. It's like turning your back on your own revolution. We'll use the United States as a recruitment center and a staging ground. Then we'll strike at Britain through Canada. The British don't have an army large enough to stop the march of the Irish veterans of Mr. Lincoln's Union Army. If the British start to try, who knows, I'll bet the Americans join in with us and kick the shit out of all the king's horses and all the king's men. There are an awful lot of Irish votes in America. We seize Canadian territory, and in return for it we get a free Irish republic. That is Roberts' plan."

"And how do Métis and Indians gain from this?"

"Well, the British will be kept busy and out of Rupert's Land. You'll get the time to organize yourselves, your own republic if you want it."

"It sounds wild to me," Craig said shaking his head.

"Where is your sense of adventure?" Kevin complained. "It'll be fun."

"Have you ever seen war, my friend?" Craig asked.

"Have you?"

"Not really. I've seen tribal squabbles, warrior counting coup on another, sometimes killing, sometimes not."

"Isn't that fun?"

"Fun is not the word. It is part of the red man's culture. My people, the Métis, the half-breeds, keep some of it and drop other things. It is true we like a good fight."

"You'll join us, then?"

"You mean the U.S. Army?"

"That too. But I really mean join the brotherhood."

"But I'm not Irish."

"So I've noted, lad."

"Stop calling me 'lad.' I'm older than you are, I suspect."

"How old?"

"Twenty-one."

"So you are, but we're both lads. You have my permission to call me 'lad' too. Well, will you join us?"

"Why the hell not? I've got nowhere else to go."

"Bella," Kevin shouted, "get me an oath. I'm about to make us another Fenian."

"Not 'til you talk to Phoebe," she responded.

"I will, but first things first."

Michael Brant sat in the parlor. His wife entered the room and took her place in the easy chair opposite him.

"Has she fallen off?" he asked Willy.

"She was exhausted. I don't think the poor child slept all night."

"Did you have a talk with her?"

Willy nodded.

"Well, what happened?"

"Honestly, Michael, I resent the fact that you felt free to discuss anything and everything with that child, but as soon as anything unpleasant happens you turn her over to me."

Brant shook his head as if to clear it of an unacceptable thought. "But she refused to tell me where she had been. She was obviously upset."

"Of course she was upset, but she's all right now."

"You're sure?"

"Yes, I'm sure."

She sat silent for some minutes more.

"Where is Craig?" she asked finally. "I hope *you* spoke to him—or did you expect me to do that too?"

"He's not here. I have no idea where he is."

Willy rose in her chair and went to the window to look out. "Dear, it's not like him not to tell us where he's going. I hope he is not going to make a habit of last night's rowdiness."

"Precisely what I feared. That's why I threw him out. He won't be coming back."

"You what?" she yelled.

"I've sent him away."

"How could you do such a thing?"

"Isn't that obvious, given what happened to our daughter?"

"He didn't force her into that tavern, you know. She has a will of her own."

"No gentleman would take a lady to a place like that in the first instance."

"He didn't take her!"

Michael made some blustering sound. Finally he stammered, "How the hell did she get there?"

"She went on her own. She followed him there."

Michael looked stricken. "Why didn't he say so? Oh my God, I never really gave him a chance. I was so frightened for her—and so angry."

"Michael," Willy said as her hand went to her mouth, "what have you done? Quick, go after him and bring him back!"

Michael left the room hurriedly. He grabbed his coat and hat from the closet in the hall. He was in such a rush that he forgot to close the front door. Willy came to the foyer. She walked to the door. She stuck her head out to look up and down the street, hoping against hope to see Craig's trim figure coming down the sidewalk. But all she saw was her husband, his shoulders sagging, walking back toward the jail where he had last confronted his nephew. Something told her that he would be too late.

III

Southern Pennsylvania, June-July 1863

They were somewhere on the road between Emmitsburg and Hanover. Craig wasn't sure whether they were still in Maryland, or if they had crossed into Pennsylvania. Kevin rode immediately in front of him. He could tell by the bobbing of the Irishman's head in time to the slow gait of his horse that he was sleeping in the saddle, something they had learned to do since May. The four of them—Craig, Kevin O'Connor, Sean Lavery and Big Jim Hickey—had taken a ship from Yarmouth, south of Halifax, to New York. Then they had gone by train to Washington, then over land to the Rappahannock River where the Army of the Potomac under General Joseph Hooker was encamped. Facing it was the Army of Northern Virginia under General Robert E. Lee.

Having heard the news of the rout of the Army of the Potomac at Chancellorsville just weeks before, Craig had expected to find a demoralized, straggling force. Instead, he found an incredibly well–equipped and well–disciplined army. Constant defeats had weakened the soldiers' confidence in their leaders, but not in each other as fighting men.

Kevin had sought out the Michigan Cavalry Brigade and found it at Brandy Station on the Orange and Alexandria Railroad west of Fredericksburg in Virginia. When Craig questioned Kevin's choice, the Irishman had given only vague answers. Craig had assumed that it had something to do with Fenian plans.

At Brandy Station, all four of them were turned over to the tender mercies of Sergeant Van Hook. He was a large man, almost as large as Big Jim. His hair was flaxen blonde with occasional streaks of grey. He was a Reformed Church man from Grand Rapids who neither swore nor drank.

He looked at his four shabbily dressed recruits. "Line up,

78

the four of you," he said in his thick Dutch accent. "You are now horse soldiers of the Sixth Regiment of the Michigan Brigade. Where are you from?" he said, pointing first to Lavery.

"Here, there and everywhere," the actor responded.

Then Van Hook turned to his clerk. "Put him down from Detroit."

For Van Hook, Detroit, the eastern metropolis of his home state, was the equivalent of Sodom, and from Lavery's flightiness he was sure he would be at home in either Sodom or Detroit.

Next he looked at Craig.

"Red River," the Métis responded.

"Never heard of it," said Van Hook. Craig was about to explain his origins when Van Hook's clerk interceded.

"That's Detroit too," the clerk said.

"How do you know?"

"I took French in school. There's a place south of Detroit called River Rouge. That means Red River in French."

Van Hook looked warily at his clerk and then at Craig. The Métis merely nodded. "Another Detroit man," Van Hook said. "What about you other two?"

"Detroit," Kevin said quickly.

Jim looked confused.

"He's from Detroit as well," Lavery said quickly of his friend.

"Can't he talk?" Van Hook asked.

"Sometimes he's a little, you know . . ." Kevin was tempted to say 'Dutch,' but checked himself.

Van Hook nodded. "Detroit. All four from Detroit."

"Now," Van Hook called out, "we'll see if any of you city boys can make a horse soldier."

As Van Hook had been questioning recruits, more and more of the troopers had been accumulating along the rail fence that ran past the tents of the encampment. Almost one hundred men had gathered by the time Big Jim Hickey had been turned from a Dubliner into a Detroiter by Sergeant Van Hook.

The crowd cheered when a large greyish white stallion was led into the camp ground. The horse stretched its long neck and stared wild-eyed at the cheering men. A trooper grabbed the stallion's head and forced a bridle over it. Strangely, the stallion seemed to be calmed and quieted by the act. Quiet enough, in fact, to allow a second trooper to place a saddle on its back.

"Now," Van Hook said turning to the recruits, "who'll be the first to take the test?"

"Allow me," said Lavery.

Sean ignored Van Hook's hand when the sergeant, with exaggerated politeness, offered to assist him into the saddle. Lavery placed his left foot into the stirrup and drew his right leg up over the saddle and into the other stirrup.

It was as if someone had kicked the stallion with spurs. The horse dashed forward and gave a vicious twist of its hind quarters and sent Lavery sailing through the air. He landed on his rear and side with a thud. He sat up, a look of shock and disbelief coming to his face.

"So much for you, Detroit," Van Hook said. "The rule is fifteen seconds on Old Stonewall to be a trooper of the Sixth Michigan."

The clerk chimed in. "We named the stallion after the Reb general—you know, the one that just died—'cause he was crazy too."

"You, Number Two Detroit," Van Hook pointed at Kevin. "You're next."

Kevin studied Old Stonewall. He was grateful for Lavery's bravado. It allowed him to study the stallion. A horse like this one would try to rid itself of its rider immediately. The twisting hindquarters was its best trick. With the knowledge Lavery's ride had given him, Kevin might pass the fifteen–second test.

Without any warning either to Van Hook or to Old Stonewall, Kevin leapt astride the horse. Old Stonewall bellowed in surprise and tried his favorite tactic. Kevin countered the twist. Now it would be all new. The horse threw his hindquarters into the air and managed to twist first to the right and then again to the left before his feet returned to the ground. Kevin could feel himself coming out of the saddle, but he held on fast. His knees gripped the horse's sides tightly. The next maneuver would unseat him. He pulled on the stallion's mane with all his might. The horse bellowed a second time and reared on its hind legs.

"Time," the clerk yelled. Kevin let his feet slip out of the stirrups and slid to the ground. He walked away from Old Stonewall grinning from ear to ear. It had been a spectacular performance, and several of the troopers broke into applause.

"You'll do," was all that Van Hook said to Kevin.

Kevin walked back to where he had left Craig and Jim Hickey. "Not bad, eh?" he said winking at them.

"Good ride, even if a brief one," Craig said casually.

Kevin's temper flared immediately. "I suppose you could do better?"

"I don't know if I'll ride better," Craig responded, "just longer."

Kevin's temper subsided. He really didn't know what to make of this half–breed. He was not all show, like Lavery. In fact there was no show about him at all.

"Next," Van Hook called out looking at Jim.

"Oh, Sarge," a trooper yelled, "have a heart on Old Stonewall. That fellow will bust his back."

"Everyone must pass the test."

Jim looked wild–eyed at Stonewall. The horse looked wild–eyed at Big Jim. Then Jim started to back away.

"No, not me. Not on that thing," he said slowly.

"Jim, you must," Kevin teased, "or else you don't get into the Sixth Michigan."

"I'll have no part of that creature. He has a devil. I can feel it in my soul," Jim said.

Van Hook wasted no time. He turned to the clerk. "Wash him out," he said.

"Now you," he said to Craig. "You ain't no darky, are you?"

Craig looked up at him in surprise. "No," he responded.

"You're a dark one but I guess you're all right. You ain't got any nigger features. Can't have any darkies in the regiment. They got one of their own units. They fight pretty good at that but we can't have them in no proper white man's regiment. How come your skin is so brown?"

"Everyone's skin is brown next to yours," a trooper yelled. They all started to laugh.

Craig paid no more attention to them. He concentrated instead on Old Stonewall. He tried to remember what his grandfather, Eagle Face, the Assiniboine, had taught him about breaking horses.

"Do not be afraid of the horse," the old man had said. "The horse must fear you instead."

He rose into the saddle slowly. The sergeant let go of the bridle. Craig too had learned much by watching, especially watching the double twist Old Stonewall had used to try to unseat Kevin. The animal had a pattern. The single twist was followed by the double twist. Craig survived both maneuvers.

Now what? Stonewall charged forward with a burst of speed and then stopped suddenly again throwing his hindquarters into the air twisting. Still Craig clung to the saddle.

"Time," the clerk called out again.

Still Craig stayed in the saddle.

"Hey, someone help the lad," Kevin called out. "I don't think he knows how to dismount."

Old Stonewall was charging madly about the camp area, sending troopers scurrying in all directions.

The stallion caught sight of the picket fence, and ran toward it. At first Craig thought the beast would leap the fence, and he prepared for that. But at the last moment Old Stonewall veered and started to run parallel to the fence getting closer and closer to the railing. The horse intended to pin Craig's leg between his body and the picket railing. He had only a split second to react. He pulled his right leg from the stirrup, then his left. He slid out of the saddle, holding onto Old Stonewall with a death grip with both arms around the stallion's neck and with both feet resting on the horse's rump. It was a trick Eagle Face had taught him that allowed a warrior to use his horse as a barrier against the arrows of his enemy.

Old Stonewall did not realize what was happening until too late. The animal screamed in pain as his flanks were torn by splinters from the rough wooden rails of the fence. Blood began to run down its side and down its leg. As soon as it changed directions away from the fence Craig allowed his feet to slip from the horse's rump and touch the ground—using the force of hitting the ground as a spring to throw him erect and back into the saddle.

Old Stonewall was weaker now, and some of the fight had been taken from him. He slowed down, and Craig took advantage of the respite to leap out of the saddle and land on his feet.

"Goddam," the clerk said in awe.

"Watch your mouth, damn it," Van Hook said, without realizing what he himself had just said.

Several troopers let out howls of appreciation. Suddenly someone screamed out an order that was totally unintelligible to the newcomers, but that meant something to everyone else, from Van Hook on down. Everyone snapped to attention. Craig turned, to find himself confronted by an outlandishly garbed officer. Instead of federal blue, the officer wore a black velveteen jacket and pants. The legs and sleeves were bedecked with gold stripes. He wore a scarlet cravat about his neck, and a loose, floppy, wide-brimmed black velvet hat, also covered with gold braid. The hat covered long, blonde curls that reached down to his neck, and his blonde moustache drooped down at the corners of his mouth. On each collar, and on the hat, there were the single white stars of a brigadier general. Craig Miller was staring into the face of the commanding officer of the Michigan Brigade.

"Who are these men?" the general asked Van Hook.

"Recruits from Detroit, General Custer, sir," Van Hook shouted back, still stiff and at attention.

Custer did not put his men at ease.

"No one from Detroit rides like these two," he said pointing to Kevin and Craig, "especially this last one. I've only heard about such riding skills. We studied them at West Point. Maybe Mongols or an American savage—no white man."

"He's no nigger sir," Van Hook shouted again.

"I'll take your word for it, Sergeant," Custer said sarcastically.

"Thank you, sir," Van Hook responded.

"Welcome to the Michigan Brigade, gentlemen," Custer greeted Kevin and Craig. "You joined at just the right time, just as I take command. Let's hope we are lucky for each other. I have always been lucky. Now that I am a brigadier, and in command, I intend to stay lucky. Carry on, gentlemen. You two, your names?"

"Kevin O'Connor."

"Craig Miller."

"Good, good," Custer said. "Carry on," he repeated and stepped away toward his tent.

Once the general was out of earshot Van Hook made a sound to indicate his disgust. "Just out of diapers and he's a general. What's happening to the Army of the Potomac? First they take away our only real general, George McClellan, and now they promote captains to generals. One day he ain't even got a regiment of his own, and now he has the whole brigade."

The company clerk stared at him wide-eyed. "Is he ours?" he said finally. "I thought he was a Reb. That hat he is wearing is a Reb hat. I've seen them."

"Oh, he's ours, all right. You just met George Armstrong Custer, our brigadier. He's regular army. He didn't pay his own way like us volunteers. No, he's a West Point man, although

I've heard he finished last in his class. We got one of them mercenaries, lives off the government."

Kevin paid no attention to Van Hook's diatribe. He stepped closer to Craig.

"Well," Craig said looking at him.

"Well, what?" Kevin said absentmindedly.

"What did you think of my ride?"

"Not bad, but I wished you'd told me we were in a contest. I'd have shown you some real riding. But I haven't time for show-offs. I have my duties to the Brotherhood. I have to find a place for Lavery and Hickey."

"Sergeant," he called out to Van Hook, "do you think Miller here and me will make good troopers?"

"With a little discipline and hard work I can see you being passable."

"Son of a bitch," Kevin mumbled so that only Craig could hear. "What about our other friends?" he asked in a louder voice.

"Off to the infantry with them," Van Hook laughed.

"Are there any other arrangements possible?"

"Like what?"

"Isn't there a battery of U.S. artillery assigned to this Brigade?"

"Ja, six three-inch rifle guns, Battery M, Second U.S. Artillery," Van Hook responded. "What's your point?"

"Don't you think someone Big Jim's size would be good handling those guns?"

"You've made your point," Van Hook said. He signaled the clerk. "The big one stays with the brigade in the artillery unit."

Jim looked nervously at Lavery. "Does that mean I have to get on a horse?" he asked.

"No. You can ride in the ammunition wagons on top of the shells," Lavery responded.

Jim smiled.

Lavery merely shook his head. "Captain," he addressed Van Hook.

"It's sergeant," said the Dutchman.

"Excuse me, sir. Your bearing betrays an injustice. You should have higher rank. What about me?"

"You, sir, can go to blazes," Van Hook said, his body shaking with laughter.

"You see, Major," Lavery persisted, "I serve as Big Jim's interpreter. There is no telling what he'll do without me by his

84

side. You may order him to turn the gun on the Rebs, but he may not understand. He might turn the gun on you instead."

"If he tries that, Lt. Pennington will have him shot," Van Hook retorted.

"That may well be the case," Lavery argued, "but you will derive small comfort from that if you are already blown from here to Georgia. Now, if I'm with Big Jim he does what I tell him. And you may rest assured, Colonel, that I will always tell him to do things that discourage Lt. Pennington from putting a bullet into my head."

"I've heard enough. There is no doubt in my mind," Van Hook said shaking his head, "that you are the greatest scoundrel I have ever met and that I shall truly regret this decision. However, you may go to Battery M with your friend."

Lavery bowed.

"He's right on all counts," Kevin whispered to Craig.

Kevin had a difficult time trying to fall off to sleep that first night. There were no tents available yet for new recruits, and they had to bed on the hard ground, cushioned only a new issue woolen army blanket. He could hear Jim Hickey's snorts as he slept across from him, separated by the glowing embers of the early evening fire. Craig Miller snored too, but more evenly, and with considerably less volume than Big Jim.

Kevin was uncomfortable. He had never liked sleeping out of doors. Even as a boy, when the other lads had urged him to join them and play "wild Indian" and camp out all night, he had rejected them and preferred the warm glow of his mother's peat fire and the softness of his straw mat. But now he had little choice but to try to make do with the hard Virginia ground.

"Kevin," Lavery whispered to him. The Dubliner had switched himself around to be head to head with Kevin before the embers, after Kevin had complained about the stench that arose from Sean's unwashed stockings.

"What now?" Kevin moaned. "I want to get some sleep before the bloody sun comes up."

"How come you can't sleep?"

"Because you talk too much."

"It's the Irishman's curse."

Kevin snorted in contempt.

"We did all right today, didn't we?" Lavery continued. "I mean, it all went according to plan."

"Well, almost," Kevin responded. "I got me into the horse soldiers and you, me and Jim are still together—even if you two are in artillery."

"Mounted artillery, sir," Lavery corrected him.

"Even if you can't sit a horse," Kevin teased.

"I thought it brave of me to try," Lavery responded with mock haughtiness.

"Damn near got yourself killed."

"Well, you weren't the best man in the saddle today, either." Kevin grew annoyed at the reference to the Métis' skills. "I'm the match of any savage no matter where he puts his red ass down," Kevin said harshly.

"Calm down," Lavery whispered. "You're too much of a hothead."

"An Irishman's curse," Kevin retorted.

Lavery chuckled. "He still performed better in the saddle than you did today."

Kevin's anger almost spilled over again. "That makes us even, then."

"How's that?"

"I outperformed him in a different kind of saddle—with a certain young lass in Halifax. You know, the one that dressed like a man and for whom our savage lad still longs."

It did not matter to Kevin that he stretched the truth to the breaking point. If Lavery had known that Kevin had come nowhere near doing what he now bragged of, and that Kevin had even run from the chance and faced him with the lie, then Kevin would merely have dismissed the untruth as another curse of the Irish. Instead Lavery turned onto his back and grew silent. The sounds of the night intermingled with the sounds of hundreds of sleeping men. Finally Lavery mumbled something to Kevin.

"What did you say?"

"I said that it would be better for all of us if the savage, as you call him, knew nothing of your behavior with the Halifax lass. His feeling for her, now that he has stopped being angry with her, is clear enough even for a blind fool to see. And that original anger at her was too great not to have erupted from a more gentle emotion."

Kevin paid little or no attention to his friend's ramblings.

Besides, finally his eyes were growing heavy with sleep. He remembered no more conversation with Lavery that night.

All that had happened days ago. It seemed like years ago as they rode single file on the Emmitsburg Road.

The Rebels were on the move. Word had finally come from General Hooker's headquarters. Lee had moved west into the Shenandoah, then north up the Cumberland Valley, putting South Mountain between himself and Federal forces. The Southern invasion of Pennsylvania had begun. The newspapers spoke of panic in Philadelphia. One report had the rebel general, Early, overrunning the town of York, and Confederate cavalry units on the Susquehanna River opposite Harrisburg and Columbia. But now the Army of the Potomac had turned its focus—slowly at first, but then with surprising speed and determination. It had moved to the north following Lee.

But the Michigan Brigade, as part of Kilpatrick's Third Cavalry Division, was not worried about Confederates in York or before Harrisburg. If they heard the cry "Rebels up ahead," it surely would be only the invincibles of J. E. B. Stuart, Lee's cavalry, Lee's eyes.

Craig was almost mesmerized by the bobbing of Kevin's head immediately in front of him. One advantage of their recent arrival was that they were issued mounts no one wanted—slow, tired nags with no pep. For this type of maneuver, steady along the trail, sleeping in the saddle, there was no better kind of horse.

Craig checked his rifle, a Spencer repeating rifle, which could fire seven shots before needing reloading. The Fifth and Sixth Regiments were now both equipped with these new weapons, these new wonders of technology. It more than compensated for the nag he rode.

"Hey, Kevin," Craig called out.

The other boy's head jerked upward.

"What do you want? I'm sleeping."

"Where are we?"

"How would I know?" the Irishman complained.

"We're south and west of Hanover, Pennsylvania." The company clerk, Private Churchill, who rode immediately ahead of Kevin, called back over his shoulders.

"There, are you satisfied?" Kevin asked. Suddenly they were startled by the sound of rolling thunder coming from the northwest.

87

"Storm?" Craig said in surprise looking up into the cloudless sky.

"Storm, my ass," Churchill said, looking around to see if Van Hook was within range. He seemed relieved when he saw no sign of the Sergeant. "Those are big guns. It means we've found the enemy or he's found us."

He pulled a map from his vest pocket and spread it over his horse's neck. The roar of the cannons became louder and stronger.

"That's no little skirmish over there," he called out. "Let's see, we're here." He pointed with his index finger to a small spot on his map and then traced a line toward the left-handed corner of the map. "That fighting is happening at a place called Gettysburg," he called out.

"Let's hope they keep us riding in the opposite direction," Kevin said.

They didn't. About ten minutes later, General Custer rode to the head of the column and turned it toward the sound of the guns. They came up behind the main column of the army at Gettysburg and added to the confusion in the rear lines. Finally, Custer was ordered to the Union right flank to protect it from any Rebel flanking maneuvers, such as those that had led to the rout at Chancellorsville. The Michigan Brigade arrived at its assigned position at Hunterstown at sunset.

They were immediately attacked by Confederate skirmishers. The Sixth Regiment was in the van when the first shots were fired. A volley of muskets roared out and passed over their heads. Kevin ducked involuntarily. Van Hook, who had joined the head of the regiment, started to laugh.

"If you can hear it, it's already too late," he joked. "It will do you no good to duck."

"It won't do me no harm either," Kevin said defensively.

Custer came galloping past them to the front of the column. His hair had escaped the back of his sloppy velvet hat and was blowing about in the wind. He reined in his horse when he reached the van and the horse reared. He called out in a high-pitched, stammering voice.

"Company A Sixth Regiment form a line of attack."

"Oh, no," said Kevin, "that's us."

"Don't worry," Van Hook said. "There'll be no attack. We still don't know what's up ahead of us. Generals don't go rushing off to attack an enemy without some knowledge of what's in front of them."

Kevin felt relieved as he joined Craig and Churchill and they fanned out in the ranks across the road to Hunterstown.

Custer had ridden farther down the line and ordered other companies of the Sixth to dismount and take the high ground on either side of the road. He ordered the Seventh Regiment to do the same thing. His last regiment bringing up the rear was ordered to stay in reserve. Then the general rode back to the front.

"All right, men of the Michigan Brigade," he shouted, "I'll lead you this time. Come on, you Wolverines."

The men returned his shout. He drew his saber and spurred his horse.

"My God," Van Hook called out. "The fool, the rotten fool is going to attack."

The ranks moved forward at a fast trot. The bugles sounded the charge and the horses broke into a gallop.

Craig, who had not ridden at a pace faster than a walk since joining the cavalry, felt exhilarated at first. The sky was purple and red. The July heat was dissipating with nightfall and the rushing air cooled his flushed face. He drew his saber. He could see no enemy yet. In fact, he could see no one, only the charging horses of Van Hook and Kevin in front of him and Private Churchill, who was by his side.

Then suddenly the first rank was gone. Kevin's horse went down screaming, blood pouring from its mouth. He saw Van Hook cut in half by a shell from a field piece. All about him dirt shot into the air and his ears were filled with the whine of shells and the screams of bullets mixed with the bellows of frightened horses and the cries of men in pain.

Craig looked down at himself, amazed that he was unharmed and still mounted. He was still moving forward but only at a trot now. The whole of Company A's charge was stopped by a volley of fire that could only have come from a force many times their number. Up ahead he could see Custer. The general had dismounted and stood waving his sword and calling on his men to continue the charge.

Suddenly from out of the dusk hundreds of grey–clad horsemen began a countercharge. They would be surrounded and cut off from any help in less than a minute. Churchill spurred his horse and rode directly toward Custer. He raised his rifle and fired almost directly at the general. At first, Craig was convinced that Churchill was determined to kill their leader for drawing them into this trap. But Churchill's second shot blew the head from the shoulders of a Confederate rider bearing down on Custer. Out of the corner of his eye Craig saw Churchill reach the general and swing him onto the saddle behind him.

Craig had turned his horse. It made no sense for a company of one hundred men to meet the charge of at least five hundred enemy. He spurred his mount back toward the safety of their own lines. He recognized Van Hook's grey standing over the corpse of its rider. He began to search the ground for Kevin. Then he saw him. He was on foot, staggered by his fall. He was walking in the wrong direction, right toward the Confederate charge.

"Kevin," Craig screamed out. It was useless. Nothing could be heard over the firing of the Confederate volleys.

Suddenly the guns of Battery M opened up. The world about Craig was in chaos but his instincts took over. He kneed the sides of his horse. The poor nag was slow, but she was an experienced cavalry horse. An untrained mount would have bolted in panic as shells exploded everywhere and men and animals raced by screaming. Craig let her have her head as she galloped back toward the enemy. The ground between him and the oncoming Confederate seemed to narrow with frightening speed.

Finally he was just a few feet away from Kevin. He leaned below the neck of his horse and grabbed his friend under the armpits, hauling him across the saddle. But now the Confederates were on top of him. He pulled his rifle from its case and held it at his hip. He saw the flash of an enemy saber coming slashing toward him. He fired the rifle, but he could not control it with one hand. The gun exploded from his grip and fell to the ground. The bullet, however, found its mark. It tore into the chest of his assailant, who fell from his horse, his sabre landing flat–bladed across Kevin's exposed rump.

Craig did not wait any longer. Swinging his horse about with one hand, and steadying his still–dazed friend with the other, he raced back toward the Union lines. He heard several bullets scream over his head but he tried no diversionary efforts. He made a straight line for the safety of the Fifth and Seventh Michigan. After he had crossed their defensive perimeter, he stopped, dropped Kevin to the ground and dismounted.

The Irishman seemed to have regained his wits. He rubbed his hind quarter and looked up at Craig grinning.

"That was a close one, wasn't it?" He laughed.

Craig was in no mood to laugh.

"You saved my bloody life, didn't you," Kevin said. "I guess I owe you one."

Craig shook his head. "Among my people the obligation is now mine."

"How's that?"

"You were supposed to die. I intervened. From now on you are my responsibility."

"I like that," Kevin said nodding his head in approval. "It makes us like kin."

Craig's response was drowned out by the roar of Michigan fire. Soon the Confederates halted, then withdrew. Finally, darkness fell and the scene of Custer's first charge was covered by night.

The four Fenians sat by their campfire just outside Hunterstown. The night was warm but the fire was reassuring. Both Kevin and Craig had been badly shaken by the disaster of the charge while Sean was exuberant about his first action. Because Sean Lavery was happy, so was Big Jim.

"You should have seen the Rebs run," Sean carried on. "We lobbed the artillery right in their laps, didn't we, Big Jim?"

The other man grinned in agreement.

"I couldn't have seen it," Kevin said sarcastically. "I was too busy trying to pick up the pieces of my horse."

"Will there be replacement mounts?" Craig asked Churchill who had joined the fire.

He looked scornfully down at the four men. They were all novices in war compared to him. Besides, he had just saved General Custer's life. He could almost feel the sergeant's stripes weighing down his arm—especially now that Van Hook was gone.

"Did you see the man's courage?" Churchill said ignoring Craig's question. "I have never seen anything like it. A general, a goddamned general, leading a company, a captain's command, right into the teeth of the enemy. He was right out there for every Reb marksman to see. That red tie around his neck almost called out to them: 'See. It's me, Custer. I dare you.' But not a scratch on him. Custer's luck, they're calling it already."

"He'd be dead if you hadn't saved his ass," Craig interrupted. "I saw it all. You did just what you said he did. You saved him."

"Today was his blooding," Churchill said almost in rapture. "It was just the beginning. He won't make the same mistake again, attacking without first getting intelligence about the force he is facing. What he did today was to inspire his brigade. J.E.B. Stuart, you've met your match at last. No one will be laughing at Yankee cavalry before long."

Kevin turned to Craig and whispered, "I think old Churchill here got hit on the head today. This guy Custer is likely to get us both killed if we stay with him. And that ain't going to do the cause any good."

"Why did you join in the first place?"

"To get experience," Kevin said defensively. "How was I to know that the brigade I picked was about to be turned over to a nut? One thing I know for sure, I have no intention of ending up as fertilizer just to help some darkies get free of what nature probably intended for them anyway."

Craig took a swig of the hot coffee from his cup. "You know, O'Connor, you're a bigot, and the Assiniboine part of me resents it."

"Why?" Kevin asked. "I hate the English part of you a lot more than the black part of you."

"Most people describe the Indians as 'red'."

"Red, black, what difference does it make? They're all niggers to me."

"Is there anyone you do like?"

"Sure, white folk. Irish folk."

It was clear to Craig that the one group was not a part of the other. Kevin equated white with Irish.

"You're hopeless," he said.

"Accept it. I do." Kevin laughed. "Then he turned to Churchill. "Where do I get me a horse?"

"They'll send around a list tomorrow for all those who have been dismounted or lost their weapons to sign. You don't think Custer will allow men in his brigade to go twelve hours without horses and rifles, do you?"

In fact, he allowed them to go thirty hours. The next day Custer joined the rest of the division guarding the Army of the Potomac's right front. In the afternoon they heard heavy fighting on the left flank. Word came for the division to mount and move to guard the left flank beyond Seminary Ridge at Little Round Top.

Kevin still had no horse. Churchill said he thought General Buford might have extra mounts. Last he had heard, Buford was supporting the center of the line on Seminary Ridge. Churchill, like most men on this July 3rd, was confused. In fact, Buford was miles to the south guarding the Emmitsburg Road. Kevin did find a mount, however. He stole it from a supply wagon along with a rifle for Craig. It appeared to be more mule than horse but it was fast enough to keep up with Craig's old mare.

Once they were both mounted, Kevin made it clear to Craig that he had no desire to follow their division to the flank. He intended to stay in the heavily defended Union center.

"How do we explain ourselves if some officer stops us?" Craig asked as they rode along. "They shoot deserters in this army, especially if you desert during a battle. And this is one hell of a big battle."

"No trouble at all. Just watch."

Kevin called out something in a language Craig had never heard before. Responses came back from different parts of the line.

"Take your pick!" Kevin offered. "Those are brothers—members of the brotherhood. They'll cover for us."

Craig merely shrugged. "You choose."

Kevin clucked at his mule. They were soon enveloped in the New York line. The regiments from New York were filled with Irish, many of them members of the Fenian Brotherhood. But in taking Kevin and Craig the Brothers were not taking them into a safe haven. Across the cornfields from Seminary Ridge, Lee had brought together his entire uncommitted reserve. After being thwarted on the right flank and on the left, Lee would move against the center.

Unaware of the Confederate forces aligning themselves against them, Kevin and Craig hobbled their mounts and joined a group of men from the west of Ireland.

"You horse boys don't want to be here when the real fighting starts," teased an older man by the name of Daly. He was from Galway town, and claimed to be in the inner circle of John O'Mahoney, the American Fenian leader and one of the heroes of 1848.

Kevin refused to respond to the teasing even when Daly started to brag about his relationship with O'Mahoney. Kevin was a Roberts man, and he was certain that Roberts and O'Mahoney were headed for a policy clash about Canada.

"They'll be coming right for us," Daly said. "You best be going. We wouldn't want to break a record."

"What record is that?" Craig bit.

"Haven't you heard? No one in the whole damn army has ever seen a dead horse soldier." He laughed and slapped his thigh.

"Well, I just have," Craig said angrily. "His name was Van Hook. He was cut in half by rebel army artillery."

As if the words were a signal, the attack started. The ground seemed to leap up at them. One hundred and fifty heavy Confederate guns across the fields on Seminary Ridge opened fire on the Union Center.

Kevin screamed and dropped to the ground.

Round after round was fired at them. The ground shook, and occasionally dirt was flung into the air, as a missile landed close by. The noise became even more deafening when the Union guns responded.

Craig lay on the ground. He looked over at Kevin. There was terror in the other man's eyes.

"Relax," Daly shouted to both of them. "At least for now. The rebs haven't the right range. Most of those shells are passing over us."

It was true. There was massive confusion in the rear among supply trains. They were being badly mauled. But thus far the front lines seemed to be the safest place to be. Kevin nodded toward where they had hobbled their mounts. There was only a large crater there now. Kevin shrugged his shoulders. Craig felt sorry about the old nag. She had saved his life in the last battle.

For one hour the guns on both sides roared at each other. Craig watched the union gunners sweating, stripped to the waist, firing round after round across the cornfields and into the woods on the opposite ridge. The explosions sent branches and dirt into the air, but still few of the Confederate cannons found the Union front line. Finally at two p.m. the Union guns grew silent. The decision was made to conserve ammunition for what all knew was coming. Shortly after two the rebel guns grew silent as well.

Now it was the silence that was stultifying. Gradually both Kevin and Craig worked up the courage to raise their heads and stare across the cornfields toward the opposite ridge. At first they noticed nothing. But then they heard it. The *rat-a-tat-tat*—the tin roll of drums. From out of the woods they came, out into the open fields, fifteen thousand strong, marching in ranks, the best troops left in the Army of Northern Virginia after two days of fearful fighting. George Pickett's whole division, augmented by other brigades, advanced across the cornfield. The only sound was the beating of military drums, heightened now by the thud of fifteen thousand pairs of feet striking the ground. Closer they came and closer. Craig watched them approach, hypnotized by the deadly beauty of it all. He wondered when the order would come or if it would come. Perhaps the generals themselves were as mesmerized as he was by the advance of the enemy.

The heat of the day grew intense. Craig could feel the droplets of sweat trickle down his armpits and soak into the blue woolen shirt he wore. He smelled rancid from fear and from the fierce heat.

What if he did not survive this wretched hot afternoon? What if he never saw the prairies again and felt the wind off of Lake Winnipeg? What if he never again saw the stern face of his grandfather or the winning smile of his mother? Never heard the cackling laugh of Warrior Woman, his grandmother, or felt the friendly wetness of his father's kisses? All of that meant so much to him. He had been away from it for so long. He had been too long in the east, too long away from the swaying grasses and the rolling hills.

But in the east he had been with the Brants and they were good people. There he had met Meg. He had thought of her often since he had left Halifax. At first he had raged against her. But, with the passing of time, his anger softened and then he realized that he missed her—missed having her around, peeking into his bedroom, starting arguments. Damn it, why had he been so impulsive and joined this crazy Irish conspiracy and this even crazier war? He looked up at the advancing Confederate line. What made him do it?

The heat grew even more intense. In front of the Union position, the heat haze rose from the scorched earth. It distorted the movement of fifteen thousand pairs of legs, giving them a jerky, almost jiglike appearance as they advanced across the beaten-down stalks of corn. The drums still beat a slow, sad rattle. Then the cry of rebel officers broke the silence. The beat of the drums quickened, and the high-pitched yell, the rebel yell, released by thousands of throats, descended upon them.

But then the Union guns opened up. Huge gaping holes appeared in the ranks of the Confederates. They merely closed on each other and continued to advance toward the ridge.

"Look at the bastards come at us," Daly shouted to no one in particular. He shook his head, partly at the waste involved, partly in admiration of their courage as one Confederate soldier fell in the ranks and another rushed forward to take his place. Now the rifles of the Union front rank joined in the deluge of noise. More and more Confederates fell but still they came on.

"Never again," Kevin said and once again ducked his head.

Craig emptied a whole magazine of his Spencer at the advancing line. There was no need to aim. Any shot fired into the line was sure to hit someone. Then they were twenty feet away, then ten feet. Once again the high wail of the rebel yell pierced the noise of the rifles and the flanking fire of the artillery. They came on the run at last to avenge their comrades and let the Yanks taste some rebel steel.

Craig rose to his feet. He wasn't going to be bayoneted in the back while lying on the ground. A shoeless soldier in a ragtag butternut uniform came toward him. Craig raised the butt of his Spencer above his head and brought it down on his attacker's shoulder. The man grabbed his belly and ignored the shoulder when Daly's bayonet pierced his stomach. Then he fell and disappeared from Craig's view. There was noise everywhere. Men cursed and grappled hand to hand.

Craig felt the bullet strike his scalp. It felt like a dull thud. Suddenly his face was covered with blood and he couldn't see. The next thing he knew he was sitting down, too weak to get back up to his feet. He was afraid he would be overrun and captured. But the Union line held. The front of the Confederate attack had reached the rim of the ridge but it had nothing left. Those who reached their destination were quickly surrounded, killed or surrendered. The last act of the massive Battle of Gettysburg was over.

Craig was never sure how he found himself mounted on a fine brown gelding moving away from the Union Front but there he was. His scalp wound was bandaged, and next to him on a black mare was Kevin O'Connor. When he gathered his wits once again, Craig managed to question his companion.

"Where are we going?"

"Back to the regiment," Kevin said without looking at him. "Custer may be crazy and he may have almost gotten us killed, but riding a horse into battle sure beats being on the ground waiting for some Rebel bastard to come and stick you in the ass or marching straight at the guns like those poor sons of bitches. Nobody should have to do that."

Craig was quiet for some moments. "I don't think there is any safe place in the army, Kevin. Anyway, isn't this what you came here for—to get experience?"

Kevin was silent. "A lot of good experience will do me if I am dead. No, Craig, my boy, you and I have fought our last battle. I am going to arrange something safer for you and me, and for Sean and Jim too. Somebody told me the Quartermaster Corps was the place to be. You and I are going to learn all about supplying an army. After all, that's going to be the big problem for us once we move on Canada. If we attack Canada we are going to have to learn to keep an army in the field. We should gain experience in that."

"We won't have that problem in Manitoba. We'll live off the land."

"To hell with that," Kevin cursed. "We're spending the rest of this war behind the lines. How would you like to be posted in Washington?"

IV

Quebec City, October 1864

The city seemed to come alive every day at sunrise. The shops of the Lower Town opened earlier and earlier as people attracted to Quebec for the conference on confederation took to the streets to shop early before winding their way up the bluff to the Citadel and the public buildings of the Upper Town.

Meg Brant was up with the first light. The *Auberge* where she was staying in the Lower Town was owned by their cousins, the Stieglers, and was run by Marc Stiegler's niece and nephew by marriage.

The Brants were family, therefore, and if Meg wanted breakfast at dawn, breakfast it would be. Fresh-baked hot rolls and honey, bacon and eggs and freshly ground and brewed coffee would be waiting for her as soon as she descended the stairs to the dining room. But first Meg had to get everyone else up. She poked her head into her parents' room. Drapes were drawn across the room's single window.

"Mama, papa, aren't you getting up?"

Willy rose on her elbow and looked bleary-eyed at her daughter. "Not today," she whispered so as not to waken Michael, who had trouble sleeping in strange beds. "Today we visit Isle d'Orleans, the old homestead, to visit the family."

"Oh, damn," Meg cursed.

"Meg!" Willy admonished her.

"I'm sorry, mother, but today Craig promised to walk the Plains of Abraham with me and to show me where Wolfe was killed and where Montcalm fell."

"Do that first and then join us on the island. I'll tell Cousin Marc that you're coming across later. I'm sure he'll send another boat for you."

"Oh thanks, mama," Meg said and ran across the room to hug her mother.

Michael groaned and turned on his side and started to snore.

"Hush," Willy said, "don't wake your father. Have the innkeeper awaken Craig so that you can have an early start. Have a nice time but don't be too late. Remember, most of these relatives you've never met before."

"Yes, mama," Meg squeezed her mother and rushed from the room.

"And it's just as well you haven't met them. A bunch of vipers."

"What's that? Did you say something to me?" Michael asked.

"I was just thinking out loud," she mused. "It comes from sleeping together in the same bed. We ought to try it more often."

"And here I thought you insisted on one room instead of two in order to conserve funds. I did not know you had ulterior motives, misplaced though they were given my age and my condition."

"Fiddlesticks," she said, "you're every bit the man you were when we took our first cruise together."

"I behaved like a perfect gentleman that night."

"And for years after that, to my regret."

Michael snorted and turned his back on her. "I'm going back to sleep. I need all the strength I can muster to face the family today." He was sound asleep again within moments.

Meg had no intention of waiting for the innkeeper to get Craig out of bed. She had done that often enough herself when he lived with them in Halifax. The worse moment in her life had been that day a year ago after the brawl in the tavern. It had been months before she could forgive her father for not allowing Craig to return to them. Nor could she forgive herself for her own behavior. Her anger had become monumental when she received the news that Craig had joined the American army and had been at Gettysburg. She accused her father of wanting to see Craig dead. Then she noticed the look of fear on his face. She was behaving like a child again. After all, it had been her impulsiveness that had placed her in Bella MacSorley's tavern to begin with. Her father had known the violence of war, and his fear for Craig was genuine. She rushed into her father's arms and they cried together. She never mentioned Kevin to anyone—especially not to Craig. But she did get Craig's address from Bella MacSorley and wrote to him explaining her father's mistaken notion about her presence in the tavern that night.

Father and daughter made peace and took consolation in the fact Craig's response was posted from Washington. He had joined his Irish friends from Halifax in the Quartermaster Corps there, away from the fighting and the endless slaughter that the Americans seemed unable to stop.

Michael had also written to Craig and apologized, and suddenly he was home. No one asked how he had obtained his release from the American army, or even if he had obtained a release. No one cared—so long as he was back home.

She knocked softly on his door. There was no response. She opened it a crack. He stood stripped to the waist before the basin across the room. He was shaving. She had never seen him do that before. His beard was extremely light despite his black hair. She knew it was almost as improper for a young lady to stare at a half-naked man as it was to peek at a man totally nude. But Meg rarely worried about impropriety until the results of her actions came down on her head.

He was beautiful to look at. He wasn't excessively tall, just right, she thought. His waist was narrow and men had such funny little rears. Her eyes rose upward. She took in the breadth of his back and shoulders. His skin was smooth and unmarked by blemish or even freckles like those that dotted her shoulders and back.

"Those are not appropriately sisterly looks you are giving me." Craig said suddenly.

At first Meg was startled by his words. Then she realized he could see her face and had been watching her stare at him in his shaving mirror. She blushed.

"I've embarrassed you, Meg. I'm sorry."

"It's all right. I deserved that. Come down to breakfast when you're dressed."

She descended the twisting stairway of the auberge and found the proprietor waiting for her at the bottom. He spoke no English, but had no problem communicating. She could smell the cooked bacon and hot coffee and followed the innkeeper into his dining room. He held her chair for her and she sat. The early sun poured into the dining room. It would be a warm day.

Craig took the chair opposite her before she could take even her first sip of coffee.

"I'm sorry," he apologized. "Most times you can be teased. I guess I haven't been around you long enough to know when you can't."

She reached over the table with her linen napkin and wiped some shaving soap from the lobe of his ear.

"Did I miss?"

"Yes, but I don't see how. You're such an expert with a mirror."

This time he blushed, and she started to laugh. Before long they were both laughing.

"Forgive me?" he asked her.

"For what?"

"For not being a gentleman."

"I forgive you." She paused. "Do you forgive *me*?"

He seemed surprised. "For what?"

"For not behaving as a lady should."

A gentleness came into his eyes and he looked at her face for some time. "Meg," he said finally, "something happened to me when I was away."

"I don't want any confessions," she said afraid to hear what he might say next.

He remained silent and they ate the breakfast quickly.

"Come. We've only half a day to see the sights. Then we must get a boat for Isle d'Orleans to meet the family."

He rose and helped her from the chair.

"It is odd, isn't it, Meg, that we have the same family even though we don't really have any blood ties."

"Yes, it is. My father was foster brother to your grandmother but they were not related at all. Your grandmother was adopted by the Brants."

"Yes, I know." It was clear that the issue had been on his mind.

They left the auberge and walked along the narrow streets. The sun poured through the tiny alleys between the houses and created shafts of light. Carriages and wagons had to give advance warning as they rounded curves to allow pedestrians to make room for them and avoid any mud that the horses' hooves and wagon wheels might send flying in their direction.

The two young people came to the stone steps that led to the bluffs overlooking the St. Lawrence. They began the long climb up.

Halfway up, Meg stopped to rest. Craig took her arm.

"I can get up by myself," she said testily.

He smiled at her. "Independent Meg," was all he said.

"Damned right," she responded and started to renew the climb.

By the time they reached the Upper Town both Craig and Meg were perspiring from the exertion and the warmth of the sun. They walked upriver until they came to the old stone walls of the city at St. Jean gate.

Now the road widened considerably. Quebec had slipped beyond its ancient limits and houses had been erected outside the walls. They left the roads behind them and entered the fields below Cape Diamond and the Citadel which capped it. For two hours they searched out places familiar to Meg from her reading of Canadian history. In some instances, she was able to add episodes from the family's lore to the historical events. She told Craig the story of the Swiss mercenary and his relationship to great–grandmother Nowell. It was said he had died in these fields somewhere.

"What would great–grandmother Nowell be to me?" Craig asked her.

"Let's see. She'd be your great–great–grandmother. Actually she is no relation of mine at all, since the Brants descended from another one of great–grandfather Nowell's escapades."

"He sounds like quite a character."

"Those stories my father tells me sound so romantic—a woman torn between two loves, forced to choose between them. The price she paid for her love was very heavy."

"Sounds sad to me."

"Sad and romantic have much in common."

They continued to stroll over the fields. "I am tired," she said finally.

He spread his jacket on the ground. "Here. Let's sit for a while."

"Just for a little while," she said. "We have to get going soon."

They sat quietly looking at the clouds pass above the Citadel with its fluttering Union Jack. She looked at him.

"You're quiet today."

"You intimidate me," he said. "I don't know when I'm going to get into trouble with you for opening my mouth."

"I'm sorry. I don't want that for us. I want to tell you all my deepest thoughts and I want to hear yours."

"What deep thoughts do you have?" he teased her.

"First, you tell me yours."

102

"Well, there are my plans."

"What are they?"

"Number one, finish school."

"And after you've become a gentleman scholar?"

"Then I want to return to Manitoba and go back to my people and work for them."

"You could do much for them in Ottawa. I am sure this confederation proposal will be adopted. Canada will include the Maritimes, and then Rupert's Land, in the far west too."

"I'm not sure I want Red River and Assiniboia to come under white rule."

"Oh, Craig, I think that's inevitable. It will be either Canadian or American."

"There's not much choice between them. Why can't we have our own republic, our own laws, laws that make sense to Indians and Métis if not to whites?"

"You know my father. He's a just man."

"When he gets his facts straight," Craig chuckled.

Meg smiled. "When he gets his facts straight," she repeated. "For all the noise he will make about being a Nova Scotian first, and the nasty things he says about Upper Canada, deep in his soul he understands that these little provinces cannot continue to survive alone. He has said so privately to me. He'll oppose confederation publicly, but he acknowledges its inevitability privately. The same is as true for your Manitoba as it is for his Nova Scotia."

"But my land is not small, Meg. It is almost impossible to describe. In some parts, it is flat, in others, rolling. But everywhere it is endless, free, unbroken. There's food on the hoof, yours for the taking—the best meat you've ever tasted. That is, if it's cooked right, like my mother and my grandmother cook it."

"Craig, you can't have it unless it's Canadian. The Americans will take it as they have taken everything else in the past thirty years—Texas, New Mexico, Arizona, California. Why, Mexico is half the size it once was because of American expansion!"

Meg decided to return to the subject that really interested her. "When will you go back?"

"Just as soon as I graduate or sooner."

"What do you mean 'sooner'?"

"I can't say much about it but there are forces gathering, Meg, forces that will support my dreams for my home."

"Is there any place for me in your dreams?" There, she had

said it. It had been on her mind for months. She was glad she had the courage.

His eyes widened in surprise. "There will always be a place for you. When I first realized that, it shamed me because we were related. I was afraid of disgracing myself and dishonoring my father before the eyes of your parents. It wasn't until just after I left that I began to understand that I loved you and that we were free to love each other. I remember being so jealous when Kevin O'Connor made eyes at you."

"Who?" she feigned ignorance.

"You remember, the Irish boy with the black hair, the handsome one that night at MacSorley's."

His mention of O'Connor had frightened her.

"I'd forgotten his name."

"We went off to the army together."

"Do you still keep in touch with him?"

"Yes, why?"

"Don't let father know. MacSorley's was reported to be a hangout for Fenians, and O'Connor's Irish. He is probably a Fenian like all those Irishmen. If there is one group father is intolerant of, it is Fenians—and besides, I did not like him."

Craig grew instantly alert. He had said too much already about knowledge of O'Connor. He could not allow this connection with the Irishman to come between himself and Meg.

"I'll change my tune for your father and the family. I'll be a Canadian patriot. I'll even go *that* far in order to have you."

"You feel the same as I do then?"

"Meg, I love you."

"You'll not let politics come between us?"

"Nothing will come between us. I won't allow it."

He leaned over and kissed her chastely on the lips. "We belong to each other forever," he whispered in her ear. He was overcome by the perfume of her hair. He would dearly have loved to pursue this moment but he knew he would destroy everything if he did. He stood up instead and offered her his hand.

"Come on," he said. "We have a boat to catch."

Willy Mackay Brant sat in her bed waiting for Michael to quit puttering about the washstand and join her. She knew the day at the Stieglers' had tired him and that he would have no trouble sleeping tonight. He turned finally and approached the bed. As he pulled back the covers to make way for himself, he smiled at her.

"This is getting to be a habit, madam, this sleeping together."

"Yes, we ought to take it up again when we return to Halifax," she said sarcastically.

"Who knows," he responded, "things might happen, some sort of miracle for me. After all, you're still young enough to have children. Wouldn't you like to get yourself a little nipper, someone to carry on the Brant name? I'm the last of my line, you know."

"Nonsense, Michael, there are hundreds of little red Brants running all over Ontario, all of Joseph's grandchildren and great–grandchildren."

"None of them keep the high holy days," he joked.

"Neither do you, since you became a warden of the Anglican church."

"Not even before then," he laughed, "although there were times I do believe that my mother tricked us into celebrating Christian holidays while she in fact turned them into Hebrew ones." He turned on his side.

"So much for little nippers," she teased.

"My goodness, woman, I'm over seventy. What in God's name do you want with a son?"

She chuckled. "There is an easier way to gain a son," she suggested.

"How's that?" he responded, asleep already.

"Your daughter could marry."

"I fully expect some day she will, when she finds the right man, and I can make arrangements with his family for his own protection."

"She has already found the right man. She confided in me today."

At first she thought he had not heard her but then she realized that what she had taken for a snore was a snort of surprise. He sat bolt upright in bed.

"Who?"

"Craig," she answered.

His eyes grew wide. "Preposterous," he shouted. "Why, they're related. They are like brother and sister. He is my sister's grandson."

"Michael, there is no blood tie. You and your sister, much as you love each other, are not in the least related."

"But we were just like brother and sister. That's how it should be with them. It is indecent otherwise. He'd have to leave our home and come only by invitation. They could not be together without chaperone."

Willy sighed. "If that's the way it must be, then let it be. I am happy for Meg, Michael. She's ecstatic. It's so wonderful to see your own child in love. It's like reliving your own romance."

"Or like having your first romance vicariously," he said sadly.

"Oh, you old fool," she said placing her head on his chest. "What I've had with you I would not trade."

"Not even for a great romance? Don't you regret not having it?"

"Never," she lied. She had known the feeling Meg had expressed to her. True, she was younger and those feelings had never been reciprocated, but she had known Meg's joy. She was sure that Michael had never known her feeling for Joshua, Craig's father. She was wrong, of course. Michael had always known.

They lay still for some moments.

"Michael, are you awake?"

"No," he said in his grouchiest tone.

"Well, get awake," she nudged him.

"Dammit, woman," he complained, "I've had a hard day. I had to be nice to Charles Miller for several hours, and that will take the stuffing out of any man."

"You were good. Marc Stiegler was really frightened that he had bitten off more than he could chew bringing you two together."

"I truly despise that man, Willy. He destroyed my sister's love for him and nearly destroyed her. Certainly he drove her into another man's arms. He killed my mother. I swear to God he will burn in hell for his treatment of that woman. He even tried to destroy Joshua, his own son. Only my intervention saved that boy and let him grow to manhood with self-esteem. How could one man achieve so much evil in one lifetime?"

"He's had a long one. But I think he's met his match in Allison."

"Oh yes, I forgot. You have some grudges in her direction."

"Not at all," she lied. "But didn't the children stand up to him and to all of us. I was so proud of how they spoke of Canada and its future."

"Not Charles's son. He's a cipher. Yet there was one moment

when he showed his true feelings behind Charles's back. Such hate! I would not want to know that a son of mine felt that way about me. That boy is dangerous. But then Charles Miller deserves such a son. He never deserved a Joshua. Maybe he was right after all. Maybe Joshua was his brother's son." Suddenly he realized the implication of his remarks for his sister Elizabeth. "Listen to me. My mother would have had my head if she could have heard me."

He changed the subject. "Wilhelmina Mackay, I gather that you are determined those children shall have each other. I can hear it in your voice, and I have never been able to thwart that once I hear it. I surrender."

"You have no objections then to an understanding?"

"I have many. When will their marriage occur? Obviously not until he finishes school. How does he intend to support himself and a wife? Where will they live?"

"Why, Halifax, of course. I thought he might read law with you. You could use a partner. Brant and Miller. Sounds good to me."

"You have it all figured out. And Meg agrees?"

"In the essentials, yes."

"And what will Joshua and his dear Rainbow say about losing a son and to Willy Mackay?"

Willy grew silent. In truth she had discussed none of this with Meg. She had assumed all of it. It was what she wanted for her daughter and for herself as well. She would not be thwarted. Joshua had other children. She had only Meg.

"We'll talk to the children in the morning," Michael said sleepily. "We have much to discuss."

He turned his back, and Willy knew that all further talk for this day was over.

V

Toronto, March 1866

Charles Miller felt as old as he looked. He sat in his favorite maroon leather chair in his study in his Bay Street house. It also revealed his age. He could not abide new things. He had come of age in the eighteenth century. It was not his fault that he had seen six decades of the nineteenth century as well. He lit his room by candlelight. It was an affectation. A generation earlier he had introduced oil lamps into the house. But he did not want to remember that failing. The rest of the house might be converted to gaslight, but candles were back in vogue in his study. He also insisted on using quills, although they were getting bloody hard to buy. No matter, his current supply would outlast him.

He was confined to a chair or to his bed now, and he was weary of life. His had been a long one. His desk was cluttered with mementoes of uselessness. Everyone who had ever meant anything to him was gone now. His mother, Amy Nowell, had been dead for over twenty–five years. He could still remember her as a young woman with her twin sons. But he also remembered her coldness toward him for turning on his stepfather, Ethan Morin.

"They hanged him," Charles said aloud. "Well, the bastard was a traitor. He deserved it." But his mother never again said a kind word to him even when he returned a hero after the war against the Americans.

He laughed aloud. "Christ's blood," he cursed (he had taken to eighteenth century cursing as well), "if you say it often enough you begin to believe it yourself." He had been punishing himself privately for years for his lack of courage at the battle of Lake Erie. But that was not the public's view of him. Charles Miller of Miller Shipping, of the Welland Canal, of the Grand Trunk Railway, millionaire, that Charles Miller was a war hero.

His twin brother, Stevie, was gone now, done in by drink and women just as Charles had always predicted he would be. Elizabeth, Charles's first wife—he laughed aloud again—his only wife in reality, still lived out in Vancouver Colony. They had never been divorced, even after she ran away with his brother. She had been reported drowned and he had remarried. It wasn't until years later that he heard that she still lived. God, how it made Allison nervous. Suppose her marriage to him was not valid. Did that make his son, Alex, Charles Miller's bastard instead of Charles Miller's heir? It was a thought that troubled her dreams, not his. Let *her* worry about it. He knew his marriage was legal. He had checked it out with his attorney. But he never told her. Sometimes he was sure the uncertainty kept her from doing him in.

He had another son, Joshua, but he dismissed that thought. He could not believe that Elizabeth's child was his. Not after she ran away with his twin brother. Who could tell Charles Miller's son from Stephen Miller's son anyway, for God's sake?

Well, Joshua lived like a savage out on the prairie with his squaw woman and his papooses. He didn't matter. It had been a shock, though; to meet Joshua's boy at the family reunion at Quebec City last year. He had heard the boy was coming to Toronto—after a stint with the Americans fighting in their civil war.

He thought of the rest of the family, those still alive, all brought together last year by the Quebec Conference on confederation. He didn't give a damn about the family reunion. He had gone as an Upper Canadian industrialist determined to bring the stubborn Maritimers into the union. Michael Brant so typified the stupidity of the easterners. But no matter, the confederation was now inevitable. True, one or two of the Maritime provinces might balk, but inevitably they would be part of a Canada from sea to sea connected by railways built by his firm with lucrative federal contracts. He would not be around then, but nothing could stop it now.

He read the *Globe* with amusement these days. All this scare about wild Irishmen attacking Canada to force Britain out of Ireland. If the United States had been trying to pressure Britain, he would take the threat seriously. The Americans had huge armies still armed and mobilized after their recent fratricidal bloodletting. But the Irish threat to Canada? He laughed aloud again. "When will my people realize they are a nation?" he spoke. "Nations do not bend before thugs, especially Irish thugs."

The door to his study opened and Alex, his son, entered the room quietly.

"It's time for bed, Father," he said.

"I won't sleep. I just lie there and think. I may as well sit here and think."

"What would people say, Father, if I just let you sit up all night? They would say I was a very unloving and undutiful son."

"Oh yes, my Alex, you are a dutiful son."

"Put your arm around my neck and I will lift you."

"Damn it, boy, I don't want to go to bed."

Alex sighed and sat down in the leather chair opposite his father. "What *do* you want to do?"

"Alex, go out and get a job. Earn your living and leave me to the care of strangers. Be more like your mother. I know you can't stand me any more than she does. Why do you hang around me?"

"I don't have to work," Alex said with no emotion whatever in his voice. "I am the son of a wealthy man. There are rights and privileges that go with my position."

"Like being a nurse?"

"Being your nurse gives me a certain amount of power."

There was not even a bit of menace in his tone but Charles grew suddenly frightened. Once before in his life he had allowed someone's control of him and it had nearly cost him his life. It pained him, but only briefly, to think so ill of his own son. And besides, what did it matter?

"I don't believe you really are my son, any more than Joshua Miller is my son. In fact," he laughed aloud, "he can probably claim a closer blood tie because his father is my own twin brother. But with a mother like yours, God only knows who your true father might be."

"People say I favor you."

Charles studied Alex's eyes.

"For once, Alex, tell me what you really feel for me. Tell me that you hate me for the things I say to you and about you and about your mother. I think I would feel much closer to you if you hated me. At least I would understand you. I bully you, I curse you, I call your parentage into doubt and you merely smile at me and tell me it's time for my nap or my hot soup. Damn it, boy. Let out the hate. I do. It is good for you."

Alex merely shook his head. "I don't hate you, father. I know when you say those things it is merely your own way of relieving your tensions."

Charles was silent for some moments. Finally he spoke. "I know about Lord Carringdon, you know."

Panic crossed Alex's face but then disappeared.

"He was murdered by some Irish rogue," Alex replied. "They say it was his own bastard."

"Your mother confided in me, Alex. She told me that you killed Lord Carringdon."

"You're hallucinating," Alex said. He rose from his chair and walked to his father. He placed his hand on Charles's forehead. "I do believe you are feverish."

"Oh, for Christ's sake, stop it. I don't hold it against you that you killed the Irish whoremonger or that you bedded his wife. In fact, it is one of the few things you've done in your life that I can point to with some fatherly pride."

"You would take pride in your son's involvement in a murder or adultery?"

"Damn right," Charles said. "At least it shows you're alive and a man."

Alex went back to his chair and collapsed into it. "I will never understand you, Father," he said. "I am not guilty of what you accuse me of, and I will defend my name and position against such falsehood with all the weapons that I possess, but that you should take pride in such false accusations overwhelms me."

"Good, at least something touches your soul. Let's be honest with each other. When I was your age, I used to like some wench to take a whip to my butt. By God, I'd get so hard . . ."

"Father, stop it," Alex said.

"I don't know what you saw in Lady Carringdon. She had a face like one of her horses, but she must have had some body, eh, boy?"

Alex had recovered. He would not let his father touch him again. He remained silent.

"You're no man. And if you're no man, why would I want you for a son? I'd rather acknowledge that crazy Indian grandson of mine. I'll bet he wouldn't deny that he screws women and takes what he wants from other men. Nothing

111

should get in the way of what a man wants. That's the way I've lived my life. I'm not ashamed of anything that I've done. I'll stand on the roof for all York to hear."

"The city is called Toronto today. It has been called that for a generation."

Charles sat back in his chair. He had had the young man going for awhile, he was sure of it.

"I'll go to bed now," Charles said.

Alex smiled his benevolent smile. He went to Charles. The old man put his arms about his neck. Alex lifted him from the chair and carried him from the room and up the stairs to the bedroom.

He slept alone. He had never shared a bedroom with anyone. Not since he and Stevie were youngsters. Both his wives had kept separate bedrooms. Alex pushed open the door with his foot. The covers of the canopied four poster had been turned down. Charles never dressed any longer. He was in his nightshirt already.

"Do you want a clean shirt?" Alex asked him as he placed his father in his bed.

"Why not?" Charles said.

Alex unbuttoned the top buttons of the shirt and pulled it with some assistance from his father up over the old man's head. Then he walked across the room to the dresser drawer to find a replacement.

Charles looked down at his ravaged and emaciated body. He remembered how he used to look.

"It's time," he mumbled.

"What's that, Father?" Alex asked.

"Nothing. Hurry up and get me my shirt. I'm freezing my ass off."

Charles complained continually while Alex struggled to get him into the clean nightshirt. When he completed his task the young man went to the door of the bedroom, taking the oil lamp with him.

"Good night, Father."

"Close the door when you leave."

He lay in the darkness. He could hear the old clock on the landing tick away. What did it remind him of? Some other clock in some other place earlier in his life. He couldn't remember such things anymore. What did it matter? What did anything matter anymore?

112

Once again, he would have to wait for sleep. He would lie here and wait for the clock to chime every fifteen minutes. Sometimes well after midnight, he would hear the key in the latch of the front door and Allison's latest lover would bring her home. At least she didn't bring them in the house with her. He could be grateful for small favors.

The door of his room opened a crack.

"Are you asleep?" he heard Alex whisper.

He did not respond. His eyes were adjusted to the dark, and he could see his son groping in the darkness. What was he reaching for? There, he had picked it up. It was the extra pillow Charles kept at the foot of his bed. Alex approached him, the pillow held at arm's length in front of him. Charles smiled to himself as the soft down came firmly over his face. He had known it would be this way, but he realized his fears had been misplaced. He had feared the mother more than the son.

Alex ransacked his father's study. He knew the will was kept somewhere in this room but he could find no loose papers anywhere. Had the old bastard finally succumbed to his lawyer's suggestion and placed it in the law firm's vault? No, he knew his father too well. He would never follow someone else's suggestion in business affairs. He had kept control of everything over the years, even the damned bankrupt railway stocks.

Then it dawned on him. There was another way to know his father's mind. He was so old–fashioned; he kept a copy book of all letters and important documents. The large leather–bound, folio–size books lined the walls of the study. In them were years of correspondence painstakingly copied down for his files before mailed.

But where to begin?

He reached for the volume that lay on its side, the last one on the shelf. He opened it. It was too heavy to hold in his hands. He took it to his father's writing desk and sat down. He had been right. The front page was dated 1866.

He paged through the volume carefully. He realized why his father spent hours in this room alone. Alex had been his secretary, and had seen the originals of less than half the letters copied here. Then he froze. There was a note in his father's hand addressed to his mother. "My dearest Allison," it began.

If you are reading this, it is because I am dead and you are looking for evidence of my fondness for you. Although I was not always affectionate to you while living, I want you to know the true depths of my feeling now that I am gone.

Your husband was a complete misanthrope. There was really no one in the second half of my life whom I did not loathe, including you. But since life is a trial, and since I want it no different for you, I am leaving you one third of my estate. You are free to leave it to that misbegotten whelp you have tried to pass off as my son all these years. No son of Charles Miller would be as weak as "our" Alex. Joshua, the "son" another wife tried to advance, may be a wild Indian, but at least he has balls. You ate Alex's at birth. You were my legal wife (you did worry about that, didn't you) so I give you your legal third. If you wish to squander it on the lad (?), so be it.

The rest of the estate I will leave to Craig Miller, Joshua's half–breed boy. He is either my grandson or my grandnephew. He is in either case, my mother, Amy Nowell's great–grandchild. There at last my dear Mother, maybe now you will forgive me, wherever you are.

All of this is in my will. Since I know you will now ransack my study looking for the document, I will save you the effort. A copy is folded neatly in my 1865 letter book. Alas yes, I said a copy. The original is with my American attorney, Cousin Conrad Nowell in Washington. He has instructions to forward it to Toronto upon news of my demise. So you see, if you are reading this, it is on its way right now.

Alex sat staring at the message. "By God, old man," he said aloud, "if anyone deserved killing, it was you. My only mistake is that I waited so long to do it. So I end up—still the beggar, dependent now on the mother as I was on the father. Well, it will not be so. You won't outsmart me so easily."

The solution was a simple one. Only two men in the world could deny him what was rightfully his. One was the half–breed nephew from the wilderness of Red River. He had little to fear from him at this particular moment. But the other was not readily at hand. The Washington lawyer was the major threat. He could handle the dilemma. But time was an enemy. He could not wait too long to act. But first he had to plan. He had to get his hands on the will. With no will, if Charles Miller were to be declared intestate—then Allison would still get her third. That too would eventually be his. But the remaining two thirds would come to him—as Charles Miller's only son and heir. But he was not the only son—again the western Millers would plague his peace. But not for long. He would take care of his supposed half-brother Joshua and his half-breed son.

VI

Washington, April 1866

The sun baked the city with a tropical heat that drove all to
shelter except those who had business in the streets or who
made their way to other shelters. The still unfinished capitol
building seemed enshrouded in a heat mist. It felt more like
mid-July than early April.

Nowell Conrad struggled his way across K Street. He could
feel the sweat drenching his shirt and vest underneath his
black coat. His bushy red side–whiskers were mottled with
sweat as well. He was a large stocky man whose clothes never
seemed to fit him. His high stovepipe hat sat unsteadily above
his wavy red hair.

His office was only a block away now. Miss Dawes, his
spinster secretary, would have some lemonade ready for him as
soon as he stepped through the double oak doors. She always
did on days like this.

There were colleagues of his in the Congress who were
scandalized by his hiring a female secretary. Many whispered
about improprieties. Conrad did not give a damn about the
whispers. His mother, Margaret Nowell Conrad, rest her soul,
had taught him never to buckle under to innuendo. She had
been an independent woman until the day she died nineteen
years before. All her life—from her Indian girlhood to her
ventures in trade in the Ferryman empire—she had done what
she wanted and to hell with the gossips. Besides, they were
right. He had bedded Miss Dawes on her third day in the
office, and he had been doing it regularly ever since, despite
his fifty-three years, his oversized belly, and his bad heart.

He chuckled at the thought of Miss Dawes and the gossips.
If they only knew what he and Miss Dawes accomplished back
in the bedroom behind the outer offices. That painfully plain
woman, brown hair tied in a neat bun, seemed to metamor-

phose once all the pins left her hair and it came tumbling down onto her bare shoulders. He shook his head as if to clear the image of her from him. It would not do to keep that up, for in addition to Miss Dawes' lemonade he expected a number of associates to be waiting for him in his offices.

He came to the red brick three–story building which contained his office and his home. He had purchased it back in 1855 when he first came to Congress representing his home state of Massachusetts, the same district his father had represented before him. His mother's bequest to him of half her fabulous Ferryman wealth had made it possible for him to purchase this Washington home and to purchase from his Canadian cousins, the Brants, the old homestead in Charleston. Maggie, his mother, had foolishly left it to them along with most of the Nowell fortune that she had inherited from her grandfather. The Brants had returned to Canada after the price had been removed from the head of that old Mackenzie rebel. Too bad the old rebel had been reconciled with the establishment in his own home. Conrad could have used a man like old Brant right now.

The grey stone steps leading from the street to the office level of Conrad's house were steep. He halted at the bottom before beginning the ascent. His heart was pounding. He had to catch his breath. His legs felt weary and strained. He should have taken a carriage back to his home. But the distance was too short. It embarrassed him to tell a cab driver that he wanted to go the short distance between the capitol and his house. He would have to become a lot sicker before he would endure that daily humiliation. Some of the drivers were recently freed slaves, and Conrad resented their insolence. He had a very low regard for Negroes. True enough, he was a Republican, elected from an abolitionist district, and he had railed against the secessionist South, voting his devotion to the cause again and again. Still, he had thought Abraham Lincoln a giant buffoon until near the end and then, too late, he realized his greatness. Yet he had voted for the Wade–Davis bill against the President's wishes. Conrad had an even lower opinion of Lincoln's successor, Andrew Johnson.

The Congressman started to climb up the steps. Maybe, if he could be rid of his guests, Miss Dawes would refresh him with something more than lemonade. But before he could get out his key, the door swung open. Emily Dawes stood in all her blandness before him.

"Good afternoon, Congressman," she greeted him formally. "I provided you with some refreshments in your study."

"Thank you, Miss Dawes," he greeted her equally formally.

"Senator Sumner does not drink cold lemonade," she continued. "I prepared some tea therefore as well."

Conrad nodded. Leave it to crazy Sumner to drink hot tea in the middle of a Washington heat wave. The man had not been the same since he had been beaten to a bloody pulp on the floor of the Senate before the war. "The first victim of southern treason," Sumner liked to call himself. The beating had heated a dislike of the south and its institutions into a fanatic hatred. But Sumner was titular head of the Massachusetts delegation to the capital and he had to be dealt with carefully.

Conrad walked down the darkened corridor. The house actually seemed cooler. Emily had kept the curtains and drapes closed during the heat wave. Keeping the sun out seemed to help keep the cool in.

His study doors were closed but he could hear Sumner. He was orating. Even on the hottest day in a decade the old windbag had to create more hot air. Conrad fixed a smile on his face and threw open the double doors.

"Charles," he called out.

"Nowell, my good fellow, what kept you so long?"

"The business of politics, Senator. Our short term makes it imperative to keep in touch with our constituents. I had a voter from Charleston in my office. Seems he didn't like my stand on the Alabama claims."

"You stand with me on that, don't you, Congressman?"

"Of course," Conrad said hastily although he would have preferred to follow the lead of the secretary of state on that matter.

"The British must be made to pay for prolonging the war. Confederate privateers ravaged our shipping. They sailed from British ports, and they kept the war going. It cost the American taxpayer an additional billion dollars not to mention the lives lost."

The senator walked over to the window that was covered with white wooden shutters and peered through the slats. Then he stopped speaking. Only the ticking of the mantel clock, the brass ship's clock given to Conrad by his mother, interrupted the silence.

"Which, of course, is why we are here today," Sumner continued finally. "The payment I desire from Britain is not

118

cash. I want the natural destiny of the United States fulfilled. Britain must be chased from this continent. The first step is to get control of the whole west, not just south of the forty–ninth parallel, but north of it, Rupert's Land. From the lakes to the Rockies. Once we have that, everything else will fall into place. Eventually Canada and the puny little Maritime provinces of the east coast and the colony of British Columbia all will become part of one great American empire from the Rio Grande to the North Pole."

Nowell Conrad had heard Sumner ramble like this before. He resented, nevertheless, losing the rest of his afternoon to this nonsense. He longed for Emily to throw her arms about him. He could think only of the coolness of her flesh.

"Your cousin Brant, the fellow I met at Charleston, dark complexion, I thought maybe he had a bit of Negro in him. He's a Republican. Ask him to help us."

"Michael? You misjudge him, Senator. He's not a black. He's part Indian and part Hebrew. He is also a Canadian patriot."

"Nonsense. He told me he fought for Mackenzie. He's a Republican. Strange blood line. Indian and Hebrew? And the man can't be more than ten years older than I am."

"He's got to be approaching eighty."

Sumner was silent for a moment. He picked up his delicate white china teacup and sipped his tea. "Fine cup of tea," he said absentmindedly, "compliment to your Miss . . . Miss?"

"Dawes," Conrad interrupted.

"Ah yes, Miss Dawes. You write to him anyway, that Brant fellow. I want Canada and I want Republican Canadians and all those with American backgrounds to rally to the cause just like the Texans did and just like we did in West Florida."

"Brant's not your man," Conrad suggested. "I have other Canadian relatives. One young associate of Brant's, a young man named Craig Miller, my first cousin's son. A good boy even if his mother was a wild Assiniboine Indian."

"My God, Conrad, everyone in your family seems part savage."

"I know. I just missed it. My mother was raised by Seneca, and my father came from Kentucky. Anyway, this Métis boy, he's a more likely candidate for causing the British trouble. I hear reports that the Métis and the Fenians are in thick with each other."

Sumner shook his head. "I don't have much truck with Fenians."

Conrad felt like saying that that was a luxury congressmen

119

from Irish Boston couldn't afford—unlike senators. Senators didn't have to face the people every two years—only the legislature once every six years.

"Métis, what does that word mean?"

"It means a half–breed. Some say it means a man and a half; half white, half red, half devil. They are the people of western Canada in Rupert's Land. You get them interested in America and you'll get yourself an ally. Control the Métis and you control the west."

Sumner was listening intently now. "I doubt if young men will be of much use to us. We need leaders."

Conrad nodded agreement. "But we may have the answer there. Even if my relative, young Mr. Miller, is no use to us, his folks in Manitoba may be. And Fenian involvement in Rupert's Land—united with Métis sentiments, may bring about an irresistable union of forces."

There was a soft knocking at the door. Emily entered with a tray holding more tea and lemonade. Conrad smiled at her. She merely nodded in return. No one could see him, but she had no intention of adding fuel to the gossips' fire. The congressman took the tray from her. He allowed his hand to linger on hers on the edge of the tray.

"Thank you, Miss Dawes," Conrad said formally.

"Marvelous tea," Sumner chimed in.

His aide mumbled in agreement. Congressman Jennings, who had been seated silently in the corner listening intently, rose and reached for a second glass of lemonade.

"Well, Ted?" Sumner addressed the Minnesota congressman. "You've been sitting there saying nothing. What do you think?"

"Conrad is on to something," said Jennings.

"About what?" Sumner said testily.

"About the Métis. But if you think they can be turned into American agents, you've got another thought coming. They dislike the Canadians more than us only because they see Canada as a bigger threat to their land and their way of life."

"What is their way?" Sumner asked.

"Hunting the buffalo, following it in Red River carts, planting the soil along the river banks, speaking in French. They are seminomads and they are wild."

"They sound as bad as the Sioux," Sumner said chuckling.

"They're worse because they've got civilization. They wear clothes like us, mostly, yet some braid their hair just like Indians. They get the best of the white man's culture and the best of the Indian's culture, but they've also got the worst of the white and the worst of the red all rolled up in one son of a . . ." He stopped himself, realizing that Miss Dawes was still in the doorway. She turned and walked out, closing the door softly behind her.

"Handsome woman," Sumner said, although he really thought her mousy looking.

"How could you know so much about these devils, Jennings?"

"My district is the quickest way to get to them. The railroads reach out to Minnesota, thanks to you and our party, Senator."

Sumner bowed smiling.

"And from St. Paul on the Mississippi it isn't far to the Red River. It flows right through Métis country. It's quicker to get to Fort Garry on the Red River, their capital, from New York than it is to get there from Montreal via Toronto. The route to Métis land is through Minnesota. That's why it should be ours."

Sumner sat down in the chair next to the window. The sun shone through the slats and threw a strange pattern on his face. "Half devil," he said chuckling. "They may be the answer yet."

"You'll have to use the Fenians to get to them," Conrad responded.

"Oh, well," Sumner said, "if our cause is just, sometimes we must pick dubious means to achieve a just end."

"I'll alert my contacts in Boston immediately, Senator."

Sumner finished his second cup of tea. He reached for his hat. Thank God he's going, Conrad thought. Before many more minutes passed, he would be in Emily's arms.

Conrad lay back against the pillows. He stared down at the bulge in the sheets over his groin. He was still hard. He amazed himself. Ten minutes earlier he had exploded in ecstasy in the arms of Miss Dawes. Never in his life had he experienced anything like it. As a young man he had indulged himself in every way money could buy. Now, in his middle age, he had come upon the essence of pleasure. And she didn't charge!

Well, he would have to be careful. He had never lost his erection after the last bout, and he had a bad heart. But, by God, if she were by his side right now, instead of down in the kitchen making more of her infernal lemonade he would be ready for another go at it.

Emily Dawes entered the bedroom. She held her ever-present tray in her hand. She had iced the lemonade and the glass into which she had poured it was frosted. Conrad reached over to take it from her and nearly knocked the glass from the tray. Emily steadied it.

"Be careful, Nowell," she chided him.

"Be careful is right. I might have spilled it onto my crotch and cooled it down a bit. That would surely be a disappointment to you now, wouldn't it?"

Emily blushed.

It angered Conrad that the woman could do almost anything without shame but just even hint at anything verbal and she blushed like a virgin. Well, she was no virgin. Conrad reached for her breasts. She pushed his hand away.

"I thought you were thirsty."

"I'm always thirsty."

Again she blushed but handed him the glass of lemonade.

He noticed the tremor of her hand as she held the drink out to him. By God, she was a passionate one, he thought. He took a large gulp of the drink and offered the rest to her. She shook her head.

"You are the thirsty one," she said smiling at him.

Conrad lay back down against the pillows after placing the remaining lemonade on the nightstand. He burped loudly, and belatedly covered his mouth with his hand.

"Such a pig am I," he said laughing.

Emily lay down on the bed next to him. He took her hand and placed it on his groin. "See what you do to me," he whispered in her ear.

She clutched at him, opening and closing her hand over his hardness.

Conrad sighed, "Slake my thirst, woman. Give me relief."

He gasped as he felt her warm mouth close on him. The pleasure began to swell. He felt a tightening in his chest which grew in intensity to correspond with the warmth that flowed from his groin. He almost belched again. He could taste the sourness of the lemonade in his throat. He gasped a second time, but this time with pain. He clutched at his chest, and then at his throat.

"Emily," he cried out.

The woman raised her head and smiled at him. It was the last thing that Nowell Conrad ever saw.

VII

Toronto, May 1866

Kevin kicked the covers off his body. The late afternoon sun poured into his garret room in the Front Street boarding-house. He blinked and put up his hand to block the sun. He ran his tongue over the film on his teeth. He had been out late last night drinking. It was his first night back from his trip to the Niagara and Fort Erie. He looked over at the other side of the bed. When he had crawled under the covers last night, that side of the bed had been occupied by Craig Miller.

It was good to have Craig back with him. Craig had arrived in Toronto at the beginning of May bearing his college diploma in hand. He was supposed to be traveling back to Fort Garry to see his parents. He intended to announce his decision to marry and read law with his uncle in Halifax. Kevin remembered the girl. How could he forget her? He had wanted to have her himself. She was stunning and she had turned his friend into a celibate. Well, to hell with that, if that was what falling in love did to you.

Craig would not make it to Manitoba this summer. The brotherhood needed him. In fact, it had summoned him to Ontario.

The latch of the door turned and Miller entered.

"Rise and shine, fellow conspirator," Craig called to him.

Kevin grimaced. He did not like to be reminded that he and Craig were extremely vulnerable here in Toronto. Spying for the brotherhood, in advance of the projected invasion, could earn one the noose if one were caught. Sometimes he felt he had been running away from the noose all his life, ever since that night back in Carringdon Hall. To hell with it too, he thought.

"Shut the damned door and shut your damned mouth," he greeted his friend.

"Ah! The hangover has gotten to you," said Craig, with what to Kevin seemed like painful cheeriness.

"Don't rub it in, Craig. I feel awful. I feel like someone used my mouth to piss in."

"They probably did. Probably couldn't resist the temptation, with you passed out on the barroom floor with your mouth wide open."

Kevin sat up on the side of the bed and held his head at each temple.

Craig placed a small bundle of food on the table in the center of the room. "I have some fresh milk and bread. Will that help?"

"It will, if your desire is for me to puke up all that piss."

Craig started to laugh. He sat down next to Kevin on the bed. "Good trip?" he asked.

Kevin nodded.

"Christ, Craig, this whole province is open. General Sweeney could walk the brotherhood army across the border. The whole goddamned thing is ours for the taking."

"Sweeney insisted at the last senate meeting that he had to have ten thousand men, three artillery batteries, two hundred rounds for each man and five hundred rounds for each cannon. That's only in order to strike at London and Niagara. Then another force of sixteen thousand are to strike at Montreal. Are we ready?"

"How the hell would I know? All I do is check on the defenses of Upper Canada. I can assure you there aren't any to speak of."

"You can't fail, Kevin. The Canadians close in on my people more every day. The papers are full of John A. Macdonald's demands on Britain to force the transfer of Rupert's Land. Manitoba and Ireland are tied together."

"You really believe that? I did sell you a load of goods, didn't I?"

"I'm not a fool, Kevin. I know damned well that no one in the high command in the brotherhood gives a hoot about Manitoba, but I believe in it. I believe that the Canadas and the Maritimes, even if confederated, are up to their asses in the swamps of Irish politics. That will give my people time to organize. I have been in touch with my father. He's discussed it with old man Riel and his son and other leaders at Fort Garry. They agree with me and encourage me with this work. Play the role of a good Canadian. I went to my family reunion in

124

Quebec and spouted that stuff. I made my peace with Uncle Michael, and even allowed my recently deceased English grandpa to give me his blessings for saying all the right things."

Kevin rose and went to the chair on which he had thrown his clothes. "I swear I think you are a better Fenian than I am, and I'm the one who brought you into the brotherhood."

"No, my friend," Craig responded, "I am not a good Fenian at all. As you've known all along, I don't care about Ireland. Fenianism is a means to an end for me. Now, for God's sake take a bath and put on some fresh clothes. This place smells like an armpit."

Kevin sniffed himself. "I guess it's me," he said. "But what difference does it make? It is the smell of the working class, and we are all of the working class."

"What the hell are you talking about?" Craig joked. "We haven't worked since we joined the American army."

Kevin had finished dressing. "Now those were the days, weren't they? Especially after we got out of the line of fire and back in the Quartermaster's operation in Washington. That was the life. Any kind of comfort we wanted."

"Yeah, it is a shame something good like that had to end," Craig said sarcastically.

"Well, the brotherhood takes care of us. Sean and Jim, you and me, we've lived good."

"It hasn't been so good since then," Craig complained.

"The politicians went and disbanded most of the army. They sent a lot of our organization back into civilian life. It won't be long now, though, before we are in power here. Everything is ready."

"Nothing is about to happen tonight, is it?"

Kevin looked at Craig in puzzlement.

"I was just wondering if we had time to attend my grandmother's little party tonight."

"You can go if you want. I haven't got time for tea and crumpets with little old ladies."

Craig howled with delight. "Oh my God, she'd have apoplexy if she could hear you. She's no little old lady. She's a strikingly beautiful and scandalous woman. She's not really my grandmother. She is my grandfather's second wife. He was forty-three years older than she. He died in March. They think it was a heart attack. You remember? I went to his funeral."

"I vaguely recall your mentioning it. I was out of town as usual."

"Her party is the scandal of Toronto. My grandfather has been in his grave only two months and she's entertaining. Everyone is outraged and everyone who is anyone has been invited and will be there. No one would dare miss it."

"I'm no one and I'm missing it."

"Come on, Kevin. You'll meet a dozen useful sources of information you can tap without their knowing it."

"You have a point there."

Craig stretched out on the bed. "Kevin, I don't know. Sometimes I get so hopeful. You read newspaper accounts of the strength of the brotherhood; you hear that they will attack Canada at any moment. But nothing ever happens, and when it does, it's a fiasco like the raid at Campobello in New Brunswick."

"You know better than that," Kevin argued. "You're one of us. You know the New Brunswick raid was attempted by the breakaway wing, the few who still support O'Mahoney, the Ireland–only leader. We're the majority, the William Roberts followers. We control the Fenian movement, the Fenian army and the Fenian funds. When we strike, it will be different."

"But when, Kevin? When?"

"Soon. It will be soon. Word is out. The centers are already on the move heading north. O'Neill and his Tennessee and Kentucky boys have been ordered to Cincinnati and will move from there onto Cleveland. That's just across Lake Erie from us."

"It's got to be soon."

"It will be, but not so soon that you and I can't attend your little old grandmother's scandal."

"But not unless you bathe," Craig teased.

The Bay Street house was alive with light. Allison had disposed of all of her dead husband's ancient possessions. He was no sooner buried in the churchyard at St. James than she went shopping. The stuffy leather chairs, the dark wood, all were replaced with the finest new upholstered chairs and love seats in the gayest of colors. All the latest imports from Paris and London had made their way to New York and Buffalo, up the Erie Canal and finally to Toronto and Bay Street by Charles's own vessels and his own pet project, the Welland Canal. The whole house was painted inside and out. New curtains and wallpapers were hung. The house was taken from the eighteenth century to the second half of the nineteenth century within a month.

Allison assumed at first that Charles's will would be discovered. But nothing turned up in Toronto. A search was made of his American attorney's files as well. Nothing. It was so unlike Charles. But since he was intestate, his whole estate passed to Alex with one third for herself during her lifetime. He had disowned the western relatives years before, but the Millers, Joshua and Craig, could still cause trouble. Charles had acknowledged only her and Alex as his heirs during his lifetime. She was sure of her position. She had consulted her attorneys and they had reassured her. But he had been such a difficult old man. She could not be sure he had not made a secret will. Well, if he had, he had not hidden it in the house. She had torn the place apart looking for it and found nothing. If any new surprises did turn up, however, she was prepared to fight for what was hers—and her son's.

Alex had been a problem at first. For two weeks after Charles's death he had moped about the house looking for something to do. Almost all his life he had been secretary and companion to his father. He seemed lost. Then word came of the death of Charles's American attorney, and finally came the news of the fruitless search for Charles's will. At that point Alex came to life.

He sought and received a commission in the Upper Canadian militia. He also began to play an active role in several of Charles's companies. She should not have been surprised. Alex had done most of Charles's correspondence over the past seven or eight years. No one knew his affairs as well as Alex. Yet it still surprised her. She had never thought him capable of decisions. She wondered about the changes in her son. Had he "arranged" any of this? She thought him incapable—not of killing, he had done that before, she knew— but rather she thought him incapable of "arranging."

The party had been partly his idea. He wanted to show off all her new things. All Toronto knew that Charles Miller was wealthy and stingy. She wanted his hometown to know just how wealthy she was now. But she had hesitated. It was really indecent after all. But then Alex explained that it would advance his militia career. They would invite Major General George Napier, British commander in Upper Canada, and Lieutenant Colonel Peacocke and Captain Charles Akers. They were all Regular British Army and could help Alex's career. He was persistent and she finally agreed, knowing it would create a scandal, but not really caring.

It was her idea to invite Craig Miller. An invitation accepted might indicate the acquiescence of the western relatives to the settlement of Charles's estate. She was delighted when Craig accepted.

But she was still wary.

The house looked splendid. She had hired several new housemaids and a new cook. The food was ready. Several musicians sat in her parlor ballroom warming up with the latest music from Vienna, which people loved to dance to. She, of course, as a recent widow, would accept no invitations to dance. But that was no reason for discouraging others—even her Alex. Perhaps he would find some pretty young girl among the guests. Up to this point he had shown no predilection for anyone, not since Lady Barbara Carringdon. Perhaps that unfortunate experience had chased him off.

She did know that she wanted to invite Charles's grandson, Craig Miller, to the party. He was in Toronto and she wanted to show off the family's wealth. What he saw would surely get back to the Brants in Halifax and perhaps even to the Stieglers in Quebec. Maybe even to the old lady in Victoria. It would serve her right to know how much she had missed. Allison had never known Elizabeth Stoddard Miller, Charles's first wife, but she still wanted to punish her for running out and leaving Allison to put up with so much. Her dislike for the unknown Elizabeth was irrational, she knew, but she didn't care. She hoped Craig would write his grandmother and tell her of the sumptuousness of it all. When he asked if he might bring a friend, she agreed readily.

Kevin had borrowed a suit from Craig. His own clothes were to be found on the floor of their room in various states of repair and cleanliness. He did not take kindly to Craig's insistence that he could have no loan of apparel without first bathing. He removed his clothes and wrapped a towel about his middle and waddled barefoot down the flight of stairs, then down the corridor to the one indoor facility. He removed the foul taste of last night's beer from his mouth. He lathered his face and shaved the stubble from it. He did a quick wash of those parts of his anatomy that were likely to give offense and then retraced his steps back to his room. He found Craig already dressed.

"Well, I'm ready," Kevin said as he entered the room with his towel draped over his arm.

128

"You wouldn't even be noticed," Craig responded.

"Hey, I take exception to that slur on my privates." The words startled him, reminding him for the first time in a while of Father Thomas Doyle and of his mother, Mary O'Connor.

Craig saw his change of expression and misunderstood, thinking his friend was truly offended by his joke.

"I'm sorry, Kevin. No offense intended. I was just joking. We could all walk into that house naked and be unnoticed. They have eyes and ears in this town only for the scandalous Widow Miller."

Kevin rushed his dressing. His friend was anxious to get going, and he might as well get this over with.

Before too many minutes had passed they were strolling through the spring evening along Front Street to Bay Street. They turned left and walked away from the lakefront. Bay Street was alive with lighted carriages and strolling couples.

"The house must be awfully big if it is going to hold this crowd," Kevin quipped.

"Oh, they are not all invited," Craig responded. "Most of the strollers are just that. They'll walk by and gawk to see if they can see anything."

"You're kidding."

"I'm telling you. This is the event of 1866."

"I certainly hope not. I have a mind to help the brotherhood place the Widow Miller's party in perspective."

"Hear, hear," Craig responded.

They were at the Miller house now. The door was manned by a very elegant-looking gentleman in butler's dress uniform.

"Do you know," said Craig, "it was either this house or one further down the street that my grandfather sold right from underneath Uncle Michael and his mother. They were his first wife's family and he was still married to her."

"Sounds like a lovely fellow. He was lucky to die of natural causes," Kevin joked.

"Come on, we may as well go in."

The young men gave their names to the butler who seemed to have the names of the invited guests memorized. He seemed to hesitate at Kevin O'Connor but then smiled.

"Oh yes, madam told me that her stepgrandson would bring a gentleman friend. You must be the young gentleman in question."

"I must," said Kevin mockingly.

"Mrs. Miller is greeting her guests in the drawing room, sir."

Kevin walked through the foyer placing a value on most of the furnishings. His year and a half in the Quartermaster's Corps had given him an eye for valuables.

"Craig, my dear," he heard the voice and froze. She might just as well have said, "tonight, eight o'clock." He could never forget that voice.

"Mrs. Miller," Craig said, "I want you to meet my very best friend, Kevin O'Connor."

"Mr. O'Connor," she said extending her hand for him to kiss. "It is marvelous to meet my grandson's friends—especially when they are such dashing young men. Tell me, my dear Mr. O'Connor, are you a visitor to Toronto? I don't believe I've seen you before."

Kevin tried to remain calm. Was it possible she did not remember him? Perhaps the six years had changed him? True, he had been a boy then and now he was a man. But he had not forgotten her. If it was possible, she had grown even more beautiful. The honey–colored hair was piled on her head and the light from the drawing room reflected in the diamond and gold earrings and matching choker she wore on her neck. Her dress was velvet, a deep wine–red in color.

Kevin did not know what to say. Several guests had lined up behind him to greet their hostess.

"Glad to meet you, ma'am," was all he could croak. He ignored her question about his residence as just so much polite chatter. Already her green eyes had left him and were searching the faces of guests behind him. He followed Craig past her and heard her delight in meeting a Captain and Mrs. Akers. She greeted them exactly as she had greeted him. He was angered by that. But why? He had not seen her since the night his father was killed. But it had been his first time, and nothing like it had occurred since. There had been many girls, more than he cared to remember, but there had never been another Allison.

Obviously for her there had been many Kevins, perhaps more than she cared to remember. No, he could not believe that. It had been special. He had to believe that.

Craig walked straight through the drawing room and into the dining room where giant platters of freshly baked French pastries awaited those who grew hungry. Craig didn't wait to be invited to partake. They had forgotten all about the loaf of bread and can of milk and had come straight to the party. Craig, at least, was hungry.

"Do you believe this?" Craig laughed as he looked around at the incredible variety of baked sweets. "My grandfather must be spinning in his grave."

Kevin paid no attention to his friend. His mind was still back in the foyer.

"I'm going to find someone interesting," he said to Craig.

"Suit yourself. Frankly, I think I am very interesting."

"I mean someone who can help us out with the . . . project."

Kevin walked out of the dining room and into the drawing room once again. The line in front of Allison was even longer, and she had been joined by her son. He was dressed in a militia officer's uniform. Kevin smiled. If bland Alex Miller was what Canada could throw at them, the project was as good as accomplished. At one point he saw Allison turn around. He thought to catch her eye but she ignored him and went on greeting her guests. He walked down the hall and practically bumped into the butler as he carried armfuls of ladies' wraps into the cloakroom.

"May I help you, sir?" the butler asked.

"I was just looking for the . . ." It dawned on Kevin that he had no idea how a butler might refer to the facilities. He was sure he could not use his old army terminology on a stuffed–shirt butler.

"Oh, yes—down the hall and then turn right before you come to the kitchen." Then he shot past Kevin to take the wraps to the cloakroom.

Kevin turned left instead and opened the door to Charles Miller's old study. It was the only room that had been left much as it was. Alex had taken it over for himself, and he liked to emulate his father's habits.

Kevin sat in Miller's rough-grained maroon leather chair. "Pretty comfortable," he said aloud. He would have to get himself one of these after he became quartermaster general of the brotherhood army.

He looked up and saw her standing in the doorway.

"Cunliffe said you were down here. He is too much of a gentleman to suggest that you were using the convenience, more of a gentleman than you are for entering a private room closed off from the guests."

"I could not believe that you had forgotten me. I wanted you to follow me someplace where we could be alone."

"Forget you? No, I could never do that."

131

"You mean I wasn't just a one-night affair?"

"Actually, my dear, that is just what you were, not because I wanted it that way, but because fate intervened. When I saw you enter the house with Charles's grandson, my heart leapt inside me."

"One could hardly have told that from the exterior."

"I've learned to control the exterior. One does not live with a man like Charles Miller for as long as I did without learning to control the exterior."

He got up from the chair and came to her side. The bodice of her dress was low-cut and hid very little. In addition she had laced her corsets as tightly as she could stand, creating even more to be revealed. He leaned over to kiss her but she pulled away.

"Think of my lip rouge. Not until later, much later tonight."

"Where?"

"I hesitate to say down at the summer house after what happened the last time we were supposed to meet."

"That's not funny."

"No. Well, we can't meet here. Poor Alex never goes out, and it would not be seemly for him to run into his mother's lover."

"Is that what I am to be?"

"That depends on how much you've learned and how good you've become."

"I'm very good."

"That's for me to determine. But where?" she said this last really to herself.

"I share a room with Craig. I could ask him to stay out tonight. We have done that on occasion for each other. Not recently. He seems to have become a celibate in recent months. You could come to my place, Front Street. The place used to be a tavern, Meacham's Tavern. It's a boarding house now."

"It was no better than a brothel when Meacham had it," she said. "Does that make me a whore, if I sleep with a man in a former brothel?"

"Only if you take money from me," he joked.

"Yes, I like that idea. I want you to pay me," she said excitedly.

"Pay you? You're the only one with money. I've just got talent, and such talent it is that you'll be wanting to pay me."

She laughed. "Wait for me," she said, "after the party

132

tonight. It will be very late but I'll be there. Make sure Craig isn't."

Kevin practically skipped along Bay Street back toward the lake. He would have to clean up the room and air it out. He couldn't bring her to a place that looked and smelled like his room. Craig had teased him when he asked for the room for the night. He had reminded him that they had come to Miller's to aid the project, but then he had agreed to find himself some other bed before the night was over.

O'Connor had never thought to connect Craig Miller with Allison Miller, even though they had the same last name and both came from Canada. There must be hundreds of Millers in Canada and then he always connected Craig with Manitoba and with his Uncle Michael Brant in Halifax. He never associated him with Toronto.

He laughed out loud. He was getting ready to have sex with Craig's grandmother. The idea tickled him. She wasn't really his grandmother, so it wasn't going to bring any shame on his friend. Besides he had done it before. The memory of that first time overwhelmed him and goaded him to run the rest of the way home.

He spent most of the evening tidying up. He opened the windows of the room and gave it a good airing. He even changed the bed linen. Finally his chamber was the way it ought to be if it was to be dwelt in, even for one night, by a lady as grand as Allison Miller.

It was late before he finished. But once the work was done, he grew impatient and began to pace back and forth. Finally he threw himself down on the bed and waited impatiently for the sound of footsteps on the rickety staircase.

He never heard her come. He did not remember falling asleep, but he could not forget waking up. Somehow or other she had managed to remove his pants without waking him. She ran her cool fingers up and down the insides of his thighs from his knees up as far as her hand could go. When he awoke, she sat beside him on the bed. She was as naked as he and she played with him. He pulled himself up and sat back against the headboard.

"Hello," he said somewhat dazed by the circumstances.

"I said I'd be late, but I didn't expect to find my lover snoring away with his clothes still on."

"I don't snore," he protested.

133

"I suggest you ask your roommate."

"Now?"

"Now what?"

"Now may I kiss you?"

She did not give him his answer in words. She leaned forward and kissed him on the mouth. Her lips parted, an open invitation. He thrust his tongue forward tentatively at first, then with growing passion.

They lay in each other's arms as passion subsided. It had been the best sex of his life, of that he was certain, because up to this evening his best experience had been his first with her too.

She leaned over and kissed him on the chest. "Where have you been all my life, Kevin O'Connor?"

"Running away from people who wanted to hang me."

"How did you get away? When I came back to that farmhouse you were gone. No one would even speak of you."

"We Irish have developed means to take care of each other."

"Where did you go?"

"To Nova Scotia. Then I served in the American army."

"I'll bet you were brave. You were brave that night in coming back to help your father."

"You believed me then."

"I knew you hadn't hit yourself on the head with a rock."

"I think it was you who suggested that people would think it was my father who hit me after I had stabbed him."

"They probably would have said that. They really were determined to blame the death on you, you know. They seemed fascinated by the thought of the bastard boy murdering his father, just as people tonight were fascinated by the scandal of my party. But I never believed that you killed him."

"Why not?"

"You're a lover, not a killer."

"And you are a flatterer."

"Besides, that knife wound was a fatal one. No one stabbed like that would have had the strength to bop you on the head hard enough to knock you unconscious."

"Ah, the real reason comes to light. Somehow or other I like the first reason better."

He lay quietly for some minutes. "They never looked for the real killer, did they?"

"They didn't know there was a real killer. They looked for you."

Kevin shifted his arm from under her head and sat up. "You know, I sometimes wonder what would have happened if I hadn't run away but had gone to the constable and told my story. You know, it was your idea to flee."

Allison fixed her green eyes on him. "Then thank me for your life, Kevin O'Connor. They would have taken you and hanged you by the neck until you were dead."

"But I'm very much alive," he said smiling at her.

She reached between his legs and touched him. "I can tell," she said.

The second time was even better.

Allison listened to his soft snore. It was true, he did snore, but it was soft, an almost soothing sound. She snuggled her face against his neck and rested her head on his shoulder. He made a comfortable sound in his throat. She had pleased him. She knew that. She could please men. She had done that all her life. Very few, with the exception of Charles in their first years together, had reciprocated. They were always in such a hurry. Not one of them was willing to take the time that good lovemaking required. Poor Kevin was no different. He was such an amateur. But no man's ego could withstand that knowledge. He would never find out from her. She had praised him, moaned and groaned when she thought it was appropriate. Not that it was all bad. There had been some good moments. But they alone had not been enough to bring her to the resolve she had just made. She had other reasons for deciding that Kevin O'Connor, whether he realized it or not, was to become her permanent lover. Permanent at least for the time being.

The answers he had given her about Irishmen having means to take care of each other, his service in the American army, and his presence in Toronto, just as the newspapers were filled with Fenian invasions . . . She thought it a brilliant piece of deduction but she was sure of it. Her dear Kevin was a member of the Irish Republican Brotherhood, the Fenians. And he would have information of use to her dear Alex and the Canadian militia.

135

VIII

The Niagara Peninsula, June 1866

"Wake up!" Craig shook Kevin's shoulder.

Kevin sat up in fright.

"It's started," was all Craig had to say.

Kevin was instantly awake. He rose to his feet, tossing his bedding aside. He had fallen asleep fully clothed to protect him from the night air. He looked up at the stars. The weather would be clear and sunny tomorrow. There was not a cloud in the night sky. He walked to join Craig at the edge of the bluffs. The Métis had a seaman's night glass trained on the Niagara River below them.

"They're on their way," Craig said softly.

Kevin strained his eyes. Yes, he could see dark forms on the river.

Craig grinned broadly and clapped Kevin on the back. "It's begun at last," he laughed. "After all these months, brother, we are taking the first steps. How the bastards laughed at us and mocked us. 'Leaders without brains,' they said. 'Followers without moral character.' Now we'll show them."

Kevin continued to stare at the river. "I see some boats, Craig, but there should be more of them."

"That's just the first wave. The Fenian invasion of Canada is now a reality." Craig started down the slope of the bluff.

"Where are you going?" Kevin called out.

"You light the signal fire. I'm going down to lead them up the bluff. This is supposed to be the first encampment, and I'm making sure that they don't lose their way."

Kevin could not share Craig's enthusiasm. There *were* supposed to be more of them.

When Craig reached the banks of the quick–moving Niagara, the first boats had already touched Canadian soil. He was challenged by a sentry. He gave the password and was allowed

136

to pass on to find the commander, Colonel John O'Neill. Craig found him sitting on the prow of his longboat, using a plank across his lap as a desk. He was a tall, handsome man with a high forehead and a drooping cavalry moustache.

"Are you the scout we were told to expect?"

"Yes, sir," Craig saluted awkwardly. He had grown out of practice since his days in the cavalry. "Lieutenant Craig Miller reporting, Colonel."

"You don't sound like one of us, boy," O'Neill said suspiciously in his broad Irish brogue.

"I was born in Manitoba, sir, not in Ireland, but I've been a member of the brotherhood for three years."

"Yes, I've reports on you. You and a Captain O'Connor are to lead my cavalry."

"He's up on the bluff, sir, lighting the signal fire to mark the first encampment. I'll lead you up the path."

More and more boats arrived from Black Rock on the American side, and he could see more dark forms on the Niagara.

"Is General Sweeney or President Roberts with you, sir?"

"Not in this wave," O'Neill said vaguely.

"Miller!"

Craig turned as his name was called out. He recognized the cape immediately.

"Sean." He greeted his friend with a bear hug. "Is Big Jim with you?"

"I'm here," the huge Irishman spoke for himself.

Craig switched his hug to his second friend and felt lost in the embrace.

"We are," Lavery said after all the greetings had been exchanged, "the commander of artillery and his second, even though at this point our army has no artillery at all."

Craig was shocked. "But General Sweeney's plan called for heavy guns."

"Indeed," said Lavery, "but we have a substitute plan now."

"What's that?"

"We capture them from the bloody English," Jim said laughing.

"Let's not discuss strategy here on the beach, gentlemen," O'Neill ordered.

"Miller, lead the way to the encampment. We'll discuss our plans with the officers once we've settled down."

Craig led the advance party of Fenian officers and men up the narrow path from Freeburg's wharf to Newbigging's farm. Kevin awaited atop the rise, and was reunited with his old companions as well.

O'Neill set up his headquarters tent and immediately called a council of war for all his officers. The officers wore a variety of uniforms, but most were from the recently victorious forces of the American Union. O'Neill stood in the crowded tent surrounded by the others.

"Gentlemen," he said in his melodious Irish accent, "*the* great moment of Irish history is at hand. The freedom of our nation is dependent on our actions and our courage. We must defeat the English here on this soil and in those other parts of Canada that are today being invaded. We must force them to trade our conquest here for the freedom of our oppressed brothers across the sea. This is what we have all been waiting for. This is why we have risked our lives in a brutal apprenticeship of war in our second home just across the border. This is our sworn responsibility before God."

There were nods of silent assent from the others.

"It will not be easy," O'Neill continued. "We have many fewer than we had hoped."

"How many, sir?" Kevin asked.

"We are about eight hundred, Captain."

Kevin blanched.

"And we have no big guns as we had hoped. Captain Lavery's experience cannot be put to good use until you fellows capture some for him."

"Please do," Sean said with a tone of nonchalance in his voice.

The others laughed.

"And just as serious, we have no horses to form cavalry units."

Craig was now truly alarmed. He looked over at Kevin and saw his concern as well.

"But before Captain O'Connor and Lieutenant Miller start to complain, we do have a plan to get some horses. My second in command and good friend from Kentucky, Colonel Owen Starr, is to move on the village of Fort Erie at first light. He is to seize every horse and mule in that town that can be ridden and get us a cavalry."

Several of the officers started to clap. "And," O'Neill

continued, "we have a proclamation from General Sweeney to read to the peoples of this land. I would like you all to hear it."

"To the people of British America," O'Neill read.

We come among you as the foes of British rule in Ireland. We have taken up the sword to strike down the oppressors' rod to deliver Ireland from the tyrant and the despoiler, robber. . . . We have no issue with the people of these provinces and wish to have none but the most friendly relations. Our weapons are for the oppressors of Ireland, our bows shall be directed against the power of England. . . . We do not propose to divest you of a solitary right you now enjoy. . . . We are here neither as murderers or robbers for plunder and spoliation. We are here as the Irish Army of Liberation. . . . To Irishmen throughout these provinces we appeal in the name of seven centuries of British inequity and Irish suffering. . . . To stretch forth the hand of brotherhood in the holy cause of Fatherland and smite the tyrant where we can.

Several of the officers began to cheer.

"We have printed many copies," Colonel Starr called out, "and we want as broad a distribution as possible."

"I have some questions, Colonel," Kevin spoke up.

"Yes, Captain," O'Neill said.

"What will be the reaction of the Americans?"

"We have some assurances that they will remain neutral and look the other way. And these assurances come from fairly high places in Washington. The Americans want us to lick the redcoats, gentlemen. It is an old American tradition. Now, you gentlemen try to get a few hours of sleep. Some of you will accompany Colonel Starr to Fort Erie at first light, especially you, Captain O'Connor, and you, Lieutenant Miller. I want that cavalry troop mounted as soon as possible."

Allison rose from her bed as soon as she heard Alex walking down the stairs from his bedroom to the first floor. She opened the heavy oak door and peered into the dark hallway. She could see nothing.

"Alex, is that you?"

The voice responded from the foyer below. "Yes, Mother. I've been summoned to a council of war at General Napier's headquarters. As you predicted, the Fenians have landed at the Niagara frontier."

"How interesting. I hope you have relayed all my other predictions to General Napier."

"I have."

"Let's hope he puts the others to better use than he did this one."

"I believe that after tonight, Mother, your star will be on the rise at headquarters."

"I would hope so, after all I've had to put up with to gain my special knowledge."

She knew perfectly well that Alex never revealed the source of his information. He would take full credit for its accuracy for himself. It was a pity, she thought. Had they known that the initial information was from her they might have taken it more seriously.

"When you return tonight, Alex my dear," she called to him, "try to make a little less noise. I am really very tired."

"Mother, I hate to disappoint you but I won't be coming back tonight."

"You're not going gambling, are you?"

"Mother, it may be of little significance to you, but Canada, our country, has been invaded tonight."

"I know that. Wasn't I the one who . . . 'predicted' it?"

"I am marching with the Toronto militia, of which I am an officer."

Allison was halfway into her room when he spoke. She stopped dead in her tracks. "You can't be serious," she said returning to the railing of the staircase to speak down into the gloom of the foyer.

Alex lit the hallway lamp. He was dressed in his militia officer's field uniform.

"My God, you are serious, aren't you, Alex?" She started down the staircase toward him. "You can't."

"Did you doubt that I would do my duty?"

"But you were always such a frail child. You could be hurt. This is dangerous business."

"Mother, stop it. I'm no child and all that frailty was a facade you created and I accepted as a means of keeping that vicious man off my back. He's gone and we need no longer keep up pretenses. I will do my duty by my country. That much of my father I inherited."

She was frightened by the look on his face. She had never

known her husband as a young man—after all, he was so many years older than she—but she imagined that he must have looked somewhat as Alex looked now—arrogant and haughty. He frightened her.

"I don't need your protection from the world, Mother. I never did. I needed you only to protect me from him. Even there, ultimately, it was not you but I who resolved our problem."

Allison surprised herself. She was not shocked by his statement. She had not initially believed he could do such a thing, not to his own father. But then she should have guessed; there was always Lord Carringdon.

"I know what you are thinking. You are about to remind me of how you saved me from a murder charge in Ireland."

"You can't deny that without my quick thinking you might have found yourself in a great deal of trouble."

"It was never really necessary. The foolish Mr. O'Connor fled all on his own. Besides, who would have believed the word of a bastard stableboy who hated his father against the word of a visiting gentleman from Canada, especially since the murdered man's widow was quite willing to be supportive just so long as she was not implicated in any way. I was always safe. You and Father need not have done anything."

"You weren't so cool that night."

"I was twenty, and I had just stabbed an Irish baron, but I would have thought my way through it. I think my way through everything." He buckled on his sword.

She rushed to him. "Alex, don't go."

He ignored her and started for the door.

"By the way, have you told O'Connor about your role back in Ireland? Don't look so surprised. I know all about the "source" of your Fenian information. Well, if you haven't—then don't." He opened the front door.

"Please, son," she begged, ignoring his comments, having at last realized that he was determined to fight his war. "Take care. You're all I have. Without you I'll be all alone."

He turned toward her and blew a kiss. "Have no fear, mother. I shall take care of myself. I always have and I always will." And then he was gone.

Allison stood alone in the hallway for some minutes, then slowly she climbed the staircase to the second floor. She was terrified. Alex could no longer be controlled. He was now in charge. He had killed Charles. It had never crossed her mind that by giving Alex the information she gathered about the Fenians she would make him Napier's resident expert and indispensable to the commanders in the field. Perhaps she had promoted his career too well. She knew she would not go back to sleep this night.

The village of Fort Erie was situated across the headwaters of the Niagara River from Buffalo in New York. The alarm was raised in the village as soon as the Fenian columns were seen moving the three miles from the camp toward the village.

Kevin and Craig marched in the van of Starr's column. Kevin seemed unhappy. Craig found it difficult to understand his attitude.

"It will be good to get some horses, eh, Kevin?" Craig said trying to cheer up his friend. "Once we're in the saddle, it will be just like it was with the Michigan Brigade but minus crazy Custer."

But Kevin was paying no attention to him. "What's that?" he said when the morning quiet was split by the shriek of a train whistle.

"It's the train," Craig said. "Fort Erie is the rail head of the Erie and Ontario and the Huron and Buffalo railroads. My grandfather was a major investor in those lines."

They saw the steam rise from the engine as the train pulled out of the village. Colonel Starr came running to the head of the column. He put his field glass to his eye.

"Damn," he said. "How could they have gotten organized so quickly?" He collapsed the glass in anger. "It looks like the whole bloody village is escaping on that train. Four engines pulling every car in the rail yard. I am sure they are carrying everything of any value out of Fort Erie. Double time, men. We have to get there before what little is left disappears."

Kevin was given the task of cutting the telegraph lines into Fort Erie. Craig was to attempt to round up horses. He went to livery stables and to private barns, but all the mounts had disappeared; they were heading north to safety on the cattle cars of the Erie and Ontario.

Craig was close to tears. So much depended on having a mounted force. Without one, they could not strike quickly against the Canadian militia and consolidate a strong position before the British Regulars could take the field.

He sat on the steps of the office of the last livery stable in the village, his head in his hands. Out of the corner of his eye he saw an old man sneak out of the side door of his house and look about carefully. Seeing no one he moved quickly into the backyard and through it into his neighbor's. What attracted Craig's attention was that the old man carried a Spencer repeating rifle. That was a modern military weapon, not something a villager or even a farmer took with him when he went out hunting ducks on the riverbank.

Craig rose and followed the old man's steps. The old man moved swiftly for someone his age, heading parallel to the riverbank, then south toward the railway yards. When Craig reached the opening between the station house and the water tank and emerged out into the open yard he looked about in confusion. All about him were tracks—some of them worn shiny silver and others rusty from lack of use. But no old man. He was nowhere to be seen. Suddenly Craig was startled by the report of a rifle. He knew that sound. He had fired that weapon himself. Then he heard the scream of a horse in mortal pain. It came from across the siding and down a ravine.

He raced as fast as he could in the direction of the rifle shot. He tumbled down the steep side of the ravine and drew level with the old man just as he was about to fire for the second time. The surprise blow from behind sent the man face forward. His shot went harmlessly into the air.

Craig rose to his feet and quickly grabbed the rifle from the stunned man's grasp. He looked about himself in amazement. The ravine had been used as a kind of a corral for the worst collection of escapees from a glue factory that Craig had ever beheld. Every old nag not worthy of saving had been driven to this spot. Obviously, this oldtimer had been given responsibility of putting even this poor herd out of reach of the Fenians.

There were about twenty of them. One had been shot in the neck and was down but not dead. Craig hated to do it, but he finished the job that the old man had bungled. That left him with nineteen horses in a variety of conditions, none of them good.

Four should be put out of their misery right away, he judged, but about fifteen were salvageable if not pushed too hard. Not good but better than walking. He fired the rifle several times into the air to attract attention. It frightened the horses and they crowded against the side of the ravine, but none of them had the strength to climb up the slope.

The old man had regained his senses and sat on his haunches. He was clearly afraid of Craig. Craig walked over to him.

"Are there any more horses in the village?" he asked.

The old man shook his head vigorously.

"Sort of stretching a point to refer to these nags as horses. How come you didn't finish them off before we arrived? That was your job, wasn't it? Isn't that why they issued you the Spencer?"

"One of them horses is mine," the old man finally spoke. "I didn't fancy putting a bullet in him. I'm not rich like some of them high–and–mighty fellas. I don't see any of them staying around to meet the enemy."

"You wanted to sell them to us, didn't you?"

"Sure beats killing them."

"What made you decide to shoot them?"

"Heard you guys weren't paying, just taking. No sense not being a patriot under those terms."

Colonel Starr arrived at the top of the ravine.

"Good lad," he called out in his strange combination of Irish brogue and Kentucky twang. "But they're not much to look at, are they? Back home we never let them get this old."

Craig laughed. "Put saddles on them, Colonel, and get your mounted troop. We'll find better ones later on."

Kevin returned to Newbigging's farm at noon at the head of his cavalry troop. Craig was at his side. Colonel Starr's men carried with them every scrap of food that had been left in Fort Erie. The spirits at the encampment were high. With the coming of daylight, more boats had crossed the river, bringing more men and ammunition and foodstuffs. So far there was no sign of organized resistance from the Canadians.

O'Neill called Kevin and Craig to his tent shortly after they returned.

"Congratulations," he said greeting them at the entryway. "Colonel Starr told me you were the ones who found the mounts."

Kevin pointed to Craig. "He gets the credit, sir, although I'm not sure I'd want credit for such a sorry lot."

O'Neill chuckled. "Yes, I hear they're pretty bad, but they'll have to do."

He walked over to the maps that were spread out on his camp desk. "I want you to take a ride for me. I need to know where the enemy is, gentlemen. It is true that we've surprised them—although from what Starr tells me about Fort Erie I have some doubts about how widespread that surprise is. But I

144

want you to take half your mounted troop, Miller, over here."
He pointed to the river road. "Take it as far as you can until you
make contact with the enemy. I suspect Napier will rush forces
to Chippawa in order to defend the Welland Canal.

"You, Captain O'Connor, take the other half of the troop and
follow the railway tracks to Ridgeway here." He pointed to
another section of the map. "You can ride beyond toward Port
Colborne and the Lake Erie terminus of the canal, but you'll
meet militia resistance if you go too far in either direction."

There was a shout from outside the tent. Suddenly the flap
was opened and a sentry entered.

"Colonel O'Neill, sir, there's a boat in the river."

"Good, we can use more men and supplies."

"It is not one of our boats, sir. It is a gunboat."

O'Neill raced out of the tent toward the rise overlooking the
Niagara. There on the river was a gunboat flying the Stars and
Stripes. Colonel Starr joined him and Kevin and Craig. All
watched as the American Navy turned back an attempt from
the American shore to reinforce the Fenian position.

Starr was distraught. "George Meade is the military commander of the Northern district. I can't believe George
Meade, the man who licked Lee at Gettysburg, would turn his
guns on former comrades in arms."

"Don't fret, Owen," O'Neill reassured his second in command. "We always anticipated that the United States would
have to make a show of enforcing neutrality laws once we
undertook this invasion. We've still got friends in Washington.
We can call them off. We just have to get word to our friends in
Buffalo."

Suddenly O'Neill's calm faded. "But, damn it, that boat got
here fast. I hadn't anticipated American gunboats in the river
for another thirty-six hours. How did they get the news and
send that damn thing here so fast?" He shook his head. "No
matter, to the task at hand. O'Connor, Miller, you have your
orders. Find the enemy for me."

"Yes, sir," both men said simultaneously.

"And, gentlemen, this is an intelligence mission. I expect
you to return here with full complements of men and beasts.
Don't do anything rash."

Craig felt almost as weary as his ancient mare. They had not
ridden that far. He had his six troopers fan out on the road
every few miles to look for any militia concentrations but there

145

was nothing. He took his glass out and turned it on the town of Chippawa. It was the last village above the falls of Niagara. The Welland and Lyons Rivers flowed into the Niagara just at this point, and both gave access to the locks of the Welland Canal. The village was a strategic one. There were no signs of military actually in the village. Aside from its own people it was undefended. If O'Neill would move rapidly, the village could be seized. He sent a trooper back ten miles to Newbigging's with the word of Chippawa's vulnerability.

Darkness fell without any word from Newbigging's farm. In fact the messenger never returned. About 9 p.m. a weary Sean Lavery, very uncharacteristically disheveled, his shirt turned dark with sweat stains, arrived at Craig's lookout post.

"Craig, I had no idea you were so far away. If I had, I never would have allowed myself to be volunteered."

Craig's impatience had taken hold of him and he had no time for Sean's theatrics. "Where is O'Neill? It is dark, but the town could still be taken."

"What town?" Lavery said peering into the darkness. "Oh, yes, there is a town there, isn't there?" he said once he viewed the flickering lights.

"Did you come in response to my message?" Craig immediately recognized the foolishness of his question. The camp was ten miles away and Sean was on foot.

"Since they seem to think I am expendable as lieutenant of artillery without artillery, they sent me to tell you that we've moved camp from Newbigging's farm on Frenchman's Creek to a field away from River Road on Black Creek."

"Why?"

"What do you care?" Sean said. "You are three miles closer to camp. Be grateful. At least those pathetic horses of yours should be grateful."

"Why did O'Neill move?"

"It was something about a central position in our lines of communication and some other nonsense. It seems that Kevin returned from his scouting with a report of heavy militia concentrations at Ridgeway near Lake Erie. Apparently the Canadians will try to retake Fort Erie from the lakeside by boat."

Craig was silent. He did not envy O'Neill his choice. Surely regular troops would be coming from Toronto to Saint Catharines and then down the river road to Chippawa. And now with heavy concentrations of militia on the other side, he was in serious trouble.

"Thanks for the news, Sean," Craig said sarcastically. "Does O'Neill want us back?"

"Yes, immediately."

"I don't know," Craig said turning back to look at the flickering lights of Chippawa. "I think I would rather have militia at my back than regulars. I think I would rather take Chippawa and try to hold it and the Welland Locks. But that's not my decision to make."

"Lieutenant Miller, sir." A trooper from Starr's Kentucky Center whom Craig had placed at the advance position loomed from out of the dark.

"What is it, Private?"

"They are regular troops in Chippawa, sir. They just entered the town. The whole village turned out and cheered."

"Well, that does it," Craig muttered. "Let's mount up, Private. Spread the word. We'll follow Lieutenant Lavery to our new camp."

"You have an extra horse?" Sean said in surprise, recalling his last experience atop one of the beasts in the American war.

"No such luck," Craig teased. "You walk. But remember what you said. You should be grateful. We are three miles closer to camp now."

O'Neill moved his forces before daylight. The entire Fenian army headed south until they met the ridge road that ran southwest toward the village of Ridgeway. O'Neill's meeting the night before with Starr, his scouts and other officers had convinced him of this strategy. He was between two enemy forces, one to the south and one to the north. His prime objective was to prevent them from uniting and overwhelming him by sheer numbers. He must defeat them individually. The southern group of opponents were militia. They were closer and they were weaker. He would deal with them first. A victory would also boost morale and perhaps bring more volunteers from the many Irish who lived on the Niagara frontier.

Craig and Kevin rode a mile in front of the Fenian army. Three of their tiny troop had been sent out even farther in advance to bring news of the enemy as quickly as possible to Colonel O'Neill.

"You've been grim ever since we got word in Toronto that

the invasion was on, Kevin. I don't understand." Craig broke the silence that had prevailed between them ever since leaving camp.

Kevin dismissed him. "You're imagining things."

"I am not. You think we're going to lose, don't you? That's what is depressing you?"

"Damn it, Craig, this whole thing is harebrained. Who could think of invading a nation of over three million people with eight hundred men and no horses and no guns? Our own general, General Sweeney, who is conspicuous by his absence, said we must have ten thousand men and artillery at our disposal. Where is everyone? I see just you and me and a bunch of idiots. I wanted to take part in a grand invasion. I expected to be part of an unstoppable horde. Then it would have meant nothing if the Canadians knew about it in advance. In fact, they'd have been sure to know. It would be too big to hide, too big to stop, too hot politically for the Americans to do anything but ignore. That's what I planned for, that's what I wanted. Not this."

"We don't know what is going on elsewhere," Craig rationalized.

"From what's gone on here I can guess. O'Neill was the best of them, my lad, and he's got us in a pickle. Whoa," he reined in his horse. The rest of the troop followed suit. "What was that?"

Only a complaint from one of the tired horses broke the silence. Craig was about to tease Kevin for hearing things when he too heard it. It was a bugle call, a call to assembly. It was coming from the direction of Ridgeway.

Kevin spurred his horse and signaled the troop forward with his hand. The cavalry unit went forward at a trot. Soon they saw some of the advance scouts riding back toward them.

"It's the Canadian militia," a scout shouted. "They're moving along the ridge road heading this way."

The first trooper pulled up in front of the two officers.

"How many men?" Craig questioned.

"Hard to tell. The column looked about as big as ours when we started out this morning."

Kevin ordered the troop to turn and report back to the main army. He reported his news to O'Neill, who rode at the head of the van.

O'Neill took the news calmly. He looked over the terrain. There were woods on either side of the road and open fields in front of the woods. Directly ahead of them there was high ground, more of a rise than a hill, and too far off to be of much consequence.

"This place looks as good as any. We'll meet the enemy here." O'Neill said. "Spread out," he called to his officers. "Take cover in the woods. We'll form a line of defense here for the glory of Ireland."

The officers and men in earshot cheered. Soon men were scurrying off the road to the right and to the left to groves of maples and oaks finding suitable positions for clear shots and looking around for places that offered them cover from the enemy's weapons. When the entire army had left the road, O'Neill turned to the cavalry officers.

"You gentlemen have done your duty," he said grimly. "Now the battle will be fought, as usual, by foot soldiers slugging it out. Take your troop off to the left flank and hold it in reserve."

Alex Miller thought Lt. Col. Alfred Booker, the regular army officer who commanded this Canadian militia army, was a fool. They had met at Port Colborne where Alex had led the Toronto militia contingent. Booker and his second in command, Lt. Col. J. Staughton Dennis, together had cooked up their own scheme for defeating the rabble. The idea was to win without any interference from their commanding officer, Lt. Col. George T. Peacocke, and his regulars. Peacocke had six companies of infantry regulars at St. Catharines along with a battery of royal artillery, enough force to blast the invaders right off Canadian soil. But there would be no glory in that for Booker and Dennis. They planned instead to reclaim Fort Erie. Dennis was to move on the village by steam tug with the Welland Canal battery while Booker moved his nine hundred militia over the Buffalo and Lake Huron railway.

Alex knew the line well. It was part of the Grand Trunk system. If the glory were to come to the Canadian militia, Alex had no problem with Booker's plan. He, after all, was a leader of the Canadian militia. But Booker and Dennis, by excluding the regulars, were placing success in question. Who could guarantee that nine hundred Canadian amateur soldiers could defeat eight hundred to a thousand mercenaries trained in the armies of Grant and Sherman.

That was why he had just sent a telegram to Peacocke— without signing it, of course—informing him of Booker's plans.

He had worried when the response from St. Catharines was delayed. Later, when summoned with Dennis to Booker's headquarters, he discovered why. Peacocke had advanced with his regulars to Chippawa.

Booker was in a rage. He stormed about his temporary office denouncing his superior as a glory hound. Alex found him amusing but nonetheless dangerous. Peacocke had sent a telegram, ordering Booker to send his troops forward by railway to Ridgeway. There he was to detrain, march to Stevensville, and unite his force with Peacocke's regulars. Together they would move on the enemy encampment at Black Creek.

Alex was relieved.

"What do you think, Miller?" Booker addressed him when he had finished outlining Peacocke's command.

Alex was immediately alert. He knew Booker wanted to disobey. If he did, and it went badly, he would need some excuse, some scapegoat. Alex was determined it would not be the men of the Toronto militia, which included young men from some of the leading families of the town and also a rifle company of students from the university. And the scapegoat was certainly not going to be Alex Miller.

"I think the commanding officer is following correct military procedure in combining his units to create of them a maximum force to bring to bear against the enemy."

"What textbook did you get that from?" said Dennis. "Miller, don't you realize that if we obey the bastard, all chance of being credited with the defeat of the Fenians will be lost by your men, the men of Canada? You know what we British are like in dealing with colonials like you."

Again Alex smiled. "You underestimate us colonials, Colonel. British Regulars under Brock saved this country back in 1812, but we write our own history books. If you read them you'd think that Brock was a Canadian and all he had was militia. I suspect what we did in 1812 we will do again in 1866. But it is much easier to turn a British victory into a Canadian one than it is to turn a Canadian defeat into a victory—although I daresay we would try that too if we had to."

Booker sat down at his desk with a sigh. "I'm doing it my way," he said, "Colonel Dennis, take the battery and the naval brigade on that tug and patrol all of Fort Erie until I arrive."

"Yes, sir," Dennis said and left the room.

"Am I to assume that you are taking full responsibility for ignoring Colonel Peacocke's orders?" Alex asked Booker.

"I am. There are certain discretions given to a commander of a separate unit in the field. You must use your own judgment in the face of the enemy."

"You must also choose correctly."

Booker looked uncomfortable for a moment and then dismissed Miller with orders to deliver his telegraph response to Peacocke.

It was this last action that convinced Alex that Booker would lose it all. Having taken the decision to disobey, he did not break contact and do what he had determined to do. He had attempted to hedge his bet by explaining his actions in advance, hoping perhaps to receive belated approval or at least tacit permission. This man was no leader. But his weakness saved Alex the necessity of sending a telegram of his own to Peacocke. He would send Booker's.

He decided not to go to bed, despite the fact that it was three in the morning, after he delivered Booker's message to the telegraph office. In fact, he decided to wait at the office itself. He knew it would not take long. At 3:45 the clerk nudged him awake as he sat sleepy–eyed on the bench in the telegraph office. He took the sealed envelope immediately to Booker's office. The Colonel was still awake. He took the paper from Alex and read it. Miller could tell the contents by the Colonel's face. He was angry. But most of his earlier defiance seemed to have folded. He would comply. His sole act of disobedience was to send the force by tug to Fort Erie, but they could do little harm.

"Miller, get your men embarked on the railroad cars," Booker said.

"Destination, Colonel?"

"None of your goddamned business."

The destination was Ridgeway. They disembarked from the train at six in the morning. They had four hours to make their rendezvous with Peacocke at Stevensville.

Alex ordered the militia company commanders to detrain and form ranks in the center of the sleepy village. About twenty houses surrounded the train depot and a flour mill. These two institutions were the reasons for the town's existence, although some of the citizenry might have offered its taverns as a better excuse.

But there would be little sleep on the morning of June 2, 1866. Booker ordered his buglers to sound assembly. The townsfolk came out of their beds to gape at the "fancy boys from Toronto" in their uniforms. Alex was about to give the order to have these "bumpkins" dispersed back indoors when the lieutenant colonel came riding on his chestnut mare into the village square.

One of the citizens recognized the uniform of the Regular Army and—perhaps old enough to remember another time more than fifty years before on the Niagara Peninsula—gave a feeble and lonely cheer that started some of the militia laughing.

"Quiet in the ranks," Booker exploded.

"Miller," he called to Alex. "I want those men who laughed disciplined."

"As you command," Alex said indifferently. He couldn't have cared less if Booker ordered the flesh off the back of every young gentleman in Toronto especially the University boys, they were the worst of the lot. But he certainly wasn't going to order it himself.

Booker brought his horse closer to Alex. "I thought you might like to know, since you've been my messenger up to now, that they have received another telegram from Peacocke at Port Colburne. They wired it up to me here. Seems the poor chap has been delayed and wants me to delay my operations until later in the day."

Alex looked at Booker warily. This last message changed things again. The lieutenant colonel was in the field at the time and place specifically ordered by his superior officer. If the superior failed to show, Booker was no longer on the hook. He was free to act as he wished.

"I think we ought to get some breakfast for these men, Captain Miller, at least for those who know enough not to break discipline by laughing in the ranks."

If that's all he intends as discipline, Alex thought, he'll never control these self-important sons of bitches.

One citizen of Ridgeway collected his courage and called out, "If you take your time to have a meal you might find yourself swallowing a Yankee bayonet along with your bacon."

Booker looked in annoyance at the citizen.

"The bloody Irishmen are on their way to Ridgeway right now," the man explained. "We got word from Black Creek earlier this morning."

"There's nothing earlier than this," Alex mumbled. He had not slept all night and he was tired.

"Nonsense," Booker dismissed this random piece of intelligence. "The enemy is over by the river road and threatens Fort Erie. Captain, get your men fed. I want to be on the ridge road out of town within the hour."

Alex did as he was told. Within the hour Booker's buglers again gave a signal to advance and nine hundred militiamen began pouring out of Ridgeway to join up with Peacocke, who Booker knew could not get to Stevensville until much later in the day. Fate might determine it all differently. The ridge road ran to the northeast all the way to the Niagara. One could never tell whom one might meet on the way.

Alex walked among the Toronto companies. The day would be a pleasant, sunny one. The light green foliage of spring still dominated the woods even if it was already early June. Later in the summer the leaves would grow darker and more tired.

They were barely a mile out of the town when the scouts came running down the mild slope of the road signaling that the enemy was in sight. Alex raced toward the rear and met Colonel Booker, who was riding toward the van on his mount.

"Enemy sighted, sir."

"Impossible," Booker exclaimed. "Come up behind me, Miller," he said offering Alex his hand. "I want us both to get a good look."

Alex suppressed his natural revulsion toward horses and hauled himself up behind Booker. The colonel spurred his mount and it dashed forward.

"How many?" Booker asked the first scout he met.

"Can't tell," the scout responded, "but they're in strong positions on either side of the road and in the woods."

Booker continued on up the rise. He took out his field glass. Alex slipped gracefully off the back of the horse and took his own glass from its case. He trained it on the woods.

"They've gone on the defensive. Typical Yank move. That's what let Lee run rings about them. Bloody fools. Well, Miller, what do you think of Al Booker now? I'm in the field, a free agent with the enemy in front of me waiting for the plucking."

"I think you'd better take them," Alex quipped closing the glass. "What's your plan?"

"We outnumber them. We rush them and let them feel our steel."

"Imaginative," said Alex. "Frontal assault on a defensive position. I believe the only time Lee tried that was at Gettysburg."

Booker's face went an angry red. "Remain here," he

ordered. "Deploy your companies on either side of the road. Then wait for the orders, impudent pup." He reined his horse to the right and rode down the slope.

Alex continued to stare at the woods. He wondered if his mother's lover had been smart enough to disentangle himself from this mess. He had not been smart enough to find a way out of the murder charges back in Ireland. It would be just like him to ride full-blown into something he knew in advance was doomed to failure. Well, maybe today would put an end to it. If he could find a corpse it would be amusing to send a lock of his hair back to Lady Carringdon with a note that justice had been done. Of course, that would probably send her into a series of fainting spells or force her to take to her bed for two years. He had not communicated with her since leaving Ireland. He expected she liked it that way.

Alex saw a flash of steel off in the woods to his left. He raised his glass. He saw something move. By God, that looked like a horse. He searched intently but could see no more detail. Perhaps it was merely an officer's isolated mount. He must mention it to Booker.

The militia companies fanned out on both sides of the road as their commander had ordered. Booker gave the signal for his bugler to sound the advance. Alex stayed with Booker at the command post on the rise. The young men of Toronto moved forward across the open fields. At first they marched tall, but as they heard the whine of rifle shots over their heads they gradually began to crouch, and finally to run for cover behind tree stumps which still stood in the open fields. As the militia force moved forward through the field their advance carried them past the clumps of trees jutting out into the fields on the right and left. Soon they had woods on both their right and left flanks. Rifle fire started to come from the flanks. Booker could see his men's courage waning.

"Miller," he called, "take the reserve and clear those woods."

"Yes, sir."

Alex called to his men, who were leaning on their Spencers. "Follow me, men."

The militia men gave a cheer and followed Alex on the run toward the woods.

Alex heard the repeat of rifles and saw smoke rising from behind clumps of bushes. He felt no fear. He knew he would not. He drew his sword as he approached the greenery. He charged through the branches. A man rose in front of him. Alex slashed at the figure. He heard a cry of pain but the man started to run along with others. His own troops had now caught up with him. The Fenians were running, not just in the outcropping of woods but all along the front line. Alex's men started to fire into the woods on their left.

"Hold your fire," Alex commanded. "Our own boys are in those woods now. We've got the enemy on the run."

He heard the bugle call again.

"What the hell was that?" he called to a militia sergeant.

"It means 'form a square'," the sergeant responded with a look of puzzlement. "But you'd only do that if you were under attack by cavalry."

"Cavalry," Alex said aloud. Christ, he thought, he'd forgotten to mention the horses to Booker. The bloody bastards did have horses. Booker's infantry was scattered all through the woods ready to be run down by horsemen.

Alex could feel the mood of the men around him change. Where before they were jubilant and confident, now they were afraid.

"I think we should fall back," he suggested.

The men needed no other order. They began to back out of the woods toward the open fields.

The same thing was happening all along the line. The Queen's Own had in fact formed a square on the ridge road itself and were drawing a withering fire from the confused and shaken Fenians. Why had the Canadians, on the verge of victory, started to withdraw? They did not await a response to their question. Never look askance at good fortune. The Fenians started to advance. Alex's men were now back in the open. Slowly they retreated back up the rise toward the command post. Alex went ahead of them and confronted Booker.

"What the hell happened?"

"Keep a civil tongue, Captain," Booker said. "Someone spotted cavalry on the left flank. It looked as if they might make a flanking move for a rear attack."

"Where the hell are they now?"

Booker fidgeted with his watch chain. "Well, they seem not to be doing what we feared. Bugler, sound the call to retire. The Queen's Own must get out of the square right now and fall back for regrouping."

Once again the bugle called.

Suddenly from out of the woods the militiamen began a hasty retreat.

"What the hell?" Booker called out. "Oh my God, they've all decided to fall back. They don't understand. Go back, you men. Go back," he screamed waving his sword in the air. "There's no need to retreat. We're winning!"

But there was no stopping the retreat. Some men dropped their weapons and began to run.

From out of the woods about fifteen men on horseback emerged. They were not charging, but their presence was enough. The rout was on. Booker tried to stem it. He rode among his retreating men, pleading with them to form orderly ranks but he could not control them. Finally he joined them.

Alex decided to retreat well before his commander accepted the inevitable. To save the militia they had to reach Ridgeway, a mile to the south, before the enemy did. But the Fenians were moving slowly and they did not seem to have the numbers to take the town and hold it.

Alex was back in the depot in Ridgeway in fifteen minutes. He had walked when in view of anyone and run when he could see no one around him. He had not stuck to the road but had moved cross country. He screamed at the Buffalo and Lake Huron engineer to get up steam for a quick getaway. It took no encouragement whatsoever. Everyone in town had heard the gunfire. Many had feared a Fenian victory and were anxious to make an ecape.

The engine had a full head of steam when the militiamen came pouring into the streets of Ridgeway. They did not stop to regroup. They climbed directly on board the railway cars. Colonel Booker rode his horse right up a ramp into the cattle car. Then he dismounted and strode alongside the train toward the engine where Alex stood.

"It was your bloody militia that cost me, Miller," he said to Alex. "They don't even understand simple bugle calls. Boys playing at men. Regulars wouldn't have run like that."

"Maybe you should have waited for the Regulars under Peacocke," Alex taunted him.

"I had no choice. I followed his orders. He was the one who was delayed. I had mere boys, untrained, under me."

He's rehearsing his court martial defense, Alex thought. Well, he should consider all the angles.

"You don't think it was the arrival of the phantom Fenian cavalry that caused the rout?"

"Never," Booker said. But Alex's blow had hit the mark. He could see Booker struggling in his own mind how to explain away the "form-square" order. Booker turned to the engineer.

"Get this thing moving."

"I think we should wait for all the men to make it aboard," Alex reminded him.

"Oh, yes, see to it, Miller," Booker said. "And, Miller, please expedite it, won't you?"

Kevin and Craig rode at the head of their band of horsemen. As they entered the deserted streets of Ridgeway, they could see the departing smoke of the train convoy as it headed west to safety.

The cavalrymen were patting each other on the back and congratulating themselves. Even though not one of them had fired a shot, they had won the battle. They had defeated a Canadian army on Canadian soil. Now the British would have to sit up and take notice of their demands for Ireland.

Colonel O'Neill entered the village along with Colonel Starr. They surveyed the deserted station.

"We can't stay here," O'Neill announced. "We are too vulnerable and we have not yet faced the Regulars. I need a position I can defend. Owen, take command of the troops still in the field." He pulled out his map from his vest pocket. "Take them along the Garrison Road to Fort Erie. I'll lead those already here along the railway bed to the fort. We'll meet there this afternoon."

Kevin looked over at Craig. He urged his horse closer to his friend's.

"That's the beginning of the end," he whispered.

"What do you mean?" Craig looked quizzical.

"I mean we were almost licked back there by a bunch of untrained boys. They were pushing us back. O'Neill knows that and so does Starr. Now they have to face five thousand British Regulars. You know they are in the field. You saw them at Chippawa. O'Neill's lost his confidence."

"Hey, we won the battle. To listen to you, you'd think we'd just been beaten."

"I think we were and so do our leaders. Why fall back on Fort Erie? Why? Because it is right across the river from Buffalo and the good old U.S.A. One signal and boats will come to pick us up and carry us back home. Fort Erie is a haven and the first step on the way back home."

But the fort proved no haven. Colonel J. Staughton Dennis, while his friend Colonel Booker was being defeated at Ridgeway, had gone beyond his orders to patrol Fort Erie in his steam tug. Finding it contained almost no enemy, only a few stragglers, he seized the village and ordered the Welland field battery to dig in.

O'Neill rode with his cavalry. He had not anticipated any resistance on reentering Fort Erie. When shots were fired as they approached the village the entire Irish Army was taken by surprise. They knew of Dennis's patrol, but did not think him bold enough to take the town.

O'Neill called an immediate council of war.

"Gentlemen," he advised his officers, "we have a large army immediately to our rear only hours from us. It now seems that we have lost the base from which to fight the British Regulars. I intend to retake Fort Erie."

"We're with you," Craig called out. The others nodded.

"I don't know how many enemy are in the positions in front of us, but I suspect they are not very experienced troops. I intend to take them by assault with bayonet. I don't want to waste precious ammunition against these positions." This was the first time O'Neill had expressed concern about their supplies. They were also running low on food. As well as ammunition.

"Spread out your companies, gentlemen. We attack immediately."

Kevin smiled at Craig. "This time we get to fight too." he said. "There are not enough of us to make a charge. If we stayed on our horses we'd just get mowed down. We'll have to go in on foot too."

Craig nodded agreement and ordered the others to dismount. "We go ahead on foot. You, Coughlin," Craig said to the youngest trooper, a boy of seventeen, "you hold the horses. We may need them later. Let's go," he said to the others.

"O'Neill called out the signal to advance and the eight hundred Fenians moved as a body—their rifles held forward with steel afixed to the ends. There was ragged fire. Craig looked to his left and saw that his friends Lavery and Hickey, who were still without command because they still had no big guns, had joined them in the charge. They yelled as they ran forward.

Suddenly the ground seemed to leap into the air. Craig was knocked off his feet. He stood up again and looked down at himself. He was not injured but he was falling behind. He picked up his Spencer and ran harder to catch up with the others. Again there was an explosion and some shouting. Craig rejoined the line.

"They've got the artillery," he yelled at Lavery.

"Indeed," Sean called back smiling. "We might yet end up with some guns of our own."

Suddenly a volley of rifle fire struck them. Big Jim Hickey seemed to stagger. He looked dumbly at the hole in his chest and at the spreading red stain that grew on his shirt. Then he fell, not in pieces but all at once, like a giant oak felled by a single stroke of an ax.

Lavery grabbed his shoulder and dropped his rifle. Craig went to help his friends but Kevin shoved him forward.

"Fire," he screamed at Craig. Both men opened fire with their repeating rifles. Suddenly they were among the gunners. Someone screamed in pain as his belly was pierced by a Fenian bayonet.

Craig rushed at a man who carried a mortar shell, hoping to fire one last round. Craig stabbed at him with the bayonet. The Canadian dropped the mortar shell and tried to parry Craig's rifle with his arm. Kevin's bullet ripped through his arm almost tearing it off at the socket.

The rest of the defenders started to run. At the wharf the steam tug which brought them to Fort Eire tooted its whistle and pulled away from the dock toward the safety of Lake Erie's waters. The village of Fort Erie was again back in the hands of the Fenians.

Craig walked back down the river road. He called for his friends. When there was no answer, he left the road and wandered about the fields. He could remember some of the landmarks of the charge.

He found Sean lying on top of Jim. He recognized the cape immediately. Lavery had taken it from his knapsack and spread it over his friend before he himself had collapsed. Craig fell to his knees beside them. He felt for a pulse at Jim's throat. There was none. He pulled the cape away from Jim's face and chest and realized that there could be none. The huge man's eyes were open in death and his face seemed at peace. Craig closed

Jim's eyes. He put his head to Sean's chest. He heard his heart beating. He looked up and saw Kevin standing behind him. "He's lost a lot of blood," he said looking wide–eyed at the gore on the front of Sean's shirt. "But at least he's still alive."

"I'll help you with him," Kevin said. He had been crying. His face was filthy but the tears had washed a clean path down his cheek toward his mouth. "We'll get Sean evacuated to Buffalo. There will be doctors who can help him there. But let's hurry. It's getting dark and we will want to come back to bury Jim."

Craig and Kevin carried Sean Lavery to the hotel in the village. The local doctor, a white–haired old man, seemed to know far more about the care and treatment of animals than he did people. His suggestion for the cavalry horses was to shoot them immediately. Craig later discovered that he served the village as a veterinarian as well. The only other local doctor, the one who treated the wealthy, had fled with most of the villagers on the Erie and Ontario train. But the old man did get the ball out of Sean's shoulder and stop the bleeding.

Kevin returned to the battlefield to bury Big Jim. He enlisted the aid of several of his troopers. Craig would not leave Sean alone in the care of the horse doctor. Sean was unconscious and Craig wanted to be with him when he recovered his wits. Big Jim might not have been stimulating company, but there had never been a more faithful friend.

O'Neill ordered the army to entrench itself on the ruins of old Fort Erie, an artifact of the War of 1812. He sent out scouts who reported about midnight that Peacocke and his regulars were encamped within three miles of Fort Erie. They had artillery. O'Neill called another council of war. When his officers assembled, the Colonel jokingly told them they would have to meet around the open campfire since his tent had been misplaced in the activity of the day.

"Gentlemen, we have done our best. We did what people said could not be done. We entered Canada with not even one tenth of the numbers we should have had. Our own beloved United States betrayed us royally, boys. I want you to know your leaders are not fools. We had our understandings in Washington. They were to look the other way. Our chance to get even with Mr. Andrew Johnson and Mr. William Seward, his secretary of state, will be coming up in the elections this fall. Andrew Johnson may be a Tennessee man like me, but I've always believed he was a Reb at heart. I'll never forgive

Mr. Lincoln for putting him on the ticket and then going and getting himself murdered. But Mr. Andy Johnson stabbed us in the back and cut off our succor with his goddamned neutrality laws and his snoopy gunboats. They're in the river at our backs even as we talk right now.

"Well, boys, we kicked the shit out of them as long as the odds were even. Our Mother Ireland can be proud of her sons. We have no shame to bear, but I don't mind telling you I've signaled my superiors in Buffalo asking their advice. I'm prepared, if ordered, to make our stand here and die. I'm sure you'd stand with me, but I dont' see what purpose that would serve. I've been notified to be prepared to evacuate."

There was shocked silence about the campfire and finally some angry protest.

"Colonel Starr," one of the Kentucky officers addressed his colonel, "does that go for Kentucky men, too?"

"I'm afraid so," Owen Starr said.

"But, Colonel O'Neill, we licked them twice today, once at Ridgeway and once here. We can take them on again. Since one Irishman can lick twenty British soldiers, you could say we outnumber them already. If you break out the whiskey ration—which I'm told is stashed in the hotel in the village— you'll up that number to forty. One drunken Irishman is equal to forty British regulars. We're contemplating a massacre here."

They all laughed.

But O'Neill remained serious. "We cross at three a.m. in the darkness. Prepare your men to evacuate."

Craig sat back on his haunches. It was over. The Irishmen would give up despite their victories. He could not help but feel the fool. He had believed in this cause not because it would free Ireland, that was the dream of the impractical. He believed in this cause as a means of stopping Canadian expansion.

He worried now that what had happened might produce the opposite effect. Canadians would be an arrogant people to deal with in the months ahead. He had spent enough time in Canada now. He was educated. He had achieved what his father had asked of him. He had tried with the Irishmen to do more. He wanted most now to go home to the prairies and to his father's farm.

First, though, there was Meg to consider. He had to go to her. He had almost told her of his involvement with the Irish

161

cause that day on the Plains of Abraham. She understood his feelings for his home, even if she was a Canadian. She would understand and support his actions. He was sure of that. He would go to her and tell her he wanted her to go home to Manitoba with him.

And then there were his friends. What would happen to Kevin and Sean, especially Sean? Kevin had always taken care of himself but Sean was helpless.

"You're dismissed," O'Neill said finally.

Craig stood up. It was like a discharge from the brotherhood for him. He no longer felt moved by any oaths, any bonds. All that mattered now were his friends and, of course, Meg.

Kevin was waiting for him at the hotel. They did not speak of Big Jim.

"They're evacuating," Craig informed him.

"I thought they would."

"We're both speaking of our comrades in arms in the third person," Craig joked.

Kevin looked at him coldly. "I've learned from bitter experience, my lad, that you must always think of everyone in the third person, that is except yourself. It's me and them."

"Does that include me?"

"Only as long as we're on the same side." He laughed. Besides, we have a special bond, remember? You saved my life. You said you'd take care of me for the rest of my life."

"Unless you, in turn, save mine. Then I think the two deeds are canceled out."

"Not by my logic. It means that you are responsible for me and I'm responsible for you for life. It ties us closer. It cancels nothing." Kevin started to laugh. "It sounds almost as bad as being married."

Craig smiled. "That's what I want to do next, Kevin. Get married."

Kevin nodded. "I figured that was coming. Last time you stayed with me you didn't ask for the room from me even once. You're mopey over that pretty girl from Halifax."

Craig nodded.

"If one of us is to be hitched, better you than me," he joked.

"You'll find someone someday," Craig said in all seriousness.

"I've found her. Many times. I find someone on a Sunday and usually someone also on Wednesday and definitely on the following Saturday."

"Funny," Craig interrupted, "but they all wear the same perfume."

"What do you mean?"

"I mean that every time you've asked me not to come home until morning—which before the campaign started was becoming a regular event—I'd return in the morning and the room would smell of the same perfume. I assumed you were seeing someone steadily. I also assumed that the lady was probably married and she had to come to you all the time."

As Craig spoke, Kevin's mood changed. The light laughter was replaced by a vacant stare and a studied nonchalance. Craig dropped the subject of the mystery woman.

"You were speaking of taking care of yourself and those tied to you. That's me and it's Sean."

"I can do nothing for Sean," Kevin said. "He'll have to stay behind unless O'Neill decides to evacuate the wounded too."

"He couldn't do anything else. They should be taken across first."

"My friend, you didn't hear anything I said earlier. You've got to understand that this group doesn't act like a normal army. In most armies they evacuate their wounded and bury their dead to convince the whole and able that if they should be wounded they would be evacuated, and that if they are killed they'll be buried and not left to the buzzards. It's good for morale. But the brotherhood is filled with fanatics who don't care if buzzards eat their guts so long as Ireland is free. Their first principle is going to be save your ass and the asses of the able-bodied so you can fight again another day. And besides they haven't got enough boats."

"How do you know all this?" Craig asked.

"I've been in the Republican Brotherhood a long time. I have contacts. They've got a few tugs and barges to cross the Niagara, but a lot aren't going to make it."

"Kevin, you yourself said you have contacts. You could get a place on a boat for Sean."

"Not unless he is walking."

"That's all I need."

"I can't help you."

"I didn't ask you to."

Kevin nodded. "Both of you be at the ferry wharf at two. There will be a boat coming over early to pick up officers, although probably not O'Neill. He'll leave later—after most of the army. I tell you now, though, there won't be enough room

163

for all, and the leaders of this expedition have no intention of staying behind and getting themselves a British noose as a prize. Irishmen know enough to expect no mercy from the British."

"I'll be there," Craig assured him, "and Sean will be with me."

Craig found Sean sleeping on the floor of the taproom of the village hotel. He was surrounded by fifteen other injured Fenians. Craig let him sleep as long as he could. He dozed off himself, but awoke with a start when the clock in the taproom chimed one forty-five. He couldn't allow Sean to sleep any longer. He leaned over and touched his friend's good shoulder.

"Sean, wake up."

Sean was burning with fever and was delirious.

"Little Craig," he greeted him. "Little Craig, Big Jim." He started to laugh wildly.

"Sean, you've got to get on your feet. I want you to come with me. Kevin has found a boat for us. We're going back to the United States."

"Nonsense, my lad," Sean said loudly. "We're going to parade through my hometown, through bloody Dublin we're the liberators. Bloody Emmet can have his bloody epitaph at last." Suddenly he grew lucid. "This was such a silly enterprise, Craig. It was not worth the life of Big Jim." Tears welled in his eyes.

Craig nodded. "Can you get to your feet?"

"If I have to," Sean gasped. He grimaced with pain as Craig held on to his elbow. He rested his good hand on Craig's shoulder and tried to raise himself.

"Damn you. You better have a good reason for wanting me to stand."

"I do," Craig assured him.

"There, I've done it," Sean said, smiling through the pain. "Now what's your reason?"

"I want you to walk with me to the waterfront."

Sean started to laugh but the pain forced him to control himself. "Craig, my lad, I'm beginning to think you were behind the whole harebrained expedition. What makes you think I would want to go anywhere near the waterfront? I'm not up to strolls."

"It's Kevin. He has a boat for us."

"Ah! Your ever-faithfulest friend, Kevin O'Connor."

"You're slurring your words," Craig admonished him.

"And me an actor. All right, we'll stroll to the waterfront. If Kevin says so, then we must. Lead on, my lad."

Sean walked to the door and then collapsed. Craig raised him to his feet again.

"You know," he said lightheartedly, "I don't think the night air will be good for me. I think I'll go back to bed."

He started to turn to go back to his pallet and stumbled. Craig grabbed him to steady him. When he pulled his hand away from Sean's chest, his palm was sticky with blood.

"Oh Christ, you've started to bleed again."

Craig forced Sean's good arm around his shoulders and grabbed Sean's filthy blood–stained cape off the bar. He moved rapidly outside into the street. Sean was leaning heavily on him. He no longer moved his feet. Craig had to drag him along. The riverfront was not far from the hotel, and the ferry wharf was just a few blocks farther to the south. Once he made it to the river, Craig feared that he had not left enough time. He had not anticipated how difficult it would be to move Sean. He would be late.

Sean made no sounds at all now. Craig was beginning to doubt his decision to escape with his friend. He dragged Sean into an alley between buildings. He could hear the slapping of water against wooden pilings. He did not have much farther to go. He heard someone call out, but Sean's dead weight was exhausting him.

"Only a little further," he said aloud. He tripped and fell to his knees. Sean had struck the wooden planks of the wharf with a thud.

Craig got up and ran a few paces ahead. The boat should be right here, he thought. But there was nothing. He looked up and down the river. He had not missed the place. This was the ferry wharf.

Then he looked out into the river. He could see the boat puffing its way toward Buffalo, growing smaller, its lights growing dimmer. A man stood in the stern. Craig could make out no more than a dark outline but he knew that it was Kevin, who searched the Fort Erie shore with his tired eyes.

IX

Toronto, July 1866

Feeling in Toronto against the captured Fenians ran very high. All one hundred men, some, like Sean, badly wounded, had been placed in the Toronto jail. Those who made it to the boats and crossed to Buffalo were arrested by the American government but then released on their own recognizance. They would never be prosecuted, not with congressional elections in the fall and a million and a half Irishmen living in the United States.

But those stranded in Canada could expect a different fate. The newspapers called for swift summary executions for those making unlawful war. That was the fate demanded for the American citizens. Treason against the Crown was the crime of British subjects among the Fenian ranks. They could expect the same fate. Craig Miller was a British subject.

June and July passed without the Canadian government taking any action. Craig spent his first days caring for Sean. Then Sean's fever grew worse and he was removed to a hospital unit. He never returned to Craig's cell. In fact, Craig was kept in isolation from most of the prisoners. He was a British subject and he had been an officer in the Brotherhood Army, not just a gullible member of the rank and file.

In mid–July Craig was visited by the Solicitor General James Cockburn and informed of the government's decision to delay trials to October in order to allow tempers to cool and justice to be served. That same sweltering July day he received more visitors. He sat on the straw–filled mattress leaning against the stone walls of the jailhouse when the iron door swung open and a slight, white–haired figure stooped to enter the low doorway.

"Filthy place," Michael Brant mumbled.

Craig rose to greet him, then hesitated. He was not entirely sure how his uncle would respond. But Brant put his fears to rest by throwing his arms around Craig.

"I am sorry to find you in such a place, son," he said.

"Not half as sorry as I am to be here." Craig tried to be lighthearted.

"Sit down, boy," Brant said. "What is it about you Millers that instantly draws you into rebellions. First, your father with Mackenzie and now you with the Fenian crowd. Now, Mackenzie I could understand. Your father fought for Canadian reform against cutthroat pirates."

Brant failed to mention his part in the 1837 rebellion, a role that had forced him into exile in New England.

"But these Fenians. All they wanted was to hold Canada hostage and force a war between Great Britain and the Americans. There was nothing worthwhile in that for Canada. What did you seek to gain?"

"Uncle Michael, you seem to forget I am not a Canadian. I'm a Métis from Rupert's Land."

"But, as you yourself said in Quebec in front of the whole family, it's all got to be one land."

"One land, Uncle Brant, with equal protection for all. I just don't feel my people at Red River will get equal protection from you Canadians. At Quebec, sir, you voiced similar concerns for Nova Scotia."

"And I still have them, but we are working out a constitution that will guarantee our rights. That's the way to do it boy— negotiations—the give and take of the bargaining table."

Craig grew silent. He had come to a similar conclusion on his own. These weeks in prison had given him time to think, to try to understand in his own mind why he had cast his lot with the Fenians. He knew the answer almost from the very beginning. He had been without friends; they offered him companionship and something to belong to. He had felt rejected by Brant and his family. The Fenians had opened their arms to him. And then there was Kevin O'Connor. Kevin looked out for Kevin. Yet Craig still thought of him as his best friend. They had gone through everything together. Despite the other man's selfishness, Craig still thought of Kevin with fondness.

"That's all piss in the pot," Brant exclaimed. "I'm here to represent you, if you'll have me as your attorney. And I don't mean to fool you, lad, you need an attorney very badly."

"I've begun to think of myself as a dead man," Craig said softly.

"Not a bad beginning," Brant said without the slightest hint of humor. "Mr. Justice Wilson will preside. He's a fair enough fellow, but he is more inclined to leniency for the poor fellows who were duped into joining the expedition. He will be hard on the leaders like you."

"Uncle Michael," Craig interrupted, "I don't want to die. Please help me."

Brant looked at the boy. Craig could see tears in his eyes.

"I'll do well by you, boy," he said softly. "My time is almost up. There is someone else waiting to see you."

He stepped to the door and called the guard. The door swung open and Meg stepped hesitantly forward. Ignoring those things that frightened her about the place, she rushed into Craig's arms and kissed his face. Her father walked quietly out into the corridor. He had a small bribe to pay the jailer for allowing the second visitor in.

"Craig, how I've missed you. When we got word that you were one of the Fenians captured I was so confused. Why didn't you tell me?"

"I almost did. I am sorry for not trusting you, but I'd taken an oath. Besides you were always the good Canadian. I thought if I told you I'd lose you."

"Never. All you would have had from me was an argument. A good fight doesn't mean I'd stop loving you. But a good fight might have avoided this. I could have won you away from those Irishmen. You would have picked me over them. But I did not come all the way from Halifax to Toronto to lecture you. I love you, Craig, and I'm going to stay with you through this. When it is over we are going to begin our lives together."

"You think I'll make it through this. I've despaired for myself."

"Of course you'll make it. You have me—you have my father—the best lawyer in Canada."

"I don't want to live in Canada when it is all over," he said to her nervously.

"Where then?" she asked.

"I want you to come with me to Fort Garry on the Red River. I want you to come home with me to Manitoba."

She was surprised by the idea. "I don't know if I could do it," she exclaimed, "I'm a city girl. I don't know if I want to do it."

"My mother could show you everything. You could even learn from my grandmother, Warrior Woman, although she must be ancient now. We could build our own house on my father's land along the riverfront.

Meg smiled sadly. "I haven't said yes yet. We must think of what is best."

He looked into her eyes. "But you will. I know you will."

She pulled away from him and looked about the cell. The panic was growing inside her. It was insane to be talking about their lives together when his life was in such danger.

He could see what was happening to her, but he refused to go back to his old depression. He had a good lawyer, the best lawyer in Canada, some said, and the woman he loved, loved him still. In spite of all that had happened, she had not abandoned him.

Mr. Justice Wilson had opened the trial with a plea to the jury for impartiality. Thus far, from Michael Brant's perspective, the plea had been ineffective. In fact, the judge's statements about simple souls who could be duped into being evil while working for what they believed a just cause had actually worked against the Fenian leaders tried thus far. There had been four trials: All four ended in convictions, and all four men were sentenced to hang.

It was Brant's belief that none would find themselves on the gallows because the American Secretary of State had already intervened with the British government and the Colonial Secretary had written to the Governor General advising clemency. But he still worried about Craig. The others were American. Craig was the first British subject to be tried.

The first witness to be called by the Crown was someone whose name Craig did not recognize.

"The Crown calls Mr. Samuel Martin."

An old gentleman rose from a courtroom seat and entered the witness stand.

Michael leaned over to Craig with a look of puzzlement on his face. Craig merely shrugged.

Mr. Graham, assistant to the Solicitor General, began the questioning.

"Your name."

"Sam Martin."

"Where do you live, Mr. Martin?"

"Who me?" the old man said pointing a finger at himself.

A look of exasperation crossed Graham's face.

"Well, right now I am staying at a boarding house on Bloor Street. Widow Johnston's. The food's not bad and neither is the widow."

The courtroom erupted with laughter.

Graham persisted. "Where do you normally live?"

"Oh, that's what you meant? Well, I've lived at Fort Erie for the last forty–five years."

At that moment Craig recognized the old man as the one who had been left to guard the horses.

"Were you present at Fort Erie on the morning of June 1, 1866?"

"I just told you I been at Fort Erie for the past forty–five years. This trip to Toronto was my first time out."

"Can you tell the court what happened to you on the morning of June first?"

"Is that the day the Papists came?"

"That was the day of the Fenian raid," Graham corrected him.

"Same thing," Martin insisted. "All them Fenians is Papist. They was planning to bring the bloody pope from Rome and set him up in Toronto."

Brant was on his feet to object but Wilson preempted him.

"Mr. Martin, just answer the question. As fascinated as we might be by your thoughts on the future home of the Bishop of Rome, I don't think they are pertinent to the proceedings."

Martin turned to Graham.

"What did he say?" he asked.

"He said stick to the question."

"Let's see. I remember it was a Friday because we usually have our Orange Lodge meetings on Fridays and it was canceled."

"Go on with your story," Graham encouraged him.

"We were called to a big meeting Friday morning early— very early. I remember the train whistles at the yard started blowing, waking up the whole town. The Fenians is coming. Shit, how everybody started running."

There was more laughter in the court.

"Your language, Mr. Martin."

"Sorry."

"Go on."

"We all went to the depot. We were told that these crazy Irishmen were coming to Fort Erie to murder us all in our beds. The big men of the town decided to evacuate. That's what they called it, evacuate. I remember because I asked my lodge brother John Ryan what evacuate meant. He laughed at me and said we were all getting the he . . . heck out of the town."

170

"We all know of the heroic efforts of the Fort Erie citizenry to deprive the enemy of any succor in the village. Right now, we are interested in your story, Mr. Martin. You did not leave town on the first of June, did you?"

"No, sir!"

"Why not?"

"Because I got me an assignment," he said beaming at the jury.

"What do you mean?"

"I got me the job of rounding up all the unfit horses, taking them down in the old railyard ravine and shooting them. They weren't worth evacuation." He smiled again at the jury when he used the word. "But we had to make sure they weren't of use to the Irish. They gave me a Spencer, one of them newfangled repeating rifles to do the job."

"And did you complete your assignment?"

Martin's face went sour. "Well, no, I didn't."

"Why?"

"Because that son of a bitch over there," he said pointing at Craig, "stopped me."

"Let the record show that the witness is pointing at the defendant, Mr. Craig Miller."

"And the record should not include Mr. Martin's epithet," said the judge. "I warn you again, Mr. Martin. Continue, Mr. Graham."

"How did the defendant prevent you from fulfilling your assignment?"

"Well, he damned near killed me."

Judge Wilson rolled his eyes but said nothing.

"After I rounded up all them horses in the ravine, I went back to my room to get my rifle. By then, the Fenians were in the town. They weren't as bad as folks feared. The few folks that didn't flee weren't molested or anything. I mean, they didn't touch old lady Meeks, but then no one in their right mind would touch old lady Meeks."

It took almost a full minute to restore order in the courtroom. It was clear though that Justice Wilson had given up on admonishing Sam Martin. The judge just wanted the man to give his testimony and get out of the courtroom.

"Go on," he said to Graham.

"Well, this fellow here must have followed me from my rooms. I got off one shot, killed an old gelding right off. But them Spencers is hard to figure out. While I'm trying to figure

171

out how to shoot again, I gets knocked off my feet by that Miller fella and he takes them horses from me. He was the leader of their cavalry. I found out later. And them old nags was used against our boys. I was sorry to hear that. Damn sorry I couldn't have finished them off."

"Thank you, Mr. Martin. Mr. Brant?"

Craig and Michael had conferred throughout most of Martin's testimony.

"Mr. Martin," Michael said as he rose from the table, "do you know for a fact that Mr. Miller was the leader of the Fenian cavalry?"

"Sure I do. Why, Sheriff Dobman told me he was before they asked me to come to Toronto."

Michael looked at Wilson.

"I was waiting for your objection after he first spoke. Why did you wait?" the judge asked.

"I just wanted to make the point again sir, that Mr. Martin can in no way connect my client with the Fenians."

"Then why did he stop me from doing my assignment?" Martin interjected.

"Maybe Mr. Miller just likes horses," Michael quipped.

There was some laughter in the courtroom.

"Mr. Martin, I have one more question for you. And remember you are under oath. Did you or did you not offer to sell the horses to my client?"

"Never."

"You never thought to make a profit from your assignment?"

"Never."

"And how long after you received your assignment did you wait before you attempted to complete it?"

Martin was no fool. He saw the trap Michael was trying to lay for him.

"Right away," he lied. "I didn't wait at all, no, not at all."

"You began to shoot the horses at dawn, then. Is that right?"

"Yes."

"May it please the court," Brant said, "I submit that either Mr. Martin is a liar, in which case his testimony should be ignored, or he should be a defense witness, since he would place my client in Fort Erie a good two hours before the Fenians entered the town. I have no further questions."

Michael sat back down looking rather content with himself.

Graham rose to his feet a bit disconcerted. "The Crown calls Alex Miller."

There was a murmur through the courtroom. Several wondered whether the witness and the defendant were related. Alex stepped into the courtroom when his name was called. He was wearing the dress uniform of a Canadian militia officer. He took his oath.

"Captain Miller," Graham said, "you are an officer in Her Majesty's militia?"

"I am."

"We should clear this up straight away. Would you explain your relationship to the defendant?"

"He is my nephew."

"Could you explain? You both appear to be the same age."

"We are. I am twenty–six and I believe the defendant is twenty–four. It is quite simple. His father and I are half–brothers. We are both the sons of the Charles Miller, who recently passed away. We had different mothers. Joshua Miller, my brother, whom I have never met, is eighteen years older than I am. I believe he lives somewhere within the confines of Manitoba. He is Craig Miller's father."

"Are you familiar with the defendant?"

"Yes, I first met him at the home of a mutual cousin in Quebec. That was, let's see, back in 1864 during the Quebec Conference."

"Have you met him since?"

"Yes, he attended a function at my home in Toronto just before the Fenian invasion."

"Did you have any knowledge of his connection with that organization?"

"None whatsoever, although with hindsight I sometimes think I should have been suspicious. He brought some rather unsavory Irish characters to the house."

"You knew them to be Irish?"

Alex smirked. "One can always tell, can't one?"

"Objection!" Michael called out.

"Sustained," responded Wilson.

"Mr. Graham, get on with it. Mr. Craig Miller is not on trial here for associating with Irishmen."

Graham looked a bit flustered. "Let's get to the point then. When did you see your nephew again?"

"On the battlefield at Ridgeway," Alex said calmly.

"Continue."

"It was just before Colonel Booker gave his unfortunate order to form a square. Someone had seen Fenian cavalrymen,

173

and since we had had no horses to counter these, the colonel ordered a square form."

"Where was the defendant?"

"Out in front of the cavalry unit. He was their commander."

"Thank you, Captain Miller."

Michael rose slowly. "Captain Miller, where were you when you say you saw the defendant at Ridgeway?"

"I was just emerging from the woods on the right flank. I had led a charge to clear out the rebels from those woods. We did a damn fine job of it, if I say so myself."

"And the cavalry unit was on your left flank clear across the entire field. Yet you recognized Craig Miller among a dozen other horsemen? Captain, that stretches credulity!"

"Uncle Michael" Alex used the familiar address to Brant for the first time in his life, "let's not overdo it. Ridgeway's battlefield is a few hundred square yards. We are not talking about battlefields such as those fought on by the Americans in their recent unhappiness. And I observed him among the enemy. It surprised me to recognize him."

"It astounds me that you could, sir. And incidentally, I am not your uncle." He sat down with a grunt of annoyance.

Craig leaned over to Michael. "That didn't go too well, did it?"

"Were you among the cavalry that day?" Michael whispered.

"Yes," Craig responded, "but he could never have seen me there. Why is he lying?"

"I don't know, but he is ruining my case."

"Mr. Brant," Judge Wilson called out, "you may bring forward your witnesses."

"I have none," he stated boldly. "Our case rests on the responsibility of the Crown to prove that the defendant took up arms against the queen. What the Crown has been able to demonstrate is that Craig Miller was at Fort Erie on June third. We do not contest that fact. On that date he was arrested in Fort Erie by officers of the queen's Regular Army. The Crown has attempted to prove that Mr. Miller was also in Fort Erie on the first, when the Fenians seized that village. Their witness is unreliable, to say the least. Indeed, I suggest he was fully prepared to sell valuable horses to the enemy. The Crown has attempted through the eyes of a respected citizen of the community to demonstrate that my client was with the Fenian forces at Ridgeway. I do not know what motivates Captain Alex Miller's testimony against his nephew. I can't and I won't begin to speculate about it. But I can say that the feat of vision he claims for himself is physically impossible. Therefore, I ask that the charges against my client, Mr. Craig Miller, be dismissed. All the Crown has proven is that he was in Fort Erie on June third. I have searched the statutes of this province and of my own province of Nova Scotia, soon to be united with the Canadas. I am sure and I have searched the precedents of the common law that binds all British subjects together, and nowhere can I find it stated that to be in Fort Erie, Canada West, on June 3, 1866, is a violation of the law." Michael Brant took his seat.

"Your motion is rejected," Judge Wilson stated after a moment of brief reflection. "Carry on with your case."

"The defense rests, sir," Brant responded.

The jury was out for twenty minutes. Craig's morale collapsed completely when they read the verdict of guilty of treason. Despite the fact that he was standing facing Judge Wilson when the sentence was read, he could not later recall actually hearing the words that sentenced him to death by hanging. He did not hear Meg scream. He remembered nothing of his uncle leaving the courtroom with his daughter. He vaguely remembered being led from the court back to his cell. What he remembered was the hissing and the jeering of the Toronto citizenry who were observers at his trial. His verdict and sentence were publicly cheered, and many expressed their hopes that the court would not allow Yankee intervention, which had probably saved the Americans, to affect its decisions regarding the fate of British subjects.

Michael came to his cell the next day. The sentence date had been set for December, he said, as he pulled off his light coat and draped it across the table that stood in the center of Craig's small cell.

"That's good," he explained. "It gains us time for an appeal."

Craig said nothing.

"I'm sorry, Craig," Brant said solemnly. "I feel I failed you."

"There was nothing you could do. Your defense was the right one. My problem is that I am guilty as charged. I just didn't think then, and I don't think now, that what I did was wrong—stupid, maybe, but not wrong."

"Damn," Michael slammed his fist on the table, "it was a good defense and I hate to be undone by a lie. Why did that little pipsqueak lie? What was in it for him?"

"Maybe he is a patriot," Craig said sarcastically.

"That little twerp? No. He's Charlie Miller's son and he behaved like Charlie Miller's son. There's got to be something in it for him, damn his soul, and I'm going to find out what it is. And it will have to do with money. What did Charles Miller's will give to Alex and to Allison?"

"I hear he didn't have one. My father was Charles Miller's son too," Craig added.

Michael Brant pounded the table with his fist. "That's it. You've given me my answer." Now he sat quietly. "No, your father is my sister's son. Never forget it. What we need to do now is to work on that appeal."

"What are our chances?"

"Of overturning the verdict? Slim indeed. Of a commutation of sentence, fairly good. You ought to know you are something of a celebrity south of the border. The newspapers are playing up the hanging story, but yours is the first that the Americans think might actually be carried out. The story of your trial, and especially your uncle turning you in, is being played up by the press in most American cities. The Fenians are having a heyday. They are describing you as O'Neill's right–hand man. His Jeb Stuart, one Fenian rag called you."

"Why? Are they trying to get me hanged?"

"Precisely," Michael said. "The cause needs martyrs. It would be the best thing that ever happened to the Fenians if you were strung up. I am counting on the government of Canada understanding it that way too. And if they don't, the Privy Council in England will."

Craig grew angry. "I'll be damned," he said. "I don't want to be any martyr for them."

"Now you're talking sense," Brant said. "I think I can prevail on the government to commute your sentence."

Craig felt relieved.

"But you ought to know the full story. The price you'll pay is twenty to twenty–five years of your life in the Kingston Penitentiary."

Craig reacted as if he had been slapped. The amount of time was enormous. He'd be middle–aged before he emerged from prison, if he ever did. He placed his face in his hands.

"I'm not sure I can face all this, Uncle Michael."

"You may get out earlier. The government may feel it useful propaganda later on to grant pardons. But I must tell you that my contacts in Nova Scotia have been in contact with the Mr. Macdonald here in Canada, and they have been told that the best we can hope for is a twenty–year sentence of hard labor."

He put his hand on Craig's shoulder in a feeble effort to comfort him.

Craig looked around in distress, "Does Meg know?"

Michael nodded. "She took the news strangely. No tears, but not quite resignation. The girl is a fighter, my boy. I know, I raised her to be one. I would not put it past her to take your cause all the way to the Queen herself."

Craig smiled but his smile faded quickly. "You've got to persuade her to give up on me, Uncle Michael. We have certain understandings, sir, but they were made in happier times before I knew what my fate would be."

Michael Brant picked up his coat. "If you think my powers of persuasion are that strong, young man, no wonder you placed your life in my hands. I do believe you expected to walk out of that courtroom a free man. My boy, it will take more than my glib tongue to get that girl to give up on you. Don't try. Be thankful that you have the love of a strong woman. I've had it these last thirty years. It has been my blessing. Now be of good cheer. I have much work to do in the next several days. Jailkeeper," he called out.

The door swung open and Brant left the cell, leaving Craig alone in his misery.

The Canadian authorities decided to move Craig Miller to Kingston even before it was announced that his sentence had been commuted. The announcement was going to be extremely unpopular, and the authorities wanted no trouble.

Craig was manacled, hands and feet, and placed between two burly detectives. He was then taken in a closed carriage to Union Station where he was placed aboard the train to Kingston, still accompanied by the detectives and still bound hand and foot.

He sat by the window as the train moved out of the town, slowly at first and then picking up speed. Outside night had fallen, and one of the guards lit the oil lamp. As a result, the window became a mirror which reflected the interior of the compartment. Craig found he could study his guards without their noticing it. Both men, he noticed, carried poorly concealed revolvers in their coat pockets.

His depression had almost overwhelmed him in the days after Michael Brant's last visit to him. He had not seen Meg but he did receive a note from her. She expressed her love, but then informed him that she would be leaving Toronto for a while and would not be able to see him.

Craig was sorry now that he had asked Michael to tell her of his feelings. He loved her deeply, and could not reconcile his need of her with his release of any claims on her love. If he loved her, he released her. If he released her, he lost her, and he would prefer the noose—a fate that terrified him. There seemed no way out of his dilemma.

The train moved quickly now along the shore of Lake Ontario. Craig recalled that his grandfather had been one of the movers in the building of the very tracks he rode. Despite frequent bankruptcies, Charles Miller had always supported canal building and railroad building. His other investments had more than offset these expensive schemes. No matter what else he had done, Charles Miller had loved this country, Craig thought. Craig bore his grandfather no malice, even if his father did. But Alex Miller, that was another story.

"Want something to eat?" one guard asked him.

He startled Craig from his reverie. He shook his head.

"Well, I do," the guard responded. "Max," he addressed his companion, "something to eat?"

"We brought nothing," the second guard stated.

"We'll be coming into Port Hope in a half hour. We'll stop to load some mail. I can get some coffee and some cheese in a shop near the station."

"How do you know that?"

"Max, I been hauling these bloody Fenians to Kingston for the past month. I know what I am talking about. You can get some bread there, too, and make yourself a lovely cheese sandwich. I've stopped at the shop on every trip."

"There's got to be more than your stomach involved," Max teased.

"Let's say there's a very pretty lass in the shop, and she'll offer you a little more than coffee if the price is right."

"Jesus, how long is our stop in Port Hope?"

"Five minutes."

Max started to laugh. "I never took you for a five-minute man, Harry."

"I said a *little* more than coffee, Max. And I meant a very little. But that sure beats nothing on a long night's journey."

Both men laughed.

Craig ignored them and continued to stare at the window.

The time passed quickly. Soon they were slowing as the train pulled into Port Hope railway station. Harry rose from his seat and left the compartment.

There were lanterns lighting the station platform. For the first time since the lamp had been lit, Craig could see beyond the window.

The train stopped. He saw several passengers disembark. No one got on the train. Harry crossed the platform and entered the station house. Craig heard him call his greetings, and a muffled response. Down the far end of the platform, where the postal car had stopped, workers were loading. They laughed at some unheard joke. There was still no sign of Harry and his sandwiches.

The conductor dropped from the train onto the platform and looked up and down the tracks. He received a signal from the mail–loaders. He waved a lantern toward the engine. The train whistle gave off a blast. Max grew nervous. He stood up and looked anxiously through the window.

"That's cutting it close," he said as he saw Harry race from the station to the train just as it started to move forward.

But Max's eyes were not as well adjusted as Craig's. Whoever it was that caught the train was dressed in Harry's suit but it was not Harry. It was a much slighter man.

Craig was now entirely alert. Max returned to his seat. He opened his mouth to tease Harry as the door of the compartment opened but he caught himself when he saw the strange face. He was reaching for his revolver when a sock loaded with sand struck him a crashing blow on the side of the head, sending him sprawling across the seat.

"That does it," said the lilting brogue that Craig recognized instantly as the voice of Kevin O'Connor. "Don't sit there open–mouthed, my lad. Where the hell do they keep the keys for those silly–looking bracelets you've taken to wearing? Our Harry didn't have them, so I assume that this dear sleeping fellow has got them."

He reached into Max's pocket. "Here's a nasty thing," he said pulling out Max's revolver.

"Try his pants pocket," Craig suggested.

Kevin did. "Correct," he said. "Excellent work, my friend. Here, hold out your hands." Kevin slipped one of the keys into the lock and removed the manacles from Craig's wrists. Then he repeated the action on Craig's legs.

"What? No thank you?" Kevin said lightheartedly.

"I've got more than thank you to say to you, Kevin O'Connor."

"We have no time for anything else, my lad. Not now."

Craig rubbed the circulation back into his hands. He had not realized how tight the cuffs were on his wrists.

"What next then?" Craig asked.

"We leave the train."

Craig looked out the window. Once again he could see nothing but he could tell the train was moving rapidly.

"I assume you mean at the next stop."

"No, we can't take that chance. Someone may find our friend Harry back at Fort Pope."

"What then?"

"Patience," Kevin replied.

"I trusted you once before."

"Now, you can't go placing blame on me for what happened at Fort Erie. You were late, and I wasn't the captain of the bleeding tug."

"You could have tried to get them to wait but I know in my bones you didn't. You were as anxious to escape as the rest of them."

"And with good reason, lad. Look at what happened to you!"

Max groaned. Kevin gave him another smash with the sock.

"Jesus, you could kill him with that."

"No, I'm killing no one. I don't want a murder charge leveled at me. Treason is bad enough. Harry's sleeping just like that one. He's stuffed into a closet. Let's hope that no one finds him for a good hour so that we have a chance to get away. Let's get going now. We're almost at the bend."

The two men worked their way down to the end of the car. Kevin opened the door and stepped out onto the platform.

"Hey, you," the conductor said, stepping out of the shadows. "You're not supposed to . . ." He said no more. Again the sock came down with a thud. The conductor crumpled at the knees and fell into Kevin's arms. The Irishman laid him gently down on the rocking platform between the cars.

"Quick, we're almost there," he urged Craig forward.

The train had slowed perceptibly. The wheels began to squeal and whine.

"Now," Kevin said. He shoved Craig forward. Craig hit the ground hard. He rolled over onto his shoulder and lay stunned for a moment. Kevin's leap was more graceful. He soon lay next to Craig. They watched the train move slowly around the bend and pick up speed for the run to Coburg.

"Quick," Kevin said, "down to the lake."

They ran the hundred feet to the lakeshore. Craig was

startled by a collection of people on the shore. Michael Brant stood beaming at Craig. Next to him, her arms around her husband, was Willy. Craig had not seen her in months. She grabbed him and squeezed him with all her strength.

"Leave some of him for others," Michael teased his wife. "We've no time for good–byes here. You go with our blessing. We don't need to know where you're going, but for our sakes be in touch once you are safe."

For the first time Craig noticed the steam tug heading directly for them. Kevin signaled the boat and it made for the stone jetty that ran from the shore out onto the lake.

"I owe you everything," Craig said to Michael and Willy.

"You don't realize just how much you do owe us," Willy said crying.

"Hurry," Kevin said. He was on the tip of the jetty. He reached for the tug and held it secure. "For Christ's sake, Craig, hurry!" he called again.

Craig turned to run to him. He stepped aboard the tug and Kevin climbed in after. The tug's wheel went into reverse, and it backed away from shore. Then it turned and headed for the open lake.

Willy hugged Michael very tightly. "Does it remind you of another night, another place?" she asked him.

"How could I forget? We did much the same thing, you and I, when we began our lives together."

"I hope they are as happy as I have been," Willy said drying her eyes with her handkerchief.

"They start out with nothing," Michael remarked.

"Just as we did," Willy responded.

Michael said no more. He was already composing his letter to Joshua Miller informing him of his right to contest the settlement of his father's estate. If Joshua could be convinced to concern himself with such matters—the two youngsters aboard the tug might not be so destitute after all.

Craig turned to speak to Kevin. He stood thunderstruck. She stood by the wheel of the boat smiling at him. He rushed to her and enveloped her in his arms.

"My God, Meg, I thought I had lost you for good."

"No, my love," she responded, "it's just the beginning."

X

Red River, February 1869

The snow swirled about the house, forming a drift against one side. Then the wind shifted and the snowdrift diminished and appeared anew on the other side of the house.

Craig sat before the fire. His heavy woolen stockings were almost singed.

"What stinks?" Sean Lavery yelled out as he entered the back door. His arms were laden down with a load of dried buffalo chips.

"Hush," Meg whispered, "you'll wake the baby."

James O'Connor Miller slept in his cradle in the kitchen next to his mother. Meg was cooking dried buffalo meat stew the way her mother–in–law had taught her. In fact, the formidable Rainbow of the Assiniboine, who lived in the great house next door, was due within the hour to test the stew. She had been invited to dine, but Meg knew her mother–in–law well enough to know that each confrontation was a test to see if her son's squaw measured up. Thus far, Meg was proud to say, she had, although deep inside her she resented the necessity.

"Are you passing comment on my toes?" Craig said softly to Sean. He too wanted James to sleep. The baby was colicky and kept both of them awake at night.

"They smell like excrement," Sean responded equally softly so that Meg would not hear the vulgarity.

"Did it ever occur to you that the buffalo shit you are carrying in your arms might be what is affecting your nose, not my feet?"

"Buffalo chips don't stink once they've dried, and I cannot say the same for your feet," he responded while tossing some of the "scentless" fuel on the fire. "Why don't you burn wood like your father if you're worried about the smell?"

Craig shook his head. "I never mentioned the stench. That

was you and you're right, if it stinks, it must be my feet. Wood is expensive. Does that answer all your questions?"

"Yes, that clears it up nicely," Sean said smugly. "Too bad you can't clear the air in here just as nicely."

Both men started to laugh.

"I guess you're inviting yourself to dinner again. Is that right?" Meg called from the kitchen. Her voice woke the baby, who began to fuss again.

"I think it may be time for you and me to go hunting again," Sean teased Craig.

"Oh, no, you don't," Meg said coming out of the kitchen with the large, red–faced baby boy in her arms. "Last time you took off, James cried for a whole week. I got no sleep whatsoever except when Craig's mother took him. You two stayed away the whole week and came home practically empty–handed."

"But well rested," Craig laughed.

"It's not fair. I carried this child. I need my sleep too."

"What we need," Craig joked, "is a wet nurse who hangs around here as much as Sean. It's a shame he couldn't grow some teats and make himself really useful."

"You're shameless," Meg said, pretending to be annoyed with her husband.

"You speak as if I lived here," Sean complained. "I've got my own domicile at Fort Garry."

Craig wrinkled his nose. "I know, I've been there. You have the nerve to complain about my toasted tootsies."

"It's a nice place," Sean said defensively. He had been living at Fort Garry since his release from the prison hospital. He came the same way as Craig and Meg had, via the U.S. railroad to St. Paul, Minnesota and then overland. Kevin had accompanied him but had returned to the United States before the winter struck. Brotherhood business was the only reason he cited for leaving.

The front door swung open and Joshua Miller entered the house dressed in a buffalo robe. His blonde hair, which he wore in two braids, was streaked with grey now. He was followed by his small, delicately featured wife and two other children, both in Indian dress: Douglas, a boy of seven, and Beth, an eighteen–year–old. The girl was strikingly beautiful, with dark hair and eyes and olive skin.

Joshua's face broke into a big grin.

"Let me have my grandson," he said loudly, startling the

183

baby who was just falling off to sleep again. The baby screamed angrily.

"Now look what you made the baby made do," Rainbow said in her strange English, which everyone but Meg and Sean seemed to understand perfectly.

"I'll take care of that," Joshua said. He took the child from Meg's arms and practically swallowed him up in his buffalo robe. The child squealed even more loudly but Joshua ignored his complaint and looked at him fondly, as if the boy were totally content. Eventually James began to quiet and to grow warm and happy in his grandfather's great robe. A bond was growing between them, one that Meg found strange, as she found her father-in-law strange. Although his wife bossed him mercilessly, Meg realized that on some issues he could not be bucked.

Craig had named the baby after a friend who was killed in the Fenian attacks. Meg had agreed to this gesture even though she did not like the name Jim, which everyone immediately stuck on the baby. She wanted to call him Jamie, but without explanation Joshua had said no. No one had the nerve to cross him. Even Rainbow had agreed with him. They called the baby James instead.

Meg, although somewhat awed by both her in-laws, nevertheless was not afraid of them. They were, after all, Craig's parents and she loved their son. She confronted Joshua and demanded an explanation but he would give her none. It was Rainbow who later told her of Jamie McAllistair, Joshua's friend, who had gone mad and had killed his own wife and tried to murder Joshua and Joshua's mother Elizabeth. He had eventually been killed by Joshua's Uncle Stephen. Rainbow failed to mention that Meg and Craig were now living in Jamie's house. She was not superstitious about it; after all, she and Joshua had lived there themselves when they first came home to live at Fort Garry. She had cast spells to placate the spirit of Jamie's wife and had seen no manifestations. She knew the woman's soul was at rest, but still was not sure the white woman would understand. There was no need for her to know more anyway. Meg felt close to Joshua. He after all knew her father and had been a child with her mother. He and Michael Brant continued to correspond about his father's estate—but the distance in miles between them and inconsistant mails forced Meg to conclude that little but trouble would come from the suit Michael had filed.

Meg had tried to feel close to Rainbow. But she remained bossy and difficult. Meg, however, would always remember that it had been Rainbow who sat at her side when James was born. And it was Rainbow who gave her the rawhide to bite on when the pains came. At first she thought the woman was determined to kill her. Rainbow had insisted that Meg walk and squat. But when James was born, Rainbow was there to catch him and tie and bite the cord. She washed him and wrapped him in warm blankets. Meg could forgive most of Rainbow's tests when she remembered the birth of her son.

Rainbow took James from Joshua and started him squealing once again.

"Take off that buffalo. It makes it too hot in here. Too hot for the baby," she said.

She strolled into the kitchen area with James on her shoulder, burping him. She did not believe that Meg did this properly. She also believed that white woman's milk gave gas. She reached this conclusion because she had never heard a white woman break wind. It stood to simple reason that if all this gas was held in, it would have to find an outlet someplace. She dipped the ladle into the pemmican stew and brought it to her lips.

"It more salt needs," she said loudly above the baby's wail. Actually it was almost perfect, but she didn't think it a good idea to give too much praise to her daughter–in–law; it would spoil her if she was praised too young. Her own mother had treated her this way and she had turned out well.

She took a pinch of salt from the bowl on the shelf above the stove. She dropped one half of it into the stew and the rest she put back into the bowl. It would not do to make the stew too salty.

The baby grew silent again and Rainbow placed him back in his cradle. Meg decided to ignore her mother–in–law in the kitchen. She turned instead to Beth. The girl, unlike her mother, was very shy.

"My father sent a bolt of cloth from St. Paul, Beth. Would you like to see it?"

The girl nodded and the two of them went out into the lean–to room which served as a storage place. They were chatting away before long.

Joshua joined his son and Sean before the fire. Douglas, his younger son, found his way into the kitchen with his mother.

"I'm glad your Meg is fond of that girl," Joshua said nodding toward the bedroom. "She needed a sister. It gets lonely for a young girl out here. I wanted to send her back East like I did with you, Craig, but your mother fought me on that one. She even brought her own mother in. No winning when the two of them gang up on you."

"How are grandmother and grandfather?"

"Last I heard, pretty good. Old Eagle Face told me he and his band would winter on the Pembina near Swan Lake."

"That's far west for them, isn't it?" Craig asked.

"Damn right, but you have to go out far now to find buffalo. An occasional winter kill can make all the difference for your mother's people. I like the life on the open prairie, but not at this time of the year. There was a time when your mother complained when I made her come to Fort Garry for the winter, but I don't hear those complaints anymore."

"The stew is ready," Rainbow announced. She started to spoon it onto plates.

Meg came out of the bedroom with Beth. She looked at Rainbow with annoyance written all over her face.

Craig went to the ledge above the fireplace and took the large jug of whiskey down. The jug was passed to Joshua. He took a large swig. He gave it to Sean who grimaced at the inelegance of the method but banished his misgivings and took a swallow. Craig took a drink also. He looked at his young brother who sat by James's cradle rocking it. Then he looked at his father.

"Why not?" said Joshua. "He'll have to learn sometime. Here, Doug," he said to the boy, "take a swig."

The boy's eyes lit up at the prospect. He took the jug from Craig and, trying to hold it as he had seen the men do, he took his first drink. The jug slipped from his hands but Sean caught it before it could hit the ground. The whiskey came shooting out of his mouth. The boy gagged and coughed. Craig thought for sure he was about to heave the contents of his stomach onto the cabin floor and rushed to get a pan from the kitchen.

"Welcome to manhood," Joshua said laughing.

"What you do to the boy?" Rainbow came rushing to her baby's side.

"I gave him some whiskey."

Douglas's face was red and he was still coughing. Rainbow held his head to her breast and patted his back.

"Joshua Miller, you big fool. Doug, my baby," she whispered in his ear in Assiniboine. If she had been in the big house up the road, in her house, she would have told Joshua what she really thought, but she could not embarrass him before his children and strangers. She took Doug by the hand and led him back into the kitchen with her.

"Sorry, Pop," Craig said. "I guess it wasn't a good idea."

"I guess I'll catch it later," Joshua said nervously.

"It was a disastrous idea," Sean chimed in. "The pup nearly destroyed our winter supply of whiskey and the winter's are uncommonly long here in Manitoba."

They sat about the long table that Craig had dragged to the center of the room. Outside, the wind and snow continued to build in intensity. Ice caked the insides of all the window panes making it was impossible to see through them.

"I think we could all use some more whiskey," Craig suggested after the stew had been devoured and the gravy sopped up with pieces of freshly baked bread.

"Not me!" Doug cried.

They all laughed.

"You get none at all, boy," Sean admonished.

The boy looked immensely relieved.

Sean took possession of the jug and poured some of its contents into pewter mugs. He took a kettle of hot water from the stove and poured some into Meg's and Beth's mugs. He started to do the same for Rainbow but she waved him off.

"Well, my children," Joshua said as he sipped the liquor, "it is good to have you all with me again. This is the way it was meant to be." He looked at the frosted windowpanes. "The colder it is outside and the more the snow falls, the cozier it becomes in here. God, I love this place. It's been so good to me. I left Canada as a boy with no one to love me and with a price on my head. I came here looking for the faded memory of an uncle who once cared. Instead I found my mother, who I thought was dead. She insists now on living on the other side of the world but I know she's there and content. And I found true love here."

He reached over and touched his wife's hand. Her face broke into a beautiful smile which allowed everyone present to understand how Joshua Miller had fallen as deeply in love with her as he had.

"And I get me three ugly brats, and now the oldest brat has gone out and found his own beauty of whom he is not worthy. The warm smile disappeared from Rainbow's face as she saw the pleasure fill her daughter-in-law's visage.

Meg bowed teasingly.

"And they have gone on and produced the greatest brat of all, my grandson."

"Shh," everyone at the table said almost in unison. And then they all laughed.

"But most of all," he said as he poured himself a second and larger mug of whiskey, "I am grateful that I live only a few hundred feet from this house because I intend to get pleasantly tipsy tonight, so tipsy in fact that I may need the assistance of my dear wife and daughter and son to return home."

Meg thought Rainbow would become annoyed. Certainly her mother would have resented any attempt by her father to get drunk, although it was difficult to think of Michael Brant drunk. But Rainbow merely laughed with the others.

Suddenly Joshua stopped laughing. He held up his hand for silence.

"Someone's coming," he said.

The only sound that Craig could hear was the howling of the wind, but he knew his father well enough not to challenge his instincts. If he said someone was coming, then someone would arrive shortly.

Then he heard the snort of a horse in front of his house. He rose and went to the front door. He opened it wide. Snow came swirling through the door followed by two huge snow-covered men. Joshua stood up.

"John," he greeted one of the newcomers, "where are you coming from on a night like this? No matter where it is, it is already too far. Sit down, have a drink. You know my wife and my younger children, but I don't think you've met my oldest boy and his wife Meg. And this is their friend Mr. Sean Lavery of Dublin in Ireland. Children, this is Dr. John Christian Schultz. And you, sir"—he turned to the second man—"I don't believe I know you."

"Thomas Scott," the second man introduced himself. He was a large man, larger than either Craig or his father.

Craig watched Schultz as he was introduced to him. He greeted Joshua warmly enough, and he was attentive to Meg, but he wasted no time whatever on the rest of them.

"Won't you sit down, Dr. Schultz?" Craig said. "We were just having a little whiskey. Can I offer you some?"

Schultz shook his head but Scott jumped at the opportunity. Craig poured him a healthy mugful.

"Are you all the way from Winnipeg tonight?" Joshua asked again. Winnipeg was the village, mostly settled by Englishmen, many of them from Canada, that had grown up a mile or so downriver from Fort Garry.

Schultz nodded. "I didn't come all this way, Joshua Miller, just to sell you a subscription to the *Nor'wester*."

"Oh, not that rag," Lavery started to laugh, "I've read it. It has very little respect for small items like the truth."

Scott glared at Sean. "Dr. Schultz is publisher of the *Nor'wester*," he said. "You're from Dublin you say?"

Sean, who was not easily embarrassed, was flustered by this turn and merely nodded.

"I thought so," said Scott, "my family are Ulstermen."

Schultz decided to ignore both Lavery and Scott. "Joshua, I've really come out to see you because you're a damned hard man to find once the snows go. You're off to the Minnedosa or Saskatchewan or some other godforsaken place. I need a commitment from you."

Joshua's eyes narrowed. "A commitment to what?"

"To Canada," Schultz responded.

Joshua remained silent.

"You're one of us, Miller. You're a Canadian. I know it and we must stick together."

"I was born here," Joshua said stubbornly.

"Of Canadian parents, and you were raised in Toronto."

"I fought for Mackenzie."

"I applaud you. The crazy little man was a patriot, even if he did have some strange flirtations with Republicanism. William Lyon Mackenzie was the true Canadian back in '37. He put Canada first. Representative and responsible government is what you fought for back in 1837, Miller, and it is what I want for the Red River settlement now, a generation later."

"Why not let things be, John?" Joshua said. "We've lived all these years here in the north under the Hudson's Bay Company. Ever since the days of the North West Company fights, we've lived in peace, all of us—Indians, Scot Selkirkers, Métis, company men, Americans, Canadians. Why stir up trouble?"

Scott started to rise. "He's with them," he said to Schultz. "Why waste any more time on him."

"Sit down, Tom," Schultz insisted. "No Englishman, and certainly no Canadian, should have to live under a charter given to a fur-trading company with a governor appointed by that company, a council appointed by that company. We deserve representative democracy."

"It will come in time," Joshua argued.

"The time is now," Scott said.

"The man is right," Schultz insisted. "The Canadian Confederation is a fact. I've word that the company will be selling its holdings to Great Britain, which in turn will turn them over to the federal government in Ottawa."

"The company wouldn't do that without telling us," Joshua insisted.

"I'm telling you it's already happened."

Joshua sat in stony silence.

"Well," Schultz said looking at him.

"Well what? You said your piece. Maybe it will happen your way. So be it. I just hope we can maintain the peace we've enjoyed these years."

"That's why I'm appealing to men like you. We must organize and guarantee the peaceful transfer of power from the company to our motherland."

Joshua said nothing.

"You know what I'm talking about, Joshua. It's men like Louis Riel I'm talking about. Frenchmen, Catholics."

"Métis," Joshua shot back.

"This has nothing to do with race, Miller. I want that very clear. It has to do with having people in power who understand English and Protestant institutions like common law and parliament and the rights of Englishmen. We must secure those rights from those who would take them from us."

"There are other rights," Joshua said angrily. "There's the right to hunt the buffalo in the spring, to ride the prairies freely, to raise your crops along the river of your own land without some government surveyor telling you it is not yours and trying to make you pay taxes on your own land."

Schultz smiled. "I see you have not remained as aloof as I had been told. You are spouting Riel's arguments."

"Louis Riel is a Métis like my children," Joshua said with vehemence.

"Riel is a Frenchman, educated in Quebec."

"And I'm an Englishman educated in Nova Scotia," Craig chimed in, "but Louis Riel and I have something in common—mixed blood."

Scott sneered at Craig.

"Joshua," Schultz persisted, "we English have a common

cause. Our freedom is at stake. We cannot let these potential tyrants like Riel deceive us with false issues."

"Has not the government of Canada started a road from Lake Superior to Lake of the Woods? Have not Canadian government surveyors attempted to block out our townships in a manner that will distort our claims—if they ever accept our claims?"

"All of this is in anticipation of receiving sovereignty in these new lands."

"They have never spoken to us. We own the land. This is our land, Schultz."

In exasperation the doctor turned to Craig. "You've been educated Canadian. Can you make them see sense?"

"I'm hardly the one to do it, doctor." Craig offered no further information but continued, "The company will go. I suspect you are right about that."

Schultz smiled. "Finally a Miller who talks sense."

"Don't be too confident of that," Craig jested. "I started to say that if the company rule is at an end, we have two choices: a takeover by the Canadians or one by the Americans."

Scott bristled. "I am suspicious of every Irish Catholic at my back if it is the Americans. Fenians, every one of them, doing the pope's and the president's work."

Craig grimaced. He hadn't heard such claptrap since his treason trial in Toronto. He decided to ignore it, although he could see that the normally placid Sean Lavery was beginning to flush with anger.

Craig continued as calmly as he could. "Faced with a choice between a Canadian and an American takeover, I'll take Canada. I've been in the United States. In fact, I served in the Army of the Potomac and the Michigan Brigade. I've seen the way Americans have governed themselves. First, they governed themselves into a civil war, and now they have a military dictatorship over half their nation. No, despite its failings in what I regard as a gross national arrogance, I'll take the rule of her majesty's government in Ottawa."

"Spoken like a man," Schultz almost shouted. "If only more of your people would see it that way."

Joshua made a disgusted sound.

"But," Craig continued, "Canada must not be allowed to dictate the terms of the takeover."

"Christ, I knew there's be a catch. Now he sounds like Riel."

"No, I sound like Craig Miller."

Meg grew nervous as the voices rose in anger. She stood behind Craig's chair. He reached up and touched her hand to reassure her.

"Canada must consult the people of this territory," Craig went on, "about their needs for secure land tenure, their needs for guarantees of language and religion."

"If you agree to that now," Schultz said angrily, "then the French will have created another little Quebec out here on the prairies. Let the land fill with good Canadian stock and then we'll establish our rights."

"But that's precisely the point," Joshua said. "They'll be *your* rights, maybe even mine, damn it. I may dress Indian but I've got ancestors that go back to Puritan Boston. I've got Quakers and Family Compact members from Toronto in my family tree, but what about my wife? 'Girl Asleep in the Meadow Awakened by the Rainbow after the Storm,'" he repeated the name in Assiniboine. "And what about the rights of her father, Eagle Face, and her mother, Warrior Woman, and all the people of the Assiniboine? What about the Cree and the Piegan, and what about my children, my dusky–faced children? What rights have they in your white man's Manitoba? When I saw my son Craig for the first time it was on the shores of Lake Manitoba. The first time I held him I lifted him up to see this land of his. I told him then that it would be his land, not a red man's land, not a white man's land. I hoped then and I still hope that our peoples will merge into one blood, half white and half red. This will be a Métis land. I still dream of that for him, and for my grandson. By God, it is a better future for this Manitoba than the one you fight for, Schultz."

Scott was already on his feet. Anger contorted his face. "He's a goddamn savage, Schultz. Don't waste anymore time on him."

"Get out of my house," Craig shouted. "No one insults my father in this house."

Scott lunged toward Craig, but stopped in his tracks when the barrel of a small Derringer was jammed against his temple by Sean Lavery.

"Leave," Craig said softly.

Schultz stood up. He picked up his fur coat which had been drying near the fire.

"Sean. Craig. See to it that our guests get their horses out of the shelter and are on their way," Joshua said coldly.

Scott stormed out of the house into the night. Sean,

wrapped in the blanket he grabbed from the divan, went with him. Schultz stood in the doorway before he left and turned to Joshua.

"I am sorry you won't be with us in this, Miller. I had hoped that all the Canadians here would forge a united front."

"Your way is not my way, John," Joshua said.

"But I intend to have my way," Schultz said and he left followed by Craig.

"I have no doubt," Joshua said sadly. "Rainbow," he called out loudly and awakened James.

The Indian woman, who had remained silent throughout the whole encounter, looked up at him from where she sat.

"Your wise old father told me that the tribes have found buffalo on the North Saskatchewan last spring. I believe you and I will skip the Fort Garry hunt next spring and go with your father and the Assiniboine. Who knows, it might just take a whole summer. I think I'd like to be as far away from the Schultzs of this world as I can."

Rainbow rose and put her arms around him. She nodded to Doug and Beth.

"Time to go home it is," she said.

Craig had not liked the way the Irishman Scott had behaved. He was a bully, and Craig worried that he might try to sneak back and do some mischief. He and Sean spent two hours watching from the barn before they concluded no one was about in the ever-increasing storm. Sean had already fallen asleep fully dressed on the divan in the cabin's main room.

Craig shivered as he removed his woolen shirt and buckskin pants in the dark of the room.

He climbed naked under the buffalo robes piled high on the bed. He could feel the warm glow of Meg's body next to him. She had fallen asleep while nursing the baby. Now James lay between them fussing without crying.

We can all keep each other warm on a night like this, Craig thought. Meg moaned in her sleep. He reached over and touched her breast which lay exposed from the nursing. Normally her breasts were small. Craig had often teased her about them. But now they were swollen with her milk. She had become somewhat vain about them—showing off their girth to him at a moment's notice when no one else was about. It was only then that he realized how seriously she had taken the earlier teasing. He vowed he would remain forever silent about the topic once her nursing days were over. He smiled to himself in the dark. It was rather nice to have a wife with large breasts, even if it was a temporary condition. He leaned over farther and bent down to kiss her exposed nipple. He received a baby foot in the face. It was as if James was warning him off. He looked at his son, red–faced and angry even while dozing.

"You know, boy," he said to the baby. "I could easily get to dislike you."

"You could just as easily learn to do without a spouse," Meg said.

"You were awake all along," Craig said.

"Of course, with you around, a mother must be alert to protect her baby's food supply."

They lay quiet listening to the wind howl.

"Craig," Meg said turning on her side to face him, "I was frightened by those men tonight."

"So was I."

"There's trouble coming, isn't there?"

There was no point in trying to fool Michael Brant's daughter.

"Come spring," Craig said.

"What's going to happen?"

"I don't know. But if men like Schultz and Scott continue to push and the Canadian government is foolish enough to try to govern without consultation, there'll be bloodshed. The Métis are a conservative people. A man like Riel is far more radical than the other Métis. They are more like my father. They would rather go hunting than have a political battle. But they won't have the land taken from them. They'll fight Schultz, and the Canadian government if necessary."

"Will you?"

"No," he responded.

"I thought you might still have a grievance against my country."

"I've grown up a bit, Meg. I learned something from my flirtation with the Fenians. We must inject a little reality into things. What I said earlier tonight still goes. It'll be either the Americans or the Canadians. Dreams of an independent Assiniboia are as realistic as the Fenian conquest of Canada to free Ireland."

"I've one more question and I need a true answer," she said seriously.

194

He looked into her eyes. He was about to joke, but even in the darkness he could see the tears in her eyes.

"What?"

"You are through with them, aren't you? For good?"

"I swear it, Meg. I am through with them for good."

She sighed with relief. "I had to know. I could not face anything like Toronto again." Then she sat up. "What about Kevin and Sean?" she asked.

"They are still dyed–in–the–wool Irishmen, my love. I was a Fenian for the sake of Manitoba, and I will renounce them if renouncing them is in the best interests of Manitoba. With my friends it is different."

She relaxed again. "At least you're free of them. We can put that part of our lives behind us."

Craig lay quiet for some more moments watching her. It had not been that long since James's birth.

"Do you think you could find some place for our son on the other side of you?" he asked her.

"Why?"

"Because I'm not sure he should see what his father is about to do to his mother given the fact that he kicked me for just touching you."

Meg laughed. She scooped James up into her arms and deposited him on the other side of the bed. It was colder there, despite the blankets, and James complained for several minutes. When his parents paid no attention to him, however, he soon fell back to sleep.

Craig sank into a deep sleep almost as soon as they had finished making love. He always did. At first Meg had resented it. She was always wide awake and ready to talk. Tonight she had wanted to continue to talk about Canada. She fought back the tears that rose in her eyes. God, how she hated it in this wilderness. She longed for Halifax—for the comfort of her mother and the warmth and security of her father's great house at the foot of the Citadel.

"In time," she whispered. "In time. The Fenians will be forgotten or father will get him a pardon and then, my babies, we can go home."

XI

Red River and Toronto, Fall 1869

The winter had left the prairies reluctantly. The sun had
warmed the snow–covered rolling knolls, and tufts of grass had
pushed their way upward to meet the sun, but then from out of
the northwest the clouds gathered and raced across the lakes
and dropped more and more snow. When they disappeared,
spring would try again.

For once Joshua and Rainbow did not accompany the Métis
buffalo hunt. Instead they left Beth in Craig and Meg's care
and departed with Douglas for the winter camp of Eagle Face's
band. They planned to return before the snow came again in
the fall. Joshua wanted to take Beth with him, but Rainbow
had seen their daughter sneaking glances at Sean Lavery. He
was a strange man, she decided, but her mother had thought
the same of Joshua. If he was the one she wanted, then it was
best that she be in close proximity to him to allow nature to
function.

Craig was left with the task that he knew his father hated,
planting the wheat in the fields that bordered the river. The
locust plague of the summer before last, and the return of
those insects last summer, had discouraged many of the Métis
from planting anything. It was easier for them to ride out on
the prairies and shoot their winter supply of meat. But Craig
had insisted on obtaining seed from St. Paul. He plowed and
planted it as he had done many times as a youth. Sean had
insisted on helping Craig with the plowing even though it
nearly killed him. The stage in Dublin had not prepared him
for the deep sod of Manitoba. Craig tried to give him an easy
excuse to avoid the work, sending him once to Winnipeg to
buy supplies and once to Fort Garry. The trip to Winnipeg was
a disaster. Sean tried to make his purchases in Dr. Schultz's
store and was thrown out for insulting the proprietor. Despite

this and other minor mishaps, however, the crops were planted and then raised to their maturity and harvested before any troubles began.

In fall a message arrived for Joshua from the fort. It asked him to attend a meeting of landowners with Governor Mactavish of the Hudson's Bay Company. There was no sign of Joshua's return, so Craig decided to attend in his stead.

Fort Garry, with its stone walls and stone buildings, its courthouse, its company stores, was the heart of the Red River settlement. It stood at the junction of the Red River and the Assiniboine. The square fort was crowded with landholders from all the settlements—white, Métis, English–speaking and French–speaking. But conspicuous by their absence were any members of the Canadian party of John Christian Schultz.

Mactavish, the governor of Rupert's Land, held his commission from the Hudson's Bay Company. There was not, however, a man present who was unaware that the company had sold its rights to the Canadian Confederation. Mactavish's authority, therefore, was badly weakened.

But it was not Mactavish who was destined to lead the discussion. Before the meeting could begin there was an enormous commotion at the front gate of the fort. Cheers were shouted and rifles fired into the air. A young man dressed in European clothing came riding into the fort accompanied by an armed force of Métis, most of them French.

"Riel, Riel," they cheered.

Craig had met Louis David Riel before. In some ways their careers had been parallel. Riel was born across the Red River in St. Boniface. He had been identified as a good student and had been sent east to be educated. He studied at the College of Montreal, hoping to become a priest, but had rejected that calling and returned to the home of his father on the Red River.

Craig and he had joked about the similarities between their careers. Craig liked the Frenchman immensely. His devotion to the Métis people was genuine, although Craig had a far better claim to Métis blood than Riel. Riel's mother was completely white and his father was French Canadian with a small infusion of Indian blood. But Riel was determined to protect the interests of the half–breeds of Manitoba. In this, Craig was completely in agreement with him.

Mactavish could not compete with Riel, nor did he attempt to. The meeting belonged to the Métis.

"Louis, what is happening?" someone called out.

"We've been putting a stop to the sale of our rights and of ourselves like so many chattels," Riel shouted.

The crowd cheered.

"All these months, my friends," he said swiftly in French, "all these months we've heard rumors the Canadians are coming. Schultz and his cronies have begged their friends in Toronto and Ottawa to come here and make themselves our masters. We heard about the road to the Lake of the Woods. Then this summer surveyors from Canada came and suddenly we found our land title in question. Well, my friends, we are ending all that. In the past two weeks we have stopped the survey. Any Canadian surveyor who enters our land does so at his own risk."

Some Métis fired buffalo guns into the air while others cheered.

Riel held up his hand for quiet.

"We have organized ourselves into a *comité national des métis*—a group headed by my associate, Mr. Bruce. We want all of you—English and French, Métis and whites, yes even our own Canadian countrymen—we want you all to know our aims. We enjoyed good times under the Hudson's Bay Company. We would have continued peacefully under their rule but they sold us out. They have forfeited our obedience."

"Throw them out with the Canadians," someone shouted.

"No, my friends," Riel said, "we must not be outlaws. We must not reject Canada but neither must we be chattel to be bought and sold. Canada may some day, and some day soon, govern us, but not until they meet with us as equals and listen to our demands."

Again there was a roar of approval.

Craig watched Riel as he spoke. His oratory was flamboyant but so was his audience. Some were dressed in buffalo robes and others in European suits with vests and gold watch chains stretched across their bellies. Some had close-cropped hair, including those in Indian garb, while others had long, braided hair, even some in European dress. But Riel was the center of attention. He seemed to mesmerize all of them. They followed every word and reacted to each and every demand that he made. In addition Craig observed more and more men entering Fort Garry. Many he knew to be French-speaking Métis, supporters of the orator. He looked for Sean. He wondered what his friend thought about the number of armed men at strategic points. But Sean seemed to have disappeared. Then he saw him across the parade ground talking to W. B. O'Donoghue, a man Sean already identified to him as the ringleader of the Fenian movement at Fort Garry. Craig was distressed for the first time. He was finished with the Irish, yet it seemed they were not finished with him. He liked what Riel was saying, but he would like it less if it received Fenian support.

"I announce to you, therefore," Riel continued, "that we cannot allow the Hudson's Bay Company to control our lives any longer. We are seizing this place in the name of the Métis people. It is with us that Canada must now negotiate." He repeated this last remark in English.

There was a growing roar from the crowd. First the French speakers raised their voices in agreement and then there was a mixed chorus among the English, some as enthusiastic as the French, others voicing complaints.

Riel continued in English. "We are all brothers, my friends. We will all share the same fate if we do not confront Canada with our strength. I invite the English of the settlement to select delegates to meet with our *comité*. We will meet in the courthouse. As brothers we will deal with our future."

This last gesture sat well with the English speakers and soon they too were roaring their approval.

"And remember," he shouted over the crowd, "we accept no officials from Canada, no governor, no government until Ottawa deals with our demands."

The thunder of buffalo guns was now deafening. Riel had all the listeners with him now.

That very night Joshua Miller returned. He arrived with two Red River carts loaded with pemmican, one driven by his wife and the second driven by his son. Behind him rode a small band of heavily blanketed Indians.

Craig searched their faces until he recognized his ancient grandmother. He rushed toward her. She opened her blanket and received him into her arms. He turned to Rainbow and asked for Eagle Face.

Rainbow looked away. Then he looked at Warrior Woman's hands. She had recently lost two fingers. Craig knew instantly that his grandfather, Eagle Face, was dead. He looked to his father who rode Eagle Face's favorite stallion for an explanation.

"He insisted on one more buffalo hunt. He should not have ridden. He was too weak in the saddle. We found a small herd. We rode into them and stampeded them. But the old fellow just wasn't up to it. He slipped from the saddle under the hooves of the beasts and was trampled."

Joshua dismounted and called to Douglas to lead the horses and carts to the barn.

"If you ask me," Joshua said more quietly, "I think he did it on purpose. It was the way of a warrior. I don't think he could have survived another winter. He knew it and he wanted to die as he had lived, not of starvation and decrepitude."

"Why did you let grandmother chop off her fingers?"

"Might as well try to stop her from breathing. It's the way of her people. A squaw loses her man, she cuts off a finger or two. It would dishonor his memory not to do it. It was all I could do to keep your mother from cutting off one of hers. I still won't let her handle a knife. Your grandmother will be wintering with us."

"And all the others too?" Craig said nervously thinking of how fast the hard work of the summer could be consumed by half a tribe.

"No," Joshua laughed. "They are just visiting. They came as an escort but I know they're also just damn nosy to see where I live."

"You've heard what is going on here?"

"Couldn't miss it. As I came in from the open prairies I kept bumping into folks returning home from the meeting. I think Riel did the right thing."

Sean came out of the house by himself to meet Joshua. Rainbow looked at the Irishman, then at Craig. She spoke to him rapidly in Assiniboine.

"Has your friend spoken for your sister?" she asked him.

It was the first that Craig had heard of Rainbow's plot. He shook his head.

"Ach," she said, "I must myself do it."

She walked to her wagon, which Douglas had not yet returned to the barn. She pulled out a rawhide sack. It was bloodstained.

Craig laughed when Rainbow took Sean by the arm and started to lead him toward Meg's kitchen. His friend was about to be treated to an Assiniboine gourmet meal, probably roast buffalo tongue. The meal, of course, would be cooked by Beth and supervised by Rainbow. She called to her mother to accompany her. She was sure she could pull this off by herself but there was no harm in having the wisdom of Warrior Woman brought to bear on the problem as well.

Craig and Joshua were left alone again. Doug received the task of showing the curious Assiniboine about the farm.

"What should we expect next?" Craig asked his father.

"Oh, I think we will all hear from Dr. John Christian Schultz before long."

"No doubt," Craig said smiling, "but there's another element, Father. Sean. He has told me all along that there is a Fenian interest in all of this. O'Donoghue is in thick with Riel. If Louis is sincere about wanting negotiations with Canada, why would he work with O'Donoghue? The Fenians want no good for Canada."

"Sometimes you take the hand that is offered you," Joshua suggested.

"Provided you don't turn your back."

"You really are through with them, Craig, aren't you?"

"Meg has made me see the error of my ways. They used me to their own ends. There were better ways to help my people. The way Louis Riel has chosen. To negotiate with the Canadians is the better way. I worry now that they'll use him too if he's not careful."

Kevin snorted and woke himself up. The room was dark, but he knew instantly where he was. The scent of jasmine surrounded him. His rough beard rested against her. His lips made almost involuntary kisses into the softness of her breasts. She stirred, contented in her sleep. Her hand touched his face, tracing the line of his eyebrow with her thumb. Her other hand reached lower. She sighed contentedly when she felt his hardness.

He knew she did not love him. That ought to have bothered him, he knew, but it did not. It was all right so long as she let him lie with her, their legs intertwined, his groin pressed all night against her, his hands free to touch her anywhere, his mouth close to her breasts, neck, and face. If he could breathe her scent with every breath, then she did not have to love him. He abandoned himself into the soothing, floating comfort of her presence. He needed nothing more than to spend these hours in her arms.

He drifted off to sleep again. She shifted her body, turning her back to him. He was aware of it through his sleep. He snuggled up against her backside. He worked his arms around her and his fingers rested on her breasts.

The door of the room was opened. Alex Miller stood in the doorway. He still wore his greatcoat over his militia uniform.

"Mother, dear," he said loudly while raising the oil lamp he held in his hands above his head to get a better view of her bed.

Allison awoke with a start. She sat up frightened and pulled the covers up to hide her naked chest and to prevent her son from seeing her lover.

But Alex already knew that O'Connor was back in Toronto. He also knew that as soon as Kevin returned to town he would seek out the comfort of Allison Miller. Alex could have pretended not to see the bulge under the blanket in the darkness behind his mother, but he had no time for niceties.

"Mother, I do hope you're taking precautions to avoid giving me a cute but unwanted Irish half-brother. He'd have no share in my father's estate, you know."

"That's no way to speak to your mother."

He smirked at her. "Neither is that any way for a mother to behave," he responded pointing in Kevin's direction. "It is O'Connor, isn't it?"

Kevin sat up in the bed.

"I'm relieved," Alex said. "It's always good to see a familiar face in mama's bed."

"What is it, Miller?" Kevin finally spoke. "Do you want to speak to your mother in private?"

"I have nothing more to say to my mother," Alex said. "It's you I want to talk to. I just made an educated guess that this would be where you might be found. After all, I heard you were in Toronto."

"Alex, damn it. Stop it. You sound more and more like your father," Allison shouted.

"I find it easier to sympathize with him since his passing. Anyway, you insisted that I always be at his side. One would have to be a dolt not to pick up his ways."

"What do you want to speak to me about?" Kevin asked as he placed his hand on Allison's bare shoulder in attempt to calm her anger.

"We need your assistance again. Your friends at the Red River are flirting with revolution."

Kevin placed his feet on the floor and rose turning his back to Alex. He put on his pants. "And I expect you want me to go and undermine any Fenian effort to stir up the Métis."

"Quite the contrary," Alex said. "I want you to go back there and cause as much trouble as you can."

Kevin turned and looked at him in surprise. "Why?"

"This time the Fenian cause and the Canadian cause are one. As much chaos and commotion as possible. The Fenians hope rebellion will lead to American intervention, which is not likely to occur."

"Some powerful folk in Washington have employed the brotherhood to raise a fuss. I don't think their hopes were entirely unfounded," Kevin said as he pulled on his pants.

"The Irish are dreamers, and the Fenians are Irish. They fall for those dreams again and again. Those same Americans promised before Ridgeway that they would look the other way. Then, lo and behold, there was *The Michigan* in the river and General George Meade on the shore arresting all violators of American neutrality."

Kevin walked over to where Alex stood in the doorway. Miller backed away out into the hallway. Allison rose from bed and pulled on her dressing gown.

"Why should I do what you want me to do?"

"Because if you don't, I just might tell the leaders in your brotherhood that you told me about every single plan for the invasion of Canada and that you, more than any other single person, thwarted the Fenian attack."

Kevin grabbed Alex's collar and pulled his face up next to his own. "I told you nothing, you little piece of shit."

Alex was shaken. He reached his hand into his pocket for his knife with the spring blade but Kevin shoved Alex away from him. Allison stifled a scream and Kevin turned to see her standing in the doorway.

"Oh Christ," he said in disgust, "I don't know why I keep coming back here," he said to Allison. "You don't love me. You and that . . . that . . ."

"He means me, Mother," Alex said regaining his composure.

"You use me," Kevin shouted at Allison.

"You're well paid," Allison said.

He stared at her in confusion. "I've never taken money from you," he protested.

"You've had other things from me. You would not deny that I've pleased you."

"You don't love me!"

"I don't remember either of us ever requiring love. You always seemed quite content to satisfy your lust." She approached Kevin and placed her arms about his neck and played with the hair at the back of his neck. As she did she signaled to Alex with her hand. The young man obeyed her and closed the door as he left.

"You're a bitch," Kevin said just before she kissed him on the mouth. She pulled him back down into the bed.

"I want to go home," he said.

"No, you don't." She started to work on the buttons of his pants.

"Why should I go to the Red River?"

"Because I want you to."

"Why should I do anything more for you?"

"Because of what I do for you," she responded.

"There are other women," he lied.

"Not like me. Not who will do what I do." She teased first his eyelids then his lips with the tip of her tongue.

Then he pulled away from her. "But why?" he asked. "What good will it do the Canadians to have a revolt at Fort Garry?"

"I don't know for sure," Allison said frustrated by his lack of response. "Maybe a revolt will force them to send British troops in."

"That would be expensive. The new Dominion government will be in no position to afford it."

"You forget the stakes that men like my husband, and now Alex, are playing for. We are talking about control of an empire larger even than the United States. There are land grants and railroads and canals. All those things at stake. Canada will find the money to suppress a rebellion." She reached over and grabbed him. He gasped.

"Now let's go back to where we were before that atrociously rude child interrupted us."

Kevin groaned as he gave in to her touch. He pulled her roughly onto his chest. "You're still a bitch," he said hoarsely into her ear. "I'll do it just like I always do because I can't live without this." He grabbed her roughly. "But I warn you I've got friends in the west. If anything happens to them I'll put the blame where it belongs. I'll cut off your little boy's balls and return them to you as a trophy."

Alex waited at the door until he heard the noise of their lovemaking. Then he smiled. O'Connor would do her bidding again. Rebellion in the west not only served his ambitions but would help him once and forever to put to rest the challenge to him presented by Joshua and Craig Miller.

The fire in the hearth roared as a precious log was thrown onto it. The fiddler struck up a tune from French Canada. He tossed his head from side to side with the rhythm of the song. His braids waved almost at counterpoint to the beat of his moccasined foot. He saw nothing incongruous in a French–speaking three–quarter Cree playing a tune he'd learned from his half–Cree, half–French father from Quebec. His father in turn had learned it as a lad, a tune whose origins could be traced to the bagpipe–playing inhabitants of the shores of Brittany.

The front door of Joshua Miller's house flew open, allowing wind and drifting snow to pour into the main room. Three fur–clad men entered the room.

Joshua yelled a greeting to them over the music. He stood next to the fire with two other men. In the corner beneath the side window a small group of Assiniboine sat on the floor wrapped in Indian blankets playing bones. They drank heavily from a small cask they passed to each other and laughed loudly or moaned with each cast of the bones from a small wooden bowl.

Rainbow stood near the hearth. Beside her was James's cradle. She rocked it with her foot while she tended an antelope carcass on the spit. But she looked frequently over toward the plain wooden stairs that led to the second floor. She turned to her mother, Warrior Woman, and handed her the basting spoon. She crossed over to the stairs and disappeared rapidly up them.

Warrior Woman grinned when she took the spoon. She tasted the basting sauce with it, she wrinkled up her nose and spat it out into the crackling fire. She searched the shelf above the stove. She frowned and looked about for Joshua. The master of the house laughed at a joke told by one of his comrades but his little group broke up when the white men's wives emerged together from the backroom where they had gone to deposit coats. He saw his mother–in–law gesture to him. He started to walk to her but she gestured again. He looked behind him and saw that she wanted a keg of blackberry brandy. It was his own mother's cure-all and he knew that Warrior Woman was particularly fond of the taste and even fonder of its effect. He was about to deny her request when the door flew open again and a grey–haired man dressed in furs stepped inside. Joshua rushed to greet him.

"Monsieur Abbé," he called, "mighty glad you could make it."

The priest held his hand out for Joshua to kiss, and seemed flustered when Miller grabbed it with both hands and shook vigorously.

"Normally my daughter would have had a good Protestant ceremony, but being that Lavery is one of yours, I was glad that you would do the honors."

The Abbé nodded at Joshua and spoke in a heavily accented English.

"Monsieur Lavery is of course marrying a woman who is not of the church. Thus, no ceremony could take place within the confines of God's house. Even so, it is most unusual."

"Neither you nor the Bishop of Red River nor the Pope in Rome could have stopped it. If you hadn't agreed, then these two," he pointed to Warrior Woman, forgetting that Rainbow had retreated up the stairs, "these two would have married her Indian–style. I wanted my daughter to have a Christian wedding."

He glanced over at his mother–in–law. She had raised a brandy keg to her face and placed its opening on her mouth. He could not hear the gurgle but he could see from the motion of her throat that she was draining it.

"Well, too late now," he mumbled.

"You are wrong," Monsieur Abbé continued to misunderstand, "it is never too late for a Christian wedding. I am surprised to hear you think it too late. If that scoundrel Lavery has lied to me . . ." he paused trying to recall if his conversation with Sean had been under the seal of confession. "It was right of you," he continued, "it was very right of you to desire for your daughter the blessings of a Christian marriage that you yourself have enjoyed."

"Me and Rainbow?" Joshua looked at the priest in surprise. "Hell, no. We got hitched Indian–style. I bought her for a string of the best Piegan ponies her father ever saw, including one fine stallion. Old Eagle Face rode that horse until it couldn't walk any more, then he shot it and buried it. Wouldn't let anybody eat that black stallion. It was quite a horse. Saved my life once, and my mother's."

The Abbé stared at him in shock. "The bride has been

baptized, hasn't she?" he said with a growing look of horror on his face.

"My Beth?" Joshua became silent and thoughtful. "Sure, she was," he lied. "The first preacher we met did it. As soon as we got back to the fort from the buffalo hunt. Her mother had her out on the prairies. I helped on that one. That girl is very precious to me."

Joshua was glad of his lie about the preacher as soon as he saw the relief on Monsieur Abbé's face. For the life of him, he could not remember if his Beth had been baptized or not. Well, if the lie made the Abbé feel better, then no harm was done.

Rainbow returned from upstairs. She frowned when she saw her mother sitting on the floor next to the hearth. When she passed Joshua, she complained the meat would be overdone, even burned on one side, because he had failed to keep an eye on his jug.

Joshua was offended. Why did she never find fault with her mother's drinking instead of his failure to hide the drink from her successfully.

Again and again the door swung open as more guests arrived. They represented every group in the colony, Selkirk Scots, Americans, French and English Métis; even some of the moderate Canadian supporters from the village of Winnipeg.

The noise level in the house rose. The fiddler was soon joined by a group of Frenchmen who broke into song. Several others started to dance a jig. The English stood more sedately in the corners and watched the dancers with amusement. Not so the Indians. As soon as the dancing began, several of them rose to their feet and staggered forward in among the dancers. One warrior grabbed a French buffalo hunter in his arms in a bear hug and swung him around. The Frenchman howled with laughter. Soon all the Indians found partners. Even the Abbé took a swig from the jug that was being passed around the room.

Joshua let loose with an Indian war cry. The fiddler stopped as did most of the dancers. One very drunk couple tripped and went crashing into the table and chairs that had been pushed into the corner of the room for the occasion. The audience cheered this graceless end to the frontier ballet and then quieted down.

"My friends," Joshua called out, "I know not everyone is here yet. The weather is probably holding them up. Even so, I get the feeling that we better begin this show or there won't be a sober soul left to witness it, except the Abbé, and we can't be too sure of him."

The crowd roared with laughter but the butt of Joshua's joke sniffed the air as if smelling something offensive.

"So let's begin."

The fiddler took his cue from Joshua and began to play the only march he knew—from Chopin's Second Sonata. The door opened upstairs. First down the stairs was Kevin O'Connor, who had just returned to the colony. He was followed by Craig Miller. Both were dressed in their best clothing. They were followed by Sean Lavery in a black suit. His hair had been allowed to grow long and he had tied it in a ponytail in the back. But the most dramatic aspect of the groom's attire was the black cape with the red silk lining. Somehow or other he had managed to salvage a replacement for the long gone and sorely missed cape of his earlier days.

The three men walked solemnly to the strains of Chopin to where the Abbé stood.

Again a door opened and closed upstairs. This time little Douglas and Meg Miller descended the stairs. She was dressed in a dark green gown she had last worn to the lieutenant governor's reception in Halifax. Her mother had shipped a trunk containing her clothing and some of Willy's best chinaware all the way to Red River. Meg was followed by Beth Miller. She wore a white lace gown which Meg had made for her. She had worked on it with scissors and needle and thread for several weeks to get it right.

Joshua beamed at his daughter when she reached the bottom step. Even Rainbow smiled. She would have preferred that Beth wear the same doeskin jerkin that she had worn so many years ago when she took Joshua into her teepee. She had folded it and saved it. But the white ways were different, and her daughter, after all, was half white. It had been good enough to get her a husband. Besides the girl looked beautiful in the white gown. It highlighted her brown skin.

Joshua and Beth walked over to the Abbé. He took Lavery's hand and joined it to Beth's. At that point, as far as Rainbow was concerned, the youngsters were married. The Indians far gone into whiskey shouted approval, and one made a vulgar gesture with his hand. Warrior Woman shouted to the spirit of Eagle Face to announce the occasion.

The Abbé stared them into silence. He began to recite

prayers in Latin. He made the sign of the cross over the couple. Beth's Assiniboine relatives murmured their approval, the white medicine man was making powerful magic. The girl would give birth to mighty sons.

Then the Abbé switched to his accented English and led the young couple in making their vows. He turned to Craig and asked him to produce the ring. Craig looked surprised and looked to his fellow best man. Kevin looked deeply perplexed.

"Oh no," Sean said with exaggerated frustration. "You have one task to worry about and you can't perform it. Look what I have to face. I must take on the ordeal of membership in this crazy family. I am afraid of our first fight. I may end up totally bald—win or lose."

Even Beth started to laugh.

"Here," Joshua said from his place next to Rainbow. "I have the solution." He opened his shirt and reached behind his neck. He removed an ancient gold locket. It was held around his neck by a string of rawhide. The old gold chain had broken once too often years ago and he had had no chance to replace it.

"This has been in my family for generations. It is time it passed on to the next." He looked at Craig. "Do you mind, son?" he asked.

Craig merely smiled and motioned his father to go ahead.

Joshua placed the locket around Beth's neck.

"It's not a ring," the Abbé complained.

"Of course it is," Sean insisted. "It is a neck ring. Where in your little black book does it say it must be a ring for the finger?" He reached over and tried to grab the prayer book from the priest.

The Abbé reacted sharply and pushed Sean back into place.

"Say after me, 'With this ring I thee wed and promise unto thee my troth.'"

Craig could see the amused look in Sean's eye when he heard the word. Craig nudged his friend in the side. "Repeat it," he warned.

Lavery did as he was told. For once in his life he resisted an overwhelming temptation and swallowed a quip.

"I pronounce you man and wife," the Abbé said. Then he repeated his phrase in French.

Everyone cheered including the Indians. Then they started a rhymic clapping. Sean reached over and kissed Beth on the lips. She blushed as, again, the crowd cheered.

The fiddler, overjoyed to leave Chopin behind, began a happy tune. Sean turned to his audience and swirled his cape in a flash of scarlet. Then he scooped Beth in his arms and lifted her up, kissing her passionately on the lips.

This time the assemblage roared. Sean, who could never resist an audience, allowed Beth's feet to touch the floor once again, then made a sweeping bow of acknowledgment. Everyone laughed, even the bride.

Joshua stood on a chair. "Break out more jugs," he called to Rainbow and Warrior Woman. Soon almost everyone in the room had a mug of whiskey or blackberry brandy.

"A toast," Joshua shouted signaling to the fiddler to be quiet. "To my daughter Elizabeth and her new husband. She is my pride and my beauty. He had better treat her well." He repeated his words in French and Assiniboine. After this last, Warrior Woman let out a hair-raising war cry, staring at Sean.

"Only one person by her absence mars this occasion," Joshua continued. "I truly wish Beth's namesake, my mother, were present to see her granddaughter married, but I know she blesses what occurs here. It would have been she who would have suggested that Beth wear the old Nowell family locket. My daughter, wear it well. And when the appropriate time comes—and you will know when that time is at hand—pass it on to the next generation. I wish you beauty and truth, my child. May you never know anything else."

Again the fiddler took up the tune and all downed the contents of their mugs.

Sean led Beth to the middle of the floor and started to dance.

Everyone began to clap in time to the music.

No one heard the horses arriving. A great roar arose from the guests when Louis Riel, accompanied by O'Donoghue, the Fenian leader, entered the house.

"My friends," he called out holding his hands in the air, "this is an occasion I could not miss. I am only sorry I am late for the ceremony."

"But not for the celebration, Louis," Joshua responded, and shoved a jug of whiskey into Riel's hand.

The Métis merely held it in his hands. Riel walked over to the fire to admire Rainbow's antelope. As he did, he signaled Joshua to walk with him.

"Louis?" Joshua said quizzically.

"I didn't want to upset your guests, my friend, but I am late for good reason. We have trouble."

"What kind?"

"That bastard Schultz, he has convinced many of the Canadians to join him. He has barricaded himself and friends in his storehouse in Winnipeg. He says he is guarding the property of the government of Canada stored with him.

Joshua started to laugh.

Now it was Riel's turn to look questioningly at Joshua. "You're amused?"

"Aren't you? What a bold stroke. He barricades himself. So what? Whom does he threaten?"

The two men were joined by O'Donoghue, who was followed by Kevin O'Connor and Craig Miller.

"Let him stay barricaded," Joshua continued to laugh.

"But it's a provocation," Kevin insisted after he had been briefed. "They could claim to be under siege and demand British troops to relieve them."

"Indeed they could, and those claims would be accurate if we lay siege to them."

"No siege," Kevin responded, "just blast them out."

"Ach!" Joshua said in disgust. "The Irish answer to every problem. Violence."

"Father Miller," Sean said as he joined the group, "do I hear you casting aspersions on my race?"

"Don't you 'Father Miller' me," Joshua said with considerable vehemence. "I'm not your bloody father. I've already got three children. I'm not taking on any more."

Sean pretended to be offended. Actually he liked Joshua Miller very much. "You mean I am an orphan again, so soon after I had thought at last I had discovered a family?"

Joshua laughed. "God help us. We have let a crazy man into the family."

"What do you plan to do about Schultz, Louis?" Craig asked.

"O'Connor is right," Riel said. "I just can't allow this challenge to my authority to go unanswered."

"For Christ's sake, why not?" Joshua demanded. "Let crazy Schultz sit in Winnipeg for the whole bloody winter. The colony would be better off not having him to deal with. I'd love to have a few others lock themselves up permanently."

"No, Joshua," Riel said, "no response will encourage them to move on to more dangerous escapades. I have no choice but to respond. I'm heading to Winnipeg just as soon as these festivities are over."

Lavery smiled. "I was hoping to keep the party going for the rest of the week."

O'Connor started to laugh. "What's the matter, Sean? Are you shy about the first night?"

Joshua looked uncomfortable. Craig nudged Kevin.

But Sean was oblivious to his new father–in–law's embarrassment.

"No, not at all," he responded. "We're going to follow an old Irish custom and abstain on the first night. We intend to kneel by the bed all night and pray, offering up our celibacy to the Virgin."

Joshua's eyes grew wider and wider as Sean spoke.

"Father," Craig finally interrupted, "Sean is teasing. They will do nothing of the kind."

Joshua looked away with feigned indifference. "What do I care what they do now? They are married. It is none of my business."

"Rainbow," he called to his wife, "I shot the damn antelope. The least you could do is have it ready for me to eat before spring sets in."

The snow was piled deep against the walls of John Christian Schultz's storehouse. Inside, the adult males of the Canadian party, most of whom were from the English village of Winnipeg, nervously awaited word from their leader. They had joined Schultz to protect the Canadian government's stores, which had been sent ahead to Schultz for his keeping. Next summer, these goods would be essential for the advance of the road–building and surveying. To the Canadians, these foodstuffs and supplies were like a link to home. They were the guarantee that the mother country, the new Dominion of Canada, would extend her authority into this wilderness.

Schultz reentered the storeroom from the office which he had made into headquarters ever since they had received an anonymous tip that Riel and his wild men were about to seize the goods in Schultz's store just as they had seized the entire stock of the Hudson's Bay Company earlier.

Damn it, he wished the government in Ottawa would stop fooling around. If it wasn't for him, Canada would have lost the northwest to the savages. If they had, the Americans and their Fenian henchmen wouldn't be far behind. John A. Macdonald, the prime minister, had every excuse to act, to send troops. The governor of the territory had been blocked from entering his own colony. He now sat helpless in St. Paul, Minnesota, and, damn it, if that didn't sum it all up, a Canadian governor had to go through the United States to come from Canada to Canada's northwest. If Ottawa did not lay claim immediately and build roads—and, even more important, build railroads—all would be lost. The savages and their American supporters were in open rebellion. The prime minister had to act.

He went to the barred window of his storehouse. The young sentry, Thomas Scott, stepped aside to let him look out.

"See anything?" he asked Scott.

"They're out there," Scott said.

Schultz peered into the darkness. He was more convinced than ever that he had done the right thing. No sooner had he barricaded himself than Riel and his men arrived. Well, he had not been a fool. The Canadian stores were safe. He resented deeply the messages he had received from Colonel Dennis of the British army and his surveying party. He was even more convinced now of his earlier feeling—that the Canadians must take care of themselves. They were too dependent on the British and the British army. The British had had too much their own way. They grew soft. Canada needed her own army with her own officers, not weaklings like Dennis. Imagine an officer in the British army telling him to disband his men. That would be handing Canada's property to the savages. Well he did not intend to obey.

"What's that?" Schultz said pointing to a group of men bearing torches and dragging something bulky into position before the oak doors of the storehouse.

Scott shoved his head next to Schultz's and stared. "That is a field piece," he whispered. Then he shouted, "The bloody savages have got themselves a cannon."

Schultz looked nervously about the room. His supporters were clearly thunderstruck by Scott's announcement. They would panic if he did not remain calm and exercise his rightful role as their leader.

"Savages with a cannon," he laughed. "They'll be able to use it just about as effectively as they used a telegraph key."

There were some halfhearted chuckles among his men. Then they all grew silent.

"Schultz!" He heard his name called out. He recognized Riel's voice instantly.

"What is it?" the doctor responded.

"I demand you surrender."

"By whose authority?"

"There is no legitimate government here, Schultz. The Hudson's Bay Company has abandoned its responsibility and Canada has not yet assumed its authority. We are left without authority. When that occurs, the people themselves have to pick up the reins of government. That is what we are doing here. You, sir, are resisting the will of the people. Your lives are forfeit if you continue to do it."

"We've committed no crimes and we've violated no law. This is a peaceful assemblage in this warehouse. We're protecting the property of the government of Canada, the legitimate government of this colony."

"Not yet, it's not. For now, we are in charge." Although he had not said so everyone present in Schultz's storehouse knew that Riel's next step would be to establish a provisional government.

"You will attack us?" Scott called out.

"In exactly fifteen minutes, unless you come out with your hands in the air."

"You would not dare, sir."

"Try me."

Scott looked over at the nervous John Schultz. "You're not going to give in, are you?"

Schultz waved him quiet with impatience. "It might not be so bad at that. If Riel seizes this property, he has committed a crime against the government. Ottawa will be forced to bring in troops. Maybe we should let him take us."

"Not me. No half–breed is putting his hands on me."

"Gentlemen," Schultz called out ignoring Scott, "we are called on to surrender. I know some of you would prefer to resist, and die here fighting for Canada, but there would be little profit and much loss for Canada if we opted for that course."

"You telling us to give up, doctor?" someone called out.

Schultz stared long and hard at the young man. "Never. What I am suggesting is that we accept this temporary setback so that we may live to fight another day."

"But I thought it was important to keep the Métis from getting their bloody hands on the stores," another Canadian shouted.

"It was. It still is. It is damned important," Scott joined in the chorus of shouts.

Schultz raised his hand in the air for silence. The men obeyed him.

"Gentlemen, we have done our duty. We have tried to protect the property of our country, but the rebels—and make no mistake about it, Riel has committed treason by rebelling against his queen—the rebels have surrounded us. They can blast us right out of this building. They can probably kill every one of us without doing any harm to themselves."

"You said they didn't know how to use those guns," Scott said.

"They don't. But those bastard Papists, the Fenians among them, they probably do know how to use them. Most of them were in the Yank army."

This last remark swayed the group. Very few now called out for resistance.

"But don't despair, boys. We may have achieved more than we could hope. Let Riel steal the stuff from Canada," he said waving his hand at the crates of supplies. "The prime minister will have no choice but to declare him a rebel. Then he'll have to call in the army and put down the rebellion."

"Let's surrender then."

"The fifteen minutes are almost up."

There was a quick movement toward the front door.

XII

Red River, December 1869—January 1870

Meg sat before the fire in her cabin. She had opened the front of her dress to give James access to his dinner. She loved this moment of the day. All the chores were over. The evening meal was cooked and eaten. The dishes were washed and put away. Craig had strolled over to visit his father's house and smoke a pipe with him and Sean. Meg was all alone with the baby. The pleasure her son's hungry mouth brought to her nipple spread throughout her entire body. She relished the sense of complete relaxation that came over her. All she was conscious of was the crackling of the fire and the soft, slurping sound the baby made. Sometimes she almost fell off to sleep sitting in the comfort of the buffalo robes which covered the hard frame of the rocking chair her father–in–law, Joshua, had built for her.

Even in this moment of complete relaxation, however, the anger would not leave her. Tears welled in her eyes and ran down her cheeks. Nothing was right anymore. Nothing had worked out as she planned it. The winters were endless in this wilderness. Night seemed to last forever. The sun seemed to struggle daily just to raise its head over the horizon, and then, as if the effort had exhausted it, it fell down again in the midafternoon and brought on darkness once again by its failure.

She should never have came to Rupert's Land. She should have prevented Craig from fleeing here. He could have gone to New England or New York, where he would have been hailed a hero and escaped from British tyranny. He could have followed the example of her own father and gone into American exile, but no, he had to return to this wilderness.

Even his family seemed alien to her. Joshua, her father–in–law, was good to her. She had come first to respect him and then to love him for his kindness, but Craig's mother she did not love. The woman's interference and her demands on Meg had been unbearable. True, she had helped Meg through James's birth, but at that time Meg would have preferred the soft, caring touch of her own mother, Willy Mackay Brant. Rainbow of the Assiniboine was uncaring and crude. True, she was Craig's mother, but that changed Meg's opinion for her not one whit. She longed for her own mother and for the smell of the sea air as it blew inland from the Atlantic stirring up the whitecaps in Halifax harbor.

Now the tears flowed freely, tears of loneliness mixed with tears of frustration. She could not talk to Craig. How could she tell him that she hated his beloved Manitoba, or, even worse, that she hated his own mother? She hated the silence. She wanted her books, her bedroom, her own parents.

She felt a cold draft as the outside air came rushing into the cabin.

"Craig?" she called out.

There was no answer.

She turned her head and Kevin O'Connor was staring at her. She blushed and immediately began to button the front of her dress. James cried out in protest at this interruption of his supper, but he had almost filled his belly. Meg put him in his cradle, and after a brief wail, he grew silent, barely able to keep his eyes open.

"You surprised me," Meg said. She sat forward in her chair keeping her back toward O'Connor. He slowly stepped further into the room, enjoying every moment of Meg's frantic effort to hide her exposed breasts from him.

Finally she called out to him in exasperation, "Kevin O'Connor, you are no gentleman."

"Right you are." He grinned. "But then I never claimed the distinction for myself, so don't try putting burdens on me because of it."

He still moved forward facing her.

"Kevin," she called out. "Please don't embarrass me any more than you already have."

Kevin shrugged and moved back toward the door. "Maybe I should start all over again," he jested. He swung open the door and stepped back out into the cold night. Then he rapped his bare knuckles on the wooden door post. Meg quickly finished her buttoning. Again Kevin knocked. He called out in falsetto, "Come in, handsome stranger. I'm sitting here with my bosom exposed to all comers." He opened the door. "Thank you, ma'am," he said lowering his voice to deeper than normal, "I'm gentleman Kevin O'Connor, and I sure do appreciate exposed bosoms."

Meg was mortified by his comments. "You wouldn't speak to me that way if Craig were here."

"Oh, come on, Meg. You haven't always been so standoffish with me. Don't you remember when we first met that night on the Halifax docks?"

"You tried to take advantage of me then too."

"You're right, I did. And I almost succeeded. It was only my own sense of self–denial that stopped me. I sometimes wonder what would have happened if I had succeeded. Maybe neither of us would be stuck in this godforsaken icehouse trying to keep our joints from freezing stiff. Maybe you'd have married me and we could be living in a warm house by the sea."

A fleeting image of the Brant household flashed before Meg and she stifled a sob.

"Aw, I struck home. Meg, my girl, do you hate this place as much as I do? Will you run away with me to the south? We'd keep going south until the ice in your veins melted and you could fold yourself into my warm body."

"You're a scoundrel, Kevin O'Connor."

Again the door swung open. Craig, accompanied by his parents, entered the cabin. They stamped their booted feet on the floor to knock off the loose snow.

"Kevin," Craig greeted his friend. Joshua nodded to the Irishman, but Rainbow gave the two adult occupants of the cabin a wicked stare, then moved toward her grandson's cradle.

"I just fed him," Meg addressed Rainbow.

"Get up gas," the Indian woman responded. "White milk for strong boy too thin."

Meg grew angry. She knew her mother-in-law had a low regard for her as a wife. After all, she did not know how to cook buffalo intestines and she was not accustomed to hauling burdens like a packhorse, but no one, not even the fabled daughter of Eagle Face and Warrior Woman, was going to belittle her as a mother.

"I said don't pick him up. He's just been fed." This time Meg raised her voice.

It was the tone rather than what she said that brought Rainbow up short.

Kevin saw the fire in both women's eyes and could not resist a quip.

"Well, we're going to have a scalping," he said.

"Shut up!" Craig said angrily. His words were addressed to Kevin, but Meg knew that in her husband's mind they could just as easily have been addressed to her.

"Now, girls," Joshua chimed in. He stopped abruptly when he saw the thin line of his wife's mouth. All hell was about to break loose. He moved swiftly to the cradle and swooped the small body of his grandson up into his bearlike grasp.

"Looks fine and hulking to me," he said. "Spitting image of his grandpa." He handed the child to his wife. "Don't you think so, woman? Feel him. He's solid. Good bones, good stock, strong milk."

Meg could not believe the three of them. She knew Joshua was trying to avoid a blowup between his wife and his son's wife and that he meant well. But despite his good intentions he had played right into Rainbow's hands. She stood there holding James in her arms, against Meg's expressed desire. Meg turned away from them all and walked to the lean-to bedroom. She closed the door firmly behind her.

Kevin sat quietly, protected from the wind's bite by a snowdrift. The smoke curled upward from the innumerable chimneys in Fort Garry, but no smoke was coming from the storehouse that was being used as a temporary guardhouse for the forty-five or so young men seized in Winnipeg.

"Poor bastards, they must be freezing their asses off," he commented to himself. Then he laughed at himself. At least they were indoors. He had bribed old Lanctot, tonight's assigned jailer, with a jug of rotgut brandy that only a confirmed drunk like Lanctot could find alluring. He had consumed some of this foul stuff with Lanctot, and it still burned his throat and stomach.

Kevin was cold even with the whiskey in him. He was also nervous. Up to now he had worked with O'Donoghue, the chief officer of the Brotherhood at Red River. There had been no reason not to. Their goals were the same: stir up trouble between the Métis and the Canadians. But O'Donoghue was delighted with the arrest of Schultz and his followers because it put an end to the opposition to his friend Riel. But Kevin's orders from Alex Miller were to keep the opposition active.

His plan was a simple one. He was going to arrange a jailbreak. The guards were lax. It would not be difficult to do.

The very thought of Alex Miller made Kevin want to puke. How had he let himself get involved in all this? First, it had been Allison. God, how he loved and hated her at the same time. She was a viper. She took his love and she drained him, not only physically but morally. When he held her in his arms, it was she who controlled him. First, she had just asked inquisitive questions. Then he had slipped and gone too far. She guessed his connections. She led him on, twisting him to her will, until he found himself telling her everything she wanted to know.

Initially, the information she had wanted was harmless. Then, before the Battle of Ridgeway, she had become more and more demanding. She threatened never to see him again. He had stormed out of his own boarding house in anger, leaving her behind. But before an hour was up, he had returned and she was not there. He panicked and followed her home. She agreed to let him into her house only if he promised to tell her everything. He rationalized it all. Canada was too weak to resist the grand invasion even if it had advance knowledge of what was to take place. She had rewarded him that night. Oh God, what a reward it had been.

But then had come the invasion. He knew its failure was largely attributable to the poor strategy of the leadership, but he could not hide his self-loathing. He was a traitor. He was a betrayer of Ireland and of the Republican Brotherhood. He deserved the fate they reserved for traitors. The knife drawn quickly across the throat. When Big Jim died, much of Kevin O'Connor died with him. Saving Craig's life had been an act of independence he no longer dared repeat.

But now things were even worse. To be Allison's slave had had its rewards. She had let him touch her golden body. She had returned his love with equal fervor, at least while they lay in each other's arms. But suddenly he had found himself not only Allison's slave but Alex's tool. He truly despised that pompous young man. It was hard to remember that he had once pitied him for bearing the brunt of his father's constant harping.

But he was in too deep. Allison, the bitch he loved, had turned him over to her son. It was Alex who controlled him now. No longer did he obey out of lust, now it was fear that drove him. If Alex merely mentioned in the wrong place what he knew of Kevin's role, then Kevin was a dead man and there were times when he wished he was dead. He thought of Allison, her hair, throat, her eyes, her breasts. Suddenly, he realized it was not Allison he saw with his mind's eye, but Meg. He stood up to clear his head and to banish the thought of his best friend's wife.

He was sure that by now Lanctot had passed out. He normally did about this hour, even without the brandy. Kevin moved away from the corner of the drift. Crouching low he ran toward the guardhouse.

The door was slightly ajar. Kevin pushed his way through. Lanctot was sprawled on the floor snoring. Kevin reached for the keys on his belt. The old man stirred, mumbled something about the buffalo hunt. Kevin waited, then tried to unhook the key ring from the old man's belt. It was no use. The belt itself had been looped through the ring. Kevin glanced nervously at the open door. He rose from his knees and closed it. Then he bent down again. There was only one way to do it. He hoped the old man was too drunk to know what was going on. Kevin rolled Lanctot onto his back.

The Métis complained loudly. Kevin opened the belt buckle and pulled the belt firmly toward him. It came through the key ring and the keys clattered onto the floor.

Kevin grabbed the keys and ran quickly toward the large cell which held about sixteen men. He opened the door and slipped back into the shadows.

"Schultz," he whispered.

There was no answer. He could hear some men stirring.

"Where is Dr. Schultz?" Kevin spoke out again. "I have a message for him from Toronto."

Scott came toward the door.

"Stay back," Kevin pointed his pistol at Scott. "I am very nervous. It is fatal to be recognized. Even more fatal for the one who recognizes me."

Scott stopped dead in his tracks.

"Schultz isn't here. He escaped earlier."

"How?"

"None of your business."

Kevin saw the open window. It was on the opposite side of the storehouse from that which he had been watching for so long. So Schultz had gone out the window. That took courage. It was a long drop. He was lucky if he had not broken his head.

"The jailer is drunk. You are free to escape. I suggest you flee as quickly as possible."

"I don't flee," Scott said angrily. "In fact, I have a good mind to go find that Frenchie Riel and finish him off right now."

"Might not be a bad idea," Kevin said stepping back more deeply into the shadows. "Except he's not at Fort Garry."

"Then his luck is still with him," Scott said. He joined the others as they rushed out the open door into the guardroom and out into the snowy courtyard of Fort Garry. It would take them the rest of the night to make their way past sleeping sentries back to the English villages of Winnipeg and Portage la Prairie.

There were other prisoners in the fort kept in smaller groups, but Kevin decided he had done his work for the night. He closed the door to the jailroom and returned to Lanctot. He still snored. He replaced his belt and keys and then left him alone to sleep it off.

As he stepped into the fort's large open square he caught sight of Thomas Scott. He was peeking into the few lighted windows of buildings within the fort.

"He's looking for Riel," Kevin said aloud. Scott was a man who might come to be useful to him, Kevin thought, during the short ride back to Craig Miller's house on the Red River. All the way back he kept thinking of Meg and of her full white breasts.

He loved to have them all together around the table for dinner. Any occasion would do. He had not only celebrated Christmas but he had decreed a Christmas Season. He would celebrate the Feast of the Holy Innocents, St. Stephen's Day and every other feast of the season he could dredge from his Anglican boyhood memory. Rainbow complained, but he knew her well. It was when she stopped talking and got that thin-lipped, angry look on her face, that was when he would become anxious. She and Meg were still not talking and barely tolerated each other. But this too would pass.

Rainbow went into the larder and pulled out pemmican for the stew. She found a bushel of last summer's apples stuck in the corner of her cold storage bin. They were mostly soft, some had even started to rot. She was just about to throw them out when Meg arrived at the big house bearing James in her arms. She took the apples from Rainbow and began to make dough and peel the apples for an apple pie, a Willy Mackay Brant special.

When dinnertime came, and the family was together again, Joshua surveyed them all, his wife, his daughter and son–in–law, his sons and daughters–in–law and his mother–in–law.

Beth had no home of her own yet. Living in the big house with a mother and grandmother had left her inclined to let others do the work. She enjoyed sitting and listening to the men talk. Her preference annoyed an already angry Meg and they had some sharp exchanges about washing dishes and preparing food.

Joshua thought at one point he might have to speak to their husbands. But it was Meg herself who put an end to that tension. She too would have preferred to sit listening to the men talk. Even more, she would have liked to join in that talk. But politeness and an earlier desire to fit into Rainbow's idea of a daughter–in–law, and her responsibilities with James, had caused her to sacrifice what she'd like to do for what she thought was expected of her. Beth, having grown up in this house, did as she pleased. Meg decided to leave the girl be.

Meg got up to take her pie out of the oven. She set it out to cool, then sat back down at the large table next to Beth and Craig. She placed James's cradle at her feet. She reached over and touched her husband's knee.

"That smells like a fine pie," Joshua complimented Meg. "You must teach Beth here how to make it."

"I can do more than just make a good apple pie." Meg said testily. "Craig will tell you I'm Michael Brant's daughter. I've been raised to be a thinking, talking person."

Joshua smiled. "You're also Willy Mackay's daughter, which has to make you one of the orneriest, stubbornnest people on all God's earth."

Now it was Meg's turn to smile. "Mix Mohawk, Jewish, and Scots–Irish together, and if you don't have an explosion, you'll at least get toughness."

Kevin leaned back in his chair. "I didn't know you were Ulster–Irish, Meg."

"On the Mackay side," she admitted. She did not like the sneer that formed on his lips.

"Nothing wrong with the Scots–Irish, young man," Joshua said. "They're fat–headed and difficult, but no more so than the Catholic Irish, like yourself and my esteemed son–in–law."

Lavery smiled and bowed his head to Joshua.

"You wouldn't defend them if you knew what they have done in Ireland," said Kevin.

"Maybe, but I have seen what the Catholic Irish are doing here in Manitoba. The Fenians are making it hard for us to have peace in this colony."

"Papa," Douglas Miller interrupted, "the boys at school say the Canadians are going to send an army here and chase out the Fenians."

"What?" Sean said in mock horror. "Chase me out? Canadians? Quick, Kevin, pack your things. The Canadians are coming."

"Are you a Fenian, Sean?" Douglas asked in awe.

"You'll never know, my boy, not unless I tell you my secret."

"Tell it, tell it," the boy said excitedly.

"To become a Fenian you must undergo an awful ritual, a torture that leaves your shoulders scarred for life. A Fenian has this terrible scar which runs from here," he pointed to where he had been shot at Fort Erie, "up to here."

The boy's eyes widened. "You have a scar there. I saw it when you were washing."

"When did I do that?" Sean laughed.

"Do they torture you, really?"

Rainbow and Warrior Woman stopped serving the food to listen to Sean.

"I'm teasing," he said finally, disappointing three of his listeners.

Rainbow went back to her stew, and her mother made a sound of disgust which tickled Joshua.

"You have fallen in the esteem of my mother-in-law, young man. I do believe she thought you were about to tell her a tale of self-inflicted torture such as we hear the Sioux carry out in their sun dances."

Rainbow passed Sean the stew.

"My goodness, it's pemmican," Sean mocked. "What a nice surprise. It's been so long. Let's see, was it lunch or breakfast that we had it last? Do you recall, my dear?" he said leaning over toward his wife.

Again they all laughed.

"Have you an argument with the Brotherhood, Mr. Miller?" Kevin asked the question that had been gnawing at him through all the banter.

"I do," Joshua said very firmly.

"So do I," said Craig.

Kevin looked at one, then the other.

It was Craig who undertook to explain. "You press Riel too hard and you press him not because you wish, as he does, to help our people. You do it because you wish to use him for your own ends—Irish ends."

"We have a common enemy," Sean interrupted.

"No, we don't," Craig said angrily. "Louis has said it very well. We are loyal to the queen."

"My ass," Kevin said.

"O'Connor!"

"My apologies," Kevin turned to Meg and Beth.

Meg was used to Kevin by now and just smiled but Beth actually blushed.

"That's precisely my point," Craig continued. "Your argument is with Great Britian. Ours is not. We accept British rule. Riel even stated, after he established the provisional government, that we will eventually deal with Canada. We may accept Canada's rule, but only if they deal with us as equals. We must be admitted to confederation as a province with our own laws, our own language rights, our own schools, and especially our land titles intact. If Canada gives us that, Canada gets us."

Joshua signaled for silence. He rose. "We'll be having a visitor," he said as he walked to the front door. The frost on the windows was so thick there was no chance of looking out of them until spring arrived. Joshua opened the door and peered into the dark.

Kevin shivered as the cold air entered the house. He had never in his life felt cold like this. Sean described it as cold enough to freeze ice.

"Papa," Beth called out, "shut the door. A visitor can find his own way."

But Joshua ignored her. The night was dark, and it could be hard to find one's path without benefit of moon or stars.

"Hello there," he heard a voice call out.

"Over here," Joshua responded.

A horse's hooves made dull thuds in the powdered snow. "Have I reached the home of Joshua Miller?"

"You have, sir," Joshua responded. "Enter and warm yourself."

A man draped in racoon furs, including a hat pulled down over his ears, dismounted from his horse.

"Douglas," Joshua called to his son, "take this man's horse to the stable. Rub it down and feed it."

Douglas grumbled under his breath. He did nòt relish the trek to the barn and the long, cold task his father had just given him. But he rose from the table and went searching for his coat and boots, feeling miserable that he was the youngest and the person to whom this chore always fell.

"I don't believe I've had the pleasure," Joshua said, ushering the man into the house.

"No, we've not met, although we have friends in common. I'm Donald Smith of the Hudson's Bay Company. I bring greetings from Mr. Michael Brant."

"Father!" Meg said clapping her hands together. "You've seen him. How is he? Have you seen my mother too?"

"He is very well, complains about creeping old age, but otherwise Miss . . . ?"

"Margaret Brant Miller but everyone calls me Meg."

"Mr. Smith, won't you join us in our meal? It is pemmican stew."

"I've heard of it, sir, but I've never indulged."

"Then you are in for a double treat, because for dessert we'll have my daughter–in–law Meg's apple pie."

Smith took a place at the table after he was introduced to everyone except Douglas, who was still in the barn with Smith's horse.

"What brings an official of the company to Red River?" Kevin asked. "I thought you fellows had sold out to the Canadians?"

"I have a dual role. I have instructions from the Prime Minister of Canada as well."

"So you are the Canadian envoy at last," said Joshua.

"I am."

"What do you offer us?" Craig asked.

"An ear," Smith responded.

Kevin started to laugh and Sean joined in.

"I'm afraid that won't be enough," Kevin responded.

"Prime Minister Macdonald wishes to know what has been happening here in the colony, why the governor has been rejected, and who is in charge. He needs to know all these things."

Craig looked at the ruddy–faced, mustached gentleman in European clothes. His complexion could well have been the result of the terrible cold on his skin as he rode downriver from the fort to reach them.

"Mr. Smith, have you met with President Riel?" Craig asked him finally.

"Yes, we had our first interview."

"And?" Joshua asked.

"The gentleman seemed a bit disappointed that I'd come without authority to negotiate a settlement. But he has called a general meeting of the settlers for next month."

"Why did you ride out all the way here?" Kevin asked suspiciously.

Smith looked him over from head to toe. "It's O'Connor, isn't it?"

Kevin nodded.

"Well, Mr. O'Connor, Michael Brant and I go back a long way. When he asked me to deliver his greetings to his daughter, a little cold and a little snow will not stop me."

Rainbow placed a plate of stew in front of him. He breathed in the aroma. "My, that smells good," he said.

Everyone began to eat, and the conversation lagged. Doug reentered the house, kicking snow from his boots. "His horse is bedded down, papa," he said as he rushed to his place to begin his dinner.

The meal was passed in light talk with Sean entertaining all of them with tales of his brief career on the Dublin stage. He slipped once and mentioned the name of a girl, a Peg Mullins, with whom he had been close but he caught himself before Beth could fully understand the implications of that relationship.

After the stew, they devoured the apple pie. Meg had to make the slices small so that all could have some.

Craig put down his fork and patted his stomach after he finished the pie. "I knew I was right to marry this woman," he said.

She glanced at him, then turned to Smith.

"Do you come to us from Halifax, Mr. Smith?" Meg asked anxiously.

"No, Mrs. Miller."

"Please call me Meg."

"Meg. No. I set out from Ottawa and I came via St. Paul."

"Then where did you see my father and mother?"

"Why, they're in the capital. Your father came along in some capacity with Mr. Joseph Howe. He sends his love and a letter.

Your mother said to tell you that another trunk of your things and some gifts had been sent on."

Meg's face flushed with pleasure. She pumped him for every piece of information he had about her parents and the events in the east. Finally Craig intervened and said it was time to go home.

"Kevin, you too," Craig said. "I don't want you traipsing into the cabin late and waking us up. I particularly don't want you waking up the baby."

It was clear that Kevin was reluctant to leave, but finally he rose and joined Meg and Craig and James. As he put on his coat and boots he motioned to Sean to join him by the fire. They spoke a few seconds, and then Kevin walked over to Donald Smith and shook his hand.

"Good night, sir," he said. He seemed almost to exaggerate his Irish accent as he spoke.

"A pleasure meeting you, O'Connor," Smith responded.

Then the young people left. Warrior Woman gave an enormous yawn, which always announced her bed ritual: a swig of brandy and then a slow, complaining climb up the stairs to her room. She slept on the heavily carpeted floors on an Indian sleeping mat.

Rainbow finished cleaning up and then chased Doug to bed. She knew Joshua would sit up with their guest. Sean and Beth had occupied the guest room upstairs and Doug had received his own room after Beth's marriage. The guest would have to sleep downstairs on the couch, but it was a comfortable one. Already her son–in–law had spent two nights on it. She chuckled at the thought. But he had pronounced the couch very comfortable.

Lavery stayed up as long as he could listening to Joshua and Smith talk. He could hear the door to his bedroom open and close several times. He knew Beth grew annoyed with him. Well, at least this time she couldn't force him to the couch. There was no room on it for both Smith and himself.

Finally she called to him. Sean rose. He knew from the tone of her voice that she wanted him. He had better things waiting for him than listening to two middle-aged men discussing Canadian politics. He said goodnight and went up the stairs.

"I thought he'd never leave," Smith said.

"I think he was told not to."

"Well, Mr. Miller, Michael Brant says hello to an old Mackenzie rebel and asks if he is still a rebel?"

"Mr. Smith, there is no rebellion here in Manitoba."

"That is not the prevailing opinion in Canada."

"That's because Canada is truly ignorant of what is happening among the Métis."

"That is why the prime minister sent me."

"Good. You must see it for yourself. But I can give you an outline."

Smith nodded for him to begin.

"Primarily," Joshua said sitting back in his chair, "these are a free people worried about their way of life. And make no mistake about it, Smith, it is a wonderful way of life. I know, I've lived it since I was a youth. It is a life of following the buffalo every spring, getting enough meat for the winter. But it gets harder to find the buffalo. My Indian in–laws swear it is the Great Spirit who is punishing them by depriving them of the buffalo. I think it is more likely the result of slaughtering the herds across the boarder in the United States."

"It's policy there, my friend. Destroy the plains Indian's food supply and you destroy the plains Indian."

"My people are feeling the effects here. But we are not complete nomads. We have this," he said waving his hand around the room. "Mine is more elaborate than most, but the Métis have built their homes and staked their claims on long, narrow strips of land bordering the rivers. You Canadians, with your land surveys using the American system, throw all that into jeopardy."

"What must we do?" Smith interrupted him.

"You tell Prime Minister Macdonald to deal with these people fairly. Grant them their land. Give them political status, the right to have their own representatives in a legislature and then eventually in Parliament, and then give them what you've given Quebec—French language, Catholic schools. They are devoted to their priests."

"That last might be harder to do."

"Tell Mr. Macdonald to bend. If he does, he'll have Rupert's Land in the palm of his hand. The Americans and their Fenian jackals will be left in the cold, not knowing what happened to them."

"What of Riel?"

"Work with him. He has an ego, and he can't stand to be crossed, but he's not disloyal. He wants justice. Give him justice and he'll give you Manitoba."

"He has that much support?"

"He has everyone, English and French, everyone except Schultz and his diehard Canadians."

"God save us from the likes of John Christian Schultz. It's hard to think of him and his friends as our only supporters."

"He thinks he is helping," Joshua offered.

Smith laughed and touched Joshua on the arm. "Is there any group in Manitoba you don't support?"

"Yes, the Fenians. They're the one group I'll have no truck with."

"Why is that? You don't strike me as an Orange lodger. For that matter, you don't quite seem like a Canadian patriot either."

"I am neither. But the Fenians nearly got my son Craig hanged when he was back East."

"Yes, I know. Brant implied that the boy was in thick with them."

"He was. Now he's home and he isn't. But the same isn't true of my son–in–law Lavery. He still takes orders from the 'Head Center'."

"Given your feelings, I am surprised you accepted him into your family."

Joshua smiled. "Those things are not exactly within my area of control in the family. You couldn't tell much about my wife Rainbow from your brief encounter."

"Except that she cooks a mean pot of stew," Smith interrupted.

Joshua smiled again and continued. "Well, she's a small woman but, by God, she has a will of her own. The only person in the world who can make her change her mind is her own mother. Those two agreed on Lavery. He was their man. Poor Beth. Thank God she fell for him."

Smith chuckled. He pulled a pipe from his pocket. "Do you mind?" he asked.

"Not at all, if you don't mind sharing some tobacco, I'd like to join you."

Smith opened his pouch to Joshua.

"My supply always runs short about the beginning of the new year. Well, as I was saying," he stopped to light his pipe with a taper from the fireplace, "Lavery is in the family without consultation with me. But that's just as well. He's relatively harmless, not like the other one."

"O'Connor?"

Joshua nodded. "He's clever and he's dangerous. I don't trust him."

"Yet he lives with your son and his wife."

"They're bonded. They've saved each other's lives. I have no choice but to accept my son's best friend." He shook his head. He was clearly disturbed. He looked over at Smith. "Well, what's your plan?"

Smith puffed on his pipe in silence. "I think what you've told me is helpful. Riel said he would call a meeting of all the men to discuss the future. I am to be there to speak and to listen. I've heard much from you. The concessions you ask could be obtained, if the Métis ask for them and no violence erupts. I might be able to get the prime minister to agree."

Joshua sat back in his chair. "Thank God," he said. "Mr. Smith, Mr. Donald Smith, I'm very glad you've come to us."

Meg lay back against the cool of the linen pillowcase. The fire in the hearth had reduced itself to glowing embers, which illuminated a few feet in front of it with a faint crimson. The baby was in his crib and sleeping at last. She could hear the logs of the house cracking in the cold. She was covered in buffalo robes, but she shivered through most of the night. She stayed on her side of the bed, denying herself the comfort of Craig's warmth. They had barely spoken to each other in the days since Meg's clash with Rainbow, and the nights had seen an estrangement that was new except for the few weeks before and after James's birth.

Craig had already risen, and Meg could see his strong back outlined against the embers' glow as he sat on the edge of the bed putting on his boots. She threw off her covers reluctantly and started to rise.

"Don't bother," Craig said almost in a whisper, fearful of awakening his sleeping son. "You may as well try to get some more sleep. You were up so long with James."

Meg had started to lie back down, but the vision of a disapproving mother–in–law poking her nose in and finding her sleeping late while poor Craig rummaged for himself was more than she could bear. She swung her feet onto the ice–cold floorboards.

Craig sighed when he saw her rise. "I'll get a fire going," he said. He tossed some dried buffalo chips into the fire. At first it looked as if their bulk would completely smother the embers. Craig kicked them with his booted foot. The embers sparked and caught. Soon the whole room was glowing from the flames. Smoke billowed from the fireplace and started to pour into the room.

"Damn," Craig cursed. He started to cough. He reached for a large fork which rested by the hearth and hoisted a section of burning dung onto it. He raised it up into the flue.

"It's so cold the smoke won't rise up in the chimney," he said wiping tears from his eyes.

"Ssh," Meg worried, glancing at the cradle.

"How long will you be gone?" Meg asked after some moments of silence.

"A day or two," Craig responded.

"The meeting will last that long?"

"Meg," Craig said, outwardly patient, but seething with impatience at her question, "you know how these political meetings go. First there's drinking, then there's talking, then some more drinking, maybe some brawling, and then more talking. It all takes time."

"While I stay alone here with the baby."

"My mother and grandmother and sister are here."

"Maybe it has slipped your mind, but I'm not on the best of terms with your mother right now, and if that's true of her, it is doubly true of that savage you call a grandmother."

Craig turned to his wife. She had never seen such an angry look on his face before. Even in the gloom of the early morning, Meg saw from the expression of his face that she had gone too far. For a moment she feared he would strike her. She could see him balling his hands into fists, but he turned instead and walked to the nightstand where he had left yesterday's shirt. He quickly donned it and stuck the tail of his shirt violently into his pants with quick thrusts of his trembling hands. He took his woolen coat and buffalo robe and placed them around his shoulders before storming from the house, heading for the barn.

Meg sat down again on the bed. She glanced over at the baby, who breathed rhythmically in his sleep. Neither her harsh words nor Craig's door-slamming had disturbed him. Meg hid her face in her hands. She wanted to cry. The frustrations were overwhelming her. She should be able to cry, but no tears would come. She wanted to go home to Halifax. She wanted to see her mother and father once again. She wanted to leave this icy desert.

She did not hear Kevin' slow descent from the loft. Despite

the fire from the hearth he could still see his breath. He shivered. The silent motion seemed to catch Meg's attention at last. She raised her face and seemed not at all startled to see the Irishman standing out in front of her in his long underwear.

She rose slowly to her feet. Suddenly she found herself engulfed within his arms. The tears finally started to flow.

"Oh my God, Kevin," she wept. "I hate this place so much, I should never have come here."

"There, there, lass," Kevin comforted her. "You're getting the front of my undershirt all wet with your crying."

He started to back away from her, but she clung even more closely to him. He could feel the tension growing within him.

"Lass," he whispered in Meg's ear, "remember the first night we met? Is this going to be a repeat? I could barely walk after our first encounter."

Meg said nothing, but clung even more closely to him. She heard the sound of Craig's horse's hooves striking the icy ground on the road to Fort Garry.

"We're on our own now." Kevin's voice sounded more husky. He could stand it no more. He swept her off her feet. His fingers felt her smooth flesh under the shift she was wearing. He laid her gently down upon the bed. Then he lay down on top of her, allowing his weight to settle onto his elbows and knees, but covering her shivering body with the full length of his.

She reached behind him and pulled the heavy robes up over his rump and onto the small of his back. Kevin touched her eyelids with his lips as if to close them so she could not see what he was about to do to her. She gasped as he touched her lips with his insistent tongue. For a moment she clenched her jaw to resist him. If she kept her mouth closed to his caressing tongue, then she would be safe, but if she opened herself to Kevin O'Connor then nothing could ever again be the same. Again his warm tongue probed. She gasped as his fingers touched her tender nipples. With the gasp his tongue gained entry. Meg felt herself sinking downward, sinking in to the disquieting warmth of his embrace.

She still wept. He had used the bed linen again and again to dry her tears. He had remained on top of her, covering her, protecting her even after they had finished and all the stiffness had left him. She hoped he would never move. If he remained where he was, she could blot out the whole world beyond him.

She fell asleep with him there, her chest rising and falling with the involuntary gasps of her slow, quiet tears. She heard no one at the door until it swung open and the ice blast of cold seemed to fill the vacuum of the room.

"Lovebirds, rise and shine," Sean called out in his rich Dublin brogue. "You're already late to hear Riel give it to the Canadian envoy."

Meg stiffened, suddenly wide awake and terrified.

"Don't move," Kevin whispered in her ear. "Just call out that you and your husband deserve a little bit of privacy."

Meg started to call out but her voice cracked.

"Come on, Miller. Get a move on," Lavery said again.

"Sean, leave Craig and me to our privacy," Meg finally blurted out.

Sean smiled. "At least you have something to demand privacy for," he bemoaned his own fate aloud, "With me it's a promise rarely fulfilled. At least I can get that besotten countryman of mine, O'Connor, out of his warm bed and into the heartnumbing cold of this wretched morning. "O'Connor," he bellowed. James awoke with a start and commenced screeching in anger. "Now what have you done," Lavery excused himself. "You've gone and awakened the little one with your lying abed. Arise."

"He's already gone," Meg lied. "He took Craig's horse and rode him to the fort."

"Damn," Lavery cursed, "Well, Craig, my lad, that leaves you to get up." He walked over and placed his hand atop the buffalo robe which covered Kevin.

"Sean," Meg cried out, "have you no sense of decency?"

Lavery hesitated. "No, I have none. But I do have a strong sense of self–preservation, and I don't think I'd like the fist of Craig Miller in me face. Are you getting hot under there, Craig my lad."

"Go," Meg said in annoyance, "I've got to get up and feed the baby."

"Ah, yes, the noisy namesake of an old companion of mine."

"Go," Meg said again this time using a menacing tone in her voice.

"All right, all right," Sean laughed and started toward the door. "I'll wait for you in the barn, Craig," he said as he started to step out into the snow.

"Don't wait," Meg shouted. "He's staying with me a lot longer."

Lavery threw back his head and started to laugh. "Don't let me interfere."

Meg fell back into the pillows when Lavery closed the door behind him.

"Well done," was all that Kevin offered her.

"Do you think he suspected?"

"No," Kevin said, "you've got the makings of a great dissembler in you."

Meg started to get up again to go to James, but Kevin grabbed her and pulled her back down onto the bed covers.

"Meg, it's cold outside and it's a warm delight down here with you. Stay a bit longer."

Meg knew she should not, but James decided it all for her. All of a sudden he stopped crying and fell back to sleep. There was no longer any need to rise and care for him.

Craig rode his horse through the gates of Fort Garry. The animal was covered with ice. Its own perspiration had frozen on its body. Craig could never remember being this cold in all of his life. His nose was running from the cold, but before it could reach his lip it turned to ice. He had come early to the meeting because of his words with Meg. He was anxious to find a stable for his horse and for the horses and wagons of the others. His father, Sean and Kevin would arrive later by sled. He worked his way through the huge crowd that already thronged the parade ground. Everyone was here. He heard both English and French being spoken, along with the strange mixture of both which both English and French Métis were capable of speaking. He saw supporters of the Hudson's Bay Company, Selkirk–Scots, Americans, Fenians and Métis, hundreds of Métis. The only group missing were Schultz and his hard–core Canadians.

Schultz himself was a fugitive. No one had seen him since his escape, but the rumor was that he was planning to head back to Canada to stir up support for his cause. It was also rumored that those prisoners who had not escaped would be released. Except for them, all the men of Red River were certain to be at this meeting.

Craig moved as close as he could to the speaker's platform. He recognized many of the faces on the dais. Riel was there, of course, and Thomas Bunn, an English Métis, and Judge Black, the Recorder of Assiniboia.

Craig wandered about the fort, entering as many of the

buildings as possible to talk to his friends, and to seek in each the warmth of the hot stoves which glowed red from the constant burning. Finally, word was received that the meeting would start. As Craig left the old Hudson's Bay Store, he was nearly run down by his frozen brother–in–law, Sean Lavery.

"By God it's cold." Lavery's teeth chattered as he spoke. As soon as he saw Craig, his shivering gave way to surprise. "How in the name of the Lord did you get here so fast?" he asked.

"I came by horse, as I expect you did. Unless you came on sled with my father and Kevin."

"Kevin? Sled?" Sean looked confused at first, then his face went blank.

"Are you all right?"

"Of course, of course," Sean blurted out. "The cold is affecting my mind. See you later. I have to warm up."

Craig looked at him with some puzzlement. Lavery was acting peculiar, but then again what was unusual about that? He closed the door of the company store behind him and stepped out into the cold.

Sean turned and stared at the door for some moments after Craig had left. He shook his head finally and called out to the proprietor, "Landlord, have you any Irish whiskey to warm my heart and my bowels?"

The meeting began. In quick order Bunn was chosen chairman and Donald Smith was called to the platform to explain his mission. Smith began by reading the papers from the Canadian government authorizing him to hear grievances. Craig looked up at the flag of the provisional government fluttering above his head, a *fleur-de-lis* and a shamrock on a white background. Nothing to comfort Smith in that combination.

The cold was mind–numbing. It must have been twenty to thirty degrees below zero, yet, as Smith read, Craig could feel the crowd's attention was with him. When he finished there was a scatter of applause. Smith now had to bring the crowd over to his side. His father and he were of one mind on this. Smith must succeed. He must bring grievances of the Métis back to Ottawa so that the Canadian government could meet the needs of these people. If they did there would be no rebels in Manitoba.

"I come here," Smith now spoke in a loud ringing voice, "to bring about peaceable union, an entire accord among all the classes of people in this land." This was greeted by some cheering. "Her Majesty's government of Canada will hear the grievances of the peoples, all the peoples of Manitoba, white and red, Métis, French and English. I will tell the prime minister how you resent road builders and surveyors coming into your land and disrupting your ways."

Several rifles were fired in the air in support of Smith's statement.

"I will tell Ottawa that, as in Quebec, there are French–speaking and English–speaking peoples here in Manitoba." More cheering. "And I will tell Ottawa that the people of Manitoba will not be bought and sold like a tired old mule. They are a free people. They must be dealt with as a free people in a Canadian territory."

There was a sudden upswell of roaring approval. Craig joined in cheering Donald Smith. He was saying and doing all the right things. It was almost as if he could read the minds of the throng of men assembled at Fort Garry.

Craig watched as O'Donoghue, the Fenian leader, approached Riel. It was clear he was angry and did not like the way the meeting was going. Riel tried to calm the Irishman down, but O'Donoghue stormed off the platform. Craig watched him depart. He caught sight of several known Fenians who joined their leader near the courthouse steps. They spoke for a few moments while on the platform other speakers rose to respond to Smith.

Then it was Riel's turn, and Craig lost interest in O'Donoghue. Riel spoke in French and then in English.

"I am happy to hear that Mr. Smith is willing to report our concerns to his government. I am angry, however, that Mr. Macdonald sent a man who could only listen and not a man who could act."

There was a murmur of support of Riel's words.

"We waste so much time with such talk and no action," he continued. Now the crowd warmed to Riel's words and there was cheering. "Canada already knows our grievances. We want our own land without the fear the whites from Canada will come and take it from us. We don't need to be a Canadian territory. If we are," he continued, "parliament will make our laws for us. Do you want lawyers from Ottawa or Montreal making laws for the Métis of Manitoba?"

With one voice the crowd roared no.

"Manitoba should be a province equal with the others. Then

our way of life, the lands, our language, our religion will be safely in our hands."

Smith looked disturbed. Riel was pushing very hard. Manitoba had a tiny population. It would be hard for him to get the prime minister to agree to this. He looked about the audience. He could see many small conferences going on. It was clear that Riel had sprung this on his people without advance preparation.

"I can promise you nothing of that nature," Smith called out. "And it would be criminal to have our understanding break down over a question of mere status. Manitoba will, of course, become a province in confederation when it is ready."

"We can't wait," Riel shouted in anger. "I've heard what the Canadian, Dr. Schultz, says. He says, 'Just get a territorial government in place, give us the policing power and send the migrants, thousands of good Canadians, and we will overwhelm the half-breed savages!' I will not let that happen to Manitoba. If Canada wants peace, Canada must take us as an equal partner in confederation."

There were more shouts of approval but there were some others who disagreed. The disagreement seemed to follow linquistic lines.

O'Donoghue came back to the speakers' platform and sat down behind Riel. Craig saw that O'Donoghue's anger seemed to have fled. The opposite was happening to Riel. He was facing opposition from his own people for the first time. His face grew flushed and he started to shout in anger.

"Follow me or the devil take you," he said in French. Then he seemed to stare into space. One of the French Métis on the platform reached over and touched his shoulder. Riel seemed confused.

One of Riel's followers made a motion that twenty English speakers be elected to join with Riel's French committeemen, and that a convention be called to draw up a list of grievances for Donald Smith to carry back to Ottawa. By then Riel had recovered. He spoke in favor of the motion, and the crowd roared its assent. The cheering went on for two or three minutes punctuated by occasional whistles and rifle shots into the air.

Then Riel quieted the crowd down. There was a sudden hush. "Before this assembly breaks up," he said, "I cannot but express my feeling, however briefly. I came here with fear. We are not yet enemies."

The crowd cheered.

"But we came very near being so. As soon as we all understood each other we joined our English fellow subjects in demanding our just rights."

The crowd cheered its approval. He silenced them again.

"I am not afraid to say *our* rights, for we all have rights. We claim no half rights, mind you, but all the rights we are entitled to. These rights will be set forth by our representatives, and what is more, gentlemen, we will get them."

The crowd renewed its celebration. Maybe it was the cold, but the meeting was turning into a party, friends clasping each other and patting each other on the back. Caps were thrown into the air and jugs were produced.

Craig saw his father standing close to the platform. He reached up and shook Donald Smith's hand. The Canadian representative looked very pleased with himself. Craig reached Joshua's side and hugged his father. He too reached up and shook Smith's hand.

Manitoba would be part of Canada. There would be no violence. Louis Riel had won a great victory for the Métis if John A. Macdonald, prime minister of Canada, was as wise a man as he should be. Only the scowl on the face of O'Donoghue, the Fenian leader, disturbed Craig's confidence in the future.

XIII

Red River, February–March 1870

Kevin had been drinking for two hours with the Portage la Prairie men. He had been doing this almost nightly for a month. He hated these endless winters. The cold wind and the snow seemed to have penetrated his soul. Old Doyle had been wrong when he said hell was a place of everlasting fire. Hell was a place of everlasting ice and snow and cold. Hell was Manitoba. Damn it, he thought, the Canadians should let the Fenians have it. The Fenians would beg the Canadians to take it back. Possession of it should be a form of punishment. Best of all, let the bloody Métis keep it.

But that was not what the 'Head Center,' President Roberts, wanted, and it was not what his other superior, Alex Miller, wanted. He was not sure what either of them wanted in the end but it was clear that both had the same immediate goal—violence in Manitoba. For the first time in years, Kevin could approach his task knowing that if he succeeded he would satisfy both his masters. It was a relief to him.

It had not been easy for him to continue to sleep in the loft just over Meg and Craig's bed. At night he'd lie awake listening, but they had never touched each other, of that he was sure. But neither had he and Meg repeated their lovemaking of the last month. In fact she barely looked at him any longer. Once he approached her while Craig was out in the barn. She had developed a distant look in her eye and tactfully ignored his advances. Well, to hell with her, but, by God, it sure would be nice to be in that bed feeling her against his body. It sure beat sitting in the saloon drinking bad whiskey.

Tom Scott, who sat next to him, was nearly drunk.

"O'Connor," he said in his slurred speech, "you're not such a bad fellow for a Papist."

"I'm a bad Papist, Tom," Kevin said. "I haven't been inside a church in years."

"Neither have I," Scott said putting his arm on Kevin's shoulder. "Let's drink to not going to church."

Kevin laughed.

"Barkeep," Scott called out to the tavern owner, "another whiskey for my friend O'Connor and another for me. In fact, whiskey for all my friends," he roared drunkenly at the twenty or so other men in the tavern.

"Attaboy, Tom," someone called out.

"What about a toast?" Kevin said. "Tom, you give a toast."

Quiet settled down in the saloon as Scott held his shot glass in the air and looked intently at it. "I've got it," and then he smiled. "Up Louis Riel's ass."

The other men roared and repeated his toast and downed their whiskey.

"That offend you, O'Connor?" Scott asked.

"Not a bit," Kevin responded.

"I think he's a crazy. Some say he's some sort of mystic, he hears voices."

"Men like him scare me," Kevin said.

"Well, they anger me. Look at him, president of a bloody provisional government. Manitoba is part of Canada. We bought it fair and square. This Riel, he spits in the queen's face flying that fucking flag. No decent British subject, no man loyal to Queen Victoria, should have to tolerate what has happened here."

"You're right, but we are going to tolerate it," Kevin said.

"What do you mean?"

"The Métis, they're fearsome fighters, and they have O'Donoghue's American mercenaries, the boys who whipped Robert E. Lee."

"Up O'Donoghue's ass too," Scott shouted raising his empty glass for a second toast. His friends cheered.

"Strikes me that you talk a lot and do little," Kevin said.

Scott grabbed Kevin's shirt. "I'll bust your nose, you piece of Catholic shit."

Kevin smiled into Scott's face. "How about busting Riel's nose?"

"I'll do that, too," Scott said.

"When?"

"Right now. Bloody right now." He let go of Kevin's shirt and stood up. "Hey, boys, we're going for a ride."

"Where to, Tom?" someone asked.

"Out toward Fort Garry. I have a mind to pay me a visit to old Doc Schultz. I hear he's over in Kildonan with the Selkirkers."

"Yeah, it would be good to see the doc again," another Canadian shouted. "I hear there are still Canadian prisoners at Fort Garry. What about setting them free?"

"Good idea," Scott said. Then he looked at Kevin. "And while we're at it, we might just pay us a visit to that fucking half-breed, Riel. I've got a hankering to bust someone's nose tonight."

The Canadians poured out of the saloon. Then went to the rear where their horses were stabled. Kevin watched them go. He smiled to himself. It was so easy to rile these people up. Back east these Canadians seemed so unemotional, yet send them to the frontier, and their bellies, their hearts, their groins took over from their minds. Perhaps it was only that type of Canadian who would dare venture out into the wilderness. The less adventurous, the less daring, sat snugly safe before their hearths in Toronto or in Montreal or in Halifax.

He heard the Portage men go riding off into the winter night whooping and hollering. He smiled again. He would need to report his success to O'Donoghue.

John Schultz lay awake in the darkness, cursing the name Donald Smith over and over again. He was staying at the home of his friend Robert Macbeth here at the Scottish settlement at Kildonan.

He heard the commotion as twenty or more horses came into Macbeth's front yard. He heard someone call his name. He became frightened. Maybe it was Riel's people come to rearrest him. He breathed a sigh of relief when he heard Tom Scott bellow out, "Doc Schultz?"

He rose painfully and went to the window. His leg still hurt from his fall out of the guardhouse window the night he escaped. Schultz threw open the window.

"What brings you out on a night like this, Tom?" Schultz called out.

"Doc, we think it's time all us white folks got together and chased them half-breed frogs out of Fort Garry."

"I been waiting for you fellows to get your balls in an uproar. What has taken you so damned long? I'll be right down."

That night Schultz sent messengers to every English and Scottish settler in the region to join him at Kildonan to release the prisoners Riel still held. In the morning well over one hundred men stood in Macbeth's yard.

Three men arrived from the Miller farms on the Red River—Joshua, Craig and Sean Lavery. Schultz greeted them in Macbeth's living room.

"I'm surprised to see you, Joshua Miller," Schultz called out.

"I'm surprised to see you here," Joshua responded. "I was told that you and Smith were going to go back to Ottawa to fight it out."

"No, we're going to fight it out here."

"That's dumb," Craig offered.

"Josh, I've always thought of you as the kind of man who'd teach manners to his brats even if they were dropped by a squaw."

Joshua's face went instantly white with anger but he held his tongue.

"I know what you have in mind, Schultz," Craig said coldly. "Start a civil war here, and the Canadian militia—maybe even British regulars—will be here to finish it off."

"It's not starting a civil war. It's crushing a rebellion."

"A rebellion that has thus far seen no one hurt, not a single loss of life. Not exactly the kind of rebellion you have to call the troops in to put down. One man, Donald A. Smith, came in and settled it."

"It isn't settled as long as that man Riel flies a homemade flag over Canadian land," Schultz responded.

"Why don't you leave it be, Schultz?" Joshua finally said.

Many men had now crowded into the living room to listen to the heated argument.

"Riel has five hundred heavily armed men," Joshua continued. This time he was addressing the other leaders of the English and Scottish communities.

"Sounds to me like you Millers are afraid of Riel. More likely, you're in bed with him. A lot of squaw men in that family," Tom Scott shouted drunkenly at Joshua and Craig.

It was getting difficult for Joshua to control himself. Craig could see his father opening and closing his fist. But it was the Reverend Bishop Machray, the Anglican Bishop of the colony, who averted any more outbursts by his entrance into the Macbeth house.

"What is this all about, Schultz?" he asked.

"It doesn't concern the church," Schultz responded.

"I am not sure it should concern a man of medicine either."

"Shit," said Scott forgetting to whom he spoke, "old Doc is a storekeeper. I wouldn't come to him for the removal of a splinter from my ass."

Several men laughed but others glanced nervously at the floor, embarrassed by the vulgar expression in the presence of the bishop.

"We're going to release all the Canadian prisoners," Schultz finally explained.

The other men nodded approval.

"It's already been done," the bishop asserted. "Monsieur Riel is sending a letter to us to that effect."

"That does it," Craig yelled out. "We don't need to stand around here all day. There's no more reason for this assembly. I'm going home."

Several other men questioned the bishop about his information but none was willing to doubt his truthfulness. One by one the English leaders left the room to tell their followers to go home. Before long, only the original Portage men under Scott waited impatiently at Macbeth's. Even they were becoming more and more nervous as they saw the others leave.

Joshua turned to Sean and Craig when the bishop departed. "I think it's time to go."

"Miller," Schultz said bitterly to Joshua, "when Canada has control of this land and I'm playing the role I expect to play in a Canadian Manitoba, I will remember what you have done. You will rue this day."

Joshua laughed. "Schultz, when that day comes, God help us. But if it does, you'll come crawling to my house looking for votes." He turned and left the room, followed by Sean and Craig.

As they rode back to the farm, Sean made a lame excuse and set out toward Fort Garry.

"At least we know O'Donoghue will get a full briefing about what happened at Macbeth's," Joshua joked to Craig.

Tom Scott was furious. They had ridden all the way from Portage la Prairie for nothing. His own people did not have the guts to stand up to the bloody half–breed frogs. Well, he knew he had the courage. He was going to ride by in full view of Fort Garry on the way home. It was a show of defiance toward Riel.

The twenty riders rode through the snow past the fort. No one expected a reaction from the fort itself. They were in error. The gates of the fort opened, and about a hundred horsemen, carrying the flag of the Provincial Government and headed by the Irishman O'Donoghue, came dashing out. Scott saw the trap too late.

"Run for it, boys. Ride to safety," he called out.

But the Fenian leader had briefed his troops. With precision, they split right and left and trapped Bolton and Scott's forces against the river with no route of escape. Tom Scott was close to tears of rage. He wanted to strike out. He swore at the first man who tried to seize him. His arms were pulled up behind him. He broke loose and slashed a Fenian in the face.

"I'll kill you bastards," he screamed, "and I'll tear Riel's heart out when I get close to him."

Instead he was bound hand and foot and thrown into the guardhouse at Fort Garry.

Sean returned home finally to the Miller house. He had been excited by everything that had taken place—up to a point. He was delighted he could play a role to help the cause. It was he, Sean Lavery, who tipped off O'Donoghue and Riel about the Portage men. He had watched from the fort's firing platform as O'Donoghue captured Bolton and Scott.

He had stayed the week at Fort Garry. Bolton had been sentenced to death then pardoned. Riel, reeling under the pressure of these outbursts from the Canadians, was moving farther and farther away from his previous policy of cooperation with Smith. Before long, Sean hoped, the Manitoba rebellion would break out at last.

But then Riel had decided to shoot Tom Scott. Well, Sean was no friend of Scott's, but the crime of disobedience and threats seemed a flimsy reason to shoot a man.

Sean flopped down at the table in the main room of the house. Dawn was just breaking outside and no one was up yet. He was glad. He wanted to put off the inevitable argument as long as possible. He thought of going to Craig's house but dismissed that idea. Knowing what he knew about Kevin and Meg made it impossible for him to be with Craig.

He went to the jug on the mantel and poured himself a good

stiff drink. He could use a hot bath and a shave, he thought, as he ran his hand across the stubble on his face.

A door opened upstairs. He looked up and saw his wife on the landing.

"Oh, it's you," she said with feigned indifference.

"What do you mean, Mrs. Lavery, 'it's you.' Is that the greeting I get after a ten-day absence?"

She turned on him, her eyes flashing. "You're lucky that I don't ask my father to throw you out on your ear. Ten days, no word, no messages."

"I was about my business."

"And what the hell is that?"

She shocked him. She never cursed.

"The business of the Motherland," he responded.

"Well, Sean Lavery, I've had it. You're going to have to choose between the Motherland and your wife."

Sean started to laugh.

"I'm not joking," Beth yelled.

Sean grew serious. The lass had to be jesting, he thought. One did not present such ultimatums to one's husband. All men had to be about the serious business of politics; women had to learn to accept that. That was the way it had always been.

"You must not be serious," he said finally.

"I'll show you serious!" she yelled, then left the landing. He heard the door slam. Suddenly, banging noises came through the ceiling from above the living room. A window opened, and he saw his clothes go sailing out the window and onto the snow drifts outside the house. Both Rainbow and Warrior Woman—who listened from their beds—nodded in approval.

Joshua poured the hot water to make some tea. He decided not to engage his depressed son–in–law in any conversation about his current troubles. Douglas was out in the back doing his chores. A boy had chores all year around. Women seemed to work continuously, but with winter the men of the house had little to keep them busy. He knew it was partly boredom that had kept Sean at the fort so long, but boredom was not an excuse a new wife was likely to accept.

It was Sean who broke the silence.

"They almost shot Major Bolton, you know. O'Donoghue worked hard to see it happen."

"Louis is no fool. He wouldn't risk it."

"I'm not so sure," Sean said rather smugly. "Schultz is driving him toward violence."

"Schultz would drive me toward violence," Joshua said, "and your O'Donoghue is not much better."

"I'm telling you, Riel has changed over the last weeks. He's close to breaking."

Joshua remembered the wild outburst of anger at the open air meeting. How strange Louis had looked. He made his decision right on the spot. He went to the hook where he kept his great fur coat, then sat before the fire and pulled on his boots.

"Douglas," he shouted, "saddle two horses. Then go next door and wake your lazy brother Craig. We're riding to Fort Garry."

As they entered the front gate of the stone fortress the two Millers, father and son, were both instantly aware that something was wrong. The sentries, who for weeks since the agreement with Donald Smith had been very lax, were now extremely tense and challenged everyone who tried to enter.

Joshua rode with Craig to the courthouse where Riel had his office. He had to join a throng of people waiting to see the president. Finally the president's door opened and he emerged. He looked very grim indeed.

"Louis," Joshua called out.

Riel looked toward him, and a wan smile parted his lips. "I'm glad you're here," Riel said to Joshua and Craig. "After this morning I am going to need support among the English."

"What are you doing?"

Riel smiled sadly. "I was wrong. You haven't heard. I ordered the execution of Thomas Scott."

Joshua went white. "Why?"

"Mr. Riel, it's a mistake," Craig said immediately.

"Come into my office for a second," Riel said to both of them. Once inside he turned angrily on them. "I am the president of this state. I do not propose to debate policy already determined before a group of onlookers. You English will learn to obey the laws of the government or you will pay the price." His voice rose in pitch as he spoke.

"I did not know that my son or I was accused of violating any laws," Joshua said coldly.

Riel seemed to relax. "Of course, my friend, I was referring to the generality."

"But why are you shooting Scott? He's a loudmouthed bully but no more than that."

"You must understand. He presents the constant challenge to the legitimacy to the government. If I don't make an example of him, others will share his contempt of the government."

"Louis," Joshua said, "you don't gain respect for the government by shooting citizens."

"But you do gain fear of the government," Riel said his voice rising again.

"You would rule by fear?"

"That's better than not ruling at all."

"No, it isn't," Joshua insisted. "You cannot do this."

"What authority can stop me?"

"I would hope the authority of good common sense," Craig interrupted.

Riel looked through Craig.

"Don't ignore my boy, Louis. He's your age and he's just as smart as you are."

"Monsieur Riel," Craig continued, "this execution is a horrible mistake. You'll fall into Schultz's trap. If you kill Canadians, Canada must respond with force."

"We'll meet force with force."

"Of course you will," Craig responded, "and you give up the path of negotiations which are about to gain you everything you want. Canada will never give up this land, Monsieur Riel, nor can you resist forever. Canada will win and you will lose everything."

"Negotiations will get nowhere if we don't control our own people. The likes of Scott must be punished as an example to all. Now get out of my way. I've made up my mind. Scott dies." He pushed them aside and stormed out of the room.

Craig looked at Joshua. "We've got to stop him, Father."

Joshua's shoulders sagged. "I don't think we can," he said with a sigh.

They followed Riel in the crowd out into the courtyard. A procession of armed men came trudging across the yard toward the courthouse. In their midst walked the burly form of Thomas Scott. He was dressed only in pants and shirt despite the cold. Riel and his government officials joined the procession at the courthouse. They went out the gate.

Once outside, Scott, who trembled with cold, was stood against a wall as the sentence was read.

Joshua and Craig followed the solemn crowd out of the fortress.

"Carry out the sentence," the president of the court called out. Several Métis guards raised their rifles. "Ready, aim, . . . fire."

Scott staggered as the bullets struck him. Then he sagged and fell to the ground. But he was not dead. His body writhed in pain.

"My God," someone called out from the crowd. "Finish the poor bastard off. You do that for a horse."

One of the Métis guards approached Scott's pain-racked form as it twisted and convulsed on the ground. He placed the pistol against the Canadian's head and fired. Scott's body jerked, then was still.

Slowly the guards and members of the court started back into Fort Garry. Riel stood watching Scott's body for some time, then he too turned to go back to the fort. He stopped in front of Joshua and Craig as if he wanted to say something to them, but he just stared at them, shook his head and continued on his way. When he arrived at the gate of the fort, Craig noted that O'Connor and O'Donoghue stood waiting to greet him. Both men very solemnly shook hands with the Métis leader.

Craig turned to look at the silent form of Thomas Scott. "Poor bastard."

"I shed no tears for Tom Scott," Joshua said angrily. "He just may achieve by his death, or the manner of it, what he never could have achieved in life, the downfall of Louis Riel and the Métis nation."

XIV

Red River Settlement, August 1870

Alex Miller sat in the prow of his longboat. The lake water was calm, pressed down, it seemed, by the heat of the August sun. Lake Winnipeg had a fearsome reputation for treachery. He smiled. It should be called Lake Miller. After all had not his father's first wife drowned in it? Or had she? He could not remember. Certainly he didn't care.

He was pleased with himself. His plans were close to fruition. One grand act and he would have it all—no matter what the damn lawyers in Toronto might say. Brant had hounded him—bringing the issue to court again and again. It was always the same. If Charles Miller had died intestate, then Joshua Miller and his heirs deserved half of the estate. Nothing had been settled yet but Alex had no intention of leaving the issue for the courts to decide. He would settle his battle with the brother he had never seen directly. And why should Joshua get anything? He had fled. Not like Alex, who had remained behind and suffered the slurs and indignities of Charles Miller, their father. Joshua had run away into the wilderness and been free of the spite of that old man. He, Alex, had suffered until he could stand it no longer and then it had been Alex who had put an end to that miserable man's wretched existence. He, Alex, deserved it all. Well, he would find Joshua Miller, and the brother would suffer the same fate as the father. What matter that he had heirs? Craig and the others were bastards under the law, and were entitled to nothing. It would all fall to Alex, and with no more threat of any change, despite all the efforts of that Jew, Brant.

There were moments when he thought it would never happen. He turned and looked back behind him on the lake. There were hundreds of boats filled with Canadian militiamen and some British Regulars. The prime minister might call this a peacekeeping expedition but every man, especially Ontario militiamen, knew what this was all about. They had volunteered to round up the criminals who shot poor Tom Scott and to hang them.

Alex remembered his frustration, and the notes he had sent to O'Connor berating him for his failures, threatening him with exposure. Then Donald Smith had gone west and returned with his damned list of liberties for the Métis. Then the Manitoba Act had created a new province and granted every concession that the Métis had demanded.

He personally did not give a damn if Louis Riel were hanged or allowed to marry the queen. He had remained in Toronto fretting until O'Connor and his wild Irish friends had forced Riel into a fatal mistake, the execution of a Canadian. Then Schultz had arrived in Toronto, and Alex had taken advantage of his venom as well. He preached revenge from one part of the province of Ontario to the other. Scott was now a Canadian martyr. This army would become an instrument of punishment. Punish whomever they want, he thought, so long as the punishment extended to Joshua Miller.

There were times when he had thought he might never get here. The overland trek had been necessary because the American government would never allow British troops to pass through their territory. It was not to be the train ride to St. Paul and then the short journey down the Red River to Fort Garry. Instead, they had to repeat the great journey of the voyageurs with a whole army—crossing lakes, making portages from Fort William on Lake Superior, Rainy Lake to the Lake of the Woods, then the Winnipeg River and now Lake Winnipeg. They rode toward the mouth of the Red where it flowed into this lake. It had been an incredible journey. Men had strained and hauled, fallen ill and died, but they had accomplished it.

Only last night, word had reached their camp on the Winnipeg River that Louis Riel had fled Fort Garry. The men had been angry. They wanted to see the Métis leader hanged. O'Donoghue and his Fenians had broken with Riel earlier, when he had accepted provincial status within the Confederation and they had left.

The English of the new province would not support Riel because of Scott. The Métis had everything they wanted, even Riel would not expect them to give it all up in a vain effort to save his hide. There was only one thing for him to do in the face of the peacekeeping mission—flee and avoid the noose.

The mouth of the Red River was directly ahead. In a few more minutes, Alex would enter it. He had O'Connor's description of the Miller farm. The Irishman was such a fool. Imagine being trapped into betrayal of everyone and everything he believed in by a whore. He did not hesitate to characterize his mother in that fashion. She had sold her body for information rather than money. It did not cross his mind that she did it to help his career.

The rowers of his boat were sweating freely. They had removed their heavy jackets, but their shirts were soaked and clung to their backs and chests. It was hard to think of this as a land of ice and snow on an August day such as this one.

They were in the river now. O'Connor had warned him to look for a large house on the right bank with a smaller cabin within walking distance of the house. That would be it.

They traveled a few miles south. There were many houses along the river front, farms extending backward away from the stream, narrow strips of cultivated land.

"There, that must be it," Alex said aloud. "Corporal, pull into shore. I have some business here."

"Yes, sir."

Alex walked up the bank toward the house. It was a large two-storied log house. He would not have thought his half–breed relatives would live this well. He walked to the front door.

"How quaint," he mumbled, "it's unlocked. Anyone home?" he called out.

A man with greying hair stood up from his chair by the window.

Alex recognized him. He looked very much like their father—very much like him for that matter.

"Who the hell are you?" Joshua blurted out, then recognized the militia uniform. "So you soldier boys have finally arrived."

"Is this the home of Mr. Craig Miller?" Alex asked.

Joshua's eyes narrowed to slits as he took Alex in from head to toe.

"Who wants to know?" Joshua asked.

Alex turned back toward the door. "You and your guard may enter, Corporal."

The militia corporal and two privates came to the door pointing their Spencers at Joshua.

"What's the meaning of this?" Joshua bellowed.

"I have a warrant to seize Craig Miller, a fugitive from Her Majesty's justice. You will lead me to him."

"Like hell I will."

The door to the pantry lean–to opened and Rainbow and her mother stepped into the room carrying iron pots of liquid.

The militia stared wide–eyed at the two Indian women. Suddenly there was a wild yell from the landing. Sean Lavery swung over the railing and hurled himself from the second floor down onto the militia privates, sending them sprawling. Joshua sent a blow crashing into the corporal's face. His rifle crashed to the floor. Joshua then moved toward Alex. The younger man reached instinctively into his pocket. The knife felt comfortable in his hand and his hand felt even more comfortable as the blade sunk deeply into his brother's chest.

Joshua lurched backward, his hand grabbed at the handle of the knife to pull it from him. His white shirt was gradually turning red in the front.

Rainbow yelled when she saw her husband's wound. Alex turned to flee, to run past her and get help from other boats on the river. But the Indian woman, with a look of wild rage, threw her pot of lye into Alex's face.

He screamed. He was partially blinded, and the stench and the sting of the liquid overwhelmed him. He backed away from her and started to run. He stumbled into the pantry, knocking over sacks of flour and sugar and upsetting baskets of apples. The burns on his face were eating away at his skin. He screamed again and again. He had to find water, something to ease his pain. He saw a trough near the barn. He raced for it, and fell to his knees before it. Thank God there was water. He stuck his whole head into the slimy wetness.

Kevin had come running as soon as he heard the shouting, and arrived in the big house to find Joshua on the floor gasping for breath. Sean knelt by his side.

"Jesus," Kevin said as he knelt by the older man as well. Then he saw the knife handle. He sat back on his haunches. It could not be— But it was— It was the same knife. It had to be. It had been dark that night, but he could never forget his father's bleeding fingers trying to pull the blade from his chest. Kevin reached to touch it. He was in a daze, and Rainbow was quicker than he. She slapped his hand away. She removed the knife herself as Joshua gritted his teeth. Then she began to stop the bleeding.

"What in God's name has happened," Craig shouted as he entered his father's house followed by a horrified Meg.

"Help your mother. Get your father onto the couch before more troops come back," Kevin said to Craig.

Then he walked to the open door into the pantry. It was beginning to make sense. He knew who the officer bending over the trough by the barn would be. Alex Miller had been Lady Barbara's lover. Alex Miller had murdered his father, Lord Carringdon. The hurt almost overwhelmed him. Alex Miller's mother, Allison, had covered for him ever since. She had used Kevin. Poor, stupid Kevin O'Connor. She had used him then, and she had used him ever since. He had betrayed all he ever believed in, everyone he had ever loved, for her. But all she had done was use him.

He looked for a weapon. There was an ax by the woodpile. He grabbed it in his hands. He approached Alex.

"Miller! Alex Miller, it's me Kevin. Poor stupid Kevin."

Alex looked up from the trough. Kevin stopped dead in his tracks. The man's face was unrecognizable. It was swollen and burned. Strips of skin had already started to peel from it. One eye was closed. Kevin guessed it was closed permanently. The ax slipped lower in his hand.

"O'Connor," said Alex, "get me out of here. These people will murder me. They resisted arrest. I was only doing my duty."

"Damn you," Kevin said.

Alex looked up at him in a stupor of pain. "I'll tell them all about you. How you betrayed them. I'll tell the Fenians that you're an informer. They have a special death for informers." He was screaming hysterically now.

"Do your worst," Kevin said finally. The ax dropped from his hand. He walked past Alex and headed to the barn. He wanted only to saddle his horse and leave this place. Nothing mattered anymore.

Meg had followed Kevin toward the barn. She stood mesmerized as he approached the Canadian officer, an ax in his hand. She could not hear what was said, but she saw Kevin's shoulders slump. Then she saw him turn and move rapidly toward the barn. She did not know what had passed between them, but she was sure she would never see Kevin O'Connor again. She turned sadly to reenter the chaos that the Miller house had become. If Joshua died, there would be no one here for her now.

But Joshua did not die. He lingered for days—racked with pain and fever. The doctor from Winnipeg gave him up for dead, but not Rainbow and Warrior Woman. They searched out herbs on the prairies with little Douglas, and when they returned they made poultices and teas. Then the fever broke and Joshua Miller survived.

Alex returned to Ontario, blind in one eye and frightfully scarred. The militia authorities held him under arrest until Joshua could talk. The two brothers then confronted each other, but Joshua refused to press charges. He told Craig that any man raised by Charles Miller, their father, had been punished enough.

Alex did not seem grateful. Instead it was clear that he bore a grudge against Joshua. After all, the horror his face had become was the responsibility of his brother. His grudge and hatred grew even stronger after he returned home to find that the Ontario courts had ruled that Charles Miller had, in his own lifetime, repudiated and disowned Joshua Miller as his son. The older man had no claim to the estate. It had been Alex's, and only his, all along.

Meg had sat by Joshua's side throughout his ordeal—especially when the Indian women went searching for their special medicines. She rejoiced when his fever broke. But at the same time her father-in-law's recovery meant that she would have to face her own problems at last.

Craig had spent the days of his father's illness busying himself about the farm—anything to keep his mind off the suffering he knew was going on up in the big house on the riverbank. Meg found him in the barn, rubbing down his father's horse. He searched her face for the news he dreaded, but her expression was strangely neutral.

"The fever has broken. Your mother says he will recover now."

Craig sighed, then smiled at her. "Thank you," he said.

"I did very little. I just sat there and held his hand."

"He had to know his loved ones were with him, and you had more courage than I. I ran away from his sufferings."

Meg looked away from him. "I'm going to need even more courage now, Craig," she said. "I'm going to leave you."

Surprise and then pain crossed Craig's face. She could see tears forming in his eyes. "Is it Kevin?"

She looked at him in surprise, then turned away, ashamed to look at him.

"Sean told me of his suspicions, and even more. He told me of a conversation he had with Kevin long ago—about that first night when we met him in Halifax at MacSorley's. God, that seems so long ago."

Meg laughed bitterly. "Once again the curse of the Irish. They blab about everything. No, Craig, it's not about Kevin. It's about me. I don't belong here. I cannot abide your Manitoba. I want to go home to Halifax—to be with my mother and father. I want to be among my books and to go to plays and to meet people who are doing things that matter. I'm taking James, and I'm leaving for St. Paul in Minnesota just as soon as I can arrange it. From there I'll book passage on the train to the east."

Tears now flowed freely down Craig's cheeks. Meg's face, too, was wet.

"Don't leave me, Meg," Craig pleaded. "I love you."

"And I love you," she responded. "But I'll die here if I don't leave. I'd ask you to come with me, but I know you'd die there. We are just ill-suited lovers, my sweet." She walked over to him and tried to wipe the tears from his face. He enfolded her in his arms and pulled her close to his chest.

"Don't hate Kevin," she whispered in his ear. "He meant no harm to you, and he is so weak."

They stood holding each other until Rainbow was heard calling to both of them—demanding that the farm chores be completed before suppertime.

EPILOGUE

Dakota Territory, June 1876

Craig rode his pony down into the gully at breakneck speed. The herd was small and the buffalo were terrified. They started to run away from the stream in different directions. It frustrated him and the three Assiniboine warriors he rode with. In the big herd there were always leaders. The herd took off in one direction, making it easier for the hunters to follow and make multiple kills. But there were no more big herds. He decided to waste no more time. He fired his rifle and brought down a small bull. His companions each fired and each made a kill. Their hosts, the Sioux and Cheyenne, would feast tonight.

Craig jumped from the back of the pony to the ground beside his kill. He began a fire of dried buffalo chips almost immediately. Then he opened the mouth of the dead beast and cut out its tongue. He placed the delicacy over the fire. His companions eagerly awaited his efforts. They were all hungry, and the four tongues would be only the beginning of their feast.

Craig rode with his Assiniboine relatives every summer after the buffalo hunt, although there was no longer an organized hunt out of Red River. Most of the Métis were gone now, the French ones at least. Provincial status had not offered the protection that Louis Riel had thought it would. Eastern whites had poured into Manitoba. The Métis sold their lands and headed west to the Valley of the North Saskatchewan River where they attempted to rekindle the old ways. But the old ways were harder and harder to live as the buffalo disappeared.

That August six years ago was like a never–ending nightmare to Craig. His father's illness terrified him. He had recovered and then had begun his campaign to take his family further west—away from the white man's ways. But Craig loved Manitoba and he would not flee from it. He and his father fought continually about it. But still Joshua did not move west. Craig suspected that it was Rainbow who carried the day. She might talk wistfully about the open prairie. But she did not wish to leave the comforts of the big house on the Red River.

Nor had he ever seen Kevin again. It pained Craig to lose him even after Sean told him of Kevin's second betrayal. The story had come from the Fenian leadership. O'Connor had sold out to the Canadians on the eve of Ridgeway. But Craig had no hatred in him for his old friend. Sean was bitter, especially about Big Jim. He blamed Kevin for Jim's death, but Craig could only remember his own rescue from the Kingston–bound train and the fact that they were responsible for each other. Had they not, in fact, saved each other's lives? It was no matter that Kevin had slept with his wife. *He* had lost Meg. Maybe they had too much baggage to carry—too many barriers between them. Kevin had not caused their break. He had only taken his pleasure from it.

Sean told him the Fenians had placed a death sentence on O'Connor. They had looked for him in the American army. The story was that Kevin had gone back to his first love, his love for horses, and that he was back in the American cavalry.

Only this summer, Sean said, he had been tracked by Fenians to Fort Abraham Lincoln and the Seventh Cavalry. It troubled Craig when he learned who commanded the Seventh—George Armstrong Custer.

He had come looking for Kevin. Not to harm. But to help hide him. Meg had been right. Kevin was weak and needed his love and protection if he was to survive. The easiest way to find him, it seemed, was to ride south with his cousins until they made contact with Crazy Horse, Sitting Bull and Gall, the Sioux hostiles that a large American military force, including the Seventh Cavalry were looking for. Rather than look for Kevin, he would let Kevin and the American Cavalry come to find him.

They feasted on the tongues, then began the hard work of butchering the rest of the carcasses. They had to carry back as much as they could. The village was now enormous, and there were many mouths to feed. Four buffalo would make the Assiniboine very desirable guests. In the camp were Minneconjous, Ogallalas, Uncpapas, Sans Arcs, Brulé's, as well as

Cheyenne—five thousand strong. The size of the village was probably a mistake. It would play into the Americans' plans. They were moving their infantry by steam boats on the rivers, and there was always the terrifying yellow hair, Custer and his horse soldiers. These Indians had a special hatred for Custer. Placing themselves in one big encampment made it easier for the American army to surround them and cut off any escape. But Craig sensed a weariness among those gathered. It was almost as if they would have this one big camp to celebrate former good times and damn the consequences. And it did make it easier for him to find Kevin.

They loaded their horses down with meat and remounted. Craig looked at his cousin—Rainbow's cousin, actually. He'd take the lead.

"Follow the lodge pole trail until you come to the camp on the Little Big Horn," he said.

Kevin was sore. He had been saddle sore many times in the past six years. This was different. This was a soreness deep down in the bones that came from days and days of endless riding. Endless riding and the search of an ever–elusive objective, the Sioux hostiles.

It was ironic, he thought, that he should be back with Custer. But he could not be choosy; he needed a place to hide and the Seventh Cavalry was convenient.

Custer was as flamboyant as ever. This time he had affected a white buckskin jacket. He had also cut his hair for the campaign. The men thought it a bad omen that Old Yellow Hair could more easily be called Old Baldy now. But cavalry men were prone to all kinds of superstitions.

Kevin was more concerned with more realistic evidence of potential disaster. The track they followed was recent and wide. There obviously were an enormous number of Indians up ahead, but Custer, instead of waiting for his commanders Gibbons and Terry and their large infantry contingents, was taking out after them—alone.

Kevin knew of Custer's impulsiveness from bitter experience, but it was not just what was in front of him that worried him. Behind him was the revenge of the Fenian Brotherhood.

Custer's conference with his troop commanders was just breaking up. Troop L commander Captain Keogh rode back toward his column. He turned in the saddle and spoke briefly to the Company First Sergeant. The Sergeant rode down the line.

"What gives, Sergeant?" some of the troopers asked.

"We're going after them," the Sergeant said.

"There goes old glory hound again," said one trooper. "He's determined to make it back up to general even without Civil War."

"We go with Custer. A second battalion goes with Major Reno, and a third battalion with Captain Benteen."

"He's splitting us up?" Kevin asked in surprise. "Just how many Indians are up there in the valley, Sarge?"

"Don't rightly know, but the Colonel is going to hit them in front and then on the flank. When their villages are attacked, no matter by how many, Indians run. Custer knows that, and he's attacked more Indian villages than most men."

"All right, men," Keogh called out. "Forward."

The troop moved in concert with its sister troops. Major Reno's battalion split off and followed along a creek until it came to the Little Big Horn. L troop, with Custer in the lead, rode parallel to the river over the bluff. There they had their last sight of Reno's battalion.

Kevin rode easily. The day was hot and the flies were bothering his grey. It was good to ride at a fast pace and get some breeze. They rode in silence. Then gunfire erupted off to the left. Reno had found the camp. But Kevin rose in his stirrups to see if he could catch sight of what was happening to Reno's men. The terrain was broken here with rolling, grass-covered knolls. But he could not see beyond the hills toward the river.

Custer ordered his men down a bluff and into a coulee. Then he led his column toward the river. He was going to ford the Little Big Horn and strike the camp while most of its warriors were busy fending off Reno.

They came to the river. Custer rode into the water to test its depth. It was fordable. He swung his horse around and ordered his troop to cross. Suddenly a withering fire mowed down the front troopers. Custer seemed to hesitate. He looked to the northwest. The Indian encampment stretched out as far as the eye could see. Circle after circle of tepees, smoke rising peacefully from most, stretched across the valley. Kevin and every trooper in the battalion knew they were in trouble. The fire continued to cut troopers down. Custer made up his mind. He spurred his horse out of the water. He called for his men to follow. He would continue parallel to the river to find a better fording place farther downstream.

They rode up again into the bluffs. Now Indians seemed to appear from everywhere, coming from the village that stretched all along Little Big Horn. Suddenly fire came from in front as well. Custer came to a halt. He looked about him. There was a high bluff in front of him to his right. He signaled to his troop to make it to the bluff. Troopers were falling all about him.

A bullet hit Kevin's grey. It fell. He was lucky to land on his feet. He stumbled and groaned in pain as he turned his ankle. He grabbed his rifle and hobbled forward, bending low to the ground.

Custer ordered the troop to dismount and dig in. There was not much cover, and Indians seemed to be everywhere, cutting through their lines, cutting off little groups of troopers and then mowing them down. Young braves anxious to make names for themselves took ridiculous chances and usually paid the price of foolhardiness.

Kevin fell behind someone's downed horse. He could see Custer off to his left, up higher on the bluff. At his side was the color–bearer, an easy target for any brave anxious to get to the big medicine of the flag.

Kevin took aim. He had innumerable targets and he killed steadily, firing one round after another with deadly effect. The trooper next to him screamed in terror. The trooper rose to his feet and was cut down by three arrows, which struck him almost simultaneously. All Kevin's calm and accuracy made no difference. There were thousands of Indians, it seemed, and ten took the place of every one he killed. Then he heard groans from the troopers around him. Custer was down, a bullet in the head and another in the chest. The realization came to Kevin that he would not leave this place alive. He took it calmly. He just kept firing. He would take as many of the feathered, painted bastards with him as he could.

The arrow hit him in the back. It felt like a fist pounding at him. Then the pain came. He cried out with the fire of it and then blackness.

He awoke. No, he was still dreaming. He had had this dream before. Dust and black smoke billowed all around him. Great painted and feathered birds bent over their victims pecking at them with their beaks. His eyes cleared a bit. He was not dreaming. They were not birds. They were Sioux, and their beaks were axes cleaving the skulls of the wounded.

He felt rough hands pull at his pants. He was being stripped of his clothes. If he played dead, maybe they would not bash his head in. Another set of hands tugged at his blood–soaked shirt. He had heard stories of the Sioux castrating the corpses of their enemies in the belief that they would be deprived of pleasure in the next world if their bodies were mutilated. He hoped they were only stories.

The hands that had worked on his shirt turned his body over roughly. The arrow pushed deeper into him. Kevin could not stop the groan of pain that escaped his lips. He looked up into the smoke. A painted face glared at him. It was over now, he knew. The face said something. Another face appeared. It was painted but he'd know it anywhere. It was Craig Miller.

"Kevin," the face said.

Kevin tried to speak but he was so weak and his lips were cracked.

"You're in bad shape. I've got to get you out of here."

Craig stood and yelled in Assiniboine. A Sioux tried to shove him aside and swing a club at Kevin's head.

"No prisoners," he said in Sioux.

Craig blocked his arm. He was immediately joined by his Assiniboine cousins. The Sioux decided to find easier pickings.

Craig reached down and pulled Kevin up into his arms. Kevin gasped in pain and blood poured out his mouth. Craig lowered him to the ground again.

"I always said Custer was going to get me killed," he joked feebly.

"Don't talk." Craig's pony was brought to him. He leapt onto its back. The Assiniboine hauled Kevin up and placed him across the pony's back in front of Craig.

Craig kneed his horse and rode away from the battlefield. He did not know quite where to go. The other battalions of the Seventh were pinned down in bluffs above the Little Big Horn. They would probably share Custer's fate. He could not take Kevin to the Sioux camp. They would kill him immediately. Craig kicked the horse into a gallop that took them up into the bluffs, away from the river, away from the site of Custer's last charge.

He rode about five miles out onto the prairies. He knew he would kill Kevin if he kept it up. He halted his pony and dismounted. He lifted Kevin gently off the horse and laid him on the ground. He had to place him on his stomach because of the arrow shaft penetrating his back. Craig took his knife and cut the shaft as close to the skin as he could. He spread the horse blanket on the ground and placed Kevin on top of it. He took some whiskey and wet Kevin's lips.

Kevin's eyes flashed open. There was terror in them. When he saw Craig he relaxed.

"Sorry," he whispered. "Sorry for everything."

Craig nodded to him and held his hand. He felt Kevin squeeze it as a spasm of pain rocked him.

"Tell all," he groaned, "that I am sorry." He seemed to lapse into a delirium. "Oh my God, I am heartily sorry for having offended thee. . . ." He prayed the prayer of his youth and then he died.

Craig sat by Kevin's body until dark. He tried to scratch a grave into the baked soil of the prairie but there was little he could do. In the end, out of respect, he hauled underbrush and placed it atop Kevin's body. He knew it would do little good. Then he remounted his horse. The search was over. He would go home now. He would go home to Manitoba.

ABOUT THE AUTHOR

A Canadian citizen since 1976, ROBERT E. WALL draws on his love for Canada and his native United States in creating the saga of *THE CANADIANS*. He perceives the histories of the two nations as deeply entwined and, influenced by the writings of Kenneth Roberts, seeks to teach those histories through the historical novel. *Blackrobe*, the first in the series, is Wall's first novel, followed by *Bloodbrothers, Birthright, Patriots, Inheritors, Dominion*, and *Brotherhood*.

Robert Wall is married, has five children (one is an adopted Cree Indian, the most authentic Canadian in the family), and divides his time between New Jersey, where he is provost at Farleigh Dickinson University, and Montreal, where his family lives.